Hold Me Forever

HOLD ME FOREVER

Margaret Thomson Davis

CENTURY · LONDON

First published in 1994

Copyright © Margaret Thomson Davis

Margaret Thomson Davis has asserted her right under the Copyright,
Designs and Patents Act, 1988, to be identified as the author of this work.

First published in the United Kingdom in 1994 by
Century, 20 Vauxhall Bridge Road, London SW1V 2SA

Random House Australia (Pty) Ltd
20 Alfred Street, Milsons Point, Sydney, NSW 2061
Australia

Random House New Zealand Ltd
18 Poland Road, Glenfield, Auckland 10,
New Zealand

Random House South Africa (Pty) Ltd
PO Box 337, Bergvlei 2012, South Africa

Random House UK Limited Reg. No. 954009

ISBN 0 7126 5933 1 Hardback
ISBN 0 7126 7572 8 Paperback

Typeset by Deltatype Ltd, Ellesmere Port, Cheshire
Printed and bound in the United Kingdom by Clays Ltd, St Ives plc

Acknowledgements

I'd like to thank all the people who gave so generously their time in helping me with my research. As usual the librarians of the Mitchell Reference Library in Glasgow spared no effort to do what they could for me. Indeed, in any library I've visited I've been equally well-served. It was a librarian who drew my attention to Tony Martin's excellent work on the history of Blackhill.

Other people have allowed me to interview them and as a result I have accumulated a vast number of tapes rich in knowledge and experience that I was privileged to draw on when I was creating this novel.

I thank them all, but especially the following:

One of my most loyal fans, Ina Thomson, who also has taken many strolls down memory lane in order to enrich my research about old Glasgow.

Hughie Healy – an absolute gem and another of my sources for stories about Glasgow life and characters. Then there's Willie MacLean, who has become my expert on life in the Gorbals and quite a 'character' himself.

The ladies and gentlemen who spoke to me in the community centres of various Glasgow housing estates, or 'schemes' as they are known in Glasgow. My apologies to the ladies of Drumchapel if I seem to have done the place less than justice. In this book Drumchapel is seen through the eyes of the awful Sophie character.

Iain Brown, MBE, MA. Med. AFBPsS. Ch. Psychol. who advised me on the psychology.

Mark Hamilton of Rock Steady Security Ltd, a man of courage and integrity.

James Muir, for allowing me to use his poetry.

Robin Lloyd Jones for the title.

My son, Kenneth Davis for advice on the karate scenes.

Chapter One

Andrina didn't understand the reason for her mother's hatred of Bernard, and the intensity with which she fought to prevent her having anything to do with him. It was one thing to dislike someone at first meeting; she could understand that. But such black hatred? That's what it was. From the moment Sophie's flint-like stare fixed on Bernard O'Maley, the intensity of her feelings was obvious. All right. Her daughter was only fifteen and still at school. But Sophie had never prevented Andrina from being friendly with the crowd at the church, which included men even older than Bernard. Although, of course, 'crowd' was the operative word. In the past, Andrina had never been alone with any male person other than her father.

She'd tried to point out to her mother that she was mature for her age. At least, physically mature. This had immediately made everything worse. Sophie had an aversion to anything physical. She became acutely anxious, for instance, the moment Andrina began to develop breasts. She insisted on binding her tightly with a broad stretch bandage to try to flatten her out. She'd bought her girdles and tight elastic knickers in a determined effort to hide the voluptuous swell of Andrina's hips and control the provocative bounce and wiggle of her buttocks. She despaired of what Andrina was coming to, and what she would be like at twenty-one if this was how she was at fifteen.

Flesh, to Sophie, was not only obscene but somehow unchristian. Andrina couldn't help giggling about this with some of her pals at school, although afterwards she was secretly plagued with guilt and anxiety in case her mother would discover her disloyalty. Her mother's extreme views and constant desperation made her seem pathetic and vulnerable as well as frightening. Andrina loved her fearfully.

1

Sophie was as lean as a greyhound, with prematurely grey hair pinned back so tightly it gave the skin of her face a taut, mask-like appearance. She scorned any kind of decoration and wore only the darkest, the plainest and most severe clothes. Even her glasses were plain steel-rimmed.

'But why are you so much against Bernard?' Andrina asked, all round-eyed and innocent, although by this time she'd begun to suspect why. It wasn't that, according to Sophie, Bernard's family were 'a disgrace', and that his father and brothers had been arrested on occasion for being drunk and disorderly. Or that his mother did the devil's work by reading teacups and cards. It wasn't that they came from Garngad. *Garngad*, of all places – one of the toughest districts in Glasgow. It wasn't that Bernard was four years older than her, or even that he was a Catholic – although his religion, Sophie insisted, was the main reason for her objections.

No. It was because Bernard was too *physical*.

Andrina knew this by the way the thin thread of her mother's mouth warped as she said the words.

'He's too physical.'

The fact that Bernard was so physical was what Andrina found irresistible about him. Already he was a black belt in karate and had shoulders like a prize bull. His eyes were watchful, knowledgeable, and reflected maturity and experience far beyond his nineteen years. He stirred excitement in her. Especially when he smiled and his cleft chin deepened and a wicked glimmer narrowed his eyes. There was no comparison between him and the boys at her school. Bernard was a man.

She remembered thinking on the day they met what a strikingly attractive guy he was, with eyes as dark as his coal-black hair. She had been walking with Mary Gardner and Sheila Preston in Kelvingrove Park. His companions were a couple of gangly youths – she couldn't remember their names now. They had been laughing and kicking a ball about. Bernard spoke first.

Soon they were all talking and laughing together. Then the

2

girls began kicking the ball and it became quite hilarious. The crowd of them met in the park several times after that and fooled about and had a laugh. Often they went to a café for ice-cream. Andrina became eager to please Bernard. She felt self-conscious about her appearance and hated wearing her gym-slip and her prim, white blouse and navy tie after school hours. They made her look far too young. She pretended to Sophie that she was anxious not to ruin her school clothes but 'keep them good for school'. She pestered her mother to allow her to wear stockings, using a plea that she thought might be the most effective with Sophie: 'It doesn't seem decent to go around with bare legs at my age, Mum. I'll soon be sixteen.' The idea was that because it was summer, wool would be out of the question and so the stockings would have to be silk.

She saved her pocket-money and bought a box of face powder, a tin of mascara with a little brush, and a bright red lipstick. The make-up was applied in secret, safely away from the house, and later rubbed off before returning. She would slip up another close a few yards along the road and around the corner, away from Sophie's watching eyes at the top floor window. There she would fluff sweet scented powder over her face, and while Mary or Sheila held the mirror she'd apply the lipstick. She'd spit on the cake of mascara and rub the brush over it before carefully applying it to her lashes. Then she would take her turn in holding the mirror for Mary and Sheila in between their shared bouts of excited giggling. The girls would shield her with their jackets as she undid the stretch bandage. She'd slip it from beneath her blouse or her dress, then roll it up and stuff it into her pocket. Later, as she became more daring, she even wriggled out of the restricting girdle and knickers.

A couple of times they'd gone with the boys to the local cinema, once to see a Charlie Chaplin film, and another time to see *The Ghost Train*. Andrina had clutched at Bernard during that film and he stretched his arm around her and held her close. The muscle of his arm was hard against her, and the heat of his body made her dissolve into one giant thumping heart.

He'd kissed her for the first time then and it was like rose petals opening up inside her, sweet and beautiful. She couldn't wait for him to kiss her again. His kisses blotted out all her anxieties, her uncertainties, her fears. Everything dissolved and disappeared and she was left floating in mindless ecstasy.

Bernard lost no time in suggesting they go out on their own. He called at the house for her. He dwarfed the kitchen of the small flat in the quiet end of Sauchiehall Street, his muscular body filling the room with a disturbing kind of energy.

Andrina's father, Andrew McPherson, had been pleasant enough. He put aside his newspaper and invited Bernard to sit down.

'And where are the pair of you off to?' he asked.

'Bill Haley and the Comets are in the Regal. We thought we'd go and see what they're like.'

Sophie cut in: 'That dreadful film that's making people riot all over the place and tear up the seats?'

'Oh, I don't think Andrina and I will be rioting or tearing up seats.' Bernard's grin deepened the cleft in his chin and made his eyes narrow. It was then that Andrina saw her mother's hatred.

'She's far too young to be going out at all,' Sophie snapped. 'You've obviously left school.'

'Yes, I'm nineteen.'

'What school did you go to?'

'St Francis.'

Sophie flashed a look at her husband that said CATHOLIC in capital letters.

Anxiously, Andrina tugged at Bernard's arm. She was desperate to escape from the house before her mother spoiled everything. 'We'll miss the start of the big picture.'

Rock Around The Clock was wonderfully exciting with its deafening, pistol-cracking beat. It vibrated an energy that was instantly, wildly infectious. Andrina and Bernard had loudly belted out the words with everyone else, and clapped their hands and wriggled around and bounced about in their seats. Afterwards, they had jived along Sauchiehall Street, not caring what anyone thought. Bernard flung her high in the air, bounced her on his bent knees, down between his legs, high in the air again, then whisked her round and round. She remembered the joyous sense of exhilaration and freedom. Then she'd caught a glimpse of her mother's rigid, disapproving face. The cold stare behind the steel-rimmed glasses watching from the front room window made joy immediately wither away. Fear took its place.

'My mother's at the window. I'll have to go. Thanks Bernard. It was great.'

She flew up the stone stairs into the house, excuses and apologies agitating from her lips before she'd even reached the front room. Then she hurried after Sophie into the kitchen.

'You disgust me,' Sophie said, 'making a disgusting exhibition of yourself for all to see. Get out of my way. I don't want to be contaminated by you.'

The barrier of ice around the older woman was something that never ceased to fill Andrina with panic. The panic had taken root long ago in the nightmare mists of childhood. At primary school it had been tied up with the times she'd come home to find Sophie had gone, and each time she believed it was for ever. So she would huddle down on the stone steps of the close, not knowing what to do. She had been left on her own long before her school days, but these memories were such dangerous pools of terror, her mind's eye shrunk away from them.

Somehow she had developed the conviction that everything was her fault, including the times her mother and father quarrelled – and in the earlier days they quarrelled a great deal. Sometimes her father would say to her mother, 'You ought to be ashamed. It's the talk of the place, the way that child's been treated. It was bad enough finding out that you've been carrying on with every Tom, Dick and Harry while I was away. But to be reported to the NSPCC; to be told that the "cruelty man" was here; to learn that neighbours had found her on her own, shivering and whimpering in the dark, without anything to eat or drink, shut in a room stinking of urine and faeces. I felt

5

horrified and ashamed. But you're obviously incapable of any normal feelings. Especially for her.' Andrina knew and even had some understanding of the neglect she'd suffered, neglect that resulted in what she suffered now. Yet neither the knowledge nor the understanding helped her to cope with her present emotions. Panic overwhelmed her still.

'I've more feelings for Andrina than you, and the chances are she isn't even mine,' her father told her mother.

'You know as well as I do that she's yours,' her mother would rage. 'You're just trying to torment me. It's just your bad mind . . .'

He sadly shook his head. 'You're a fine one to accuse anyone of being bad. I was away fighting for an ideal with the International Brigade in Spain. Then I was fighting against the evil of Hitler. Only to discover I had an evil nearer home to contend with.'

More than once he'd said, 'If I hadn't been a committed Christian, Sophie, I would have flung you out on to the street years ago.'

Then Mother had become 'saved', and joined Father's church – the Church of Jesus. By that time Andrina was about nine or ten, and from then on she saw even less of her mother. Sophie, in her usual extreme way, plunged herself with almost maniac efficiency into doing good works. She was the one who laid out the dead, the one who visited the sick and ran their errands.

When she was in the house she filled the kitchen with people including, ironically enough, any neglected and abused children of the neighbourhood. Tough, snotty-nosed little boys called her mother 'Aunty Sophie'. They were made a fuss of, and sat up on the draining board beside the sink at the kitchen window. They had their noses blown, their faces scrubbed, their hair brushed. They were told what good boys they were. Then they were given a bag of black-striped balls or jelly babies.

Andrina had been darkly jealous of them, and as often as not her feelings were returned. The boys were usually angelic in her mother's presence but outside the house the language even of

6

the youngest could be foul. She remembered one little boy who, if they met on the stairs, used to spit on her. He was one of her mother's special favourites. Andrina hated him, but she was careful to hide her feelings from her mother and from everyone. Just like her mother and father hid theirs.

Sophie and Andrew McPherson still argued in private, although admittedly not so often. Her father had long since forgiven her mother – or so he said. In public, they gave the impression of being almost saintly in their devotion to one another, as well as to the church.

The only time Andrina could remember her mother turning any attention on her, and what she hoped was love, was on the few occasions when Sophie said, 'If you're very good and please Mummy, Mummy will tuck you up and read you a story tonight.' More often than not, despite straining to do her utmost to please, nothing happened. Only occasionally was Andrina rewarded by this much-treasured attention.

She had pleased her mother by promising to have nothing more to do with Bernard, although secretly she couldn't imagine cutting Bernard out of her life. To her he'd become the symbol of life itself. She admired the way he had stuck to his guns about being her friend. He'd spoken first of all to her father. McPherson had listened with that sympathetic concentration he used when dealing with union, or council, or church business. He sat leaning forward, arms resting on knees, hands clasped between them. After hearing Bernard out, he tipped back his portly body and began the ritual of pressing tobacco into the bowl of his pipe, then flaring several matches against it before puffing and drawing on the stem. All this time he appeared to be giving the matter under discussion the serious weight of his attention. Eventually, he removed the pipe from his mouth and gazed sadly at Bernard. He could do this most effectively because he had drooping 'spaniel' eyes set in a loose crêpe skin that looked darkly stained with nicotine.

'Of course I trust you, lad. Despite what some folk think, I believe you come from good stock. Your father and I are both proud members of the Royal Artillery Club.'

7

'You know my father?' Bernard was pleasantly surprised and suddenly filled with hope.

'We've spoken on occasion at the club.' McPherson smiled between leisurely puffs. 'I remember he was most generous in his congratulations when I received my VC. He insisted on buying me quite a few drinks. He would have spent his last penny on me if I'd let him. I had to explain that I regard my Victoria Cross as representing not only what I did, but as a symbol of the courage of many brave men, like your father himself.'

McPherson enjoyed thinking about the club and it showed in his face. Like most of the gunners and ex-gunners who were members (every Artillery man was a member automatically), he liked a good drink – and Patrick O'Maley wasn't the only man who always insisted on buying him one. 'I don't manage to get to the club so often now,' he said regretfully, 'I'm kept so busy with council business.'

'To get back to what we were talking about,' Bernard prompted. 'If you trust me, does that mean it's OK for me to go with Andrina?'

Councillor McPherson fixed him with another sad stare. 'If it were only up to me lad . . . but . . .'

'I know Mrs McPherson is opposed to our friendship, but can't you talk to her, use your influence?'

'Andrina is very young. I can see my wife's point of view.'

'She's almost sixteen.'

'And still very immature.'

'I'm very fond of her. And I'm determined . . .'

'Yes. I can see you're a strong-minded young man, but I'll have to ask you to leave now.' McPherson pulled a gold watch from his waistcoat pocket and took his time studying it. It was attached to a heavy chain and an amber fob. It had belonged to his late father and he liked to show it off as often as possible. 'I've people coming for advice. I'm on the housing committee and it takes up a lot of my time. Finding a decent home is such a problem for so many people nowadays. I do my best to help but . . .' He rose with a sigh. 'Like most things in life, it is more complicated than people realise.'

Bernard rose too. 'I just want to be friends with Andrina, even if we're just two in a crowd of friends. What's the harm in that? I don't understand what all the fuss is about.'

Although of couse he did. The question about his school, and the look that Sophie McPherson had flashed to her husband, had not escaped him. In Glasgow, the religion you were born into was of prime importance. Even when he was little more than a toddler, he had been faced with the aggressive question of 'Are you a Billy or a Dan?'

'There is no need for any fuss, Bernard. And no need to go on as if Andrina is the only girl in the world.'

But as far as Bernard was concerned, she was. 'I'll speak to Mrs McPherson,' he said desperately. 'But if you could just put in a good word for me first, Councillor McPherson. If you could use your influence . . .'

How many times had McPherson heard that phrase before – especially since he'd become a member of the housing committee. He nodded sagely at the young man. 'I'll certainly do my best on your behalf. That I can promise you.'

'Thank you.'

For a horrible moment McPherson thought Bernard was going to pounce on him and kiss him.

He felt sorry for Bernard. For no apparent reason, Sophie had taken an intense dislike to the young man. Yet he was good-looking, civil spoken, and ambitious to do well. He also thought the world of Andrina.

He was a left-footer, of course, but as McPherson had already pointed out to Sophie, he didn't seem a very devout one. Anyway, what did it matter? Since McPherson had been in the army and fought side by side with Catholics as well as Protestants, he no longer judged a man by what foot he kicked with.

'What does it matter? What does it matter?' Sophie had been outraged. Since her conversion she was much more bigoted than he'd ever been. 'Of course it matters. They're ignorant. They worship idols. They accept everything that man in Rome says as gospel. They blindly follow him, instead of Jesus and the

9

word of God . . .' She had gone on at some length, until he had stopped listening to her. Then she changed tack and said, 'Anyway, that O'Maley creature's disgustingly physical.'

She should talk, McPherson thought. Now he leaned towards Bernard and said, 'She's through in the kitchen, if you'd like a word.'

'No, I'll come back. I'll wait and see what you can do first. Thank you again, Councillor McPherson. It was good of you to hear me out. I know Andrina's young. I know I'd have to wait a year or two before we can be anything more than friends, but I must have a chance. If I'm not allowed to see her at all, she might find someone else and forget about me. That mustn't happen, Councillor McPherson. I want to be friends with her, and then court her, and then eventually marry her.'

McPherson gazed solemnly at the earnest young man and thought with a deep sigh, 'Oh dear, oh dear . . .'

Chapter Two

'She's still seeing him,' Sophie told McPherson.

'You don't know that. I was there when she said . . .'

'I know what she said, and I believed her. But there is something different about her recently. She's lying to me.'

'You've a suspicious mind, Sophie. Always thinking the worst of folk. It's not Christian.'

'Not Christian?' Blotches of colour burned high in Sophie's cheeks. 'How dare you say such a thing? I'm trying to do my Christian duty by her. That's why I'm so worried. It's obvious you don't care. The only people you care about or have any time for are your precious constituents – your all-important voters. You care about them all right . . .'

She could see he'd switched off. Now there was no way she could get through to him. She'd tried often enough in the past. But once that expressionless veil came down over his eyes, once he began leisurely filling his pipe, she was shut out. She was on her own.

His calm self-containment had been one of the things that had attracted her to him at first. His idealism, too . . . and his courage. What a big, fine-looking man he'd been. Not a pick of flesh on him in those days. Not like now, with his heavy jowls and bulging paunch. Of course he'd worked in the building trade then as well as in politics. The job hadn't been a sham then as it was now. He'd really sweated it out on the sites.

She'd been one of his constituents. She'd gone to his surgery for advice. His 'surgery', where he held court once a week, was an empty shop in Dumbarton Road. People came there with their problems and he treated everyone, including herself, with patience and much flattering attention. People liked their young Labour councillor, and they liked him still.

She had gone to see him about her chances of getting a

11

council house. He hadn't offered her much hope, if any. After all, she was a single woman, and when did the Corporation ever allocate homes to single women? Especially when there were so many married couples on the waiting list.

But he'd been so sympathetic that she found herself telling him more than she'd intended. It had all spilled out about the 'home' she'd been brought up in, run by the sadistic tyrant of a matron, then the string of seedy lodgings and bed-sits. She told him she didn't remember her parents. They'd died when she was very young. Of course, they hadn't died, and she did remember them, and she remembered why she'd been taken away from them and put into what had been euphemistically called 'care'.

She remembered them all right. The filth that they were. She prayed they were dead now. They had ruined her life. They had awakened in her a vile torrent of emotion and erotic desire that had taken many years to repress and control. Even now, saved by the blood of sweet Jesus, she had to be forever vigilant.

In the quiet of the night she'd see them – fumbling with one another, and with her, involving her, abusing her, arousing her. She'd remember how much she once loved them. She'd remember how confused she became. But even in her innocence she had known they were betraying her. The betrayal had been a thousand times worse than any physical pain she'd ever suffered. The betrayal and the contamination of her. Those had been the worst things.

She wasn't even old enough for school when she was caught simulating sex with children in the street. Other parents had complained to the authorities. That's how it had all been found out and she'd been taken away. Taken into 'care'. It made her laugh with bitter sarcasm.

A lot of good that had done her. Nobody had cared for her, and she cared for nobody else. Often her hatred turned on herself, and the thought of being trapped in her own loathsome body nearly drove her crazy.

The church had been – and still was – her lifeline, her saving grace. She couldn't live without it and the high regard with which she was held there. If she had been a demonstrative woman – which she was not – she would have kissed each and every church member's feet with gratitude. She had confessed her sins at the altar and they had forgiven her. All the men she'd fornicated with, all her neglect of Andrina when she was a baby. All wiped out.

It was McPherson who'd told them that her parents had died when she was a child and she'd been brought up in a 'home'. Then she had their pity as well. It was almost like love. She treasured it. And she blessed McPherson for introducing her to the church, and for his part in the saving of her. For all his faults, she'd always be grateful to him for that.

In time, he too had forgiven her. She knew it was the church who had helped him do this. Wonderful, miraculous Church of Jesus and the pure and blessed Christians who belonged to it. She'd rather die than let them down. Andrina would not let them down either. Or her mother. Never. She'd see to it.

'She's only sixteen.' Sophie refused to give up her badgering to get McPherson's attention. 'And that Pape's over twenty. He'll stir up the bad in her. I knew what type he was the moment I set eyes on him.'

McPherson sighed before lifting his newspaper and using it as a barrier between them. 'He seemed a nice enough lad to me.'

'How can you say that, knowing the family he comes from? But it's not only his background.' Sophie hesitated, her mouth twisting. 'It's worse than that.'

She couldn't say any more. Some things were beyond explanation.

Chapter Three

Sometimes Andrina wondered what made her suffer most: the first years of her life, when she had continuously longed for the security of her mother's love and attention, or now, when she had her mother's attention with a vengeance. From the age of sixteen, Andrina was put under a magnifying glass. Sophie was constantly suspicious. She inspected what Andrina wore. Nothing had to be 'provocative to men'. Friends were strictly vetted. Only the offspring of the Church of Jesus were allowed. Even then, Andrina was subjected to a 'third degree'. A Saturday afternoon at the cinema, even on her own, resulted in an ordeal that made a repeat of the outing too exhausting to contemplate. Only the few secret meetings she managed with Bernard made her otherwise unbearably restrictive life worthwhile. On the other hand, she suffered torments of guilt after each occasion. To make up for her wicked deceit she tried extra hard to please her mother. At church for instance, where her mother seemed to gain so much pleasure listening to her and watching her sing in the choir. Sophie always sat in one of the front pews, eyes bright and intense, riveted on her daughter.

She lapped up the praise afterwards too. People would say, 'You must be very proud of Andrina, Sophie. Such a lovely girl, and such a sweet voice. She looks just like an angel, doesn't she?' Sophie's smile would still hover about her thin mouth as she and her husband and daughter walked home. They walked separately. They weren't a touching kind of family. Never in her life had Andrina seen her parents kiss each other.

Sophie had a very straight, stiff back and she was always telling Andrina to straighten up. 'Don't slouch,' she'd say. 'Stand straight in the sight of the Lord.'

Andrina had hoped to widen her horizons after she left school. She had dreamed of going to university. She imagined the freedom this would entail. Now, freedom meant being able to see more of Bernard O'Maley. He could meet her on University Avenue and they could walk over Great Western Road way and along to the Botanic Gardens. All her dreams included Bernard now.

Her father had been quite amenable to the university idea. He was always quite amenable to everything she put to him, of course. So much so that she suspected he was just acting the part of a pleasant, easy-going father. He could wear an earnest and sympathetic expression while she was talking, yet she never felt she was getting through to him. She had the feeling that he wasn't really listening. His mind was occupied with someone else's problem.

Her mother listened all right. 'University? Have you not seen the wild crowd that mill about over there? You just need to look out of our window. Anyway, do you think your daddy's made of money?'

Seeing the so-called wild crowd out of their window was somewhat of an exaggeration, because although the towering grey spire of the university was perfectly visible over on the hill beyond the Art Galleries, the students could not be seen from the tenement window. Unless of course they ventured down Kelvin Way to the Art Galleries across the road, or to the park spreading out and dipping down beside it.

'But I was hoping to try for a degree and eventually become a teacher,' Andrina protested. 'I was speaking to Robert Anderson and he thought it was a good idea.'

The mention of the church, or one of its members, always made her mother more amenable. Sure enough, Sophie's voice immediately lost some of its edge. 'You mean Jean Anderson's son?'

'Yes.'

'He hasn't been to church for a few Sundays. His mother's been coming on her own.'

'He was saying that he runs a club at weekends for deprived children from Blackhill. He teaches in Blackhill.' Andrina almost added, 'and that's near where Bernard lives and went to

15

school,' but caught herself just in the nick of time. 'Robert comes to our painting group on Tuesday nights. He's a great help, with him being an art teacher. I wonder that he can be bothered after working at it all day.'

'He's a nice lad, that's why.' Sophie's voice gathered enthusiasm. 'And a good Christian like his mother, and his late father before him. Jean says he's a gem of a son to her.'

Andrina nearly blurted out that he was hardly a lad. He must have been at least fourteen years older than her. She thought better of it. If there was one thing her mother hated, it was being criticised or corrected. Along with her Christian commitment had come an extremist way of thinking and an obsession to do everything to perfection. She was houseproud, for instance. There wasn't another fireplace in the whole street that sparkled and gleamed as hers did. Every morning she was down on her knees attacking the old range with black lead, and its steel edges with an emery board. Twice a week she had all the rugs down in the back court and whacked them like a wild thing with the carpet beater. Every day (every minute, it seemed to Andrina) she was bumping the carpet sweeper back and forwards. Andrina was allowed to do very little, because apparently she could do nothing right. Even when taking the ashes out to the bin in the back yard, Sophie followed her to make sure no ashes were spilled on the stairs that she'd just scrubbed and decorated with pipe clay.

Sophie began to talk of getting another house. It would be a new house, she prophesied, with a bedroom for herself and McPherson, so that they wouldn't have to sleep in the kitchen as they did there. Andrina could have a proper bedroom too. There would be a bathroom. There would also be a room free to use as a sitting-room. The kitchen would be a place in which to cook, instead of having to live and wash and eat and sleep and do everything else in it.

Sophie was a wonderful cook. Even McPherson gave her credit for that, and not just in front of others. 'That was good,' he'd say, patting his widening girth. 'That's one thing I have to give you credit for, Sophie, you're an excellent cook.'

16

Sophie wasn't sure at first where the new house should be. She did not know about areas of Glasgow other than the one in which she now lived. Nor did Andrina. Like most Glaswegians she had never gone far outside her own district. She only ventured further along Sauchiehall Street to the centre of town to attend the Church of Jesus, or to visit a cinema, or to gaze at shop windows. Any real shopping was done locally, in the McPherson's case it was along the other end at Dumbarton Road, or in Byres Road which ran up from Dumbarton Road to the West End. It was within walking distance, or a brief tram or bus ride from the house. McPherson's mother lived in Dumbarton Road, across from the foot of Byres Road, and they often visited her there.

Of course, the Art Galleries and the Kelvin Hall nearby were places most Glaswegians knew and had visited at some time in their lives. This gave the area where they lived more of a cosmopolitan feel than the other, more closed districts. The war had widened everyone's horizon to some extent, but people still tended to keep to their own patch where all their friends and relations also lived.

It was therefore a surprise to Andrina when her mother invited Mrs Anderson and her son from Adelphi Street on the other side of the river to visit Sauchiehall Street one Sunday. And they came. Andrina wished it could have been Bernard being accepted into the house, and she told Bernard this on one of their secret assignations. He said, 'It's not so bad if it's Anderson. He's OK.' Robert Anderson was much admired by pupils and ex-pupils alike – more for his prowess at karate and his karate club than his school art classes, Andrina suspected. But he was, as Bernard said, 'OK'. In fact, she was flattered by Robert's obvious interest in her. Sometimes she even suspected that she was the reason he attended the art group at the church. He certainly went out of his way to help her more than anyone else, and more than once he'd said he'd like to paint her portrait.

'You've got such wonderful eyes, Andrina – an unusual kind of turquoise colour,' he'd told her. Touching her hair, he added, 'And that deep rich shade of auburn. I'd love to try and capture it on canvas.'

Another surprise had been when her mother bought her a dress at one of the sales to wear that Sunday. Andrina was so excited that she blurted out about the portrait Robert said he'd like to paint. Immediately the words escaped she violently trembled, fearing the coldness of her mother's disapproval – something to be avoided at all costs.

But no. Miracle of miracles! Her mother looked pleased. Andrina even sensed an aura of triumph. For the first time in her life she felt that her mother was emotionally involved with her – in a pleasant, happy kind of way. They were sharing an excitement. Happy expectation was bouncing between them.

'Stand still,' her mother commanded as she pinned the hem of the dress. Her voice was good-humoured. 'I'll be jagging you if you keep wriggling and bouncing about.'

Gratitude towards her mother for being so unexpectedly close to her gathered like a lump in Andrina's throat. It was as much as she could do to contain her emotions and not burst into tears. Speechless, she gazed at the older woman, the steel spectacles and the piercing eyes behind them, the gleaming hair pulled back so tightly that made her eyes slant a little. At forty-six she had not an ounce of surplus weight, unlike most of the shapeless forms of the other women they knew.

The tiny flat was gleaming and pungent-smelling with furniture wax on the Sunday of the Andersons' first visit. All the work had been done on the Saturday, of course. Sunday was the Lord's day, and whenever possible Sunday was a day of rest. Even the skirting boards were washed and polished. The outside toilet, situated on the landing between the top flats and the next ones down, was thoroughly scrubbed and disinfected. The disinfectant was so strong the smell of it enveloped you as soon as you set foot on the stairs. Andrina had tried to help but her mother shooed her out of the way, insisting, 'I'd only have to go over it all again. I have to make sure of everything myself.' Nevertheless, Andrina had taken a duster and began dreamily smoothing it over everything.

It was when she'd reached the window-sill in the front room and was thinking of Bernard that suddenly she saw him. He was standing at a bus stop across the road, but he wasn't watching for a bus coming. He was staring up at the window. Her pulse immediately quickened and she darted an anxious look behind her in case there was any danger of Sophie seeing him too.

A bus came and went and Bernard was still there. Andrina leaned closer against the window, caught in the hypnotic force of his unsmiling stare.

'Andrina!' Her mother's voice fractured the spell. 'What are you doing through there?'

'Coming, Mummy.' She hurried back to the kitchen. 'I was just doing some dusting.'

'I've already cleaned through there, as you well know. Anyway, they know the front room's your bedroom, more's the pity. It's high time we had a decent house with a proper bedroom each and a proper room to entertain folk in.'

On the Saturday night McPherson was told to go to the Royal Artillery Club to be 'out from under my feet', as Sophie put it. But, 'for pity's sake don't drink too much and let yourself down.'

He went without a murmur. He enjoyed any opportunity of meeting and having a talk with the other ex-servicemen who frequented the place. Old campaigns were relived and argued over with great eagerness and enthusiasm. His visits were most welcome. If trumpets could have been blown they would have heralded his arrival. He was their only VC, and they were touchingly proud of him. He only wished he could go to the club more often.

Unfortunately, the Andersons' visit had increased a hundredfold Sophie's nagging about a new house. 'You've managed to get houses for other people,' she kept saying. 'Why can't you get one for us? It's terrible not to have a decent sitting-room – or any kind of sitting-room. That front room is Andrina's bedroom. And what can I do with it when there's that big wardrobe there? It means we'll have to have the Andersons in the kitchen.'

19

He'd pointed out, 'We've been having friends and neighbours and folk from the church in the kitchen for years.' But it was no use.

'I know, and I've had enough of it,' Sophie said. 'I'm sick of being so cramped and having to eat and sleep and cook and wash in this one poky wee kitchen. It's not sanitary.'

'There's a lot worse places.'

'I'm not interested in worse places. I want a better place. And not up on a top flat. It's enough to give me a heart attack – climbing all these stairs every day carrying heavy message bags.'

McPherson knew this wasn't the reason. Sophie thrived on buzzing about all the time. Restlessness was a disease with her. It was exhausting to watch. He was glad to get out of the house and away from her fast-moving greyhound body and equally rapid tongue. He sat a lot, often with fellow councillors, in the Corn Exchange Restaurant and Bar in Gordon Street opposite Central Station. There people could approach him, and many a deal was done and favours offered and received. He could get a council house for Sophie, no bother at all, despite the fact that there was a huge waiting list. Every member of the housing committee could be counted on as a friend. He had done them favours in his capacity as a member of the licensing board. He'd used his influence to get more than one licence for Jimmy Barker, for instance, for his new pubs. It was Andrew McPherson that Bill Dodds (also of the housing committee) had to thank for his taxi licences. These were just a few of the people he'd gone out of his way to help. It had always been a case of: 'If you scratch my back, I'll scratch yours'. The housing committee knew better than not to allocate him a house if he wanted one. But he was quite content where he was: this part of Sauchiehall Street was handy for transport and near any amenity, and yet it had the nice peaceful outlook on to the Art Galleries, the trees of the park and the University beyond. But he wasn't going to get any peace now that Sophie was determined to move.

'All right,' he sighed eventually. 'We'll get a council house. I suppose you want Knightswood or Mosspark?'

20

These were the best and most respectable housing schemes the council owned. Only those, and such as those were honoured by being given the chance of a home there. That was if one became vacant – and vacancies were few and far between.

'No. Drumchapel.'

His stare widened. 'Why Drumchapel?'

'They're brand new houses in Drumchapel, I've heard.'

'Yes . . . but . . .'

'And it's right out in the country.'

'Well, it's still Glasgow but I suppose you could say . . .'

'And it's right next to Bearsden.'

McPherson had never been in Bearsden, but everyone knew it was *the* posh place to live. 'It's not that near.' He suddenly felt exasperated. 'You're city born and bred the same as me, Sophie. What on earth do you want to go and live in the country for? Once Andrina gets married we'll have this place to ourselves. Why can't you settle down and appreciate your nice wee house?'

'I could ask you the same question when you keep leaving it, either to hang about the City Chambers . . .'

'I don't hang about the City Chambers,' he interrupted irritably. 'I sit in at innumerable committee meetings. It's me and people like me who run the city.'

'Or the Corn Exchange Restaurant.' Sophie ignored his interruption. 'Or disappear for weeks at a time on one of your jaunts.'

The jaunts (all expenses paid) she referred to were the times he had visited various parts of England, and even further afield, to study their methods of running their cities, or building their roads, or their bridges, or their housing estates. Or for any reason at all that was thought necessary, or just thought up. His late father, David McPherson, had been a dedicated member of the Labour Party Council before him. He had always refused to go on any jaunts. He had been ruthlessly honest, absolutely incorruptible, and idealistic. He had been so hard-working on behalf of the people of Glasgow that he had, while negotiating one of the first housing schemes and rehousing people out of the

21

slums, even brought a camp bed into his office and collapsed in an exhausted sleep there night after night. 'And what thanks did he get for all his fast-held Socialist principles?' McPherson thought bitterly. 'Where did it get him? To an early grave. That's where it got David McPherson.' Thinking of his father, McPherson was bombarded with the usual mixture of love, admiration, guilt and anger. Once he'd been ready and willing to follow in his father's footsteps and live up to all his father's high ideals. But not any more. You couldn't beat the system. You had to go along with it. You had to do the best you could with it – for everybody, including yourself.

'All right. All right,' he told Sophie. 'We'll get a house in Drumchapel, if that's what you're sure you want. But I'm not a miracle worker. You'll have to wait until a decent one becomes vacant. So content yourself just now and leave me in peace.' More and more, anything for a peaceful life was becoming his motto at home. He went ahead and had a word in a few ears and it was, as he said, 'No bother at all'. He was eventually able to tell Sophie that it had been agreed and she'd have her new house as soon as a suitable one became available.

What he didn't tell her was that he'd come to believe that he could, if he really wanted it, put the pressure on Felderman the builder to have a house specially built for him however and wherever he wanted. He also felt confident they'd sell it to him for a rock-bottom price. But he drew the line at bought houses. The ordinary man in the street couldn't afford to buy a house. It was the duty of the council to make sure there were enough houses to rent. He was supposed to work for Felderman's, but it had been agreed that he would just say he worked for them and they would stamp his cards. It was also agreed that neither of them wanted to do anything illegal – but if McPherson, as a member of the housing committee, could do Felderman's any favours, he would. And he did.

When the construction of all the vast housing schemes had become too much for the council employees, McPherson had been the one who had sung Felderman's praises, who had spoken to this committee member and that committee member on Felderman's behalf. He had been the one who put the pressure on, and reminded the committee of favours done in the past and possibly more favours in the future. He had been the one who had eventually secured Felderman the building contract worth millions. There had been a lower tender, but he had organised that too. The Council was seen to be accepting (as they were supposed to) the lowest tender, only to have that tender withdrawn at the last minute. That left Felderman as the successful applicant.

He was glad that Sophie was not only happy with his promise of a house in Drumchapel but that she kept out of his hair while busying herself with preparations for the Andersons' visit.

She baked two Victoria sponges that were as light as thistledown, sandwiched them together with her home-made raspberry jam and dusted the top with icing sugar. Girdle scones and pancakes and salmon sandwiches also graced the table. Its scrubbed wooden surface had first of all been covered with Sophie's best white damask table cover, and her fluted, rose-patterned wedding china was set out. A pristine white bedspread with a fringed border was spread over the set-in-the-wall bed.

The fire glowed and sparkled redly in the steel edges of the range and in the brightly polished fender.

'Everything looks beautiful, Mummy.' Andrina clapped her hands in excitement, but calmed down immediately her mother snapped, 'Control yourself. You're not a child any more.'

It had been decided now that she'd leave school before the summer holidays started at the end of June. Nothing was certain about what she was going to do after that. Work in one of the posh Sauchiehall Street shops, perhaps? She quite fancied the idea of herself in a smart black frock and pearls, swanning towards a wealthy lady customer with the words, 'Can I help you, modom?'

The Andersons arrived exactly on time, something that Sophie took pleasure in remarking on. She was a stickler for punctuality herself, although Robert grinned and said that in their case it was more by good luck than good habit.

Robert Anderson was only an inch or two off six feet, and of lean build. Not that he was tough in the sense of looking common, as Sophie later remarked. It was just that he kept himself decently healthy with all that karate, or whatever it's called. His face was lantern-jawed, with overhanging brows and blue-grey eyes.

Jean Anderson was smaller and plump and motherly, with sandy hair fading into grey and face and hands blotched with freckles.

Everyone enjoyed their tea, although Andrina couldn't eat much because of nervous excitement. It was all too unusual, too much for her – her mother being so indulgent, so happy. Sophie and Mrs Anderson (just call me Jean, she'd said) and McPherson did most of the talking. But Robert addressed several queries and remarks to Andrina, and they smiled at each other in between eating and drinking tea.

Before they left, Jean invited them all to have tea at her place in Adelphi Street the following week, and Robert addressed Sophie in that confident, aggressive tone that teachers often acquire. 'Perhaps Andrina and I could meet before that. There's an interesting film at the Cosmo I believe she'd enjoy.'

And, miracle of miracles, Sophie smiled and said, 'Yes, I think Andrina would like that. Wouldn't you?'

Andrina was too confused and bewildered to make any response and her mother quickly answered for her.

'Of course she would, Robert.'

Right there and then arrangements were made. Robert Anderson was calling for her on Wednesday evening to take her to the Cosmo Cinema.

The confusion and the bewilderment did not go away. Indeed, these feelings intensified over the weeks and months that followed. But they were private to herself, mixed up with and hidden deep in the same secret place as her feelings for Bernard.

On the surface she was skating along a strange, unreal path; happy in a superficial, unreal way. She was grateful for so unexpectedly being able to please her mother, and she basked in the attention and envy of all the other girls in the church.

'You've all the luck,' they'd say. 'What's it like', they'd ask with barely suppressed longing, 'to go out with a real man?' They too had strict Christian parents. Their parents however were still imposing rigid and inhibiting rules on their lives. Andrina's life had changed completely.

'Wonderful,' Andrina would enthuse, like an actress as soon as a spotlight was turned on. 'He's strong and masterful. He knows his way around too. He takes me to such interesting places. And he's so self-confident. Not show-offy or noisy with it, you understand, not like some of the silly boys we knew at school.'

It was true that she felt proud of Robert and enjoyed going out with him. He was opening new worlds for her. She did admire his relaxed, easy manner, and also the firm air of authority about him. She was impressed by his knowledge of so many things of which until now she had been completely ignorant. But oh, he wasn't Bernard.

When Robert kissed her, the controlled gentleness of his mouth against hers was pleasant enough. But oh, he hadn't Bernard's fire, Bernard's magic touch. Bernard could not only send her blood careering wildly through her veins, but could make her feel that she was part of him – one spirit, one flesh. With Bernard she belonged.

Robert was her bulwark against Sophie. As long as she was with Robert, she was, in a way, free. She had her mother's blessing. Because of this, Robert seemed an incredible good fortune.

Jean, Robert's mother, and Sophie became bosom friends, and they couldn't hide their delight and satisfaction when Robert confided in them that he was going to ask Andrina to marry him.

'I was so happily married,' Jean told Sophie. 'It's my dearest wish that Robert will be settled in the same way before I die.'

'I feel the very same about Andrina,' Sophie replied.

Sophie couldn't wait to rush home and warn Andrina.

'He's perfect,' she enthused. 'A good Christian man. A member of our church. You'd be safe. He'd keep you safe in a respectable home. He'd keep you on the right path.'

'Mummy, what are you talking about?'

'I'm talking about you saying yes to a decent, respectable man when he asks you to marry him.'

'But I've only been going out with him for a few months.'

'You've known him for longer than that at the church.'

'Yes, but . . .' Andrina's mind groped through darkening mists. 'I don't love him,' she wanted to say, 'not the way I love Bernard.' But she hadn't the courage. 'I'm too young,' she said.

'You're near enough eighteen. Anyway, you'd not be married right away. For one thing, we've the move to the new house first.'

Word had come about a house in Drumchapel. A house exactly where Sophie wanted it – at the end nearest to respectable Bearsden.

'But Mummy,' Andrina tried again. 'I like Robert. I know he's a nice man and I've enjoyed going out with him as a friend. But I'm not in love with him.'

'In love.' Sophie spat the words out in disgust. 'You've been reading trashy romance books again. I told you how wicked they were. They fill young girls' heads with stupid, wicked nonsense.'

'No, it's not that . . .' Andrina's face creased with the strain of trying to make her mother understand without alienating her. But how could she express to anyone, far less her mother, how she felt about Bernard? The mere sight of him melted her with warm delight. Oh, how beautiful he was. So tall. His broad chest a warm welcome for her head. His hard features, his soft, sensuous mouth. And oh, those dark, glowing, knowing eyes.

She had only managed to see Bernard once or twice a month, depending on where and when he was working and how successful she was in finding a friend willing to cover for her. Sheila Preston was the only one who would oblige, the only one who even knew about her continuing relationship with

Bernard. Sheila's father was an elder in the church, and her mother was president of the Women's Guild. Sheila was a fellow member of the church choir and taught in Sunday School, but there was more to Sheila than met the eye, and certainly more than any of their respective parents knew about. Sheila was Andrina's loyal alibi. It could also, and often did, work the other way around. Sheila was the one with whom Andrina was supposed to be picnicking in the Campsie Hills. Or visiting the People's Palace Museum. Or attending a performance of Gregorian chants in the cathedral. Instead, Andrina was revelling in a few golden hours with Bernard, cuddling, caressing, sweetly kissing, or being perfectly content to hold hands. Often they didn't even talk.

To be with him was the important thing. Just to see him. To gaze at him. For oh, he was so beautiful. He was the flame that warmed her. There was no need for words. No need even to think.

Looking back, she realised she hadn't thought about anything else that was happening to her, hadn't asked herself any straight questions. What was she doing? How could she have been carried away by the envy of the other girls when they spoke of her relationship with Robert Anderson?

She hardly knew where she was, her life was careering along so rapidly. Sometimes she felt a little frightened. She'd hardly been allowed to abandon her gym-slip, ankle socks and broad stretch bandage for dresses, silk stockings and brassière, before being plunged into talk of wedding dresses and veils, and the booking of the Co-op purvey.

Not that she was afraid of Robert Anderson. But his proposal had such an air of authority about it. The desperate hustling of her mother and the eager expectancy of Robert's mother all conspired to make her agree obediently to the marriage before she'd really thought about what she was saying, or why. She kept telling herself that she'd done the right thing; her mother was so pleased with her, and she was flattered by the admiring attention of all the girls.

'You lucky devil,' they said. 'Fancy being taken out and

27

around by such a gorgeous man. Even having your portrait painted. And now you're going to be MARRIED!'

Flattery was the key word. Especially in connection with the portrait. Secretly she believed she couldn't, she didn't look as stunningly beautiful as he'd painted her. And did she really have that confused, uncertain but eager-to-please look about her?

Certainly she was confused by the speed and pressure of events, including the change from the tenements of Sauchiehall Street to the incredible space of the three rooms and kitchen and bathroom they moved to in Drumchapel. The space wasn't just inside the house either. There was miles of it outside, and hills in the distance on one side, and on the other, nestling down in the valley, were the villas and gardens of Bearsden.

Andrina had never been out in the country before. None of them had. Her father had fought in the desert during the war. Was that 'country'? She didn't think so. She and her mother wandered about in mutual confusion. Her mother kept saying, 'Isn't this wonderful? Everything looks so green and there's so much space.' Inside the house she never tired of repeating, 'Would you look at all these rooms. And look at the kitchen. And would you believe – a *bathroom!*'

Andrina couldn't. Any more than she could believe that she had allowed herself to agree to marry Robert Anderson. It wasn't just a bit of excitement to giggle about with girlfriends. It wasn't something out of the romantic novels they'd all read in secret. *It was real.* What added to her confusion was that everywhere she went, she kept imagining she saw Bernard O'Maley. She hadn't met him for months now. Not since her engagement. Yet she kept thinking she'd seen him. A dark concentration began to haunt her.

Chapter Four

'I don't know where you get all your energy from,' people often told Sophie. 'You're never at peace. You never seem to get a quiet minute to yourself. No wonder there's not a pick of flesh on you.'

This was how it had to be. She had to keep going. She had to keep lashing herself with work. She could not bear being idle. A quiet minute to herself was an anathema to be avoided at all costs. If no one was in while she was doing housework, she had to have the wireless blaring in the background. Her mind had to be bombarded with sound or occupied with some over-whelming interest, some immediate task or present problem – her own or anyone else's. Often she filled the void with feverish prayers. It was a constant battle to prevent her slipping back and down into the sewer of the past. It wasn't just the furtive fornicating in draughty, evil-smelling back closes with men from far off places, some of which she'd never heard of. All that, she realised now, was bad enough. She had been a slag, a slut, a hairy, an easy lumber. (Her only saving grace was that she had drawn the line at bringing the men into Andrew's house, Andrew's bed.) She'd danced and laughed and had a riotous good time at the Locarno or Green's Playhouse but later, after the giggling and groping had quickened into penetration, she had felt sickened, even while actively enjoying her animal-like coarseness.

Later still, in the house on her own (she never acknowledged the existence of the child crouched in the dark in the hole-in-the-wall bed), Sophie felt even more sickened. She was swamped by the filth that had been her parents. She saw them in her mind's eye, forcing her to watch them having sex, getting a thrill at being watched, forcing her to do things, doing things to her. She had been hardly more than an infant when it had

29

started. She looked back at them with a loathing that had grown and festered over the years instead of diminishing. Even her salvation hadn't cured the poison of her hatred, only driven it deeper so that it didn't show.

When Sophie was a child, her parents' behaviour had been the norm, the only way of life she'd known. That had been the reason for her behaviour with other children. Looking back, one part of her mind recognised the truth and the innocence of her behaviour. At the same time the loathing of her parents spilled over and enveloped the memories of her childhood. Until they were one and the same thing.

Neighbours had complained about their children being in moral danger. Sophie was, in their view, a source of corruption, and was therefore removed to the huge prison-like institution of Moorlands. She'd never seen her parents again – nor did she want to. If they did come back into her life she believed she would take great pleasure in destroying them, as once they'd destroyed her. But probably they were dead. She hoped they were dead. She hoped they had died a slow death of leprosy or cancer. If they were alive, and they could be alive for all she knew, her father would be seventy-six and her mother would be seventy. But the chances were that their filthy flesh would long since have been deservedly consumed by the worms.

Sophie stamped them from her mind. Crushed them out with busy, useful, good, worthwhile things. This had cleansed her. The church was a wonderful saving grace. She enjoyed the fellowship of it, and the rigid framework within which she had learned to function.

Now there was the wonderfully harassing business of moving house. There was the intriguing novelty of the new place, and all the plans she'd formulated of how she was going to decorate it. There was the problem of the extra furniture it would need.

On top of all this, there was all the work and planning for Andrina's wedding. She was doing her very best for Andrina. She had protected her against the sin of casual sexual encounters. She had arranged that Andrina should be safely settled in a good marriage with a decent Christian man. A secret part of herself, a part she refused to recognise, was glad to be getting rid of the girl. That hair, those full lips, that curvaceous body – it was her disgusting mother all over again. From the first moment she'd set eyes on the infant Andrina, as soon as she'd seen the fluffy red down of hair, she'd known.

Nevertheless, Sophie was doing her Christian best for the girl. She had decided that instead of getting the Co-op purvey, she'd do everything herself. Everyone had protested that it would be far too much work for her. McPherson had warned that she'd end up killing herself and there was no need. Admittedly they were having a lot of extra expense with moving house, he said, but they'd manage to pay for a purvey. The Co-op wasn't too dear and they still had a month or two to put a few pounds by.

Andrina too was worried. 'Please Mummy, don't do this. You'll only make yourself ill. I don't want to have you on my conscience on my wedding day. You won't have enough energy left to enjoy it.'

Robert Anderson had told Sophie bluntly that he wasn't going to invite any of his friends or relations to keep down the numbers if she didn't at least come to some sort of compromise.

So in the end she grudgingly agreed to the Co-op providing the steak pies, potatoes and peas, and the trifles. She would bake and decorate the wedding cake. And of course she would make Andrina's wedding dress. It was when she set about gathering all the things she needed that she discovered the first drawback of being in Drumchapel. There were no shops. The Council had apparently not thought of including any amenities whatsoever when they'd built the huge housing scheme. There was no community centre, no school, no church or church hall, no cinemas, no dance hall, no pub or club. There wasn't even a bus service.

It gave her something new to nag McPherson about. 'The crowd of you in City Chambers couldn't run a ménage. You've just flung up these houses and never given a thought to the people's practical day to day living. I've over a mile to walk before I can get a bus to take me to the shops. Then I've all that walk back again, weighed down with messages.'

31

It was now a terrible business trying to get to church on a Sunday. In Sauchiehall Street they simply had to go out and catch one of the tramcars that passed by their close. On a nice day they sometimes walked along to Rose Street, off Sauchiehall Street, where the Church of Jesus was situated.

'I go down on my knees and thank God,' Sophie kept repeating to McPherson, 'that Andrina is engaged and will soon be safely married. With nothing to occupy them around here, young folk will be bound to get into trouble.'

Special buses collected children early in the morning and took them to schools miles away. By the time they were brought back it was late, which didn't give children much time to do anything once they'd had a meal and done their homework. The trouble would come if they left school at fifteen and no longer had any homework to occupy their time. Already groups of youths were wandering aimlessly about. Lack of discipline didn't help either. So many mothers weren't there to keep a watchful eye on offspring, far less lay down the law and insist that it was kept.

Most people had come from single-ends or one room and kitchen, and hadn't enough furniture to fill their new Drumchapel houses. The result was that many women had to go out to work to make the extra money needed. Then the journeying to and from work made it a long day away from home for them too.

The difficulties at this early stage at least didn't worry Sophie overmuch. Indeed, she thrived on them. They kept her extra busy, hurrying here and there, getting things for the house, painting, decorating, scrubbing, polishing, cooking, baking, planning everything for the wedding.

She helped Andrina with the house she and Robert eventually rented in Monteith Row opposite Glasgow Green. It was a cobbled street of old black tenements, but it was very handy with tramcars nearby and a nice view of the Green from the front room window. They had been very lucky in managing to get two rooms and kitchen with a huge bathroom. Andrina was obviously thrilled at the idea of having her own house and especially such a spacious one.

It wasn't as big as the three rooms and kitchen and bathroom Drumchapel house, of course, although the rooms in the older property were marginally bigger and had high ceilings with carved cornices. However, the kitchen was as cramped as all the tenement kitchens she'd ever seen, with the hole-in-the-wall bed and the big black range, the iron sink, the wooden coal bunker and four-barred clothes pulley dangling from the ceiling. Once a table and chairs were put in, and a sofa against the bed, there wouldn't be enough space to swing the proverbial cat.

The bathroom had more floor-space. They really made the most of having a bathroom. Robert mirrored the walls and laid a lovely black shaggy carpet on the floor – edge to edge. It was really luxurious. Of course, Robert and Andrina were full of bright ideas; Robert was thinking of doing away with the kitchen bed and making the space into a dining area – putting the table and chairs in there, to leave more central floor space.

'Did you ever hear the likes of it?' Sophie asked McPherson. She had been shocked and silent on the subject of the mirror walls in the bathroom, but about the kitchen she was enthusiastic. 'Of course it's with Robert being an art teacher – he makes drawings of everything and plans everything out. He's really very clever and original. Andrina is terribly excited with the idea.' She added in a more accusatory tone, 'Of course Robert takes a real interest. If he had had anything to do with building housing schemes, he wouldn't have made the ridiculous mistakes that you and your crowd at the City Chambers made.'

All the same, she thought Drumchapel was a beautiful place and she was proud of her house. She couldn't have been more busy and happy. And as McPherson said, it was early days. The amenities would come in time.

The wedding plans were going full steam ahead and Sophie had made a lovely job of Andrina's wedding dress. The girl was ecstatic about it. They'd both gone to Copland and Lye's for the veil and white shoes. Andrina got quite a big discount because she was now an employee there. The Co-op florists were going to supply the bouquet of pale pink and white lilies and a deeper shade of pink carnations.

The only annoyance had come when Andrina, bubbling over with eagerness, had asked, 'What kind of wedding did you have, Mummy? Were you married in white? With your slim figure you must have looked lovely. I bet your mother and father were really proud of you.'

'They both died when I was a baby. I don't remember them.'

'Oh?' Andrina looked puzzled. 'I thought you once said . . . I understood that . . .'

'What could you understand about anything?' Sophie snapped, turning away from her, cutting Andrina out, cutting out her red hair and long lashes and shameless curves that she flaunted with every step she took.

The so-called 'Sweater Girl' bra with the pointed cups that Andrina had bought with her first week's wages had been disgusting. Sophie had told her that if she saw her wearing the thing she'd no longer be a daughter of hers. 'As long as you're still under my roof,' she'd said, 'you'll keep some decency and not behave like a shameless slut.'

At least she'd prevented her from buying the tight fitting slacks. Andrina had asked her what she'd thought of the idea. 'All the girls are wearing them now, Mummy, and they're not really tight,' she'd pleaded. 'In fact, they're very comfortable for walking and sports and . . .'

'What kind of sports do you do? And you're too lazy ever to walk to work. You're just wanting to wear these things so that you can flaunt your backside. You're disgusting. You're revoltingly fat. It would suit you better to try and hide your backside as much as you possibly can.'

If Robert didn't put his foot down and watch Andrina like a hawk, God knows what she'd be up to once they were married. Sometimes Sophie wondered if she ought to warn him. Especially now that she'd discovered Robert knew Bernard O'Maley. O'Maley had been a pupil at Robert's school. He also attended Robert's karate class. Now, apparently, he helped Robert to run it.

Sophie worried constantly about Andrina and the O'Maley creature meeting again. Right from the beginning she had seen in his eyes what a filthy beast he was. Surely he couldn't be one of the friends that Robert spoke of inviting to the wedding. If he was, she'd soon score him off the list.

Chapter Five

'Frank's always been too soft. That's his trouble.' Patrick O'Maley made the pronouncement about his youngest son during a family conference at which everyone except twenty-four-year-old Frank was present. 'I've tried everything I could to toughen him up from the moment he began to walk but it's been no use.'

'Och, he's a lovely boy. Leave him be,' Frank's mother pleaded. 'Just because he's not like the rest of you doesn't mean there's anything wrong with him. Far from it. I did his chart the other day and it said great things are going to happen to him. He's got a great future ahead of him, has Frank.'

'You and your bloody fortune-telling,' Patrick said, but in quite a pleasant tone. Then his voice gathered its anger again. 'All that's happened to Frank so far, Maureen, is that he's been regularly duffed up at school. And since he's got himself in a soft job as a pen pusher, that's not likely to increase his popularity with the lads. But the worst thing is, he's shutting himself away all night writing letters to himself. The boy's gone soft in the head now.'

'No, you don't understand, Pat.' Maureen's dramatic eyes bulged. 'He has to address envelopes to himself, see, so that he gets his stuff sent back.'

'What stuff?'

She hesitated uncomfortably, then tossed her wild bush of grey hair. 'His wee verses. Och, he's not doing anybody any harm.'

Michael, a year older than Frank (and Bernard's twin), was incredulous. 'Not doing anybody any harm? What do you think it does for me? Do you think it helps my reputation in the ring having a poof for a brother?'

'What Frank does is nothing to do with you or any of

you,' Maureen cried out. 'And he's not a poof. Stop calling him that.'

Bernard said, 'We're just thinking of his own good, Ma. Frank doesn't seem to have a clue. If he'd come to the karate club with me. Or even let me coach him at home . . .'

'He's just not interested in learning how to handle himself,' Michael shook his cropped head. 'It's not natural.'

'If he was a Ted he'd have to handle himself or he'd be minus a nose or an ear.' Tony, the eldest at twenty-six, worked in a butcher's shop and was a Teddy Boy in his spare time. After shop hours he changed from rolled-up shirt sleeves and striped apron to knee-length draped jacked, drainpipe trousers and thick crêpe-soled shoes that he called brothel creepers. He was fussy about his clothes and his hair. He was forever combing it. (Unlike his brothers, Frank didn't care about his appearance. Frank was a bean-pole topped with lank, straight hair. His clothes, like his hair, never seemed to fit him.)

Michael was a natty dresser in his own way, perhaps a bit on the flash side, with his pin-stripe suits and dark glasses and brightly-coloured ties. At least as a boxer no-one could say he wasn't tough. Already he'd won several amateur trophies and with his iron muscles, his bullet head and his craggy, broken-nosed face, he could boast as pugnacious a manner as any professional fighter. When he wasn't in the ring either training or fighting, he was on building sites doing the same brickie work as his father. He was tough all right, but he had recently come in for almost as much flack from the family as Frank.

Michael's problem was in courting Caroline Stoddart. The Stoddarts lived in Cobden Street, the next street along off Garngad Road. The moment Michael had introduced her to the family they'd been suspicious. His mother had been very pleasant though, and made Caroline a cup of tea and plied her with coconut snowballs. She asked her which street she came from, and of course when Caroline admitted it was Cobden Street she was immediately branded a Protestant.

Not that Maureen or any of the O'Maley family were bigoted. They denied it most hotly. As Maureen said, 'Many a

Protestant from Cobden Street and even as far as Springburn has been made welcome in this house in Bright Street, and has had their teacup or tarot cards read.'

However, Michael knew that the predominance of Protestant clients stemmed from the fact that Father Riley said fortune-telling was wicked. His mother, in her own inimitable way, had interpreted this to mean it was only wicked if she practised it on Catholics.

As far as his courting of Caroline was concerned, his mother warned, 'It can cause so much trouble, son. It's safest to stick to your own kind. Then if you get scratched, it doesn't go septic. What does her family think of you?'

He could have said, 'Not much', but he restrained himself. He and his brothers were all Maureen's 'lovely boys', and no outsider would dare say anything against them without her immediately and indignantly taking up verbal arms. This fire didn't need any fuel.

But the important thing was, as far as he was concerned, he and Caroline got on great. He wasn't planning to marry her family. He didn't think much of them either. Caroline's mother, Big Martha Stoddart, was built like a battleship and was well known for the unusual, the almost unheard-of activity of beating her husband. Jimmy Stoddart made up for his ineffectualness at home by being a loud-mouthed bigot outside of it. He was a grand master of an Orange Lodge. Not in Garngad, which was predominantly Catholic – an Orange Lodge in Garngad wouldn't have lasted very long; it would have lasted an even shorter time in neighbouring Blackhill – but bigger districts like Springburn could accommodate Orange Lodges and the equivalent Catholic establishments.

Michael secretly dreaded the day when the O'Maleys and the Stoddarts got together and Jimmy Stoddart found out that Tony O'Maley, not content with being a Catholic, was also a Republican. It was fortunate that the Stoddarts and the O'Maleys used different pubs, otherwise Jimmy would have found out by now. Tony was a bit of a loudmouth himself. No, that was an understatement. Tony was the world's worst loudmouth. Tony was noisy about everything.

For a time Michael and Caroline had managed to hide the seriousness of their relationship from Martha and Jimmy Stoddart. They had appeared no more than part of a crowd. Occasionally they *had* been part of a crowd, standing at the street corner when the Stoddarts passed by. Even so, Caroline had been warned to 'watch herself' because there were 'a couple of Papes in that lot'.

More recently they had been spotted on their own and the trouble had started. Caroline had been reduced to a nervous wreck. Her face was constantly swollen and blotchy with tears, until Michael braved the lions' den and faced the Stoddarts. He would have preferred to oppose anybody in the ring to confronting Caroline's parents, but he stood his ground. He told them he loved Caroline and Caroline loved him and they were going to be married. Caroline could remain a Protestant if that's what she wanted. Any children they had could be brought up as Protestants if that's what Caroline wanted. All he wanted was to marry Caroline.

What swung the decision in his favour, however (although their pessimistic misgivings remained), was the fact that he had won not only the interclub championships and the Western District championships, but more recently the Scottish middleweight title. As far as Jimmy Stoddart was concerned, even a Catholic Scottish middleweight champion was something to boast about. Big Martha stuck to her prophecies of doom, however, and insisted that a mixed marriage was a recipe for disaster and no good would come of it. A Pape was a Pape – Scottish middleweight champion or not.

Frank was now an added worry for Michael. What the Stoddarts would think of his younger brother he had no idea, but feared it would be much the same as his mates, all of their mates. Frank was a queer fish. Some people believed he thought himself a cut above everyone else. He didn't. It was just that people imagined he did. That was the unfortunate impression Frank gave and it caused a simmering resentment among the locals.

Only a few days previously, when Frank had had a drink with him, there had been an example of this resentment. The beer had definitely been cloudy, and Michael had been going to remark on this to Joe, the barman. If he had, Joe would have been apologetic and pulled another beer. Probably they would have had a friendly and interesting chat about it and Joe would have explained the reason for the cloudiness. Unfortunately, Frank was the one who happened to remark on the beer first. A look of hatred had immediately darkened Joe's face and he spat out, 'Just because you fancy yourself as a know-all writer doesn't mean you know a fuckin' thing about beer.'

Poor Frank couldn't say anything to anybody without having his writing flung in his face. If he'd managed to keep it secret it wouldn't have been so bad, but there had been times when his enthusiasm had got the better of him and he told everybody that he was writing poetry – even, to everyone's acute embarrassment (and the family's shame), he had read some of it out loud. He was only about twelve when it first happened, but tall and lanky even then. He'd also been bug-eyed and eager.

'It's called "What Waits",' he announced. Then, to the stunned crowd in the kitchen of family and friends who had been enjoying a good bevvy, he continued:

'What waits,
When this brilliant burning flame,
This flame we call life,
Is done: we finish the unfinished game,
And cede the futile strife.
What waits,
Behind the ever unopened door,
With breath and body gone;
We do not know, we wondered before,
But we shall know – anon!'

What waited for Frank was a clip round the earhole from his father and an exhortation not to be so bloody daft.

But there was a stubbornness about Frank that no clip round the earhole from his father, nor hooting and jeering from his brothers, nor playground beatings, could budge him one inch.

Frank had continued scribbling away at his poems. Maureen was angry when she found out that while she thought he was doing his homework and studying, he had actually been concocting poems. Sometimes he'd been wasting his time making up stories.

'Sweet Jesus,' Maureen cried out, 'would you look what the boy's doing now!' Then to Frank, 'Every penny we can scrape together goes to keeping you and Bernard at school. God gave you and Bernard the brains in this family and it's a sin if you don't make the most of them. Bernard works hard doing his homework, and he's doing a milk round and God knows what else as well. He's a good boy. What are we going to do with you, Frank?'

Neither Tony nor Michael had been offended at the implication that God had dished out less brains to them than to their two brothers, although Michael had no doubts that he was much better endowed in that respect than Tony. He would have flattened anyone who said it, but secretly he accepted the fact that Tony was a bit thick. The mere fact that he kept mouthing off about his support for the IRA was, in Michael's opinion, daft to the point of being dangerous. The truth was that Tony had never had anything whatsoever to do with the Republicans. He'd never been in Ireland. Indeed, none of them had (except their grandads and grandmas on both sides, but they were all dead). He'd been involved in gang fights when he was younger, and more recently the occasional fight with gangs of Teds from other districts. Compared with the IRA, however, Tony's acts of violence were child's play. They couldn't get this through his thick head. But that was nothing to the incomprehension they all felt about Frank.

'What's to be done about Frank?' had been expressed with varying degrees of anguish or anger, or a mixture of both, down through the years.

41

The whole family had nearly emigrated at one point, such was the mortification Frank caused them. He had actually taken up tennis and was seen going down Bright Street and along Garngad Road in a white shirt, white pullover and white flannels. They had all been vehement in Frank's defence to outsiders, and nobody dared to jeer or laugh or say a word against Frank when Michael or Tony or Bernard were around. Inside the house it was a different story and they did everything but physically abuse him. Patrick had threatened to beat the living daylights out of him and Frank had only been saved by Bernard grabbing his father and struggling like mad to stop him.

Frank didn't seem to care. Or at least, he always stood his ground. He did what he wanted to do and that was that. It was a kind of courage and it aroused in his brothers a grudging admiration. It had to be admitted that to walk the gamut of Bright Street and Garngad Road in white flannels took guts. Either that or it was an act of incredible stupidity, and Frank wasn't stupid. He had passed God knows how many Highers before he left school. Some of the books he read were by names no one could pronounce – like Dostoevsky.

This wasn't the first family conference about Frank. At previous gatherings it had been decided to get the priest to talk to him. That had happened, all to no avail. At this family conference, however, the idea emerged that if Frank could start walking out with a good Catholic girl, that would be sure to do the trick. If they could just get him married and involved in a family (the bigger the better), the responsibilities that would entail wouldn't leave Frank any time for all his nonsense. But what girl would have him? Patrick thought of Bridie Gallacher, one of Scobie Gallacher's daughters. The Gallachers – a monstrous tribe of them – lived in Turner Street, and Bridie's twenty-first birthday party was coming up soon. Frank – as well as Michael, Tony and Bernard – had been invited.

One of Bridie's sisters, Effie Gallacher – Michael remembered her well – had been drowned in the Monklands Canal a year after his brother Sean. The canal claimed several victims every year, but still youngsters ran joyously to it and splashed and bounced about like frogs in its murky waters. It was their only swimming pool, their equivalent of a more affluent person's seaside.

'We can't force him to go out with anybody.' Bernard shook his head. 'How can we even get him to go to the party? You know what Frank's like.'

Maureen interrupted him. 'Leave that to me. I'll tell him how much Bridie's mammy is trying to make this a good do for Bridie, seeing it's her twenty-first, and how much of a comfort the poor wee soul was to me when we lost our Sean, God rest his soul.'

Tony revealed his long, horsy teeth. 'You mean that wee fatty with the specs and the face full of plooks? Only somebody as daft as our Frank would look at her.'

'She doesn't look like that now. At least she's lost her plooks,' Bernard said. 'She's a bit like Frank in a way.'

'A bit daft, you mean?' Tony said.

'A bit of a loner. Maybe because of the mess she looked when she was younger. Neither of them hung about the corners very much.'

The talk of getting Frank paired off with Bridie made Bernard's mind turn yet again to Andrina McPherson. Since he'd first set eyes on her in Kelvingrove Park, she'd never been far from his thoughts. After her mother had laid down the law and forbidden Andrina to see him, they'd met as often as possible in secret, wonderful, exciting, dangerous assignations, as Andrina had made them seem. There was magic in the very air they breathed every moment they were together. His darling. His own beautiful Andrina with her round, childish eyes and sensual body. He wanted to marry her. He had held back from consummating their relationship, something he'd never done with any woman before. But he'd never wanted to marry any woman before.

His ability to keep control of himself sexually with Andrina had been helped in a way by the fact that they had only been able to meet on so few occasions and for such limited amounts

43

of time. But even a moment with her was precious to him and wonderful.

Even after she'd begun seeing Robert Anderson, he'd still tried to talk to her. She'd started work in Copland and Lye in Sauchiehall Street. As often as he could in the evenings he waited outside the shop door, and as soon as she emerged he caught her by the arm and urged her to come with him 'somewhere where we can talk'. On each occasion she had become more and more agitated, and kept looking furtively around as if she was doing something criminal by being seen in his company. He sensed her agony and cursed her bigoted old harridan of a mother for causing it. Even in his dreams he cursed her. It was impossible to communicate with Andrina when she was in such a state. He'd tried everything including anger.

'For God's sake, Andrina. Your mother doesn't live along the road any more. She's away out in Drumchapel. She's not likely to see us, is she? So what are you getting all up tight about? I know what's behind your mother's attitude. It's the Orange and the Green, the Celtic and the Rangers, the Billys and the Dans. Well, I don't care about all that, and I don't believe you do either. We were getting on so well. We were so happy until your mother interfered.'

But no matter how desperately he tried, he could not break through the barrier of her agitation. She seemed completely unable to concentrate on what he was saying. Her expression was miles away, withdrawn, blanked out. Then she started coming from the shop after work surrounded by a tight bunch of other girls. Giggling and chatting, they'd crowd along the street and then all crush on to a tramcar. Sometimes he managed to *will* Andrina to look back in his direction, and he'd see beyond the giggling and chatting to the deep distress in her eyes.

He was convinced that she felt for him as he felt for her, despite all her talk about Robert Anderson and how her mother was encouraging a friendship between them. He made excuses. She was young and impressionable and she was dominated by her evil old hag of a mother. But one day when she was older and stronger, Andrina would break free of that influence. She belonged to him. They belonged to each other. It was impossible to accept that she was never going to be his. All the time he lived in hope. Everything he did he did for her. After he'd graduated from the paper round he'd done while he was at school, he'd worked for all the hours God gave as a bouncer in the Empire, and then for a security firm. He'd gone abroad with them on some highly dangerous jobs. Everything he did to make enough money so that he'd be able to afford to rent a house and furnish it in whatever way she wanted.

Before the McPhersons had moved to Drumchapel, he'd hang about Kelvingrove Park and the Art Galleries, watching for her in every free moment he had. There had been occasions when he'd followed her. Once she'd been with her witch of a mother. The woman even looked like a witch, dressed in black, with dark, piercing eyes glinting behind steel-framed spectacles and skinny body leaning forward as she hurried along. Mother and daughter had gone from their house in Sauchiehall Street along to Dumbarton Road where he knew Andrina's granny lived.

Another time, Andrina had emerged with Robert Anderson and gone in the other direction to the busy shopping part of Sauchiehall Street. They had eventually disappeared inside the La Scala picture house. It tore at his gut to see her with another man. The fact that the other man was Robert Anderson, someone he admired and who had always been his mentor, was a frustrating and confusing element with which Bernard found it impossible to cope.

His pain and confusion grew as time passed and it became obvious that Robert and Andrina were walking out together. It was an agony for him to stand in the shadows and watch them, arms linked, laughing and talking, Andrina glancing up at Robert with a mixture of innocence and teasing flirtatiousness.

It was obvious the way things were going, yet he couldn't believe it when he heard that marriage was on the cards. It had been a proud and happy Robert who had told him. In a daze,

45

he'd shaken hands with the man and murmured his congratulations along with the more voluble ones from the rest of the karate club.

Robert was a great guy. As far as Bernard was concerned no better man walked the face of the earth. He would have done anything for Robert Anderson – died for him if necessary. He wished him well. He wished him everything that his heart desired.

Everything, that is, except Andrina McPherson.

The only clear-cut thing that remained in his mind, in his gut, in his very soul, was the belief that Andrina McPherson belonged to Bernard O'Maley. They belonged to each other. Yet the world kept turning. The wedding day came.

Bernard stood across the road from the church, waiting and watching, his belief overflowing into a kind of madness.

Chapter Six

The only thing that had spoiled the wedding preparations, as far as Andrina was concerned, was her mother's fury when Robert suggested inviting Bernard O'Maley.

'That revolting Pape?' Sophie spat out. 'If you have him at the wedding, you won't have me.'

Robert was astonished. 'What's wrong with Bernard? I've known him for years and I've always thought him a credit to the kind of background he's had. Garngad's a tough area, and not many turn out as well as him. He was working hard even before he left school, and since then he's really used his strength and his expertise at karate to his advantage. I think he'll end up employing people, building up a good business.'

'A good business?' Sophie sneered. 'He's part of the underworld. He's a gangster.'

Robert shook his head. 'He's tough, and perhaps he has to mix with, or deal with some tough people, but he's not a gangster.'

McPherson cut in then. 'I agree with Robert. Bernard always struck me as a decent enough lad, and his father was a good soldier. One of the best.'

'A good drinker, you mean?' sneered Sophie. 'I always know when you've met Patrick O'Maley at the Artillery Club. You come home stupid with drink. A great influence he is on you, or on his son or on anybody else. I will not have Bernard O'Maley at my daughter's wedding. If you have him at the wedding, you'll not have me,' she repeated.

McPherson took a thoughtful puff at his pipe before saying to Robert, 'When Sophie feels so strongly about it, perhaps it would be wiser to think again, Robert. She's never liked him. He used to be friendly with Andrina . . .'

'Yes, he told me he knew her,' Robert interrupted. 'When

47

they were young, a crowd of them used to meet in Kelvingrove Park.' He sighed. 'What do you think, Andrina? He's a good friend of mine and a valuable help to me at the karate club. I would like him to be at the wedding, but it's supposed to be the bride's big day. I don't want anything to spoil it for you.'

'It would completely spoil it for me if Mummy wasn't there,' Andrina cried out. 'It would be terrible. I couldn't bear it.'

Robert put a soothing hand on her arm. 'All right. All right. I won't ask Bernard.'

It took Andrina some time to calm down, she was shaking so much. Robert had stared curiously at her afterwards when they were on their own.

'Darling, are you all right?'

'Yes, of course.' She tried to laugh. 'Why do you ask?'

'I'm not quite sure . . . You're not afraid of your mother, are you?'

Andrina gave a genuine laugh this time. 'Don't be ridiculous, Robert. Surely you can see she's the best of mothers. She's worked like a slave to have everything perfect for me at the wedding. I adore her.'

'Yes,' Robert agreed. 'She's done everything she can to help us. I'm a very lucky man to have such a mother-in-law. I realise that. I'm just sorry she feels as she does about Bernard, that's all. But not to worry.' He took Andrina into his arms, smoothing his cheek against hers, not saying anything for a time before he let her go. She loved him for making her feel so comforted and secure. Everything would be all right once they were safely married. 'Safely married' was the term her mother always used, and Andrina had acquired the habit of using it. At the same time she was secretly looking forward to the freedom she imagined the marriage would give her. She didn't dare admit it, even to herself, but by freedom she'd come to mean freedom from her mother. She imagined that as a married lady she would be her own boss with her own house to queen it over. She could go in and out when she liked. She could wear whatever she fancied in clothes or in make-up or in jewellery. (Her mother thought anything other than an engagement ring and a wedding ring was wickedly frivolous.)

Oh, how Andrina longed to wear big flashy earrings. Oh, how she longed to be free from guilt and the disapproval that kept chipping away at her self-confidence, and the illogical terrors that had so often plagued her. When she'd still been at primary school, and after her mother had first been saved, her mother had told her about Hell and 'the bad burning fire' that people, especially children, would be cast into if they did bad things. Andrina no longer believed such a threat. Her mind told her there was no such thing as a 'bad burning fire'. At least not in the context of a place called Hell. Indeed, her intelligence told her there wasn't such a place under any name or description. The girls at the shop had often giggled and made a fool of the expression. They too had been on occasion threatened with 'the bad burning fire' and they all, including Andrina, agreed how ridiculous, indeed how hilarious, the expression was. (Although one of them had admitted that what really had scared her was her mother saying that the bad fire into which she could be cast was Dixon Blazes, the Iron Works that was the beacon that reddened the sky over the south side of Glasgow.)

Oh, to be free of all these dark, ridiculous things. Oh, to be free of being constantly watched and warned and questioned. To be married was going to be like having a burden the weight of an elephant lifted clean off her shoulders. It was the instant dispelling of a dense black cloud. She was filled with joy at the mere thought of it.

And, joy of joys, the marriage came with her mother's blessing. Yet over the joy hung a gauze of sadness.

She was a very lucky girl, her mother said, and Andrina was quick to agree with her. The thought skimmed secretly and guiltily across her mind that she was lucky that, by the move to Drumchapel, her mother wouldn't be able to visit her too often. Fleeting as it was she still felt shame at the thought. 'You and Daddy will aways be welcome at Monteith Row, Mummy,' she anxiously assured the older woman. 'I'll arrange for you both to come for your tea as soon as we're settled in.'

What she didn't say was that she and Robert had planned a housewarming party for their friends. She was looking forward to the event so much she just couldn't bear the idea of her mother knowing and probably taking over the organising of the whole thing. She wouldn't attend the event when it was specifically for younger people. (She wouldn't, would she?) But she could insist on coming earlier to do all the cooking and organising. Then perhaps she might stay on with the excuse of helping dish out the food or washing up the dishes afterwards. That would mean the kiss of death to the party. She would watch and criticise what everybody was drinking. She disapproved of women smoking, and so nobody would dare light up. Stolen kisses, even just for a lark, or friendly cuddles, or sitting on boyfriends' knees, would be more than frowned upon. Such behaviour would be publicly denounced.

The housewarming party would have to be kept secret from Sophie, Andrina insisted to Robert, until after the event.

'She'll surely hear about it from some of our friends in the church,' Robert said.

'I'll warn them. They know what mother's like. She does tend to go over the top a bit. They'll keep quiet about it. Anyway, I'm only inviting a few of the young ones that I know enjoy a bit of fun. Our front room won't hold all that many and I want to leave enough space for your friends from work.'

'Some of the teachers at St Francis aren't so young, I'm afraid. But they're a good crowd. You'll like them. Then there's a few lads from the karate club I'd like to invite, including Bernard, of course. I still feel rotten about not inviting him to the wedding. To be honest with you, Andrina, I would have preferred him to be my best man.'

'Oh dear.' Andrina's expression collapsed with distress. She could no longer cope with the reality of Bernard. He had become like a beautiful dream and it was better that way. Nothing could ever have come of this relationship. She'd always known it. 'I'm so sorry, Robert. But you know what Mummy's like about Catholics.'

50

'She definitely mustn't come to the party then. Most of my colleagues and friends are Catholics.'

'Doesn't your mother mind?'

He shrugged. 'I suppose she's got used to the idea. For a start, when I was offered the job in St Francis there weren't many jobs going around. My father was ill and unemployed and we needed the money.'

'It was unusual for you to be offered it, was it not? I mean with you being a Protestant . . .'

Robert grinned. 'Darling, if you knew how tough a district Blackhill is you wouldn't think it at all unusual that a school there would be glad to get any teacher with enough nerve and optimism to teach in the place.'

Andrina felt a pang of apprehension. 'Is it dangerous?'

Robert's grin widened. 'Not for me it isn't. Or for guys like Bernard. Do you know any of his brothers?'

She shook her head.

'There are four O'Maley boys – Tony, Michael (Bernard's twin), Frank and Bernard. To see them coming along Garngad Road together is an impressive sight. People automatically clear a path for them. That's the kind of charisma you've got to have in places like Garngad and Blackhill.' Robert sighed. 'Sad but true. It's a case of the survival of the fittest. I try to teach them other things as well, of course. But it's a terrible uphill struggle. Especially in my department. So many of them think anything artistic is soft and poncey. You've got to keep proving yourself. God help Frank. I hear he writes poetry.'

'Are Michael and Bernard identical twins?' Andrina asked.

'Well, they're both big, heftily built men, but that's about it. Michael had curly hair like his father, but he keeps it cropped close to the bone now. And his nose has been broken a few times with him being a boxer. He and Bernard have a different look about the eyes too.'

Soon Bernard faded from Andrina's mind again. There were so many exciting thoughts to occupy her. The preparations for the wedding went happily and busily on, as did the more secret plans for the housewarming party. The party was going to take

51

place a week after they returned from their honeymoon (two weeks at the Clyde resort of Dunoon) – just enough time to do a good sized baking. The same sponge mixture could be used in different ways: as small individual iced cakes with a cherry on top; as Victoria sponges stuck together with raspberry jam; as sponge fingers spread on top with ginger jam and nuts. Scones had to be baked as well, and pancakes made. Lots of sandwiches – tinned salmon, corned beef, mashed dates. It was going to be great fun. Andrina was looking forward more to being a busy housewife and entertaining guests in her very own home than to getting married. She hardly gave the wedding a thought. She hardly gave Robert a thought. Except when she was with him, of course. They were good friends. She liked and admired him enormously. She liked being with him.

To her he was awesomely sophisticated. He was not intimidated by posh restaurants. He spoke knowledgeably about art and artists and took her to exhibitions. He introduced her to the world of the theatre. She was grateful. Her hugs and kisses were outward expressions of that gratitude. It was easy to tell him she loved him. She was light-headed with happiness on her wedding day.

'You look like an angel,' her father told her, and kissed her and gave her an affectionate hug.

'What do you think, Mummy?' Andrina turned, shining-eyed, to Sophie.

Sophie was dressed in a black tailored coat, and a black brimmed hat tilted forward over her brow. She jerked on her black leather gloves and thought, 'Her and her red hair, and green eyes, and voluptuous curves.' Hand to mouth, she turned quickly away. 'You'll do,' she managed.

Both Andrina and her father were touched. They thought Sophie had been overcome with emotion.

They were right.

Chapter Seven

'Oh, hello, Mummy.' Andrina opened the door and stood aside. 'What a surprise!' It was her first full day back from her honeymoon. Robert had returned to work, and when the doorbell rang she had been standing in the front room feeling free and happy and proud. The sitting-room was ultra modern and in such good taste. What other house in the street, in the whole area, would have beautiful, original paintings on the walls?

'A pleasant surprise, I hope,' Sophie said, bustling after her daughter into the kitchen.

'Of course. I'll put the kettle on. It won't take long. It's still hot from breakfast.'

Sophie's eyes darted into every corner of the room.

'You haven't dusted, I see.'

'I lit the fire.' Andrina's voice quickened with eagerness, like a child hoping for praise. None came.

'Breakfast dishes still in the sink.' Sophie shook her head.

Andrina hastily explained, 'I was just going to wash them . . .'

'It's past ten o'clock.'

'. . . when my neighbour came to the door . . .'

'You don't want to encourage every Tom, Dick or Harry coming to your door, keeping you off your work. Especially in a place like this. You don't know what kind of people they are. I've heard there's prostitutes often hang about the Green.'

Andrina's mouth fell open and it was a second or two before she could find words. 'I thought you liked the place. You said . . .'

'Yes, yes, you were lucky to get a house with a bathroom and an open outlook on to the Green. But there's a pretty mixed crowd to be found in there, especially if there's a fair on, and

53

there can be a terribly tough crowd. And don't forget there's Bridgeton nearby, and the Calton over the other side of London Road. Not to mention the High Court facing the Monument. There's bound to be a right lot of riff-raff always around there. That's where they used to have public hangings. Facing that monument. Don't you ever go out at night without Robert.'

Andrina laughed. 'Mummy, there's never been any public hangings for donkey's years.' But her euphoria had evaporated. 'Mrs Slater next door seemed all right. She's invited me in for a cup of tea later on. She had to rush out this morning but she said she'd be back after . . .'

'Don't tell me she works, and her a married woman. I can imagine what her house will be like.'

Andrina gave a gasp of disbelief. 'Mummy, lots of women have a job nowadays. Surely you know that. You said yourself that during the war . . .'

'There isn't a war on now. That's half the trouble today. Women going out leaving their children to grow up any old how without discipline or being taught what's right or wrong, or given a good Christian education. Boys getting into fighting and thievery. Girls into pregnancy or prostitution. The world's full of sin and sinners. If God's will's not done there's going to be retribution, you mark my words.'

'But she's divorced and she hasn't got any children.'

'A divorcée!' her mother echoed.

Andrina poured the tea. 'Would you like a biscuit?' She nearly added, 'These are shop ones but I'm going to be doing lots of home baking this week,' but she stopped herself in time, afraid that Sophie might wonder what all the baking was for. Her heart plummeted at the thought. Quite apart from the danger of her mother spoiling all the fun before and during the housewarming party, there was the terrible business of Bernard being there. At least it would be terrible in her mother's eyes.

Her mother startled her by saying, 'When are you going to do some home baking? You don't want to fill your good man with shop stuff like this.'

'I'll probably do some tomorrow.'

54

'I'll come and give you a hand.'

'Oh no, I've just remembered,' Andrina nearly spilled her tea in her anxiety, 'I've to visit Robert's mother tomorrow. Anyway, Mummy, you can't possibly travel all the way over here from Drumchapel every day. It takes so long. How could you get anything done in your own house? Anyway, there's no need. And I don't want Robert to think I can't bake or do anything by myself. I mean, what would he think of me?'

'I suppose you have a point,' Sophie reluctantly agreed. Then her thin face brightened. 'But I can still keep in touch with you every day.'

'How do you mean?'

'We've got a phone!' Sophie announced triumphantly. 'Andrew should have had one long ago – with all his council business – and we've arranged for you to have one installed as well. As part of our wedding present. Remember we said we had something else for you – a surprise? We thought we'd have it in for you coming back but they couldn't manage it so soon. They've promised to install it for you before the end of this week though.'

Andrina was torn between the thrill of having a telephone to link her to her friends and the fear of the umbilical link it might prove to be with her mother. 'Oh Mummy, it's very kind and generous of you and Daddy, but I don't think you ought to go to all that expense.'

'Nonsense. Your daddy seems to be doing very well just now with one thing and another. I'm sure Robert will be delighted. I'm surprised he didn't think of putting one in himself, a man in his position. That tea's not very strong. You should have let it mask a bit longer.'

Suddenly something occurred to Andrina. 'How could the engineer have got into the house while we were away?'

'Oh, didn't Robert mention it? I asked him for one of your keys in case there was an emergency while you were away and I needed to get into the house.'

Andrina was so appalled she couldn't speak.

'If the place had been burgled, for instance,' Sophie went on, 'and the police needed to check on what was taken. Or needed the place locked up again, I could have come and seen to everything. I'll pour this weak stuff down the sink. Maybe it'll be a bit stronger in the pot now. Just a minute, I'll give it a good stir first.'

'I've never heard about any house-breakings,' Andrina managed. 'Banks, shops in town, bars and bookies' places, but never ordinary tenement houses in working class areas like this, have you?'

'Just because there was never any in Dumbarton Road that we know of doesn't mean there isn't anywhere else. You can't be too careful.'

Anger was trembling inside Andrina, but she tried to sound pleasant enough. 'I'm surprised you didn't use the key today instead of knocking at the door.'

Her mother stopped in the middle of stirring the contents of the teapot. 'Do you actually think I would have walked in here without knocking and risked frightening the life out of you? Is that all you think of me? After all I've done for you?'

'No, no. Of course not. I mean, I really appreciate all you've done, Mummy. You've been really marvellous. A marvellous help.'

'Did you notice I got messages in for you coming back?'

'Oh yes. I really appreciated that. It would have been too late for me to get any milk or bread or anything for Robert's supper. He really enjoyed the meat pie. I did too.' She'd left a key with Mrs Slater next door and had thought it was her that had just been neighbourly.

'I thought it would be nice for you to come home to something in the cupboard,' Sophie said. 'I noticed you hadn't got any messages in before you went away.'

'I know. I'm sorry about that, but what with all the excitement of the wedding and everything, I forgot.'

'That's better,' Sophie said, pouring out another cup of tea. 'Will I fill you up? Oh, you haven't drunk it yet. No, leave it. It's like dishwater. I'll get rid of it and pour you out a fresh cup.'

Andrina could have wept with irritation. She longed to

56

stamp her feet and cry out, 'It's my home, my key, my kitchen, my teapot, my tea.' But felt ashamed at what she saw as the childishness and pettiness of her feelings. Her mother was only trying to be helpful and caring. (Although she secretly determined, one way or another, to get her key back.) 'Thanks, Mummy,' she said.

'How was your honeymoon? Was Dunoon nice?'

'Lovely. You and Daddy should go there some time. Such a nice clean place. You'd love it, Mummy, and it would do you so much good to get away for a holiday.'

'Oh, your daddy's too busy for me. I hardly ever see him these days. What's that saying? "A shoemaker's bairns are always worst shod." He's too busy seeing to what everyone else needs.'

'You could go with him on some of his trips.'

'And what difference would that make? On the journey in the train he'd have his nose in official papers all the time. Then, when we got to wherever he was going, he'd disappear to meetings and I'd be left on my own in a strange town among strangers. He'd forget all about me. I know your daddy. It's hard enough trying to make him toe the line when he's here.'

Andrina looked at the thin bespectacled face and felt a rush of love and pity. 'Never mind, Mummy. You've always got me.'

'Yes,' Sophie echoed, 'I've always got you.'

Andrina wished she could do something or say something to make her mother relax. There was always such an intense look about her, almost of desperation. It was most unsettling. In a way she couldn't blame her father for withdrawing into himself or into council business. Probably he did it so he could get a bit of peace.

'Your daddy's got an office or some place where he does his council business now,' Sophie continued. 'He never even comes home for his dinner. I don't see him all day.'

'In the City Chambers?'

'He's says it's just a small corner in the chambers. And they've a restaurant for the councillors. I told him – it won't be as good food as you'd get in your own home. He's been staying in the chambers till late as well.' Her mouth tightened. 'I'm beginning to wonder if he's up to something.'

Andrina was shocked. 'Oh no! Not Daddy. Mummy, how could you think such a thing?'

Sophie's nostrils pinched in as she took a deep, firm breath. 'Yes, God forgive me. I must cleanse my mind of bad thoughts. Drumchapel's too far out for most folks to come to the house, apparently. Remember how they all used to come every night after we had our tea? Never a soul now.'

'Oh dear. Are you finding it lonely?'

Sophie shrugged. 'I'll soon settle in and get to know folks. The trouble is so many of the women seem to be out at work. I've said it before and I'll say it again. It's not right.'

'Robert and I will come to visit you at the weekend. Will that be all right?'

'Come to Sunday dinner. I'll get a bit of good steak. I know Robert likes a good bit of steak.' Sophie's eyes brightened. 'And I'll make one of my apple tarts. Remember he said it was the best apple tart he'd ever tasted.' She laughed. 'I don't know what his mother would have thought if she'd heard him. Of course, give Jean her due, she makes very good butter shortbread.'

'I know. I've tasted it.' Andrina couldn't help wondering how long her mother planned to stay.

'I'll rinse these along with your breakfast things.' Sophie snatched up the cups and saucers although in fact Andrina hadn't quite finished her tea.

'I'll do them, Mummy.'

'It won't take a minute. What've you got in for Robert's dinner?'

'We're going to have our dinner at night after he finishes work. I gave him some sandwiches to have in the staffroom at lunchtime.'

Her mother splashed water into the basin and rattled the dishes around. 'Oh, *lunch* now, is it?'

Andrina knew that everyone – or at least everyone she and her mother knew – had their main meal, which they called

58

dinner, in the middle of the day, and a 'high tea' in the early evening – which could consist of scrambled eggs and chips or some sort of fry up, and bread and jam, perhaps scones and pancakes as well. But times were changing.

'It's better this way, Mummy. We can both relax and enjoy our main meal after Robert's finished work.'

'I suppose it's sensible enough when you look at it like that. Yes, it's a good idea. From now on, we could have our dinner at night as well. I must tell Andrew not to stuff himself with a lot of rubbish in the City Chambers restaurant during the day. So what are you making for Robert tonight?'

Andrina felt trapped. She had been looking forward to such a lovely day on her own, doing anything she wanted and in her own time.

'I hadn't made up my mind. I've still to go to the shops.'

'Right.' Sophie put the last of the dishes on to the draining board to dry. 'I'll go and see what I can get while you rake out that fire and set it and polish up the grate. That job causes a lot of dust, remember, so give the whole place a good going over afterwards. Now, where's your message bag? Don't tell me you haven't got one. Never mind, I'll take mine.'

'But I don't know how much money to give you . . .'

'Oh don't be so gormless. I'll tell you how much everything cost when I get back and you can square up with me then. I'll bring a bit of corned beef or a nice slice or two of tongue to make a sandwich for us as well.' She laughed. 'We'll have our first *lunch* together.' She emphasised that word, as happy as a child with a new toy.

The door closed and Andrina was alone again, but no matter how she tried, she could not recapture a single vestige of the joy she'd experienced earlier.

59

Chapter Eight

The phone rang within minutes of it being installed.

'Hello Mummy.'

'How did you know it was me?'

'I haven't had time to give anyone my number.'

'I asked the exchange. I gave you my number, didn't I? Wasn't it lucky you getting the phone in so soon?'

'Wonderful.'

'What have you been doing today?'

'It's only quarter past nine, Mummy.'

'Don't tell me you've left the breakfast dishes and the fire again.'

'No,' she protested, then flushed guiltily as if her mother could see down the phone and into the kitchen. 'Well, I would have had them done, only the telephone engineer kept me back.'

'Remember to order more coal.'

'Yes, Mummy.'

'Did you see that woman after I left yesterday?'

'What woman?'

'Next door.'

'Oh yes.'

'What was she like?'

'It wasn't that she was working yesterday morning. She had to go and see the factors.'

'Had she got into arrears?'

'I don't know. I never asked her.'

'She doesn't work then?'

Andrina hesitated. 'Well, not in the morning.'

'Well then?'

'At nights.'

'Where?'

60

Another hesitation. 'In a public house.'

'A barmaid?' Her mother sounded so shocked it was as if Andrina had confessed to being a barmaid herself.

'She seems a very nice person, Mummy.'

'What kind of judge of character are you? Where is this bar?'

'Castle Street.'

'Castle Street? That's near Garngad and Blackhill. I can just imagine what a so-called nice person she is. The next thing will be she'll be tempting you into the rough circle she obviously mixes with. I feel quite ill at the thought. That whole area is a cesspool of sin, Andrina. There's gang fights and prostitution and all sorts of wickedness goes on over that end of town.' She was working herself up into a frenzy.

It frightened Andrina. 'Please, Mummy,' she pleaded, 'there's no need for you to get upset.'

'You've always been a worry to me. You worry me sick. You've always got into bad company. I've always tried to watch you and keep you from the paths of sin. I've tried, God knows I've tried to give you a good Christian upbringing. But all the time I'm fighting a losing battle. You'll be drinking next. That'll be the next thing.'

'Oh, Mummy, honestly!'

'Of course, your daddy's no kind of example.'

'Daddy's a good Christian, surely. He helps so many people, and he hardly ever misses a Sunday at the church.'

'The way he pours the evil stuff down his throat.'

'Oh, I don't think Daddy . . . I mean I've never once seen him the worse for drink.'

'He never staggers about or raises his voice. It would be better if he did. The demon drink transforms your daddy into a stupid, sly, disgusting, revolting beast.'

There were times, and more than one of them, when Andrina had the fleeting suspicion that her mother was mad. 'I don't know why you're talking like this, Mummy. If it's because you're afraid I'll take to drink, please believe me I've no intention of doing any such thing. I don't even like the taste of the stuff. I've never been in a public house in my life and I've no desire or intention of ever setting foot in one. *Not ever!* Please believe me.'

'Promise me you won't have anything to do with that woman.'

'Josie?'

'You see what I mean? You're on first name terms already.'

'But she's my next door neighbour.'

'Promise me, Andrina.' Sophie's voice withered into coldness. The coldness brought the usual spectre of panic to haunt Andrina.

She struggled to cope with it. 'Mummy, honestly, there's absolutely no need for you to worry.'

There was a silence in which Andrina lost the battle with herself and floundered into acute anxiety.

'Mummy, are you still there?'

'There's obviously no point in me saying any more.'

'Mummy?' Andrina hastily clicked the rest up and down. 'Mummy?'

Eventually she replaced the receiver. Wandering about the flat kneading her hands, shoulders hunched up with tension, she tried to remember what it was she had been meaning to do before the phone rang – but couldn't. In the kitchen she stared blankly at the dead embers of the fire.

All she was conscious of was nerves tightening all over her body, impeding the smooth flow of blood to her cheeks, making her heart palpitate, tightening in her neck, making it tenser and tenser until she felt like screaming. A headache gripped her skull like a vice.

The only release, she knew, was to phone her mother and apologise, promise, do or say anything to please her, to bring her closer again, to make everything all right. At the same time she didn't know how she could keep her promise not to have anything to do with Josie Slater, who seemed such a nice open-hearted person.

Josie's mother had recently died after a long illness, and Josie had spent every day nursing her and only went out in the evening after she'd got her mother settled. 'We had to eat, you see, hen. I had to earn a bob or two somewhere.' Josie seemed so eager to be friendly. 'Here, it's great to see somebody young in the close,' she enthused. 'It's awful depressing here with all the neighbours being older. Don't get me wrong, hen. They were all good friends of my mammy and I've nothing against them. All the same, it's great to know I'll have a pal nearer my own age. I'm a wee bit older than you, but not that much. If you run out of anything, hen, or need a helping hand, don't hesitate. Just knock on my door.'

Andrina guessed Josie was a woman of about Robert's age, certainly over thirty, not very tall, but busty and with well-shaped legs precariously balanced in high heeled shoes. She sported large flashy earrings, the kind that Andrina had always longed to wear. They dangled and sparkled and swung about as she talked. The blonde hair that framed her plump cheeks was straight, except for the ends which curled inwards. She looked a bit like Diana Dors. She had been delighted when Andrina had told her this. 'You and I are pals for life, hen. You've made my day, so you have. I needed cheering up. I miss my mammy, so I do.'

Andrina couldn't settle to wash the dishes or clear out the fire or do anything. Torn between her need to dispel the agonising tension caused by any discordant note between herself and her mother, and her inability to see how she could cut Josie dead, she stood helplessly rooted to the one spot in the kitchen. Eventually she couldn't bear it any longer. She phoned her mother. The phone rang for a long time before Sophie's voice intoned the Drumchapel number.

'Mummy, it's me. Please don't hang up. I'm sorry. I know you just want to protect me. To make sure I'm all right. I understand. I won't have anything to do with Josie Slater. I promise.' Even as she spoke she remembered that she had already invited Josie to the housewarming party. Her heart-beats made fluttery echoes in her stomach.

'It's for your own good.' Sophie's voice was still cool but not quite so cool as it had been.

'I know, Mummy.'

'I worry about you.'

'I know.'

'You're my only child.'

'I know, Mummy.'

'Now just you concentrate on your housework and have everything perfect for Robert coming home. Always start with the fire. Get rid of the ashes. Take them down to the back court right away. I hope that barmaid person's going to take her turn of the stairs. You see that she does. Not by talking to her. Don't have any truck with a common trollop like that. Put a note through her door if she misses. Say you'll report her to the factor. I bet she's a Pape. Josie sounds like a Catholic name. Is she?'

'I don't know.'

'I can tell just by looking at them. I can see the map of Ireland on their faces.'

'Gosh.' Andrina affected a spurt of bright surprise. 'Is that the time? And I haven't done a thing yet.'

'Well,' her mother said, 'I'll let you get on.' Her voice warmed. 'It's lovely having the phone, isn't it?'

'Yes, Mummy.'

'Bye bye just now.'

'Bye bye, Mummy.'

Andrina savoured exquisite relief as she put the phone down. There was still the flutter of worry about Josie coming to the housewarming party, but the housewarming party was a secret. Sophie would be none the wiser.

She tied on an apron and hurriedly began raking out the fire. Robert said that one of these days he'd have the big black range with its high mantelshelf taken out. They'd have a gas cooker put in and use an electric fire for heat.

'Think of all the work it'll save you,' Robert said.

He was so thoughtful and she appreciated it. He was even considerate in love-making. The honeymoon had been quite an adventure, especially the first night. The excitement of the unknown, the novelty of being a married lady – it was all very pleasant and enjoyable.

64

Before the fortnight was over, however, she was beginning to get tired of the sexual act. It was a bit of a nuisance really. Not that she'd let Robert know that she felt this. He seemed to get such a thrill out of it with his little moans and groans of pleasure. She didn't mind him enjoying himself. The sex act was not exactly unpleasant to her. At times it could be quite nice. She decided, however, that they shouldn't do it so often once they got home and had other, more important things to think about and take up their energies. As a result they had settled down to a more sensible level of sexual activity.

She began to sing as she worked. It was lovely having a home of her own. She was so proud of it and it gave her pleasure to see everything sparkling clean and polished. Eventually she gazed around with pride. Her mother couldn't fault the place now.

Andrina went around touching, caressing everything, the round table and spar-backed chairs in the alcove, the lace doily and crystal vase of gypsy gracing the centre of the table, the two occasional chairs, covered with moss-green tweed, one on either side of the range. On the opposite wall a modern kitchen unit in green and white with handy cupboards and drainers for dishes and cutlery gave her special pleasure. From a line of hooks along it hung shiny stainless steel pots and pans. The press over in the corner between the sink and the range was where the food was kept. The floor gleamed with a highly-polished black linoleum. Black linoleum against white woodwork: who had ever heard of such a thing! It was absolutely unique, like the modern geometric rug which lay in front of the fire.

The bathroom of course was a dream. Like something out of a Hollywood film.

Satisfied with everything, she went through to the bedroom and enjoyed the deliciously wicked experience of sitting at her very own dressing-table and putting on make-up. A dusting of powder with a fluffy pink puff, then reddening of lips and a brushing of mascara gave an impressive result. Round, slightly protruding eyes were filled with childish happiness.

Robert said her eyes sparkled like jewels and it was true. He said her hair was glorious. Not red, but a deep rich copper colour.

She enjoyed giving the luxurious, thick, wavy, curly mane a brush before rising, hands on hips, to admire her full reflection. Then she donned her coat, collected her message bag and purse and, singing happily to herself, she left the house. She wasn't yet familiar with the district and felt like an explorer as she strolled along to one end of Monteith Row where stood the impressive archway of the main entrance to the Green. She was tempted to walk along and have a look at the High Court, even go inside. Maybe there was a murder trial in progress. Instead she decided to leave that adventure to another day. Today she had special purchases to make, not only for Robert's dinner but for the baking she planned to do for the party.

Soon she found herself in Bain Street, the end of which was crossed by the London Road. In London Road she had a field day buying everything she needed.

The Calton was bounded by the Gallowgate and London Road, which met at Glasgow Cross at one end, and the equally notorious Bridgeton at the other. She enjoyed her walk exploring the area. She did not find what she'd seen of the Calton either depressing or frightening, despite its dusty broken paintwork, its crumbling black tenements, the men languishing about its street corners, its noisy children kicking tin cans, bouncing balls against walls, shouting and fighting.

Her stride had acquired a bounce to it. She was a married lady. She was a free spirit. Yet a couple of times, as if she was attached to an invisible watcher, she turned, and in vague apprehension looked around.

Chapter Nine

'I would have loaned her plates if she'd asked me,' Maureen said to Patrick. There was no need to lower her voice, indeed quite the reverse because of the racket all around them.

Bridie's twenty-first was going great guns. As well as the Gallacher family, of God only knew how many, plus mother and father Carragh and Scobie, there was Maureen and Patrick, plus all the friends of the Gallachers' offspring. The Gallachers' room and kitchen had never been so chock-a-block.

'Och, what does it matter?' Patrick was already in his cups and didn't care if he had to eat his piece of clouty dumpling off the floor. 'The tablecloth's clean enough.'

'Looks more like a bed sheet to me,' Maureen said. But she felt sorry for Carragh. After all the miscarriages she'd had and such a big family to contend with, God help her, she had more to bother her than finding plates for her clouty dumpling. Anyway, it tasted just as good without a plate. Even the rich, spicy smell of it was mouth-watering.

'Frank and Bridie seem to have hit it off.' Maureen felt really pleased about that. Her prayers looked as if they were going to be answered. Every night she'd prayed to the Holy family, 'Oh Holy Mother, Blessed Mary, ever virgin, Saint Joseph and the Infant Child, please make our Frank more normal. Please stop him making such a silly ass of himself. Please make him take a notion for Bridie Gallacher.'

She and Patrick and Tony and Michael and Bernard had all agreed that no mention of Bridie would be made to Frank before the party. They all knew that Frank was not only peculiar, he was thrawn. If Frank thought you were dead keen for him to do something, or were eager to guide him in one direction, he'd do something else, he'd go the exact opposite way. Or he'd just dig in his heels, put down his head (usually to bury it in a book) and refuse to do anything at all.

If she hadn't seen Frank being born, or at least seconds after he emerged from her body, if she'd had him in hospital instead of her own home, Maureen would have thought there must have been some mix-up and she'd been given the wrong baby. He didn't even look like her or Patrick or any of his brothers.

Patrick was a typical Glasgow working man with his short, stocky, robust appearance and rough-hewn features. Maureen was sonsy in build, 'a good armful', Patrick called her. Tony, Michael and Bernard were all well-made. One look at them told you they were men to be reckoned with. Hard as rocks. Poor Frank, although about the same height as his brothers, couldn't boast a pick of flesh. His clothes hung on him. His hair was lank and greasy. He didn't take a bit of interest in his appearance. And it was true what Patrick said – Frank had a soft nature. Maybe that's why she loved him so much. (They all did really.) Frank was the one who noticed when she was tired and made her sit down while he did the dishes or cooked the meal. He'd even, on one memorable occasion, gone down to the back court and hung out the washing. She'd been laid low with varicose veins at the time. It had been the talk of the place. For a Scotsman to do household chores, any kind of women's work, for any reason, was really beyond the pale. She knew that he would be labelled a Jessy, a Pansy, a Poof, and God knows what else behind their backs. His father and his brothers, in the privacy of their home, had on occasion called him all of these things.

Frank was the one who cut her toenails, a job she found difficult to do herself since she'd put on a bit of weight. ('But all in the right places, hen,' Patrick always assured her.) She could tell Frank her troubles. She was ashamed to admit it, even to herself, but sometimes she felt he was like the daughter she'd never had. She was glad of and grateful for his soft nature. At times like that she'd chastise herself and pray for Frank's sake.

'Dear Sacred Heart of Jesus, help me to be strong and not to take advantage of the lovely boy's soft nature. Don't let me be glad of the comfort of it. Oh, Holy Mother, help me to help him to be hard and strong like Patrick and Tony and Michael and Bernard. Dear God, Dear God, hear my prayers.'

Now she thought to herself, 'God bless Bridie Gallacher'. There the dear girl was, making up to Frank as hard as she could. Listening to him as if he was Jesus Christ delivering the Sermon on the Mount. Occasionally a little sigh would escape and a hand would give Frank's arm a quick touch as if in wondrous disbelief. Probably Frank was boring the pants off the poor girl with one of his poems. Maureen hoped Bridie wouldn't overdo it and make Frank suspicious.

Both Maureen and Carragh had long since suspected that Bridie had a notion of Frank. Although basically a shy girl, she had asked Maureen on more than one occasion how Frank was getting on. Or she'd remark, with forced casualness, 'I didn't see Frank at Mass this morning.'

It worried Maureen that Frank sometimes missed Mass. Admittedly he was forgetful. Even when he was a young child, however, he was beginning to show ominous signs. He was barely more than seven when the most awful thing happened. Frank's teacher and the priest had been going round the class examining the children to see if they knew their catechism in preparation for their first Holy Communion. Each question had an exact answer that had to be learned off by heart.

'Who made you?' the priest had asked Frank.

'God made me,' Frank dutifully answered.

'What did God make you for?'

'God made me to love him and serve him in this world and be happy with him in the next.'

'What is God?'

Apparently at this point Frank had hesitated and the priest had prompted, 'God is a Supreme Spirit.'

'But how do you know?' Frank said, shocking rigid both teacher and priest. And then he'd compounded his crime by adding the phrase he'd often heard from the lips of his Uncle Joseph concerning other questions – mostly relating to the attributes of a greyhound or a race-horse, 'He sounds like a right bummer to me.'

His mother was sent for but too late to save him from the belting he'd already received. Her plea that Frank didn't know what he was talking about and it was all his Uncle Joseph's fault did not absolve him from sin and the warnings of eternal damnation.

She remembered crying all the way home, she'd been so worried about Frank and so afraid of how he'd end up. She was relieved when he'd run around with a gang for a while. He'd got into minor scrapes and trouble like any other normal youngster. He and his pals had tied door handles together, kicked at the doors, then run away. They'd thrown stones at the pupils of the nearest Protestant school. They'd played football in the street, broken windows, been chased, caught and had their ears boxed.

But by the time Frank was twelve, he was already drifting away from normality to become a loner who wrote poems. No belting or ear-boxing could cure him of that. Bridie Gallacher might do the trick. At least she must be interested in books because she'd chosen to work in a second-hand bookshop. Frank loved books.

'If Frank doesn't know he's getting the come-on sign there, and if he doesn't take advantage of it, he's a fool,' Patrick said.

'We don't want him to take advantage of the girl,' Maureen chided. 'Just fall for her and court her and eventually tie the knot with her.'

Patrick shrugged. 'Comes to the same thing. The poor sod doesn't know what she's letting herself in for.'

'Patrick!' Maureen elbowed him in the ribs. 'Our Frank's a lovely boy and well you know it.'

'What are you two fighting about?' Big Bernard came sauntering over and Maureen gazed up at him with pride. 'Och, you know who. Do you reckon they've clicked, son?'

'Frank could do worse than Bridie. Her sister's the one with the looks though.'

'Doris? Ah-ha. Is this another romance brewing then? Och

well, she's a nice enough wee lassie. A bit la-de-da, that's all.
She thinks because she works in Daly's she's as posh as the
customers.'

'I need somebody to partner me to another do in a few days
time over at Monteith Row.'

'Who do you know there?'

'Robert Anderson.'

'The Mr Anderson you help at the karate club?'

'Yes.'

'Aw, a lovely man, so he is.' Maureen remembered with
heartfelt gratitude how this teacher had been the saving of
Bernard. She'd always worried about Bernard in the opposite
way from Frank. Bernard had brains but he had brawn as well,
and she'd been afraid of him getting into too much trouble
when he was young.

She'd never forget the day he arrived home – he was only a
young lad at the time – cut and bruised and battered and with
blood soaking through his clothes. He'd insisted he hadn't been
involved in a gang fight. He had just been minding his own
business when a crowd had surrounded him. He hadn't stood a
chance because they had weapons. If it hadn't been for Mr
Anderson coming by at the time and rescuing him, he would
have been killed. If Mr Anderson hadn't then got Bernard
interested in karate, Bernard might have taken the path of so
many other boys in the district. He would have joined a rival
gang and fought vengeance fights along with them.

The next step would be into crime. Many a lad from a decent
family had gone from gang fights to petty crime, and then to the
more serious crimes of robbing pubs and bookies and banks
and big houses in Newton Mearns. The most hardened cases
became real gangsters.

What had saved Tony was first of all getting into a skiffle
group. Then he'd gone drum-crazy and bought himself a set of
drums. This was a mixed blessing. It nearly drove everyone else
into the crime of murder. Murdering Tony.

What had saved Bernard, she believed, was getting involved
with Mr Anderson and his karate club. She'd often sent up a

prayer for Mr Anderson despite the fact that he was a Protestant.

'It's not Mr Anderson's twenty-first birthday party, is it?' she laughed.

'No. Housewarming. He got married recently.'

'Aw, you should have told me, Bernard. I would have got him a present. I think the world of that man.'

'I got something.'

'Thank God for that. Who did he marry?'

'Bailie McPherson's daughter.'

Patrick joined in the conversation then. 'I'm proud to claim Bailie McPherson as a friend. He won the Victoria Cross during the war,' he announced as if he hadn't told them this a hundred times before. 'A real hero, but you'd never think it to talk to him. Always ready to do anybody a good turn.'

'I thought he was Councillor McPherson,' Maureen said.

'Listen,' Patrick said, 'you can call a councillor a bailie but you can never call a bailie a councillor. He's on the bench now. Gold chain of office and all.'

A sudden flash of hope widened Maureen's eyes. 'Here! He'll have more clout as a bailie. And he's on the housing committee, isn't he?'

'You name the committee,' Patrick said, 'and the chances are he's on it. He works like a slave for the benefit of his fellow man, does Bailie Andrew McPherson. A fine, big man.'

'Well then!'

'What do you mean – well then?'

'Ask him to get us a nice house with a bathroom. Just round about here. I don't want to move away from all my good neighbours.'

'There aren't any nice houses with bathrooms round about here.'

'There are so. In Blackhill or Provanmill for a start.'

Patrick looked uncertain, but he said, 'I suppose I could mention it the next time I see him at the club. But he doesn't manage there so often now. He's a busy man.'

'Go and see him at the City Chambers then, or wherever

72

folks are supposed to see him about houses. Aw, go on, Patrick. For me, darlin'. It would be heaven, so it would, to have a bathroom.'

Patrick put an arm round her waist and gave her a squeeze. 'What's it worth?'

Maureen squealed with pleasure, making both Patrick and Bernard guffaw.

Bernard thought it was great that his mother and father obviously still enjoyed a good sex life. More than once when friends had been in the house having a drink and a sing-song Patrick had suddenly announced, 'Right, folks, it's been a great night and I've enjoyed your company but I'll have to ask you to leave now. I want to take my wife to bed.'

In his imagination Bernard had taken Andrina to bed and had made love to her many times. He could see her still as she'd looked on her wedding day: so radiant, so sublimely beautiful, her copper-coloured hair shimmering in the sunlight, her veil floating around her like a halo. His mind, his heart, every nerve in his body reached out to her, claimed her irrevocably as his own. He couldn't believe that she was giving herself to someone else. It was some cruel distortion of fate. Had the groom been anyone else but Robert Anderson, he would have rushed across the road to the church, snatched Andrina up in his arms and raced off with her.

As it was, he was paralysed in his agony of love, unable to do anything.

His angel. He would be seeing her again within the week.

'I'd better go and chat Doris up,' he told his mother and father.

Patrick winked at him. 'A big, fine-looking chap like you – it'll be no bother, son. She'll be eating out of your hand in no time, or my name's not Patrick O'Maley.'

Bernard crushed his way through the crowd of revellers towards Doris Gallacher. He regarded her as a bit of a pain, with her pretensions of being a lady. Apart from that she was all right. He'd known her off and on since they went to school together. She'd been in a younger class. He supposed her affectations were her way of trying to get out of her present environment. He didn't blame her.

'How are you doing, Doris?' He smiled down at her. She was drinking a cup of tea with pinky raised.

'Oh, hello, Bernard. Isn't this a terrible rabble? And no plates for the dumpling. Did you ever? I didn't invite any of the girls from Daly's. What would they have thought? Some of them come from Bearsden.'

Bernard kept the smile stuck to his face. 'How would you like to come to a party with me on Saturday?'

She had dark eyes, black lashes, and a bee-hive of cream-coloured hair. Its pale colour made the blush that spread to her cheeks all the more noticeable. 'Thank you. I'm sure that would be very nice.'

'Were you ever in Mr Anderson's class?'

'Was he the one with kind of sunk-in jaws?'

'You make him sound half dead. He's one of the fittest men I know and he's over thirty.'

'He had that kind of face though. But he was a terribly nice man. I remember he told me I drew very nice little pictures.'

Bernard couldn't imagine Robert saying any such thing unless he was being sarcastic, but he let it pass. 'He got married recently and it's his housewarming party.'

'Oh, how terribly nice!'

'I'll call for you about seven-thirty, OK?'

'I'll look forward to it. I really will.' She lowered her heavily mascaraed eyelashes and took another sip of tea. Her pinky annoyed him intensely.

74

Chapter Ten

Bernard had always worked nights, but he made sure he'd be off on the night of Andrina's housewarming party. It was a bit easier in that respect, now that he was taking on more than one pub at a time and employing Bill Doyle and Jack Rafferty. He would accept a booking for a job, the club or bar owner or manager paid him, and then he paid Doyle and Rafferty, making a profit for himself in the process. He had no regrets about starting to organise work on his own like this.

He had had no regrets about the training or the expertise at the security firm called Bodyguard Incorporated either. He had been barely sixteen at the time, and working in the Empire as a bouncer when he'd first heard about the firm. He had lied to the manager of the Empire when he'd started there because he'd been only fifteen. He looked at least two years older, and husky with it, so there had been no problem, except perhaps to get one of the Empire's red uniform jackets to fit his shoulders. The jackets were padded to make the other guys look broader. He didn't need the padding. He remembered he felt very smart with his black trousers and black bow tie. Even then he'd believed it was important to look well turned out, and he had been right.

A guy that used to come about the place had approached him one day and told him he was from this set-up called Body-guards Incorporated. They were all ex-SAS, and this man said to him, 'I've been watching you. You've got what it takes. Would you like to get involved with my firm?'

Bernard had been doubtful. For one thing he didn't want to give away his age. 'Do you not need to go into the army or anything like that?'

'No, no,' the man said. 'We've got the wherewithal to train you, and the techniques involved.'

75

So, from the age of sixteen, over a few years, he worked with these people. They trained him in close protection techniques, bodyguarding, evasive driving techniques, and firearms training. He went abroad with them and saw how they worked. He was impressed with what highly-trained professionals they were. The most valuable things he learned from them were self-discipline and one hundred per cent concentration, although he'd also become an expert in judo and a black belt in karate. He'd already had a good grounding in karate from Robert Anderson of course. He survived the close protection or bodyguarding even in the most dangerous situations – with terrorists, for example – because working on the streets of Glasgow had sharpened his instincts.

More and more he'd nursed thoughts of his own business, and he knew the place to start was on the streets. He went back to work in the bars and nightclubs of the city. He still did the occasional jobs for Bodyguards Incorporated, usually protecting a pop star who wanted to relax over a meal and a few drinks at a nightclub after their show in Glasgow or Edinburgh.

He built up a reputation for being able to deal with problems before they began. His mere presence in a bar or a nightclub usually proved a deterrent. He thought a lot about his job and how best he could deal with it. His obsession with his work became almost as strong as his obsession with Andrina. He'd always been single-minded in everything he did, especially in overcoming fear. He remembered as a child how terrified he was to go down the shadowy gaslit stair to the lavatory, especially on winter nights when the wind would be howling and moaning from the close. Inside, the lavatory was total darkness. His mother always told him to climb up and pee in the kitchen sink rather than go down the stairs. But even then, when he was only knee-high to a grasshopper, something in his personality drove him to stubbornly face his terrors head on. He'd stamp, grim-faced, down the stone stairs, then grope determinedly into the black pit of the lavatory.

Sometimes he'd repeat out loud to himself as he did so, 'I don't care about ghosts. I don't care about ghosts.' His ma and da used to laugh at him about that, especially when they were reminiscing about when the family were young.

'Bernard were always a stubborn, determined little devil,' his ma would say. 'Even as a baby.'

His absorption with his work, and the total concentration needed in carrying it out, became reflected in his outward appearance. Even when he laughed, his eyes remained cautious, watchful, ready. More often than not his face was set in a cast-iron mask – hard, expressionless. He was known around the pubs and clubs as 'The Big Man', and for a big man his reactions were astonishingly swift. He was feared for the rapidity of his responses to trouble. Yet he still appeared to keep his calm. He could suddenly bring a man down and make him howl in anguish with a finger to a shoulder nerve or a karate kick, without a flicker of an eye or the slightest change of expression. He had never been known to show anger on the job, never lost the slightest self-control. He was admired for it, even by the gangsters. Quite early on he'd sorted out in his mind his own particular philosophy, his special approach. He'd explained it to Doyle and Rafferty, because it was the lines on which he wanted his business run.

'I believe in showing a modicum of respect for everyone,' he said. 'Even to the worst drunks we have to deal with. That means I cajole them first. And if they've friends around I get them on my side to help. I try to avoid confrontation. With even the worst gangsters I show a bit of respect. You know they're scum; I know they're scum. But I don't let them see that I know. I talk to them as if they're businessmen, because that's what they like to believe they are. Remember, we have to spend night after night standing at the same bar as them. We've got to have some sort of working relationship. They've got to respect us too. That way we keep the trouble we're there to deal with to an absolute minimum.'

Working relationships were very difficult, very difficult indeed. He believed in showing respect to the police too, and in the case of some high-ranking officers, he often showed them more respect than they deserved.

The police were constantly suspicious of him. They saw him talking to criminals and gangsters, and they assumed he must be one of them. It was just as mistaken as the attitude of ordinary punters who, seeing him or his men having a drink at a bar or a meal at a club, thought they were relaxing and having a good time. They thought it was an easy job.

Easy it was not.

For a start, he was forever trying to assure the police that he wasn't running some sort of racket alongside his security work.

One officer had told him to his face, 'We know you're up to something and we'll find out what it is and nail you for it even if it takes us years.'

'Look,' he'd said, 'the only thing you'll ever nail me for is something you've set me up for. No way am I going to work anything on the wrong side of the law. Never.'

He meant it. He knew he was too intelligent for that. Apart from strongly-held principles, he also knew he had the ability to make as much money as the gangsters without joining them. They tried hard enough, of course, to manipulate him and influence him to get him on their side. He kept on apparently friendly speaking terms, but remained his own man. He kept his balance on the dangerous tightrope, the invariable dividing line. It was an art that had taken him years to perfect, and one with which he was still having to practise extreme caution and self-control. Self-control was of vital importance. Only the other night he'd been standing at a bar, to all appearances relaxing and passing the time talking to one of these gangsters. But in fact his guard was not lowered, and he was acutely conscious of everything going on in his surroundings. He was aware that the gangster's girlfriend and her sister were sitting at a table nearby. Gorgeous looking girls, but potential trouble. He had long since decided that women were *the* worst stirrers of trouble and the most difficult to deal with.

While he was talking the gangster's girlfriend got up, came over to him with a pair of nail scissors in her hand and cut his tie in half. He could have killed her with one blow. Instead, he totally ignored her. Her stupid act made not the slightest interruption to what he was saying. After the conversation finished and he had to move away to deal with a drunk who had suddenly decided to pick a fight with another customer, the gangster went over to his girlfriend and gave her a blow across the face that knocked the girl off her chair.

After that, these two girls pursued Bernard, did everything they could to latch on to him. He supposed it was because with their gangster lover no man would dare hook up with them. Any man who did would end up in the Clyde or minus some part of his anatomy. The girls had come to the conclusion that he was tough enough to deal with any trouble. And he was.

But no matter what reason they were throwing themselves at him, he didn't take them on. It was another part of his professional attitude that he didn't mix business with pleasure. To get involved with any woman on the job was strictly taboo. This wasn't easy. He came in contact with quite a few glamorous women, and he was a fit and highly-sexed man. As a result he only had sex with local girls, mostly girls he'd known all his life. Some of them had wanted marriage. They had spoken of a 'nice wee house' and 'settling down'. They seemed to think they could change him; make him into a pipe and slippers man.

A pipe and slippers man he was not. He managed to remain friends with some of the girls. Others had become bitchy and bitter when they realised marriage, or marriage with Bernard at least, was not on the cards.

The only marriage he wanted to make was with Andrina, and that would be an exciting adventure. His adrenalin began pumping at the mere thought of it. At night he had wet dreams thinking about her. Wanting her nearly drove him mad. Even with a girl he didn't love, of course he could have good sex. He was, he realised from what he'd noticed in urinals and by comparison with his brothers, particularly well endowed for sex. Not only in size. One girl had told him adoringly that she'd never known anyone able to 'keep it up for ages like that'.

He wanted sex with Andrina, but it wasn't only lust as it had been with other women. He loved her. Her marriage had been a knife in his heart. With her he was vulnerable. Thoughts of her made his hard shell crumble, his toughness melt away. During the day, he often watched her house, hungry for a glimpse of her. If she emerged he followed her, feeding on the sight of her, every moment obsessing him with desire.

He adored her. Some day, somehow, some way, she would be his. It had to be. He willed it to be. And he was a patient man.

Chapter Eleven

Scobie Gallacher, Bridie and Doris Gallacher's father, couldn't remember Bridie's twenty-first birthday party. These black-outs, the blank periods of his life, secretly frightened Scobie. He'd wake in the morning and see Carragh with a black eye and swollen lip and he'd feel immediate concern and cry out, 'What the hell happened to your face?'

He could never believe it when she told him he'd been the cause. She'd tell other folk she fell or bumped into a door, or she'd refuse to say anything at all. But in private she swore it was him.

There were other occasions when he thought he'd been sleeping on the couch or on the floor after a few drinks. But next day other people told him what he'd done and he didn't believe them either. An army of small, furtive fears was growing in his mind, confusing him. Especially the times when he seemed to have been performing quite normally. He'd apologise for taking the day off work, only to be told that he hadn't taken the day off work at all. He'd been there on the building site working away as usual.

Patrick O'Maley and all the lads would laugh, and he would laugh along with them. But secretly it gave him a hell of a turn.

One day he'd gone in for a pint to his favourite pub in Castle Street. The next thing he knew, he was in Ireland. He'd bought tickets from Glasgow. He'd negotiated a boat ticket to Dublin. Buses in Dublin too. He had the ticket stubs to prove it. Yet he remembered not one thing about either the journey or his sojourn in the capital city.

At first the laughs had kept up. Good old Scobie. Did you hear about his last caper? You'll never believe what old Scobie did the other day. Fellas would say – Aw, you're some man, you. You did this or you did that. And you said this to big Jimmy and you said that to me.

81

Big Donald McMillan or Hector McLean, the local bobbies, often took him home. They'd have a laugh with him about it the next day. More often now they were having him in and charging him with being drunk and disorderly. But it was still good-humoured. He had some good pals in the local nick. In Barlinnie prison as well. The screws were decent enough fellas. Just doing their job.

More recently, however, Scobie was becoming a Jekyll and Hyde. He apparently was doing things that were completely out of character. One of them was hitting Carragh. Poor wee Carragh, with her long skirts to hide her legs and her wrap-around floral pinnies. Christ, he loved the woman. The fact that he had no recollection of his violent behaviour meant he'd no control over it.

'It's the drink, Scobie,' Carragh would say to try to comfort him. 'It's not you, it's the drink. If you could just stick to one or two pints like your pals . . .'

He always meant to. He'd go into a bar for one pint only. Or perhaps just a half and a whisky. But after one pint or one half he'd feel he'd grown inches taller. He felt more sure of himself. His shoulders swaggered. Just one more, he'd think, no problem. But the more he drank the more difficult it became to leave the bar and go home. He'd make all sorts of excuses to Carragh when he did get back – usually minus most of his wages, or all of the wages, that she was so anxiously waiting for.

He'd say he met Patrick or Tony or Michael and couldn't get away. When he woke up next day and discovered he'd vomited all over Carragh's nice bedspread he'd blame the lemonade somebody had put in his whisky. He'd say he'd been all right in the pub. It was when he came out and the fresh air hit him. It was the fresh air that had got him drunk. The first time he woke up and discovered he'd peed in the bed he was horrified and utterly disgusted with himself. This, he knew, was totally unacceptable.

The first time Scobie got put in jail for being drunk and incapable the horror and degradation had shocked him, and as he'd lain in Barlinnie prison, he vowed to himself, 'Never, ever again. I'm here because of drink, and never, ever, will I take it again!' Yet the first thing he did when he walked down the long road from Barlinnie was to go into an off-sales and get a bottle.

Eventually the unacceptable became the acceptable. Lying in the gutter and getting locked up for the night had become part and parcel of his life.

He could still raise a laugh by saying to the guys on the building site, 'You haven't lived if you haven't gone up the Garngad Road on the ten o'clock bus after the pubs have shut.'

More times than he cared to remember now Scobie had come out of the pub in Castle Street near the Royal Infirmary with a crowd from Garngad and Blackhill. He'd be laughing and singing and staggering along with them, without thinking or caring where he was going, and he'd get on the bus with them. Sometimes he'd doze off into a drunken sleep. At other times he'd bellow out songs at the top of his voice along with the rest.

The conductress never got any money, only a share of the carry-out. 'Hae a slug, hen' was the generous cry as she passed along the aisle. Once he'd offered her the fare and she'd brushed it aside with, 'Why should you be fucking different?'

He remembered one time he'd been sitting upstairs in the smoky atmosphere of the bus in a drunken haze, his *Daily Record* rolled up on his lap. He remembered staring hypnotically at the passing glow of the orange streetlights as the bus swayed round corner after corner. The raucous noise from the front seats washed over him. They were singing, '. . . For freedom comes from God's right hand, and righteous men must make our land a nation once again. A nation once again, a nation once again. And Ireland long a province been – a nation once again . . .'

On the seat next to him sat a fresh-faced youth, his cheeks aglow, his mind no doubt still on his recent passionate fumblings in a handy close. He was softly whistling various melodies as he gazed unseeingly out of the grimy windows.

Then Scobie's drunken reverie was disturbed by a sudden bellowing from the front of the bus. 'Some bastard's whistlin' the Sash! There's a fuckin' Orange bastard taking the piss!'

Oblivious to the concentration of the front row or the deathly silence of the rest of the bus, the boy whistled on tunelessly; but yes, there was a hint of the Sash there.

A drunken tide welled down the passageway, feeding on its own rage, towards the hapless and still oblivious youth. 'Hae you, whit's yer gemme? Can you whistle wi' nae teeth?'

Shocked back to the present by his all too clear impending doom, the boy was obviously at a loss to know what offence he had caused. 'I'm sorry,' he stuttered. 'I don't know what you're talking about.'

This brought a further roar of rage from the incensed rabble. Scobie didn't like the odds. He leaned over. 'Give the boy a break, lads. He's away with it. He didnae mean any harm.'

'Piss off, you drunken old fart,' the leader of the mob yelled. 'Before ah ram yer paper up yer arse.'

Scobie's face went white as if the blood had been siphoned off. To the uninitiated it could be mistaken for fear. It was Scobie's eyes that contradicted this impression. It was said that in a drunken rage Scobie's eyes had the malevolence of a psychotic pit bull terrier.

But the leader of the mob only saw Scobie's pallor and, looking for approval from his mates, he leaned over the back of the seat in front of Scobie and wagged a finger close to Scobie's face. Before he could deliver any more insults, however, Scobie had grabbed the offending wrist, shot his head forward, and slammed his teeth down on the outstretched finger.

The high-pitched scream was abruptly extinguished as Scobie's fist rattled a short, sharp staccato beat around the base of the leader's jaw. This unexpected attack left him slumped forward over the seat with a glazed expression.

For a few seconds the mob behind him were stunned into immobility and Scobie, still not liking the odds, decided it was time for him to leave the bus. This signalled a mad rush towards him. Unfortunately, in their rush the mob trampled and climbed over their now recumbent colleague. Scobie saw the world through a red haze as he lashed out hooks and uppercuts, grabbed lapels, butted noses; he ducked and hooked as he backed off down the bus, dragging a small pool of mayhem with him. His final parting as he went down the steeply spiralled staircase was a full-blooded uppercut into an exposed groin above his head.

He dropped, running, off the back of the bus, having lost his jacket and his false teeth, presumably still attached to the finger on the top deck. And, horror of horrors, he'd lost his *Daily Record* with the day's scores.

Now Scobie couldn't even remember his journeys on the bus. He'd go in to the pub for a pint, and the next thing he'd know was waking up in Patrick's house in Blackhill. Or in the gutter in Blackhill. Or someplace else.

This time he'd been toasting Bridie's health at her twenty-first birthday party, and then suddenly he was lying sprawled all his length in a close in Cobden Street. Big Martha Stoddart was towering over him saying to Jimmy, her man, 'It's that drunken Pape from Turner Street.'

Jimmy Stoddart was a well-known Orangeman and mason, but to give him his due, he bent down and gave Scobie a hand up. Big Martha said, 'Let him get up himself. See you!' she addressed Scobie. 'You dirty drunken wee nyaff? Don't you dare come round here fouling our close. You get back where you belong, do you hear, or you'll get my fist in your face.'

'OK. OK.' Scobie flung up his hands. 'I'm going, hen. There's no need for violence.' He'd felt ashamed. He hurt inside but he managed to dust himself down and walk away as if he wasn't caring a tuppenny toss. He was wondering what he'd done to spoil Bridie's party and give her a showing up. It was usually Doris who accused him of giving her a showing up. Bridie hid herself away, usually in the lavatory with a book, until somebody came battering at the door desperate to get in.

He hoped to God he hadn't hurt anybody. 'Holy Mary, Mother of God, don't let me have battered wee Carragh.' Or Bridie, or Doris, or any of the boys. Or anybody at all, for that matter. 'And don't let me have spewed over anybody. Or insulted anybody.'

Desperately he tried to remember what he had done. But couldn't.

'Hello there, wee man.' Francis O'Donnell, one of his fellow brickies, greeted him in Garngad Road. 'Fancy a pint?'

Just one, Scobie thought. He needed something to pick him up, give him a wee lift, make him feel better. The hair of the dog. 'Aye, OK, son.'

Francis O'Donnell had three pints and then said, 'I'm away, Scobie. I've to get some fish suppers to take home. I promised the wife.'

'I'll just have another one,' Scobie said. 'And then I'm on my way as well.'

He had to ask the barman to put his next drink on the slate. And his next – he lost count of how many. He and Carragh were in debt all over the place but he always made sure when he got his wages, the publican was paid first.

Closing time came eventually, and he had to leave and stagger towards Turner Street. He felt angry – at – he wasn't sure what. It was something to do with the party. Why should he care about the shitting party? But he did fucking care. They'd better not say anything to him when he got back. They'd better not even look at him in the wrong way. He knew Carragh had done a lot of work cleaning the house and making a big dumpling. He knew it meant a lot to her. She was that anxious it would go well. His anger grew until it was unendurable and turned outside of himself. He was a time-bomb of fury, ready to go off.

As he approached his close on Turner Street, his eye fell on Kevin Connelly, the wee upstart that had cat-called his Doris –and when she'd ignored him, he'd made a fool of her, mimicking her polite voice and teetering, mincing walk. He'd heard Doris complain about this to Carragh. 'That horrible Kevin Connelly from downstairs is always pestering me and making a fool of me.'

He'd show Kevin bloody Connelly he couldn't make a fool of any daughter of his. 'See you, you fuckin' bastard,' he yelled. 'You'll no' talk about a Gallacher again!' With that, he lurched towards the suddenly wary and defensive Kevin. Scobie feinted left and lashed out a vicious kick with his steel-toe-capped boot

86

to Kevin's knee. There was an ominous crunch and Kevin's head dropped with a grunt of anguish. Like a striking stoat, the short figure of Scobie bulleted forward. Two chopping short rights to the base of the neck, followed by a flurry of short-range butts into the face, and Kevin dropped to the ground.

Scobie had just started to bury his boot into the young man's ribs when he was forcefully dragged off by a posse of neighbours rushing to Kevin's rescue.

Carragh had seen the attack from the window, and she was crying when Scobie got upstairs, and going on about how Kevin was the son of one of her best neighbours. Doris was saying how Scobie was worse than Kevin Connelly and it was terrible, just terrible. He had to give both of them a belt across the mouth to shut them up.

Next day he woke up in the kitchen hole-in-the-wall bed to the sound of voices. Carragh was saying, 'Oh, that's awful kind of you, Mrs Connelly. I'll really enjoy that, so I will.'

'That's OK, hen. I'll get the bowl later on. No hurry.'

Mrs Connelly had brought Carragh a bowl of soup. Scobie nodded a good morning to the woman but she ignored him.

Afterwards he said to Carragh, 'What the hell's wrong with her? And what's she bringing you soup for? We're surely not that hard up.'

'It's just to show there's no bad feelings against me. She's a good neighbour to me, is Mrs Connelly.'

'Hard feelings against you? What hard feelings?'

'After what you done to her Kevin.'

He had no idea what she was talking about. He struggled out of bed, pulled on his trousers and forced himself to brave the cold and draughty stairs to the lavatory. There he could relieve his bladder.

He did not know how to find relief from his fear.

Chapter Twelve

'In other days I thought I'd never
Find a love to call my own,
That I was meant to walk forever,
My lifelong path alone;
That my lonely heart should never sing
Nor know the joy that love can bring . . .'

Frank chewed happily at his pencil as a vision of Bridie swam before his eyes. He was sitting, hunched protectively over his notebook, at the kitchen table penning his latest poem. Well, to be accurate, he was fiddling about with a poem he'd written some years before. It described walking with an imaginary love on a distant hill and into 'forests hidden ways . . .'. He changed these bits, brought it up to date, but left the ending which seemed so relevant to the wonderful change in his life.

'Now all my loneliness is past,
Now both our dreams are one,
Our hope, our love, shall always last,
Till life itself is done:
Each pledge and promise be ever true,
And love shall live while I have you.'

He felt so inspired he knew he would be capable of writing much better poetry than that. He had even begun thinking about writing a play. He was brimming over with creative energy.

As Tony crushed past him, Frank hunched lower and made a wall with his hand around his notebook. Too often his father or brothers had tried to read over his shoulders, and laugh and jeer or groan and shake their heads. It was difficult to keep going with his creative work in the face of such sustained discouragement. Why did he keep on writing? After all, he'd never had anything published; never made one penny piece from anything he'd produced. He couldn't give a sensible answer to the question. He just had to do it, that was all. It was an obsession, an addiction, a need. It was the only way he was able to communicate his emotions. He couldn't even express his feelings to Bridie – not everything that was in his heart. Except through poetry.

They'd discuss the merits and demerits of a film they'd just seen together. They'd make a plan of reading for the weeks ahead. They'd decide on a list of books they'd borrow from the library, and after studying each one they'd make notes of their critical reactions and discuss them with each other in much enthusiastic detail. But he couldn't find words to fully express how wonderful it was to have someone who shared his interests, who cared about the same things as him, who took him seriously, who accepted him as he was.

Except in poetry.

Then came the most exciting thing in both their lives. He had his first poem published. It all happened because of a nightmare. He had dreamed that Bridie had died; he had lost her forever. Fear haunted him all next day. He couldn't concentrate on his work at the office. His imagination was a dark sea in which he was drowning. He'd gone round to Bridie's house straight after work. She wasn't in and her mother didn't know where she was. What if he never saw her again? He returned home and wrote a poem called 'The Legacy of Love', in which he tried to visualise what his feelings would be if Bridie disappeared forever from his life:

> 'You will not come again, and yet
> I turn my head attentive round,
> Hear voices down the wind, and let
> My hand reach out to touch the sound:
> Or else, in mist's fantastic swarm
> See shaped in shaking line your form.

I go again where we have been,
Revisit each remembered place,
Hold hands on every bridge, and lean
To see in every stream your face:
Laugh laughter that was laughed before
And press each cheek to cheek once more.

Sentience invades insentient things,
The trace of touch outlines the years;
And shapes and sounds where presence clings
Assail receptive eyes and ears:
No more than time can part from tide
Can lover from his love divide.'

It was accepted for publication by a literary magazine and they
actually paid him for it. The letter of acceptance and the cheque
had been waiting for him one evening. He had met Bridie in
town straight from work. They'd gone to Miss Cranston's
restaurant for high tea, and then to a concert in St Andrew's
Halls. The Glasgow Phoenix Choir had enchanted them both,
and Bridie said she'd never enjoyed herself so much in her life.
When he'd arrived back home he'd gone into the kitchen to see
if there was any tea on the go. His brothers and his father and
one or two of their friends were enjoying a noisy game of
pontoon round the kitchen table. The small room reverberated
with the lusty male voices. It was thick with cigarette smoke
and the smell of whisky and beer. His mother was huddled over
the fire, enjoying a glass of Guinness and a read of her *Family
Star*.

The letter was propped up on the mantelpiece against one of
the brass candlesticks. He examined its contents with disbelief,
then joyous excitement. 'Here, you'll never guess what's
happened!' he suddenly bellowed out. 'A magazine is going to
publish one of my poems and they've asked for more. Look,
they've sent me a cheque!'

The racket round the table ceased. A silence gripped the
room for a few seconds, before one of his brothers looked at his

90

cards and said, 'Fuck! Bust again!', and the game continued as if Frank had never existed.

Frank felt embarrassed, ashamed even. He almost apologised for himself. His mother hissed at him, 'You give that money back, do you hear?'

It occurred to him that there was no use arguing with her, no use expecting any of them to understand. His mother thought there must be some mistake. It smacked of dishonesty. He must have conned the money from the publisher. The others were just embarrassed. They didn't know what to think.

He didn't make a cup of tea. He didn't wash his face at the sink. He left the room as if in disgrace without even daring to bring any more attention to himself by saying goodnight. In the front room he undressed and slipped into one of the inset beds. Alone in the dark the excitement returned, making him shiver and sweat.

If he could get one poem published he could get another poem published. If he could get poems published he could get plays accepted. This was the beginning. This was all he needed. Just one bit of encouragement.

First thing next morning Frank hared round to Bridie's place and told her of the stupendous news. She was over the moon. They hugged each other in secret, furtive joy outside the front door. Bridie's house was always packed to the gunwales and privacy was impossible inside the house.

Poor Bridie had an even worse life at home than Frank had. She was an intelligent, sensitive girl among a right mindless rabble. Except perhaps her sister Doris, who at least had some ambition to get out of the place – albeit for silly, snobbish reasons.

Bridie's father Scobie, in Frank's opinion, wasn't just a heavy drinker like his own dad, but an alcoholic. Scobie was a right Jekyll and Hyde character – a nice enough man when he was sober but a devil when he drank. His wife Carragh was a poor wee soul, only an inch or two over five feet, and with a sparse straggle of hair and bandy legs that she tried to hide under long skirts. Neither Scobie nor Carragh were capable of disciplining or having any control over their innumerable offspring, several of whom were well known and feared local corner-boys.

Feared by all except the O'Maleys. Michael especially was contemptuous of the Gallacher boys. Frank had once heard Michael say to a group of Gallachers and their razor-carrying pals, 'Don't try to tell me how tough you are. I could fight and beat the lot of you with one hand, while I'm doing the crossword in the *Daily Record* with the other.'

Michael said only useless cowards carried weapons. The Gallacher boys were a weedy and unhealthy looking bunch. The saving of them was when they nicked some musical instruments from a shop in town and took a notion to learn how to play them. Already they had started to play as a group in pubs and clubs in Glasgow.

Now there was talk of them travelling further afield. Frank hoped this was true. He couldn't imagine Carragh shedding tears over their departure. Nor could he imagine her shedding any tears when Scobie was locked away in Barlinnie. It was a mystery to think what they saw in each other. Undersized Carragh with her sparse wisps of hair on top and legs like a full moon. Scobie was the same height as his wife. They resembled a pair of bookends. But his sparse wisps of hair were at the back of his skull. He had nothing on top, and his nose looked like a lump of putty squashed on to his face and given a cruel twist for good measure.

How Bridie survived in the Gallacher household, Frank shuddered to think. Half the time it wasn't just a rabble but a drunken rabble. And the place was a tip. The quicker he got her out of there the better. As soon as he made that decision, the urgency of it rapidly increased to unbearable proportions. It was unthinkable that his Bridie should stay in such appalling surroundings for one moment longer than was absolutely necessary. He proposed to her immediately, and vowed he would leave no stone unturned to enable them to get a place of their own as quickly as possible.

He asked his da what was happening with Bailie McPherson.

92

Patrick had proudly announced that the good bailie had managed to get a Corporation house for the O'Maley family in Blackhill – a two-bedroom, living room, scullery and bathroom in Acrehill Street, just across from the gasworks about a mile the other side of Garngad Road.

Frank had pleaded with Patrick to approach his friend at the City Chambers again, this time on his behalf. Patrick was outraged. 'What do you think I am? For my sake he's taken one hell of a risk of getting himself into hot water. He stuck his neck out for me. There's a waiting list for Corporation houses as long as your arm.'

Then it occurred to Frank that there might be a chance of him getting the rent book of the house in Bright Street changed over to his name when his ma and da and Tony and Michael and Bernard moved to Blackhill. He didn't have to ask Bridie what she thought, although of course he asked anyway. But he knew that her circumstances were so desperate in Turner Street she would have moved with him to a tent on Glasgow Green if he'd asked her.

'Oh Frank.' She was ecstatic. 'It'll be absolutely wonderful. Like a wee palace.'

Frank laughed. 'A room and kitchen with an outside lavatory is not exactly a palace, Bridie. But I promise you, I'll get you a better place one day. One day I'll make a lot of money with my writing. I'll be really successful. I know I will. I'm determined I will.'

'The room and kitchen will do us fine just now,' Bridie assured him. 'Fancy, just the two of us in the whole place. It's like heaven to me just to think of it.'

Even the fact that they didn't have any money to buy furniture and other necessities didn't dampen Bridie's enthusiasm. 'We'll save up, Frank. I'll put every penny by that I can. We both will, won't we, Frank?'

'I've got a few pounds put by already,' Frank confided. 'Enough to get a few basic things. But not much.'

'Och, we'll get other things in time. And we're bound to get some wedding presents, don't forget.'

93

He loved her all the more for being content with so little. He vowed yet again that one day he would be enormously successful as a writer. He would work like a slave to shower her with every luxury. One day in the future his Bridie would lack for nothing. He felt feverishly excited, as if fame and fortune were just around the corner. He also dreamed of the room and kitchen as it would be after his parents and brothers had gone. A heaven on earth. A place to write in peace. He hugged that dream to himself. It was too precious even to share with Bridie.

Chapter Thirteen

Bernard and Doris got off the tram at the end of Monteith Row. The clangour of its bell rent the air before the tram moaned away into the distance and there was silence.

'Further along,' Bernard said, peering through the fog at the numbers on the dark slits of entrances to the buildings. The closes, like the street, were gaslit. Eerie green circles of light were cast down, deepening the shadows.

Doris linked her arm through Bernard's and gave a dainty shiver. 'My goodness, it's terribly eerie. Just listen to those trees creaking over there.' She wasn't used to trees, and treated all country-type things with the utmost suspicion.

'Haven't you ever been down here before? At the Green?' Bernard asked.

'It was different then. The Shows were there. They made the place all bright and noisy and cheery. I don't go to them now, of course.'

'Why not?'

'Fun-fairs are a teeny-wee bit common. Of course everyone to his own taste.' Her blonde hair was teased and backcombed into an enormous beehive shape, and she'd taken a great deal of trouble with eyelashes and eyeliner. Underneath her short navy coat was a red and white spotted dirndl skirt and scarlet sweater. Underneath that again, a stiff nylon waist slip stuck out and rustled as she walked. Above it, a nylon 'Sweater Girl' bra with wide circle-stitched cups jutted to unnaturally sharp points. Every move was tricky and needed a certain amount of concentration because of the high heels that were necessary to give her much-needed height. She had spent hours dressing up and putting on her make-up in very difficult circumstances with other Gallachers constantly milling and crushing around. In her harassment and frustration she had allowed herself the use of very coarse swearwords, something to which she never stooped outside the Gallacher hell-hole.

She'd managed to make the best of herself eventually. Her hair looked striking and fashionable, and of course she had neat little features and a flawless skin.

'In here.' Bernard indicated Andrina's close. 'One up, I think Robert said.' His feet thumped and echoed up the stairs as he took them two at a time. Doris's heels rapidly click-clicked in an effort to keep up with him. She was thinking how big and powerful he was, charging ahead like a hefty-shouldered bull. He was thinking how wonderful it would be seeing Andrina again, to actually be near her, to be able to talk to her. He'd thought about nothing else for weeks, ever since Robert had invited him.

And suddenly there she was, opening the door to him. Darling Andrina, with her large round eyes sparkling with childish excitement. Yet also their baby shape contained a teasing sexual awareness. No other girl in the world had such eyes. They looked green if she was wearing green, blue if she was wearing blue.

'Andrina, this is Doris Gallacher,' he heard himself say. 'Doris, Andrina Anderson.'

'Come in. Come in.' Andrina welcomed them with breathless delight. 'You're the very first. It's nice to see you again, Bernard. It's been ages, hasn't it? Let me take your coat, Doris, and yours too, Bernard. What a night! I hope everybody manages. There's some free pegs here. Oh, thanks Bernard.'

She relinquished the coats and Bernard hung them on one of the pegs in the hallway. Then Robert appeared wielding a bottle and a corkscrew. 'I was just getting some drinks organised. Come away in.'

They were led into the front room which was furnished as a sitting room in contemporary style. Bernard thought the furniture looked precariously balanced on insubstantial splayed legs. Everything appeared as if it was on tiptoe. He was hesitant about testing his weight on the chairs.

'What a lovely colour scheme,' Doris called out. 'I just love that carpet. Such pretty heather colours. And these soft greys. Such terribly good taste. Of course, your husband's an artist, isn't he?'

Robert laughed. 'Art teacher. What are you having, Doris? I've sherry, port, gin, whisky, beer and soft drinks.'

'Goodness me. What a choice! A teeny glass of sherry will do fine, thanks. I just love your white woodwork. It's *the* latest fashion, of course.'

Bernard wondered how Doris was such an expert on home fashions. The house she came from hadn't even got curtains at the window. He was surprised the paper blinds had survived.

Everything pawnable in the Gallacher house was pawned when Scobie took his drinking bouts. The floors were bare boards, the whitewashed walls weren't white any more, and stained with God knew what missiles Scobie had aimed at Carragh or one of the family and missed. The house was a sordid dump. Compared with the Gallacher house a prison cell would be five-star luxury.

Bernard watched Andrina as he sipped a beer. She flushed under his steady gaze, but seemed pleased and happy to be the target of such a concentration of attention. She fluttered about like an exotic bird with her deep flame of hair and high-necked Chinese-patterned dress. Back and forth she flew to welcome in more and more guests until the front room was thick with bodies, laughter, loud talk and cigarette smoke. Bernard found it difficult to get near Andrina. So near and yet so far. His longing for her increased a thousandfold. It was a knife jammed inside him. He could hardly breathe for the pain of it. He crushed through the crowd towards where she was standing near the door, but just before he reached her she suddenly looked anxious and disappeared into the hall. He went after her only to find her speaking on the phone. Catching sight of him she put her finger to her lips in a warning sign and pointed at the front-room door. Then she said into the mouthpiece, 'It must be the wireless, Mummy.'

Bernard carefully shut the door but remained in the hall, watching her.

97

'Is that better, Mummy? I've told Robert to turn it down. Yes, of course I'm all right. Why shouldn't I be all right? When did you phone? I'm so sorry we didn't hear you, Mummy. Yes, of course I was in . . . The phone's in the hall, that's the trouble. If the front-room door's shut and the wireless is on . . . Yes, I know we usually sit in the kitchen. I meant the kitchen when I said the front room . . . I don't know why I said it, Mummy. It was just a slip of the tongue. I'm not used to the house yet . . . No, you don't need to phone back . . . Robert and I planned an early night, you see, Mummy . . . No, we're both fine. Honestly, Mummy, I'm fine . . . Yes, I'll be at the church in the morning. Yes, I'll see you then. Yes . . . all right . . . Yes, I will . . . Yes . . . I promise. Goodnight, Mummy.'

She put down the phone and rolled her eys. 'Sorry about that, but you know what Mummy's like.'

'Don't I just,' he said.

Flushing a little, she avoided his eyes. 'Do me a favour, Bernard. Tell everyone it's time to eat. I've already said but they seem to be enjoying talking so much . . .'

Just then the door was flung open and a riotous mob spilled out. Laughing and shouting, they made for the kitchen, sweeping Andrina before them.

She obviously had an artistry of her own. The table in the recess, a tea-trolley, the kitchen unit, the draining board at the side of the sink – every surface was covered with mouth-watering and attractively displayed food. There were golden, mouthwatering meat pies and little tartlets heaped with mashed fish instead of jam. Soda scones, treacle scones and even cheese scones – something Bernard had never tasted before – also delighted the palate. The pancakes and crumpets were as light as a feather, as were all the sponge cakes, whether filled with jam or cream, or decorated with icing sugar.

He thought again how truly wonderful she was. Not only had she looks and brains, she could cook. He knew in his gut she would have a talent for making love as well. People spoke to him, he answered them, but he didn't know what they said or what he said. All the time Andrina riveted his attention. Her

98

slightly protruding eyes, dancing with life and laughter and flirtation, the cheeky tilt of her head, the provocative swing of her hips, the way she crossed and slanted her long legs.

'Is this a serious affair?'

'What?' Bernard looked round in surprise at Robert.

'Doris. You can't keep your eyes off her.'

It was then Bernard noticed Doris speaking to Andrina. He shrugged. 'Doris is all right.'

'Nice figure. She went to St Francis, didn't she?'

'Aye. She lives a couple of streets away from us. Frank's going with her sister. Remember Bridie?'

Robert laughed. 'I hope she's improved in looks.'

'She's still specy, straight hair – and as smart dressed as a Guy on Guy Fawkes night. Frank doesn't seem to notice. Of course, he's no tailor's dummy himself.'

Bernard liked to be smart and was proud of the pin-striped suit and Crombie coat he'd just bought. It was important always to be well-shaved and showered and immaculately dressed. It was one of the things that impressed the punters and the hard men. When they saw you well turned-out, they thought you had your act together and they respected you. He had done a deal with a dance hall and another couple of pubs in town to supply them with bouncers. He was confident more venues would come. It all went by word of mouth. His reputation was steadily growing. He'd roped in more men for the job. He saw that his guys gave a good service and they were glad to get the money. He had recruited them from unemployed young men at the karate club, and thanks to the karate training all were able to handle themselves and were aggressively self-confident. He gave a good service himself. He kept a sharp eye for trouble. Any customer at the pub or the dance hall would simply need to take one step out of line, one flash of a weapon, and they were out on the street before they knew what hit them.

But more often than not he just needed to look at potential trouble-makers for the trouble to die down and disappear. It wasn't just his hefty build. Michael had told him, 'You've got

99

that killer stare, Bernard. You should have been in professional boxing.'

Michael could keep his boxing. It was a mug's game. Michael was riding high at the moment in the amateur scene. When he wasn't humping bricks around he was slugging away in the ring. The next thing would be the ABA championship in London. In the end, though, the chances were he'd be left punch drunk and unable even to hold down his brickie's job. Or just drunk. Michael had always had a special liking for the booze, ever since he used to get a sip of his ma or da's beer when he was a youngster.

Bernard hoped to God Michael wouldn't end up like Scobie Gallacher. The wee sod drank like a shoal of piranhas and regularly duffed up his wife. Father Riley had tried to teach him a lesson and punch some decency into him. All to no avail.

The women in that family had more spunk, including Doris. Even old Carragh could beak up to Scobie on occasion. She'd once knocked him out cold with an iron frying pan.

Everyone except Scobie knew that Scobie was an alcoholic. And a randy one at that.

Thinking of being randy aroused Bernard's own sexuality to an almost unbearable degree. He had to look away from Andrina. Just the sight of her put him in danger of having an erection. Afterwards, going home with Doris, he decided to relieve his sexual tension on her. After all, she was more than willing, so what was the harm? He would be pleasuring her, and getting some pleasure for himself. Too soon he felt sickened, disgusted at himself much more than the woman who gave herself so freely against the wall of the foul-smelling back close.

After all, and much to his surprise, she had been a virgin.

100

Chapter Fourteen

Jimmy Stoddart was in agony. So for that matter was his wife, Big Martha. For their daughter Caroline's sake they had walked from their home in Cobden Street to the next street along, to visit the O'Maleys. As far as they had always been concerned, Cobden Street was for Protestants, Bright Street was for Catholics, and never the twain shall meet. Now here they were, sitting in the enemy's camp surrounded by holy pictures. The Virgin Mary and the infant Jesus stared over their heads from one wall. Another picture on the same wall was of Jesus with tragic upturned eyes and wearing a crown of thorns. Another wall was decorated with St Francis and a crowd of animals. On one of the bed recess walls (which seemed positively indecent) was a big, gilt-framed picture of the Pope.

Statues of Mary, Joseph and Jesus crowded the mantelpiece beside a rusty-looking alarm clock, two brass candlesticks and an Oxo tin.

To Jimmy Stoddart, being surrounded by so much Popery was almost as bad as being inside a Roman church. He had to keep reminding himself that his future son-in-law was the Scottish middleweight champion, and think of all the reflected glory he could bask in as a result. The next thing Michael was aiming for was the ABA championship in London and he was going to accompany him. This was a chance not to be missed. All the same, brushing shoulders with Popery was a high price to pay. As far as Jimmy Stoddart was concerned, the Vatican and the priesthood were the cause of all the evils in the world. There was no doubt in his mind that the war had been the work of the Pope. Hitler and Mussolini were Catholics, to mention but two Papish bastards.

'Another cup of tea, Mrs Stoddart?' Maureen enquired

politely. They were all being terribly polite to each other. The strain was something cruel.

'No thanks,' Mrs Stoddart replied with a sniff, as if the query had been vaguely insulting. 'I've still got half a cup.'

She was wearing her best black dress and new corsets. The corsets were keeping her in an unnaturally erect position. She was in absolute agony, but would rather die than admit it. All she could think of to relieve her torture was the battering she was going to give Jimmy Stoddart the moment she got him home. It was his fault they were in this terrible position. It was he who agreed to the visit. It was he who had been all for the marriage in the first place. This she knew was an exaggeration, but in her torment she was beyond the niceties of total accuracy.

'A wee fairy cake then?' Maureen was determined, for Michael's sake, to act the perfect hostess.

'Aye, well . . .' Martha grudgingly selected a cake from the proffered plate. 'I hear you're moving to Blackhill.'

'A three apartment, scullery and bathroom,' Maureen beamed.

Martha knew Blackhill was a Catholic stronghold, so she wasn't in the least surprised at the move.

'I'm sure you'll be pleased at Michael and Caroline being promised this place,' Maureen continued. 'Having your girl just the next street along.'

'Aye . . . well . . .'

'You could have knocked me down with a feather after it was promised to Michael – our Frank said he'd wanted it. We knew he was winchin' Bridie Gallacher, but he never said.'

'Well, with Michael getting married first and him being older than Frank . . .'

'That's what we said, and Frank was very decent about it.'

Michael and Caroline smiled at one another. Everything seemed to be going well. The atmosphere was admittedly strained, but that was only to be expected under the circumstances and on a first visit. Michael had recently been in and out of chapel like a yo-yo, praying that everything would go well. Now he thanked God for preventing Tony and Frank from making an appearance. They had been well warned, of course. Indeed, they had been bribed to keep away. The trouble was you never knew with Frank. If his head was full of poetry (and it so often was) he could be dangerously absent-minded. Tony could forget, or renege on his promise out of sheer stupidity. Michael kept having a dreadful vision of Tony bursting into the kitchen, all buck teeth and Teddy Boy glory, yelling 'Up the IRA!', or some such insanity. The mere idea made him sweat. It would mean the end of all his and Caroline's dreams. They could still get married in a registry office without her parents' consent, of course. It wasn't like in England where you had to be twenty-one for that. Here in Scotland it was legal to get married at sixteen whether the parents wanted it or not, and Caroline was nearly twenty. But Martha and Jimmy Stoddart would prove bad enemies. They would make their lives a hell on earth. Michael couldn't see Caroline standing up against her mother. Caroline was sweet and adorable, his little Shirley Temple, and he loved her dearly, but the fact had to be faced that she wasn't the world's strongest character. He didn't blame her for being so easily cowed by her mother. He lost a lot of bottle himself when faced with Big Martha Stoddart.

'I suppose,' Martha said now through a mouthful of fairy cake, 'we'll just have to make the best of it.'

'A drop of the hard stuff in your tea, Jimmy?' Patrick volunteered.

Jimmy put his hand over his cup. 'In my book it's a crime to dilute it.'

'You're that fond of tea?'

'No, whisky.'

Both men laughed, and Patrick poured a generous glass of the amber liquid. 'Have it separate then, and to hell with the tea.'

'As I was saying,' Martha aimed each word like a dagger at the two men, 'before I was so rudely interrupted: we'll just have to make the best of it.'

'You're quite right, Martha,' Maureen soothed. 'It's a

terrible problem, so it is, but the young folks are in love and love conquers all things. I just pray to God that they'll be happy together. With a wee bit of help and good will, I'm sure everything will work out all right. Caroline is a lovely girl, so she is, and Michael's a good boy.'

Both Martha and Jimmy regarded her with suspicion. They didn't trust prayers to a Catholic god. What good could come of that? She'd better not have any ideas of making Caroline 'turn', or having any children brought up as Catholics. If they thought . . . Unknown to them Caroline and Michael had already signed a paper promising that any children would be brought up as Catholics. Even Maureen didn't know this, but it was her prayer and fondest hope that one day Caroline would see the light and, of her own free will, become a member of the true church and bring up her children in the faith.

Martha said, 'We've always been good Protestants. Nothing like this has ever happened in our family before.'

Jimmy, like Patrick, had downed his second dram. It was their way of smoothing out the sharpest edge of any problem. 'My father was once a Grand Master of the South Side Orange Lodge.' His eyes were misted with remembrance.

'You must have been hell of a proud,' Patrick said, refilling the glasses. 'When I was wee my ma and da lived for a while in the country. He was sent on a job – building one of these new roads. I remember I followed the Orange Parade on the twelfth of July. I thought it was great listening to the bands and joining in the fun in the park.'

'Good for you!' Jimmy said, warming to the man.

'It seems to be just in Glasgow that there's all this ill will. I wonder why that is.'

Jimmy thought – because there's more bloody Papes in Glasgow insinuating themselves into the police and the Council, and all the positions of power. They'll be taking over the whole city, the whole country if we're not careful. He managed, however, to refrain from expressing his thoughts. 'Beats me,' he said.

That reminded Martha. 'It's time we were getting back to

Cobden Street. It's all settled then. The wedding's to be a quiet affair, but to be blessed in our church, and you and your family are going to be there.' Martha, in fact, had only been twice in the church she claimed her own – once to get married and once to have Caroline christened.

'Well,' Maureen said, 'me and Patrick will certainly attend.' She was able to say this because she'd finally been able to persuade Father Riley (with the help of a bottle of whisky and a large donation to the chapel funds) to give them permission to go to the Protestant church for the wedding ceremony. 'Michael's brothers will have to make up their own minds.'

'The reception will be round in my house so there'll be plenty of room if they do come, and plenty to eat as well.'

'I'm sure,' Maureen agreed. 'It'll be a lovely do, so it will. Caroline's told me you make a marvellous steak pie.'

'Aye, well . . .' Martha was slightly mollified, although her words retained their usual ominous undertones. She rose, and gave a jerk of her head to indicate to her husband that he should rise too. 'We'll see you on the day. Are you coming round with us, Caroline?'

'Can I just wait for a wee while to finish my tea, Mammy?'

'Aye . . . well . . .'

Maureen and Patrick saw the Stoddarts to the door. 'It'll be fine,' Maureen said. 'Don't worry.'

'I hope you're right.' Martha gave a tragic sigh and shook her head. 'As if I hadn't enough to worry me,' she added, referring to Jimmy.

After the door shut, Patrick went back to the kitchen to have another dram and open a screwtop. Maureen went through to the front room window to give the Stoddarts a friendly wave. She stood there for what seemed like ages before they appeared.

Later, in the kitchen, she said to Caroline, 'I was beginning to think your mammy and daddy had got lost, hen. They took that long to come out the close.'

She learned later what had caused the delay. Lizzie Feeney, one of her neighbours, told her that when she had emerged on to the landing en route to go down to the midden to empty her bucket, her path had been unexpectedly blocked. Mountainous Martha had been struggling, with skirts up round her ears, to unhook herself from her corsets.

Lizzie Feeney and Maureen O'Maley laughed so much they nearly split their sides.

Chapter Fifteen

Some Teds weren't so bad, but Tony O'Maley was an eejit. Scobie decided to play a joke on him. Not only because he enjoyed practical jokes, but because what he had in mind would help his pal, Patrick O'Maley, out of a tricky situation.

'As sure as my name's Patrick O'Maley,' Patrick said, 'Tony's going to bugger up Michael's wedding.'

'Can't you tell him he's not to go?' Scobie suggested.

'He's twenty-six years of age. He does what he likes and he likes any excuse to get dressed up. He's already bought a new "drape", as he calls it. It's a black loose thing that doesn't know whether it's a coat or a jacket. And you should see the skinny string of a tie he's got. And his trousers aren't much wider.' Patrick sent a long-suffering look heavenwards. 'Drainpipes, he calls them, and brothel creepers for shoes. The soles are inches thick. And he looks a right cock-a-doodle-do with that quiff stuck on top of his head. Have you seen him done up like that?'

'Aye,' Scobie sympathised.

'It's what's liable to come out of his big mouth that worries me the most, though. To hear him talk anyone would think he was blood brothers with the IRA. What can I do, short of knocking him unconscious? He's determined to be at that wedding – and another thing, he'll want to batter away at those infernal drums of his.'

'Leave Tony to yours truly.' Scobie cupped his hands and rubbed them, then smacked them together in delight. 'I've got one hell of a good idea.'

'I don't want any serious harm to come to him, you understand.'

'Not at all. Trust me, Patrick. It'll just be my wee joke. But Tony won't be at the wedding. He won't put a foot over the door at the weekend, believe me.'

And so it was agreed.

The very next night, Scobie slunk up to Tony in the pub and, tapping him on the elbow to catch his attention (it was a bit of a strain to reach his shoulder – all the O'Maley boys were tall), he looked furtively around. 'A private word, Tony.'

'So? Fire ahead. I'm listening, wee man.'

'You've been honoured, son.'

'Eh? A VC like my da's pal, you mean?'

'Naw, ya bampot.' Scobie darted another furtive look around the half-empty bar. 'You've been chosen, singled out.'

'Who by?'

'Your friends across the water.'

Scobie winked meaningfully and began to sing in a whisper, ' "A nation once again . . ." You've been highly recommended, Tony.'

Tony was beginning to look distinctly worried. 'What for?'

'They will be in touch. They're staying over the weekend.'

'What for?' Tony's long face had now gone a shade paler.

'Tony, you're going to be approached by a brigade commander. If you want to know, I'll tell you. He's from the Belfast Brigade. They don't come any better. He's had a wee word with me, and I've assured him that all he'd heard about you is true. You're a good Republican. A man to be trusted.'

'What for?' Tony's mind and tongue seemed to have got stuck in one groove. Total confusion reigned in his eyes and his mouth hung loosely open.

'Here's what they want you to do,' Scobie confided in hushed, but very clearly formed words. 'You will get two parcels to deliver. Now, don't worry, you will get enough money for a nice month in Spain. Three-star hotel. You'll still have enough money left in the last week. You'll not be counting the pennies. Just two parcels, Tony.' Scobie smacked his hands together, making Tony wince and nearly spill his beer. 'And you won't be in the country when they go off.'

'I'm not planting any fucking bombs,' Tony howled.

'You should have thought of that before, Tony. They think you're willing to be an active member and plant bombs. Now you're telling me you're not. You're just a public house Republican.'

At this point, Tony relinquished his beer as if the glass had suddenly electrocuted him. 'I'll have to go. I just remembered. I've a train to catch.'

Scobie put a detaining hand on his arm. 'Wait a minute, Tony. Did all those people in Ireland die for nothing? For well over eight hundred years we've been ruled by foreigners. Now you're getting a chance to do something about it.'

'Fuck off.' Tony flung aside Scobie's detaining hand and disappeared with the speed of a greyhound.

'What's up with him?' the barman asked.

For a minute or two Scobie couldn't speak for laughter. 'He's discovered he's not such a good Republican as he thought he was.'

'Aye,' the barman said, 'there's a lot like that. Good at the romancing. Singing the Irish songs and buying raffle tickets. But they don't want to have anything to do with active service. They draw the line at getting involved.'

'Aye,' Scobie agreed, wiping the tears of hilarity from his eyes. 'As long as the old Murphy's stout's flowing, and the Guinness, it's hunky-dory. But when they say we've come to collect you, it's hell of a difference. Pull me another pint, son. I'll just have another one before I go.'

Tony was not at Michael's wedding. Nobody knew where he was. He disappeared on Thursday and didn't reappear until Monday night. He'd gone straight to work from wherever he'd been, and wherever he'd been he refused to say. It turned out afterwards that he'd holed up at the house in Blackhill – it was all ready to move into and they all had a key.

The flitting from Bright Street, Garngad to Acrehill Street, Blackhill happened six days after the wedding, just before the happy pair returned from their honeymoon in Rothesay. (They'd had two minds about going away at all because Clyde coast resorts could be pretty nippy in the spring, but in the end the treat of a few days at the seaside could not be resisted.) The flitting had been carried out by the O'Maleys themselves with a little help from Scobie. It wasn't too far to Acrehill Street, maybe a half-hour's leisurely walk. So they managed no bother using a horse and a cart loaned by Spud Tamson, the coal man. This was a lot easier than the handcarts trundled along by other new folk who had been moved to Blackhill by earlier slum clearances. To celebrate the success of the move both Patrick and Scobie had gone on a bender.

'You shouldn't encourage him,' Maureen scolded. 'You can stop, but he can't.'

'Encourage him? How do I encourage him? As for stopping, he's always stopping. Every time he swears he'll never touch another drop. Wait till you see, in a few days, he'll be coming here as sober as a judge and with a terrible hangover and telling us he'll never look at another drop as long as he lives.'

'I wonder if Carragh could get him to go to the AA.'

'Alcoholics Anonymous? No chance. I've told you, he keeps thinking he can stop. He'll never admit he's an alcy.'

Maureen sighed. 'Anyway, I've told Carragh she can come round here any time she's stuck. I think she feels everybody's deserting her, with some of the boys talking about joining the fair and others planning to go down South, and Bridie looking forward to her wedding. Not that any of them are much help to her as it is. Do you think Doris and Bernard will come to anything? She seems daft about him.'

Patrick made a face. 'Bernard doesn't seem very keen as far as I can make out. But then he always plays his cards close to his chest. He deserves better than one of the Gallachers. So does Frank, for that matter. The Gallachers are a right gormless lot. The whole crowd of them put together couldn't even match our Frank.'

'Frank's had no luck yet with a house and Bridie and him are that keen to tie the knot. I know you don't want to take advantage of your pal's good nature, Patrick, but if he's such a nice man, would he not be pleased to give your son a wee helping hand? I read in the paper that Bailie McPherson's had quite a bit to do with these new flats in the Gorbals.'

'Why can't they get their own places?'

'You know Bernard, he'll never ask you to do anything for him. Bernard will always see to himself. And Michael didn't ask you to speak to the factor about Bright Street. He saw to that himself. Tony's not even going with anybody. So it's just Frank. Aw, go on Patrick. Frank's such a good boy.'

'He's put his name on the Corporation list. He'll be allowed a house when his time comes.'

Maureen sent a glance heavenwards. 'Holy Mother of God! Poor Frank could be drawing his old age pension by then!'

'Bailie McPherson went out of his way to get us this house. I couldn't have the cheek to ask him again. Especially so soon. It wouldn't be right.'

'Och, Patrick . . .'

'Look, just think yourself lucky he helped us get this place.'

Maureen sighed, then abandoning any hope for Frank, she gazed around her new home with pleasure. It was her pride and joy, and already many of her old neighbours and friends had come to be shown around. Carragh had been for a bath and said it was the best luxury she'd ever enjoyed in her life. The living room in which Maureen and Patrick were sitting, one either side of a coal fire with a plum-coloured tiled surround, looked out to a back green. Beyond that was the railway line and the gasworks. Already Patrick and Tony had jumped on to some stationary wagons, split them open with axes, and stolen some cartons. But it turned out there was nothing worth selling in them. 'Better luck next time,' they'd said.

Maureen and Patrick slept on a bed settee in the living room. They pulled it out at night. It meant shifting the table and chairs back against the window, and even then it took a bit of manoeuvring to get around. But that was only at night. If the boys wanted a cup of tea or anything to eat after she and Patrick went to bed, there was the beautiful scullery with its gas cooker and wash boiler and slatted shelves for pots and pans.

Tony and Frank shared one bedroom, and Bernard had the other to himself because his work was very irregular, and more often than not he came in during the wee small hours. Sometimes he was out the whole night long and didn't appear

111

until five or six in the morning. Anyway, Bernard could afford to give her more money than the other two, and he insisted that he was entitled to the room. There was never any use arguing with Bernard. He had such a strong will sometimes it frightened her. But he was a lovely boy. Maureen had a secret admiration for him as well as love. If truth be known, he was her favourite. He had always been good to her. But at times, noticing that steely unwavering stare of his, she wondered how he was to other people. Of course it was the nature of his job that he had to be tough. Still, Michael was a boxer and he hadn't the same kind of look. She blamed the difference on the fact that Bernard often missed Mass. She suspected he only went at all to please her, and that was only after she pleaded and cajoled and openly wept for his immortal soul.

Maureen wondered again if he was serious about Doris. All the Gallachers were good Catholics and never missed Mass if they could help it. Even Scobie, while still feeling like death with one of his hangovers, struggled along to the chapel. The priest had tried his best to keep Scobie on the straight and narrow. When he was working and didn't hand over his pay packet to Carragh, Father Riley had come to the house and given him a right doing. That worked for a week or two. Then Scobie would be arrested for being drunk and disorderly and disappear for a spell into the Bar L., as Barlinnie prison was nicknamed. The local bobbies knew Scobie well and it was said that they picked him up every now and again just to give Carragh a breather.

If Bernard was serious about Doris, Maureen couldn't imagine him being married in the chapel. At the same time she couldn't imagine what Bernard could have against the faith he'd been brought up in. As a child he always seemed to go quite happily to Mass and to enjoy the Boys' Guild.

She had noticed his gradual withdrawal into a kind of secrecy. Was it linked with, or caused by his job? she wondered. Had his hard-man image crushed all his finer feelings? Yet he was such a lovely boy, with his smooth black crown of hair. And when he smiled, and that cleft in his chin deepened, he looked

112

so handsome and strong. She loved him dearly. Doris Gallacher was a nice enough wee lassie, but in a different class altogether from Bernard. Bernard was going places. Already he could claim to have his own business. Doris Gallacher wasn't for him. Although it was plain for anyone to see she'd set her sights on him.

Poor Doris, she thought, then wondered why she hadn't thought – poor Bernard.

Chapter Sixteen

'It was you who wanted to come to Drumchapel,' McPherson reminded Sophie. 'I told you Knightswood or Mosspark would be better, but you refused to listen. Anyway, you've barely been here two years. Can't you settle yourself for anywhere for any length of time?'

'If you and your crowd had built the place right, maybe I could have settled here. If you'd thought about what folk needed, like shops and churches and halls . . .' She was polishing the table near where he was sitting, polishing it desperately over and over again as if each mote of dust that landed on it tormented her.

'We've been through all this before,' McPherson groaned. 'What good does it do? You wanted to come here, and now you'll have to stay here whether you like it or not.'

'Don't you dare lay down the law to me about where I've got to spend the rest of my days. You're not sitting on the bench now. I'm the one who's stuck here all the time. I notice you make sure you don't need to spend one hour in the place more than you can avoid.'

McPherson tried to be patient. 'I've my work to go to.'

'Work?' Sophie sneered. 'When did you last lay a brick? Your hands are softer than a woman's.'

'You know perfectly well what I mean.'

'Oh yes, the busy committee man at the City Chambers. Not just a committee man now – chairman of this, chairman of that. The man who can do everything for everybody except his own family.'

'Sophie, if you're now expecting me to get you a house in Knightswood or Mosspark, I'm afraid I'll have to disappoint you. The reason why I said you'll have to stay here whether you like it or not is simply because it's impossible for me to get you a

house in Knightswood or Mosspark. People have found that
they like it in those schemes. They like living there so much I
couldn't get them to move to make a house vacant for you
unless I put a bomb under them.'

'Well . . .' She hesitated, outwardly defiant, inwardly shivering at her own outrageousness. 'A house in Bearsden then.'

She had passed many a lonely hour recently walking around
the elegant tree-lined streets of Bearsden, imagining how
wonderful it would be to live there. There could be no doubt
these people had amenities. In the central part, called the
village, there was a line of shops with tidy flats above them.
There was a town hall, churches and church halls. It was
obviously a very busy and Christian community. The halls had
notice boards telling of innumerable meetings and social events
that no doubt needed conscientious helpers. She longed to be
really needed, have something useful to do. She still didn't
know any of her immediate neighbours in Drumchapel. They
were out at work all day. Some of the others she'd come across
she didn't want to know. There were young women who during
daylight hours flaunted painted faces and bare feet with scarlet
toenails showing through open strapped sandals. She'd told
them they ought to be horsewhipped for being such shameless
jezebels. After dark she'd caught couples behaving in a
shameless and filthy manner in the back close. She'd called
God's wrath down on their heads and shone a torch like the
light of God on their disgusting wickedness. There isn't a
corner dark enough, she'd told them, to hide from the light of
the Lord. Filth had poured from the lips of the sinners. They
called her obscene names, but she knew she had God on her
side and was given strength to survive their hatred. The
mothers of these sinners were no better. Lazy sluts who never
washed the stairs and couldn't be bothered to discipline even
the youngest of their children. Children roamed wild in
dangerous looking packs or hung about shouting and laughing.
Underaged boys smoked cigarettes. Boys and girls dropped
litter and blasphemed. When she chastised them for taking the
Lord's name in vain, they jeered and made a fool of her.

115

Drumchapel was a soulless barren waste of a place. She hated it.

'Bearsden?' McPherson gasped. 'Have you gone completely out of your mind?'

'What's wrong with wanting to live in Bearsden?'

'Houses there cost money. That's what's wrong for a start.'

'We could get a mortgage.'

'You know perfectly well, Sophie, that would go against my principles.'

'Principles, principles. We can't afford those kind of principles. Anyway, just because you support the building of council houses doesn't mean you have to live in one.'

'We can't afford a mortgage.'

'You always seem to find money when you need it for yourself. Anyway, I've seen your bankbook. You're not as hard up as you keep making out. Think about it, Andrew. It would be a step up in the world for you. A man in your position should have a good address. And think how you could relax. You need more time to relax. You could join the golf club and meet decent people you wouldn't be ashamed to invite home.' Her eyes misted, imagining entertaining people to dinner or supper or afternoon tea. 'I've discovered there's a local Church of Jesus there. We could become part of a really nice Christian community.'

McPherson personally didn't think Drumchapel or the people were nearly as bad as Sophie made out. They were always decently behaved and respectful to him.

He began to think, however, maybe she had a point. He rather fancied the idea of being a member of an exclusive golf club. It was true. He didn't give himself time to relax. It might look as if he was relaxed sitting in the Corn Exchange but he was constantly on tap, constantly available for people to approach him for advice or help. And that was over and above his work in the City Chambers committee rooms and his regular stints sitting on the bench of the Licensing Court.

The more he thought of Sophie's idea the more he felt it might have possibilities. Bearsden was the place where the

116

money was and money not only talked – it gave the right answers.

Of course his old mother wouldn't like it. She never tired of reminding him what a good Socialist his father had been. Indeed there could be no denying it. David McPherson had been one of the best. A regular old Keir Hardie of a man, cloth cap and all. Hundreds of Glaswegians had turned up at his funeral.

But his high principles, his brand of Socialism, had meant grim poverty and hardship for his family. A bricklayer by trade like himself, his father had been a great admirer of the Soviet Union and a tireless worker for the Independent Labour Party. He had a strong faith in Marxism but always said he'd defend parliamentary institutions to the death.

McPherson had followed his father's footsteps into local politics but felt his own personal way forward was through the Labour Party, and pledged himself to help the people of Glasgow who lived in appalling housing conditions to be rehoused in suitable flats. He had kept that pledge and had fought for the demolition of slums and the fast rebuilding of houses. He'd fought for the cleaning up of the polluted River Clyde, he'd lobbied for more attention to be paid to the arts and for financial help for the university.

In short, he'd fought and worked tirelessly for his fellow citizens, and it had been said of him that he was a town councillor who saw the advantage of regional planning, new towns and comprehensive redevelopment, and did all in his power to put them into effect. His father would have been proud of him.

Yet sometimes when McPherson gazed at himself in the mirror, looking portly and distinguished in his dark, well-tailored suit and his heavy gold chain of office, he quailed inside as he imagined his father's sharp eyes staring back at him. The truth was the old man *ought* to have been proud of him but wouldn't have been. Yet why not? What good could you do the starving if you starved along with them? In his own way, he did as much as his father ever did for the working class. It wasn't the working man that he made any extra money from. Any gifts, any favours he received, were from businessmen; builders who wanted contracts, taxi owners, and men who wanted to open pubs or restaurants and needed to be sure of getting a licence. Men who could well afford to pay for any influence he used on their behalf. It was worth remembering that any building contract awarded, any restaurant or pub licence given, meant much needed employment for more and more people. He did his best for everybody else. Why shouldn't he do his best for himself? He deserved it.

'We'll see,' he told Sophie, and was taken aback by the immediate and feverish way her face lit up.

'I know it's the right place for us, Andrew. God has called us there. I feel it. I feel it.'

'I just said we'll see,' he repeated uneasily. 'It's as far out as Drumchapel, you know.'

'Oh, but what a different world. A world of God's chosen people.'

Sometimes he wondered if Sophie was mad. She so often went to such extremes. 'I'll have a word with Felderman's and see if they own any property out there. We might come to some arrangement that could be to the advantage of both of us.' He was thinking of the flats in the Gorbals. More and more of the old Gorbals was being demolished. Some new flats had already been built. More were on the cards. The contract for them would be worth millions.

'I'm sure you can do it with God's help, Andrew. We'll both go to Church on Sunday and pray for your success in this.'

He sighed. It was such a difficult trek to get into town from Drumchapel on a Sunday. Public transport was bad enough during the week, but on a Sunday it was practically non-existent. It was high time he had a car. It was ridiculous for a man in his position to have to struggle here, there and everywhere by bus or tram or train. Felderman had a car all right. Felderman had a black Rolls Royce. A wave of bitterness engulfed him. Why shouldn't he have a house in Bearsden and a car and any other of life's comforts? He was a better man than John Felderman. A better man by a long chalk.

'I grant you it would be a lot more sensible and convenient,' he told Sophie, 'to be members of a church on our doorstep, so to speak.'

'Perhaps it's time for us to move on spiritually as well as physically,' Sophie said, thinking of the shabby converted house in the ancient terrace along Rose Street and comparing it in her mind's eye with the noble looking religious edifices in Bearsden.

'Well, yes, I suppose one could make a case for that.' He leaned his elbows down on his knees and thoughtfully made a roof by placing the tips of his fingers together. 'I take your point. Yes, I'll see what I can do.'

Sophie was ecstatic. She couldn't wait to tell Andrina. She phoned her up right away and was taken aback to get no answer. Where could she be? It was only a couple of hours ago that she'd been speaking to her, and Andrina had assured her she would be in for the rest of the evening. All the excitement about living in Bearsden immediately shrank into suspicion. She telephoned again and again. Until eventually Andrina answered.

'Oh, Mummy.' The guilt in her tone was unmistakable.

'Where do you think you've been?'

'It was one of Robert's karate nights.'

'Do you think I'm a fool? You don't go to Robert's karate club.'

'No, I wasn't saying that. I just felt a bit lonely . . .'

'And so you decided . . .' Sophie's voice turned ugly, twisted with disgust. '. . . to seek a little male companionship else-where.'

'No! No! I just popped out to have a chat with one of the neighbours.'

'That immoral slut next door. She'd be able to supply you with what you were looking for, all right.'

'No, not Josie, Mummy. She works at night. And honestly, she's a very nice person. She's not what you think at all.'

'Anybody with eyes in their head can see what she's like. That woman's a filthy prostitute.'

119

'Mummy, please don't speak like that. It upsets me. You don't know what you're saying. You don't know Josie.'

I know you, she thought bitterly, you wicked liar. 'You promised you'd have nothing more to do with that woman and when I arrived unexpectedly to visit you last week, she was in your house.'

'She'd just popped in to borrow some sugar, Mummy. What could I do? I couldn't shut the door in her face.'

'You've always been the same of course. You hadn't left school when you were sneaking off with men. I thought being safely married would change you, but I see it hasn't.'

'If you're meaning Bernard O'Maley, that was years ago and we just met in the park a few times, Mummy. And Mary Gardner and Sheila Preston were there too. And a couple of Bernard's friends. It was all very innocent. You'd no need to worry.'

'Innocent? With a man like Bernard O'Maley?' Sophie spat the words out in disgust. 'You nearly killed me with worry. God forgive you, you nearly killed me and you haven't changed. You lied to me then and you're lying to me now. You met him on your own more than once and you painted your face when you went to meet him. I know all about what you did.'

'Mummy, I didn't mean any harm . . .'

'And you haven't changed. When I caught you with that woman your face was painted like a common harlot. You had as much paint on your face as she had, and you were wearing cheap flashy earrings . . .'

'They were Josie's, Mummy. She was just letting me try them on. It was just a bit of fun.'

'Oh? Was the disgusting bra you were wearing hers as well? Making you stick out – flaunt yourself. I was ashamed for you. You enjoy flaunting yourself and making a vulgar exhibition of yourself. I felt dirtied being in the same room as you.'

Filth.

'Oh Mummy, please don't talk like that.' Andrina had begun to weep.

Sophie banged down the receiver as if it was contaminated.

Chapter Seventeen

Bernard observed Andrina as often as he could, and when he went to karate he tactfully elicited from Robert as much information about her as possible. He learned that every Friday she went into Sauchiehall Street to have a wander about the shops and then enjoy afternoon tea in Miss Cranston's Willow Tearooms.

The tearoom was a Rennie Mackintosh masterpiece. Outside, it sparkled like a little jewel between the darker, more sedate buildings crowding it on either side. It had smart chequered edging and elegant looping ironwork combined with abstracted organic shapes so typical of Mackintosh. Mackintosh also liked symbolism and no doubt that was why he chose the motif of the willow. It came from the name of Sauchiehall Street, which meant alley of willows.

Bernard wished Andrina had been in the habit of frequenting any other restaurant in the city. The Willow seemed a very feminine kind of place, and if he knew anything about Rennie Mackintosh there would be his ladder-backed fragile looking chairs inside. However, there was no question of being put off. He waited and watched across the road from the tearoom. Eventually he saw her arrive, tall and elegant in a grey alpaca dress that fitted snugly over her shapely body in what he'd learned from Doris was the Princess line. The dress had a high horseshoe neck and over it a short white spencer just reached to under Andrina's bust. She wore white gloves and a little straw boater decorated with a broad ribbon to match her dress. She had lost much of her teenage voluptuousness, but she was still a curvaceous and strikingly beautiful woman.

He followed her inside the tearoom. He watched her hesitate under the great flower bowl that marked the transition from the front saloon to the back beyond. Then he watched as she

121

decided to climb the open-screened stairs leading to the tea-gallery above. He too climbed the stairs. The upper tea-room was sumptuously extravagant and sophisticated and it occurred to him that Andrina obviously enjoyed and could appreciate life's luxuries. This gave them something else in common. It was, he believed, linked with sexuality and sensuality, this ability to appreciate, to savour, to enjoy. He felt himself relishing and appreciating the luxury of his surroundings. One wall of long, low, slightly bay windows set with a design in mirror glass looked over the street. The other walls were lined with pale purple silk and had a frieze of leaded panels of mirrors, purple and white glass reflecting light and chairs and customers. A panel set with glass jewels and beads had such a romantic imagery that Bernard now felt that Andrina could not have chosen a better place.

She was sitting facing the window and so she didn't see him approach.

'Hello, Andrina.'

She looked up, startled. 'Bernard.'

For the briefest of seconds he saw pleasure flutter over her eyes.

'May I join you?' he asked, pulling out a chair and sitting down without waiting for an answer.

Already she had become agitated. He could feel the tension in her. 'I don't think you should, Bernard.'

'Why not? We're old friends. And I had to talk to you. I didn't get a chance at the party.'

Her eyes kept agitating anxiously towards the stairs as if she was expecting her mother to suddenly materialise on a witch's broom. She wasn't worried about Robert, or about anybody else seeing them together. Just her mad old mother.

'If my mother saw us,' she said, confirming that he'd guessed correctly, 'I'd die, Bernard. I'm sorry. I know we're just friends and it's perfectly harmless us meeting by accident and having a cup of tea together, but that's not how my mother would see it. I'd just die, Bernard. I'm sorry, but I can't help it. Please go.'

'In a way, your mother's got a point.'

Her sudden, undivided attention fixed on him. 'How do you mean?'

'This meeting isn't an accident. I've been watching you and waiting for you.'

Colour darkened her cheeks. 'You used to do that before.'

'I've never stopped.'

'This is ridiculous. Apart from anything else, I'm a married woman.'

'I'm the one you should have married, Andrina. I know it and you know it.'

She became agitated again. 'This is ridiculous,' she repeated. 'I don't know anything of the kind. I'm perfectly happy with Robert. How dare you spy on me and follow me and say things like that to me?'

'From the moment I first set eyes on you, I loved you and wanted you. Every day I hold you in my thoughts. Every night I hold you in my arms and make passionate love to you in my imagination.'

'This is madness.'

'In a way I suppose it is.'

'You must stop this, Bernard. Stop it at once. I will not have you thinking such things about me, or following me, or spying on me, or upsetting me like this. If you don't leave right now, I will.'

He rose. 'I've no desire to upset you. But I wanted you to be clear about how I feel.'

'It's time you were married with a wife of your own,' she was near to tears of distress, 'instead of pestering another man's wife. Robert of all people too. He thinks you're his best friend.'

'Yes, I'm sorry about Robert.'

'Just go.'

'I'll see you again.'

He'd said all he wanted to say. Out on Sauchiehall Street, despite her words of rejection, he felt animated, energised, inflamed by a love that he knew instinctively was burning in her blood too. Perhaps she hadn't awakened to the fire of it yet.

Perhaps she had not yet found enough courage to face it. But it was there in her exactly the same as it was in him.

The only thing that spoiled this secret union, this promise of wonderful riches to come, was the mention of Robert. The words 'Robert of all people' echoed like a Chinese torture in his mind, tensing every nerve, every muscle.

He had to go to the karate club now. He needed the outlet of karate for his pent-up energies and tensions. On the other hand, he didn't relish facing Robert so soon after making love –albeit only verbal love – to his wife.

Yet at the same time no one really mattered except Andrina. He thought of being with her in no other terms than loving ones. With Doris it was sex – a simple release of nature, like peeing. He tried to behave decently to her in other ways. He gave her a good time. He took her to posh restaurants for meals – something that thrilled her to the core. He gave her presents. He tried not to show his growing irritation with her. It wasn't Doris's fault that he didn't love her.

But Andrina, oh darling Andrina. How he adored everything about her: her baby-shaped eyes, her fiery crown of hair, her creamy complexion, her soft bulging breasts, her neat waist, her delightful wiggle of curvaceous hips, her long shapely legs. She had the mixture of innocence, vulnerability and sensuality of an auburn-haired Marilyn Monroe. He ached to touch her, caress her, stroke her, kiss every inch of her. When he made love to her, and one day he would make love to her, he would take his time and savour every precious moment.

He got off the tram and walked through the grim lines of tenements to the school hall where the karate club was held.

'Hi,' Robert greeted him.

Bernard gave him a nod as he retrieved the white baggy trousers, loose white jacket and black belt that was the traditional karate uniform. He began to undress with Andrina still so livid in his mind it seemed strange that Robert couldn't see her. Robert was already in his karate gear and left the side room to join the boys waiting in the hall, his bare feet slapping on the boards. Bernard followed, the karate discipline banishing Andrina at least temporarily from his mind. Concentrating was important in this martial art. Concentration, and a mixture of relaxation and speed.

Robert took the class through a quick warm-up session. Once loosened, they all lined up. Then with a short bobbing bow Bernard faced Robert. He gave a loud 'Ossu' and slid forward, knees flexed, ankles loose, concentrating on relaxed rhythmic breathing. Suddenly, with a rapid double shuffle, he drove forward off his back leg. A satisfying thud exploded up his extended arm as he scored a solid Yakuzuki into Robert's ribs. He immediately leapt sideways to avoid Robert's counter punch and, on the break, shot a left leg Jodan Mawashigeri into Robert's temple.

He quickly disengaged and continued his circling motion, bouncing lightly, arms and shoulders loose. Robert rushed forward with a loud Kiai and a strong focused series of punches. Bernard continued to spiral away. He knew that, despite his height and the bulk of his shoulders, he was faster, smoother, more in control. He feinted an opening and as Robert leapt into the opening, he dropped his lead hand down across the punch and threw a lightning-fast back fist onto Robert's temple.

With a wry smile Robert called 'Yame' and the class halted. 'You're getting too good at this, Bernard,' Robert said. 'What's your secret?'

Chapter Eighteen

'Andrina?'

'Mm?'

'You were miles away. There's nothing wrong, is there?'

Andrina raised a brow. 'What could be wrong?'

Robert kept his book open on his lap but did not immediately return his attention to it. He peered over his glasses at her. He had taken to wearing glasses for reading. She had never seen him looking more like a school teacher. 'You seem a bit tense and worried.'

'Do I?' She gave a half laugh. 'All I was thinking about was what to have for tomorrow's dinner.'

'Perhaps you should get out and about more. Take up some hobby. Go out with a woman friend instead of being on your own so much during the day. I feel guilty about leaving you on your own on my karate evenings as well.'

'We go out together at the weekend, or we have people in. I'm quite happy with that.'

'Are you sure?'

She smiled. 'Of course I'm sure.'

'As long as you're happy.' He pushed his glasses up to the bridge of his nose again and returned his attention to his book. In the silence she could hear the gas mantle putter and the fire creak. In the peace and safety of their home she felt affection and gratitude towards Robert. It was true what her mother said. She was a very lucky woman.

She struggled to keep her thoughts anchored in the serenity of the kitchen and the comforting familiarity of the man sitting at the other side of the hearth. She gazed at his short brown hair. It was peppered with grey at the temples and beginning to thin a little too. Robert didn't bother so much about the smattering of grey but he was anxious about losing any hair. He tried to pretend otherwise, but he had started to experiment with different shampoos and hair tonics. She worried more about his thin face, the way his cheeks sunk in, pulling his skin tight over his high cheekbones. He laughed at her when she voiced her concern and told her he was proud of the fact that he carried no extra flesh. It was healthier that way. He certainly seemed healthy enough. He had a quick, intelligent mind and a well-shaped and energetic body, despite its leanness.

She flicked through the magazine in her lap but couldn't concentrate on the printed word or the pictures. She felt restless, uneasy, disturbed. No matter how hard she tried to blank him out, she kept seeing Bernard O'Maley. Like Robert he had broad shoulders tapering down to narrower hips. But there was so much *more* of Bernard. He was solid. He had an aggressive self-confidence which, coupled with his straight unwavering stare, could be intimidating. It was impossible to ignore Bernard. He had an almost menacing presence. There was an aura about him. In the restaurant she had felt that presence engulf her to the exclusion of everything else. Even the memory of it made her breath quicken painfully and sweat break over her. Guilty and ashamed of even thinking of another man in the presence of her good husband, especially after all the outrageous things Bernard had said, she went over to the sink, ran cold water over her wrists and dabbed at her temples.

'There *is* something wrong.' Robert laid aside his book.

'No, honestly, Robert. I sometimes take these silly hot flushes, that's all.'

'It can't be the menopause. You're far too young.'

'I know. It's just a kind of nervous thing. Mummy gets the same. I've seen her face go quite scarlet and you know how normally pale she is.'

'Yes, but she probably *is* going through the menopause.'

'She's forty-nine.'

'I believe some women can have symptoms until well into their fifties.'

127

Andrina shrugged. 'It's nothing. I feel fine. Probably I was sitting too near the fire. I think I'll make a cup of tea. Do you fancy one?'

'Sit down. I'll make it.'

Andrina did as she was told, heart discreetly thumping. The whole thing was ridiculous. She took long, careful breaths.

'Mummy was telling me on the phone today she and Daddy have been looking at houses in Bearsden. *Bearsden* of all places. Can you believe it?'

'That'll cost them.'

'I suppose they'll get a mortgage.'

'Even so.'

'Sometimes I think Mummy's more ambitious than Daddy. She's got that kind of drive that ambitious people have.'

'I don't think she's happy in Drumchapel though.'

'Yes, she misses her old neighbours. Everybody knew each other up her old close. Everybody in the whole building and a few of the other buildings as well. Everybody could leave their key in the door so that the coalman or anybody else with a message could pop in if the person was out. Apparently you wouldn't dare do that in Drumchapel – or so Mummy says.'

'Everybody seems to be moving,' Robert remarked as he poured boiling water into the teapot. 'The O'Maleys – you know, Bernard's family – have moved to Blackhill. Michael's married a Protestant girl, and taken over the house in Garngad.'

Andrina busied herself with poking the fire. 'How's Bernard getting on these days?'

'He seems to be making enough money, by the look of the Crombie coat he was wearing last winter. And obviously he doesn't buy his suits and shirts at the Barras. He's got several other bouncers working for him. Now, *he's* an ambitious type.'

'Does he still go to the karate club?'

'As often as he can. It helps keep him fit. By God, he's good. He nearly floored me the last time.'

Andrina's heart thumped with anger. 'That's terrible. How dare he try to hurt you?'

Robert laughed, but gently. 'Darling.' He leaned over and kissed her. 'It's not like that. Anyway, you've no need to worry. I'm more than able to give as good as I get.'

Nevertheless she felt anxious, apprehensive. 'I love you, Robert,' she said.

'And I love you, darling.'

They drank their tea in silence for a minute, then Robert said, 'I shouldn't have arranged so many outings for the children during the holidays. I should be spending more time with you.'

'Nonsense, you'll be spending plenty of time with me. We don't need to be living in each other's pockets all summer. Anyway,' she laughed, 'their need is greater than mine.'

'Admittedly they're always in danger of getting into trouble with so much time on their hands. The sketching and painting is just an excuse to get them off the streets and out into the country.' He grinned. 'I throw in a bit of biology while we're there. Anything to hold their attention. It's keeping track of them that's the most difficult thing though. You know how thirteen and fourteen-year-old kids can be. Once away from the tenements they're like wild animals let loose.'

'I can imagine.'

'I always have to do a quick count to make sure I don't leave anyone stuck up a tree or wandering about in a cave.'

'A cave?' she echoed incredulously.

'Up the Campsie Hills. I must take you one day. We could have a picnic. You get a panoramic view of Glasgow from the top of the Campsies.'

She nodded. 'I'd like that.'

The telephone rang, making her jerk so violently that hot tea splashed over her hands.

'Andrina!' Robert took the cup from her. 'Your nerves must be bad. Go and run cold water over your hand. I'll answer it.'

She knew it would be her mother. As she stood at the kitchen sink it wasn't only the icy water that made her shiver. Panic swooped and flapped and careered about in her head like a flock of crazy birds. She knew it was crazy, but she was terrified her mother would know she'd been thinking about Bernard.

She could hear Robert chatting on the phone and then saying, 'Yes, she's in the kitchen. I'll fetch her.' Returning from the hall, he said, 'How's the hand?'

'It's fine.'

'It's your mother.'

'Oh, right.' She hurried from the kitchen, then half-way across the hall she remembered to slow her pace and take breath more evenly. 'Hello Mummy.'

'Is there anything wrong?'

'Wrong?'

'You never answered the phone.'

'I'm answering it now.'

'You know what I mean. There's something in your voice. Have you been quarrelling with Robert?'

'Of course not.' Andrina gave a genuine laugh of disbelief. 'What a thing to say.'

'Well, there's something.' A short pause was followed by her mother saying, 'You're hiding something.'

'Mummy, what could I possibly . . .'

'What have you been doing today?'

'Mummy, you've already phoned and I told you.'

'You said you were going to the shops.'

'Yes, that's what I did.'

'What shops?'

'Daly's, Copland's, Pettigrew and Stephen. I saw some lovely things but I didn't buy anything. Everything's so expensive in those big shops. In Sauchiehall Street at least. Argyle Street isn't so bad.' She knew she was chattering, but she couldn't stop. 'There's some shops in Argyle Street, especially along at the Trongate end . . .'

'Who were you with?' her mother interrupted coldly. 'As if I didn't know.'

'Nobody. I just had a wander about on my own. I like doing that. I often do that.'

'You were parading about the streets with that prostitute who lives next door to you.'

'No, no, Mummy. I swear to you. I'll swear on the Bible if you like. I haven't seen Josie all day. I'm a bit tired, that's all. The town can be tiring, you must know that yourself.'

'Robert did say,' her mother's voice acquired a grudging note, 'that he thought your nerves were a bit on edge and you needed a holiday.'

'So does he,' Andrina said eagerly. 'He does far too much for those pupils of his. We might go away somewhere.'

'Remember, Robert's not made of money.'

Andrina thought – neither is Daddy, but it would never have occurred to her to say the words out loud.

'Well, I'll phone you tomorrow and see how you are.'

'I'm fine – really, Mummy.' She had learned not to say, 'There's no need to phone' – This would only open the floodgates to more suspicious questioning. 'All right, Mummy. Sleep well.'

'You too. And don't forget to say your prayers.'

'I won't.'

Her immediate prayer was, 'Please, God, don't let Mummy find out about Bernard.'

131

Chapter Nineteen

Doris knew that it was the usual and accepted thing to do one's courting in the back close. Everyone she knew did it. Well, perhaps that wasn't totally true. The girls in the shop who lived in Bearsden couldn't do it. As far as she knew there weren't any closes in Bearsden. Anyway, there would be bigger houses there and smaller families. A girl living in a bigger house with less brothers and sisters to get in the way could probably have the use of a front room. Or a sitting room, or lounge, or whatever the best room was called in a place like Bearsden.

Perhaps they did it in the country. That was nice – at least, when the weather was good. She and Bernard had made love in the country. Although it had been a bit of a problem getting the grass out of her hair without bringing it all down. And it had been awfully cold and draughty on her bum. The weather was never all *that* good in Scotland. Surely there could be no nudist camps in this climate. She'd heard there was. She'd had a good giggle with the girls about that. Blue tits wouldn't just refer to the birds of the feathered variety, Betty Campbell had said. That had sent them all into absolute kinks.

Betty was a real scream. She was always doing or saying something to set them off, and make it terribly difficult to approach a customer with a serious face and a polite 'Can I help you, Modom?'

Now winter was here again and it meant a return to the back close. Much as she loved Bernard – perhaps *because* she loved him – she didn't want to stand there any more in the foul-smelling darkness, pinioned against a wall with her clothes up around her ears. She was worried. Bernard was different from the rest of the local men she knew. He was even different from his brothers. He had the look of a man who was going places. He was much better dressed for a start. She admired somebody who took trouble with their appearance. She took great pride in her own appearance. There was the struggle with her bouffant of hair, and the delicate attachment of false eyelashes. There was the careful washing and pressing of clothes. She never trusted Carragh to touch her things.

Despite all her care and all her efforts, physically and otherwise, to please Bernard, he'd never mentioned marriage. All sorts of worries, uncertainties and insecurities had begun to plague her.

Bernard had never said he loved her. Sometimes she became depressed about this and depression brought panic. Sometimes, drooping about the house in her slippers and with her hair down, she'd catch a glimpse of herself in the full-length wardrobe mirror. She'd see herself with all her inadequacies, and be frightened.

She'd think – how could a big handsome man like Bernard O'Maley love a wee smout like her? Was he just after one thing, and she allowed him to have it? And that was that?

She felt ashamed every time she thought of the back close. She'd never allowed such behaviour before. There had been a couple of occasions when a young man had persuaded her, after a night out at the pictures, into the back close for a few kisses. Once his hands had begun to wander, however, she had acted on her dignity and stopped him.

She was saving herself for better things. She had nightmares of being caught in the same trap as her mother and so many other women in the district: marriage; a single end, or at best a room and kitchen; one baby after another; being dragged down in poverty and misery that ruined looks, figure, everything. Especially dreams of a better life – a chance in life.

She was hoping and praying that Bernard was her chance. But even if Bernard wasn't going places, even if he didn't have a job, even if he didn't employ men, even if he didn't wear good class clothes – she would still love him. With Bernard she would be willing to be the breadwinner if he had no job. With Bernard she'd be willing to starve in a single end.

She loved him terribly. Her fear and insecurity about their

133

relationship made her instinctively gravitate to Bernard's mother. She would drop in to see Maureen after Bernard had gone to work in the evening. She'd take her a box of sweeties, and they'd sit and smoke and talk until Maureen would get tired and say, 'I'll have to get to my bed. I think it must be old age, but I feel so done out some days.'

Often Maureen would tell her about what Bernard had been like as a wee boy. Maureen liked to talk about the past when her boys were young. Doris was greedy for anything about Bernard. It fed her love for him. Knowing everything about him brought him closer, created a deeper intimacy, made bonds that could not be broken.

She and Maureen became closer. One night, Maureen patted Doris's hand and said gently, 'You really do love him, don't you?'

'Oh, yes. Oh, yes, I really do, Mrs O'Maley. Terribly.' Tears blurred her eyes. 'But I don't know how he feels about me.'

'He hasn't said anything?'

Doris shook her head, not trusting herself to speak.

'Why don't you ask him, hen?'

'I'm too frightened,' Doris quavered. 'You know what he's like.'

'Och, he's a lovely boy.' Maureen immediately went on the defensive. 'It's his job makes him seem a bit tough on the outside, but he has a heart as big as a bucket, that boy. He's always slipping me a few pounds to help me out, or buy myself something. "Treat yourself to something nice, Ma," he'll say. "Be good to yourself, you deserve it." A heart as big as a bucket.'

'I know. I know,' Doris hastily assured her. 'He's a wonderful man. There's nobody like him. Nobody in the whole world. He's handsome and strong and brave and generous. I'm just crazy about him.'

'Well,' Maureen relaxed again, 'I'm sure he's very fond of you too, hen.'

'The thing is . . .' Doris plucked up enough courage eventually. 'The thing is, Mrs O'Maley, I'm pregnant.' Immediately the words were out her courage deserted her again and she began to weep. 'And I'm frightened he won't marry me.'

'Now, now,' Maureen hushed and soothed, at the same time trying to give herself time to think. She had grown fond of Doris. She wasn't a bad wee soul. And she loved Bernard, that was the main thing. And if she was having his child (and her grandchild), there was only one thing to do. Bernard could do a lot worse than marry a nice wee girl like Doris Gallacher. And poor Carragh had enough to worry her without having to cope with a pregnant unmarried daughter. No, that was unthinkable. Bernard would have to do the decent thing. 'You'll just have to tell him, hen.'

'How do you think he'll take it? Could you not tell him, Mrs O'Maley?'

'I'll have a quiet word afterwards, if need be, but it's your place to tell him first, Doris. He'll probably be delighted, and ask you to marry him right away.'

A silence followed in which both of them struggled to convince themselves of the truth of this pronouncement.

'Anyway,' Maureen said eventually, 'he'll have to know.'

'What if he chucks me?' Doris's mascara-streaked face was so pitiful in its wretchedness, Maureen felt truly sorry for her.

'He's the father of your child. He'll have to do his duty by you. You come round here tomorrow straight from your work while he's in. You and him can go through to the room. I'll keep Patrick and everybody else out the road.'

Doris nodded. 'OK.'

She couldn't sleep that night for thinking about the ordeal to come. She'd never said so many prayers in her life. She appealed to every member of the Holy family for help. She went round her rosary beads so often it was a wonder that by morning they weren't all worn away.

She nearly took the day off work, she felt so exhausted. But apart from the fact she couldn't afford to take time off, she was dreading spending twelve hours or more at home doing nothing but worrying about what she would say to Bernard and what he would say to her.

135

By the time she arrived on Maureen's doorstep she not only felt sick, she'd actually vomited twice down the lavatory pan. She felt and looked like a nervous ghost. The thing was, she wasn't only afraid of telling Bernard. She was afraid of Bernard – period.

She hadn't realised it until now.

Maureen opened the door and whispered, 'He's through in the room. I told him you wanted a private word before he left for work.'

'Ta.' She stared saucer-eyed at Maureen, unable to move.

'He won't eat you,' Maureen said. 'Away through.'

'OK.'

Bernard laid aside his newspaper and rose when she entered the room. That was one of the things she loved about him, one of the things that was so different. No other man had ever stood up when she entered a room.

'Hi,' he greeted her.

'I had to talk to you.' Doris plunged immediately to the root of the problem. 'I'm so worried.'

'What's wrong?'

'I'm pregnant.'

'Oh.' It was a flat, expressionless sound.

'I've told your mother. I was so upset and it just came out. But I haven't had the nerve to say anything to my folks yet.'

After keeping her anxiously waiting for a minute or two, Bernard said, 'It'll be all right.'

'Will it?' Her eyes cautiously brightened with hope.

'Of course. I'll look after you.'

'Will you?'

'Yes, I'll pay for an abortion.'

'An abortion?'

'Don't worry,' Bernard said. 'Just leave it to me. I'll arrange everything.'

'But that's a mortal sin.' Doris was so shocked she forgot her fear. 'I'm not having any abortion.'

'No one need know.'

'I'd know. Your Ma would know. She'll be terribly angry at you. She'll not want me to commit murder.'

'It's not murder.'

'It is so.' She was trembling with outrage now. 'I'm not doing it, Bernard. I'd rather keep the baby and face all the shame if you don't want to marry me.' Not knowing what else to say, and suddenly overwhelmed with grief and hopelessness, she ran from the room and the house.

Later, when Maureen found out, she was equally outraged, and the words she subsequently had with Bernard were anything but quiet.

Bernard tried his best to be patient. 'But Ma, I don't love Doris. She's a nice enough girl but I don't love her.'

'You should have thought about that when you were having your way with her.'

'It is possible to have sex without love, Ma.'

Maureen was suddenly exhausted. This was happening to her more and more often recently. For no apparent reason she'd feel drained of all energy. 'Not for a decent wee lassie like Doris Gallacher, it isn't. She loves you. You're breaking her heart, so you are.'

Unexpectedly, she disintegrated into weak tears and, ashamed of her weakness, she tried to louden her voice and rub the tears away with her bunched-up apron. 'And you're breaking mine as well. The shame of it! To the daughter of old friends and neighbours too. If you don't do the decent thing, I'll never be able to look them in the face again.'

'Ma!' Bernard appealed. It shook him to see his mother so distressed. 'It wouldn't work out. Neither of us would be happy. Look, if she feels she must have the baby, I'll pay for its keep. I won't see her or the child want for anything.'

'What a pregnant girl needs is a husband to look after her.' Maureen's sobs had become uncontrollable and were exhausting her so much she could have fainted away. 'And what a baby needs is a father. Money isn't everything. I don't know who you get your hard streak from, Bernard. It's not from Patrick or me. I just don't know.'

'It's not a case of hardness, Ma. I'm just trying to be sensible.'

'Oh, aye. Sensible, is it? Was it sensible to get that poor wee girl in the state she's in today? You just took your pleasure and never bothered about the consequences, Bernard, and now your refusing to take responsibility for your actions. That's the truth of it.' She paused to draw breath and take another wipe at her nose and eyes. 'You've really let me down, Bernard. You're letting the whole family down. You're going to drag the good name of O'Maley through the mud.'

He almost laughed. The good name of O'Maley? His father and Tony were a couple of train robbers to say the least.

Nevertheless, he couldn't see his mother in such a state. She hadn't been looking her old self recently. He was sure she was losing a lot of weight. Her face at times had a drawn appearance as if she was in pain. More than once he'd tried to persuade her to go and see a doctor but she always refused. For his mother's sake he'd do anything – even, he decided, if it meant marrying Doris Gallacher.

The decision brought a weight of hopelessness and depression.

'Come on, Ma, cheer up,' he managed at last. 'I'll tell Doris we can get married. But I'll have to be honest and tell her I don't love her. If she has any sense she'll not have me in those circumstances.'

But he knew in his heavy heart that she would.

Chapter Twenty

The Salvation Army was marching along Garngad Road, blasting out 'What a friend we have in Jesus' with noisy Christian fervour. Some children were dancing and skipping after them. Others in the cobbled corners of side streets were intent on their rhymes and skipping games.

> 'Gypsy, Gypsy Caroline,
> Washed her face in turpentine,
> The turpentine will make it shine,
> Gypsy, Gypsy Caroline.'

As Frank and Bridie walked round to Turner Street a group of little girls in cheap cotton frocks were chanting counting-out rhymes. The one at the receiving of the last word was O-U-T, and had to leave the game.

> 'My mother and your mother were hanging out some
>   clothes,
> When my mother gave your mother a punch on the nose,
> Guess what colour the blood was:
> Blue!
> B-L-U-E spells blue and that's the colour it was,
> And you are O-U-T with a dirty washing clout,
> Over your face like THIS!'

Boys were racing, rattling, clanging over the cobbles with iron girds and hoops. Others were hunkered down, intent on a game of chuckies or jorries. Crowds of boys were yelling and jostling and thumping and chasing each other and scattering sedate games of ring-a-ring-a-roses and in-and-out-the-dusty-blue-bells.

Outside the black tunnel of Bridie's close (even on a bright summer day the closes into the buildings were black), a crush of ragged little girls were singing:

'I'm a little Brownie dressed in brown,
See my knickers hanging down,
One, two, three, four,
Shove the tiger out the door.
Five, six, seven, eight,
Here she's coming in the gate.'

Bridie said morosely, 'You could have refused Ma's invitation. Why is she suddenly making such a thing of inviting you to tea anyway?'

'Now, how could I have said no? Your mother would have been hurt and offended. Anyway, having tea at your place isn't all that bad.'

But of course both of them knew that it was. The noisy crush in the kitchen had always been hard enough to bear. But now Scobie had taken to battering Carragh about when he was drunk. Frank was accustomed to a brain-numbing level of noise with Tony's drums, but Patrick had never lifted his hand to Maureen. Bridie's brothers had been bad enough with their habit of boasting about their street fights and who they'd chibbed. 'You ought to have heard the Proddie bastard scream,' they'd reminisce. Thank God they all seemed to be leaving or had left home now. Of course, that kind of violence was common enough in the neighbourhood. Frank had been caught up in fights himself. Not that long ago he'd been walking along on his way home from work, minding his own business – thinking about a wonderful idea for a love poem, in fact – when he heard the shout of 'PAPE'. Suddenly alert to his surroundings and knowing all too well what the shout meant, he saw guys coming at him from all directions. As they attacked him, he backed hard against the tenement wall, intent on keeping his feet. If he fell he would be booted unconscious to the scream of 'Papist Bastard' and chibbed until he could bleed to death.

As he fought like a madman to defend himself, women leaning from windows screeched out, 'Messins. Messin bastards. Polis!', adding to the wild cacophony of screams from the gang, 'Bastard. Fucker. Pape.'

Fortunately the beat bobby had been in one of the shops having a cup of tea and was quick on the scene, brandishing his truncheon. The gang immediately melted away and Frank was left with blood from his nose gushing down over his good suit. Normally he never cared about his appearance. Unlike his brothers he had no interest in clothes. The office of Messrs Goldmayer Ltd, Wholesale Warehousemen, insisted however that their employees should come to work wearing a decent suit, shirt, collar and tie. Not having a decent suit to wear might cost him his job. If that happened, God knows when he and Bridie could get married.

'My suit,' he kept repeating in horror, trying at the same time to stifle the flow of blood with a handkerchief. 'Look at my good suit.'

'Never mind your suit, son,' the bobby said. 'Is there any bones broken?'

Frank was racked with agonising pain. His stomach felt as if it had been punched right through his spine, but all he could think of was how bad luck seemed to be dogging his plans to get married.

'No. I'll be OK, thanks. I'd better get a move on before this blood dries in. If I wipe it with cold water, it might do the trick.'

His mother had run around like a wild thing, calling down curses on everyone who'd laid a finger on him. She'd also bewailed the fact that this was God punishing him for not going to Mass.

He was becoming disillusioned with the Church – and especially with Father Monachan, Father Riley's assistant. Father Monachan had been round at Bridie's mother's, asking her why she hadn't been pregnant for a few years. Poor Carragh, who was like the old woman who lived in a shoe and had so many children she didn't know what to do. Anyway, the silly young fool should have known that Carragh was past the

141

age for childbearing. Not content with berating Carragh, though, when he'd got wind of Bridie's proposed marriage, he started lecturing her about a woman's duty to be fruitful and have children.

'If I had been there,' Frank had told Bridie, 'I would have knocked what little sense he had out of him with this . . .' and he brandished a fist.

Bridie had been terribly upset. So had both mothers. Carragh and Maureen had been horrified, and warned him that if he lifted his hand to a priest, his arm would become petrified.

'Frank, that's not like you,' Bridie wept. 'Please don't get violent like your brothers or my brothers. You've got to stay above the way they think. It's our only chance of a decent life.'

Now she said, 'I don't know how I'm going to stand it much longer, Frank.'

He knew that she meant her life – in what was euphemistically called her home. What upset Frank most was the whole depressing ambience of both Garngad and Blackhill, and the things that dragged so many good people down. Poverty, he believed, caused the drunkenness, the hopelessness, and in many cases the violence of one kind or another. Many youngsters believed that the only way to get out of the poverty trap was literally to fight their way out. The poorest areas of Glasgow had produced boxers like his Scottish Champion brother Michael, and professional boxers like World Champion Benny Lynch. But Benny Lynch, brave man that he was, couldn't conquer the drinking habit, and Frank feared that Michael one day would share the same fate. He'd always secretly thought it a mistake for his father to allow Michael to have sips of his beer when Michael was a child. Patrick had offered him the same 'wee taste', but he had grued at it and spat it out. Right from the start Michael had liked it. Often since adulthood he'd gone out drinking with his father. But Patrick was just a Saturday night drinker. Patrick always maintained, 'There's not two Saturdays in a week, son.' For Michael there was. Not that he got drunk like his father. Patrick would stagger and swing round lamp-posts and fall up the stairs. Admittedly he was never violent like Scobie, but he could make a terrible noise with his shouting and singing.

When he was drunk, he sang the old Irish songs:

'God save Ireland! said the heroes,
God save Ireland! said they all.
Whether on the scaffold high,
Or the battlefield we die,
O, what matter when for Ireland dear we fall!'

Michael could hold his drink. Maybe because he drank more often but not quite so much at a time. Recently though, since his marriage to Caroline, his drinking had increased.

As Maureen said, 'With a mother-in-law like Big Martha Stoddart, who could blame my poor, lovely boy?'

Recently Maureen had been really furious during one of her regular arguments with Martha. In defence of her 'poor, lovely boy', she'd got rather carried away and prophesied that he would show them yet. He would become a professional boxer, and one day be champion of the whole world. He'd make a fortune and be able to move away from Bright Street and buy a big house in Newton Mearns, or Pollokshields, or Bearsden.

Martha had folded her tree-trunk arms and replied, 'Aye, well, you can take the boy out of the bog but you can't take the bog out of the boy.'

On that occasion Maureen had come near to being violent. The overcrowded living conditions were affecting them all. Frank found Blackhill even worse, with its bleak grey tenements like giant gravestones, its lack of shops or any amenities except the karate club at the school. A mobile shop was the only commercial venture that braved Blackhill. There it stood, ready to serve but equally ready to rapidly remove itself.

The bedroom that Frank shared with Tony and his drums looked out on to the gasworks and the railway line. The challenge and adventure in his father and Tony's lives had increased from stealing char from the gasworks for the living room fire to regularly attacking stationary trains with butcher's cleavers. Sometimes the trains weren't stationary, but just slowing down for a few minutes. Then, like something out of an American Western, the two men would run alongside and jump on to the wagons. Sometimes they flung off crates of whisky or other valuable commodities. Sometimes, when they opened the crates, they contained nothing of any interest, like nails or washers, although they always managed to sell whatever it was to the stallholders at the Barras.

If their haul was whisky, or something of value that could buy whisky, there would be a party and much drinking (and wild drum beating) in the house. Patrick and Scobie and Tony and Michael always got stupid drunk. Even Maureen became tipsy and somewhat staggery. Bernard was never there because he worked nights. These parties depressed Frank so much he had to get out and walk the streets, not knowing what else to do or where to go. But walking the streets in Blackhill did nothing to lift his depression. He had once read a description by one of the first journalists who'd gone in to Auschwitz with the liberating army. A heavy silence of death and desolation had hung over the place. No bird sang. Sometimes he was reminded of this description as he walked the streets of Blackhill.

When the place had been built in 1936 it had looked quite neat and tidy. He'd seen pictures in the Mitchell Library. Perhaps, if the tenants who'd escaped from the decaying bug-infested slums to live in Blackhill had also escaped the brutal and harsh economic and social factors which caused their deprivation, things might have been different. As it was, their poverty, their unemployment, their social problems just moved with them.

There were still the good things as well as the bad. There was still the closeness of neighbours, who were ready to help each other and show solidarity in adversity. Frank supposed that the gang warfare that regularly flared up was a kind of tribal and territorial solidarity. At least they contained their violence within the bounds of their gangs. They seldom harmed anyone but themselves.

But this self-destruction depressed him. It seemed such a waste of human resources. And the waste spread like a pall of hopelessness and futility over the area. He didn't want to get sucked in. Once he'd found comfort and a kind of hope in the Catholic church. He'd sat in the church and absorbed the beauty of the architecture and the statues and the priests' robes. The sound of the litanies and prayers had also a kind of beauty that gave nourishment to his soul. The priest taking what could be described as an over-active part in the local community gave him occasional twinges of doubt and unease. Nevertheless, he could understand that when Father Riley's parishioners chose to send for him rather than the police when trouble arose, they had not much choice but to accept his method of dealing with it. As often as not the trouble was a husband spending all his wages on drink instead of handing over housekeeping money to his wife. Father Riley's method of dealing with this problem was to deliver to the miscreant several hefty punches to the nose, eyes and stomach, and a warning of worse punishment to come if the offence happeend again. Father Riley ran the boxing club in the church hall and did his best to keep young lads off the streets and out of trouble.

But Frank was worried by the absolute obedience, the answers to questions being unquestioningly accepted – and the rule by fear. Carragh, poor grey wisp of a woman, exhausted by childbirth and poverty, should not be afraid that she would incur God's wrath by not having any more children.

Visiting Bridie's mother's home was nearly as depressing as walking around the streets of Blackhill. He avoided it as much as he could. But the invitation to tea at the Gallacher home, which he and Bridie were at the moment reluctantly walking towards, had been a formal one. He wondered why. Bridie's arm was linked through his and he pressed it tight against his side to comfort and reassure her as they entered into the dark tunnel of Carragh's close.

145

Chapter Twenty-One

'I've never mentioned it to Bridie before, Frank.' Carragh creased her grey button face in an effort to produce a pleasing smile. 'I thought it best to speak to you, you see. You being more sensible like. Have another wee cookie, son.' She bent forward over her deformed legs in pathetic supplication.

'No thanks, Mrs Gallacher. Mentioned what?'

'Well, you see, it's like this.' Her voice acquired a 'Once upon a time' confidentiality. 'You know how young Francie, being no right in the head, has been kept in that place? And Tam and Billy and Eamon have gone to England with their group. Geordie and Haggis have got jobs with the Fair folk; they've always hung about the Fair when it came to Glasgow Green – now they're as happy as larks travelling around with it.'

'Yes,' Frank murmured uncertainly.

'What's that got to do with Frank and me?' Bridie wanted to know.

Carragh struggled to keep the smile glued to her face. 'Now Charlie has joined the Merchant Navy.'

'Oh, right. Very good.' Frank's wary uncertainty had developed into downright suspicion.

'I know all that,' Bridie said. 'What's that got to do with Frank and me?'

'Well, you see, I was just thinking. This big place'll be empty with just Scobie and me. And then I thought, there's Bridie and Frank, desperate to get married and needing a place, and what better than them having our big front room?'

'What?' Bridie's voice wobbled between tragedy and astonishment. 'What do you mean empty? There's Doris for a start.'

'Well.' Carragh lowered her voice and looked furtively around as if to make sure no one else was hanging about the kitchen, eager to listen. 'Between you and me and the gatepost, Doris is expecting a happy event.'

'Oh, God,' Bridie groaned. 'That means one extra, not less.'

'No, no, hen. I'm sure Frank's brother's going to do the decent thing and put together some key money for a place. Or a backhander, or whatever he needs to get a house – I'm sure Bernard'll wangle it.'

Frank groaned inwardly. The mass exodus of Gallachers did not surprise him. They had never supported or protected their mother. Now Carragh was pinning her hopes on him. She was afraid of being on her own with an increasingly violent Scobie.

'No way,' said Bridie. 'Big front room?' she added bitterly. 'Call that a big front room?'

'Now, hen, don't be hasty. Talk it over with Frank. It's time you two were married. Don't you think, eh? Once you were here you could still be looking around for a place of your own. But you'd be together. Do you know what I mean, hen?'

'No way,' Bridie repeated, fixing Frank with a tragic gaze.

Frank felt heart sorry for both Bridie and her mother.

'What do you think, son?' Carragh fixed him with a gaze not only tragic, but desperate. 'I'd make you awful welcome. You're like a son to me. Just like my own flesh and blood. It would just be for a wee while, Frank. Just till you got a place of your own, eh?'

Frank said, 'Bridie and I would have to discuss it, Mrs Gallacher.'

'Of course, son. Of course. I'll just run down the stairs and take in my washing. It should be dry by now. That'll give you a chance.' She scuttled across the bare floorboards and picked up a clothes basket from the top of the coal bunker. 'I'd see you lacked for nothing, son. You'd have every comfort here. Every comfort.'

Bridie rolled her eyes after she'd gone. 'Every comfort? Could you beat it? Francie's not the only one that's soft in the head.'

'She's afraid, Bridie.'

'What do you think I am? I'm afraid I'm never going to get away from here.'

'We're bound to get a place soon. Our name should be well up the Corporation list by now.'

Bridie's pale face had become positively sickly. 'Frank, you're not seriously considering living here. You don't know what it's like.'

'It can't be much worse than where I am. I'd rather share a room here in Garngad with you than share a room in Blackhill with Tony any day.'

'I know it's not easy for you either.'

'That's putting it mildly. Tony's one big mindless noise. And I don't just mean when he's battering away at his infernal drums. When he talks, when he coughs, when he sneezes – he lets it all rip-roar out as if noise is something to be proud of. Even when he's asleep that toothy grin of his is hovering over his face as if he's enjoying the racket his snoring makes.'

'What I'm afraid of is . . .' Bridie's eyes filled with tears and she removed her glasses to mop at them, '. . . that we just sink into this place, that somehow we'll be trapped, that we'll never get out.'

Frank gathered her into his arms. 'No, no. That won't happen. I promise. Quite the contrary. The way I'm looking at it is I'll have more peace here to write, now that your brothers are away. My writing is our passport out of here, Bridie. I've had quite a few poems published now as you know, but there's no big money in poetry. It's got to be plays, and I need a bit of space and quiet to work on a play. I know I can do it, but not while I'm sharing a room with Tony.' He sighed. 'I love that guy but I hate him as well. Sometimes I feel I could kill him just to shut him up.'

'Oh, Frank, I know how you feel, but do you really think it would be that much better here? There's my father, don't forget, and his drinking.'

'My father drinks as well. All right, he doesn't get violent like Scobie. But he's just as much a pest in his own way. He and Tony are a right pair when they're drunk. Bawling and singing and crashing about. The only peace I've ever managed to get at home, whether in Garngad or Blackhill, was when either of them or both of them were in Barlinnie.'

'If Bernard gets married to Doris and moves out . . .'

'I wouldn't depend on anything Bernard might do. He's a law unto himself. Anyway, if it's his bedroom you're thinking about, what do you bet that my mother and father move into it. It is hell of an inconvenience them sleeping on the bed-settee in the living room.' He cuddled her and stroked her hair and tucked it behind her ear. 'What do you say, pet? Just until I get a play published and make some money.'

'I think I'd rather be a squatter than start my married life here.'

'Now you know you couldn't bear the indignity of squatting in some old army camp with no water or electricity. Or illegally breaking into some unoccupied private house.' Since the war and the shortage of housing, squatting had become a serious problem and was constantly hitting the newspaper headlines.

Bridie sighed and replaced her spectacles. 'I suppose not. That's really the dregs, isn't it? At least here we'd keep our dignity and respectability.' Even as she uttered the words, she suddenly felt so hopeless, so painfully depressed, she didn't even believe Frank would ever write a play, far less sell it. They seemed to be sinking into the morass in which so many couples and their dreams had disappeared before.

'If I just got a run at a play. If I could just get a bit of peace and privacy.' Frank's voice was wistful.

Bridie gazed at his thin sensitive face and loved him for his innocence. 'You really think you could get that here?'

'Well, if we had the room to ourselves, I'd at least have a chance. I've no chance at all in Blackhill.'

Tears welled up in Bridie's eyes again but she struggled to ignore them and make her voice seem bright. 'Well, if it's all right with you, Frank, it's all right with me.'

'Oh, great.' His eyes glowed with optimism, and with a quick, excited movement he flicked back the lock of hair that kept sliding down over his forehead. 'It won't be for long, pet. I promise.'

Bridie noticed his dandruff was getting worse. He neglected himself terribly so perhaps it was just as well they were going to

149

be together sooner than they'd planned. She would see that he washed his hair with an antiseptic shampoo. She'd brush it for him and get it into shining good condition. She would see that he ate properly too. But all the time, the depression and the hopelessness wafted about inside her like a dangerous fog in which she could so easily lose her way.

'It can't be a big wedding,' she told Frank. 'There's no money. It all goes on drink now. And I'm not using my savings. That's for when we get our own house.'

After a moment or two's thought, Frank said, 'I don't mind a registry office, if it's all right with you.'

'Oh no, we have to be blessed in the church, Frank.' Frank didn't have her conscientiousness for attending Mass, and it worried her. It was another thing about him she'd have to work on and change. She could understand his compassion for her mother and her constant pregnancies and miscarriages – Frank was a compassionate kind of person – however, her mother needn't have suffered like that. The church taught abstinence and the safe times for sex. It was Carragh's own fault, or perhaps to be fair, it was more Scobie's fault, that no attention had been paid to the church's teaching on the subject.

'All right, pet. A quiet ceremony in the church.'

'It would have to be just you and me and a couple of witnesses – maybe Bernard from your side and Doris from mine. If we include everybody in our families the church would be packed. Then they'd have to have food and drink after-wards. That could turn out to be a right rammy.'

He smiled. 'Remember your twenty-first?'

'The only good thing about my twenty-first birthday party was that we got together.'

'All right. I'll go ahead with the arrangements and I'll ask Bernard if he'll be my best man.'

Something then occurred to Bridie. 'Perhaps Doris and Bernard will make it a double affair. That would be nice, unusual – really special. Two brothers and two sisters getting married at the same time.' She felt quite cheered by the thought. She had always been drawn to unusual things, like

150

serious music, and paintings, and poetry. That was one of the reasons she'd fallen for Frank.

'Well . . .' Frank's uncertainty returned.

'It'll be all right with Doris,' Bridie assured him.

It wasn't Doris, however, that Frank was seeing in his mind's eye.

Chapter Twenty-Two

Doris hadn't been too upset when Bernard told her he didn't love her. After all, she'd known that all along. Only now she didn't altogether believe it. He was willing to marry her, wasn't he? That was the important thing. The wonderful, exciting, absolutely marvellous thing. It must mean something. She was so happy she persuaded herself that he must have feelings for her. She told herself that once they were married, everything would be all right. No, not just all right – *perfect!*

She was so proud of him. Her head floated light as a balloon and her chest puffed out as she walked along the street arm in arm with him. He was such a big, handsome man, fit and strong in body and character.

She never tired of boasting to her fellow shop assistants in Daly's. 'My Bernard has a very strong character. Very self-controlled. You can tell that, can't you, by that dark unwavering stare of his. He's the strong, silent type.'

Actually, she was having a bit of trouble with that recently – him being silent. He'd never been much of a talker at the best of times. He always seemed quite content to let her chatter on. Now he seldom initiated a conversation, or added to it. The only time she'd seen him animated and talkative recently was when he'd gone on about Uri Gargarin and how he'd gone up in space.

'The greatest thing to happen in our lifetime,' he'd said and she'd made a really big effort to share his enthusiasm.

She couldn't help wishing he'd shown the same enthusiasm for the idea Bridie came up with about a double wedding. Although he did make one contribution to the arrangements. Or rather two: he said he wanted Robert Anderson and his wife to be there; he also insisted that he should pay for a meal for the lot of them after the ceremony.

Everyone in the O'Maley family and the Gallacher family was insulted, offended and upset at the mere idea of such a small affair. They had expected, indeed demanded, that there should be a proper white wedding in the church with not only all the relations on both sides, but all their friends as well. Everybody could have, and should have, gathered at the Co-op hall for the traditional purvey of steak pie, potatoes and peas, followed by sherry trifle. This enjoyable meal would have – should have – been followed first of all by merry speeches and much drinking of whisky, then a noisy knees-up, reels and dashing white sergeants and much screeching and heughing. And more drinking of whisky. Lemonade, Tizer and Irn Bru were always supplied for the youngsters, who increased the general hilarity and confusion by racing around playing tig between the dancers.

Bridie and Doris, even Frank, wavered in the face of family outrage ('Aunt Nellie's never going to speak to you for ages'), pleading ('the wee ones will be that disappointed'), and persuasion ('it'll please poor wee Carragh so much').

But Bernard would have none of it. It was to be a quiet wedding with only Robert and Andrina Anderson – or nothing. That decided Doris, and in turn strengthened the resolution of Bridie and Frank.

The wedding day dawned to disappointment and huff in both houses. Carragh had volunteered to give them a party and make one her cloutie dumplings. And never mind the Co-op.

'It would be no bother, girls,' she assured Bridie and Doris. 'You know how I'm used to cooking for crowds. Remember thon great party I gave you for your twenty-first, Bridie, eh?'

That definitely settled the issue. Doris spent much time back-combing and layering her creamy froth of hair. Great care too was taken on her eye make-up which was thick and black. She was very proud of her long lashes, which, thickened with false ones and several layers of mascara, looked, she believed, really glamorous. She perched a black velvet bow studded with pearls on the back of her monstrous bouffant and blessed the high hairstyle because it helped add to her rather small stature.

This was vitally important when walking with or next to Bernard. She was terribly pleased with her dress too. She'd got it at a genuinely reduced rate from Daly's. It had a terribly smart 'hobble' or 'bubble' or 'puff-ball' line. It had narrow little shoulder straps and a black velvet bodice, and a lime-green taffeta 'puff' that ballooned out from waist to mid-thigh, before changing to a tight velvet band from there to knees.

Round her neck she fastened a pearl choker to match her pearl earrings. (Pearls were in terribly good taste. Jane Dempster from Bearsden always wore pearls with her black dress at Daly's.) Long black gloves and high heeled shoes finished the picture. It had never been easy to walk in such high heels, and the tight velvet band round her knees didn't help, but she managed quite nicely.

Bridie looked plain as usual with her earnest, bespectacled face devoid of all make-up, and straight brown hair caught back on one side with a clasp. With that and her floral print dress she looked like a schoolgirl.

It had to be admitted that Andrina looked rather nice, if you liked tall girls with long auburn hair and green eyes. She was a bit flashy though, in her wide-brimmed straw hat with its cinnamon trimmings, and beige trapeze-line dress with its collar standing away from her neck and the long bow hanging down from it. That dress looked like an Yves St Laurent. But it had to be a cheap copy. After all, how could anyone afford Yves St Laurent on a schoolmaster's wage? Maybe that was why Andrina was wearing hardly any make-up. Make-up was terribly expensive these days.

Frank had forgotten to get his hair cut, but he had managed to have his awful old suit decently cleaned and pressed. He was at least wearing a new white shirt. His black tie, however, didn't go with the brown of his suit and made him look as if he was attending a funeral.

Robert was smart in a grey suit, a paler grey shirt and nicely patterned tie.

But Bernard, oh how wonderful Bernard looked in dark blue, with a waistcoat and a lighter blue shirt over the new style slender-line trousers. His tie was pure silk, Doris was sure. She couldn't believe her luck. Fancy her catching such a big, gorgeous hunk. Unlike Frank, Bernard was interested in clothes and how he looked. And Bernard wasn't dreamy like Frank. No two brothers could be more unlike. Yet . . . sometimes Bernard could give the strange impression that he was somewhere else, thinking about – she knew not what. Of course, his work needed a lot of concentration. It was terribly dangerous. She felt a sudden qualm. What if anything should happen to Bernard? She'd die. *She'd just die.* She wondered if she could persuade him to change his job. Something more nine-to-five, so that he could be home with her at night. Now that he employed quite a few bouncers he could surely let them do most of the rough work. She had to admit to herself however that the toughness of Bernard's job was part of his attraction. She'd once seen him in action and it had both frightened and thrilled her. It had been at Green's Playhouse Dancehall. Some guys had come in and started pestering girls and making a big noise and jostling and threatening and frightening people. All except two had taken to their heels when they saw Bernard striding towards them. The remaining two pulled out knives. The way Bernard disarmed them was so quick she had difficulty bringing the scene to her mind's eye. But what she did remember clearly was the way he pounced on them after he'd disarmed them. He caught them by the neck – one in each of his big hands – then literally ran them out of the door.

After the wedding ceremony they went to a terribly posh hotel that had a restaurant with a little dance-floor in the middle. They sat at a table just on the edge of the dance floor. Doris chatted non stop to Andrina about fashion (Andrina had once worked in Copland & Lye's). The men argued about boxing and football, and the possibility of more men going up in space. Bridie just sat looking uncomfortable. She obviously wasn't used to such a terribly posh place.

'See her over there,' Doris widened her eyes in the direction she wanted Andrina to look. 'That's a Dior if ever I saw one. Did you stock any in Copland's?'

'A few.'

'We had several designer labels in Daly's – Dior, Hartnell, Cardin, the lot. Of course, Daly's is *the* top class shop. I know Copland's is terribly first class too. No offence.'

Andrina smiled. 'None taken.'

Suddenly Bernard said, 'May I have this dance, Andrina?'

Andrina felt flustered. She looked over at Robert but he only smiled and said, 'Go ahead', then turning to Doris, said, 'May I have the pleasure?'

The four of them got up and left Frank and Bridie gazing fondly at each other.

The band was playing 'Always' as Bernard took Andrina in his arms, and as they moved together he whispered, 'Oh, how I wish this was our wedding day. Oh, how I wish it was you, how I wish it was you . . .'

'Stop it! Please don't talk like that.' Andrina began trembling so visibly that Bernard had to tighten his hold to steady her. As they danced, the hard feel of his body against hers thrilled and frightened her. He must be crazy to behave like this on his own wedding day.

After a few minutes she spoke her thoughts out loud. 'On your wedding day of all days, how could you?'

'You said it was time I had a wife and family of my own.'

'All right, but now you have a wife . . .'

'A pregnant wife.'

'All the more reason why you shouldn't speak to me like that.'

'Nothing's going to change the way I feel about you.'

'But what about Doris?'

'She's got what she wanted – a name for her child.'

'I think she'll want more than that.'

'Tough.'

Again Andrina experienced tremors of fear. 'You must promise to put me out of your mind, Bernard.'

'I can't do that.'

'But I'm happily married to Robert. You must.'

'I love your hair. It glows like rubies.'

'Bernard . . .'

'Your eyes sparkle like aquamarines.'

'Bernard, please.'

'Your skin is soft like velvet. My darling velvet. I love every soft smooth inch of you.'

'You're crazy.'

'I'd like to kiss every inch of you from the top of your lovely head to the tip of your toes.'

'You're mad.' She tightly shut her eyes to protect herself from his stare. But there was no way she could ignore the chemistry interacting, the heat generating between their two bodies.

Chapter Twenty-Three

Sophie mentally rubbed her hands together in glee. It had taken her some considerable time to find a place in Bearsden that suited both herself and Andrew and was within the price that he had stipulated.

'Remember,' McPherson kept saying, 'I've still only a brickie's wages plus my expenses from the Council.'

Sophie didn't listen, knowing subconsciously that this could not be true, as indeed it was not. McPherson had been on Felderman's books as a 'consultant' for months now, and was paid considerably more than a brickie. Then, of course, the expenses he claimed from the Council were always inflated. Nobody, as far as he knew, put in a claim for the exact sum for which they had been out of pocket in lost wages, or in money spent on fares or food or anything else. Nobody, that is, except his father, the late Councillor David McPherson, who although outwardly admired for his honesty, had grievously inhibited and frustrated many of his fellow councillors. McPherson had loved and respected his father but he could easily imagine a sigh of relief rising up from the City Chambers after the old man had gone.

The end terrace house in Drymen Road, Bearsden, had lain empty for some time and they had got a marvellous bargain of it. An old man had lived alone in it for years and had never bothered to paint or paper it. 'Or clean it either,' Sophie said. She was just dying to get her hands on it. She couldn't wait to plunge into an orgy of housework. Not to mention the painting and decorating. Bliss, absolute bliss! Her mind raced hysterically ahead, she saw herself like a whirlwind in her imagination. In working, cleaning to the utmost of her ability, she too somehow felt she was cleansing herself of the past and every dark and dirty corner of herself.

Structurally, the house was in very good condition. Drymen Road was the busy main road just next to the line of shops – separated only by a little side street called Kirk Road. There was a church down at the end of the side street and another church across the road. This part of Bearsden was called the village. It was the heart of the place, the oldest and busiest part and, as far as Sophie was concerned, it just couldn't be bettered. She would never have a dull or idle moment here. Even sitting and looking out of the front-room window would be bliss – or even the side window. The sitting room and dining room had side windows looking out on to Kirk Road. From there she could get a side view of the shops and people going down Kirk Road to the field to exercise their dogs. Good, smiling, well-dressed, solid people.

There were no gasworks, no brickworks, no factories, no sawmills here to pollute the air or discolour the beautiful silvery walls of the buildings. The lovely trees that rustled in the streets were fresh, pure green, as if God himself had washed each leaf until it glistened. No litter, no old newspapers, no smelly chip papers would dare flap about these pavements. The streets of Bearsden were kept pristine clean.

Sophie adored the house. She had enough imagination to see how the dark brown inside walls and floors could be transformed by light paint and attractive wallpaper and carpets. In a daze of admiration she walked through the high-ceilinged hall into the spacious sitting room, then into the dining room, then further along into the kitchen and the scullery beyond and the back door that led into her very own garden. Upstairs was a bathroom on a half landing and a bedroom. Then upstairs again there were three other bedrooms. A veritable palace of a place.

To go back to Drumchapel was like descending into hell. Even the inhabitants looked drab and seedy and neglected. There were people in the streets, yet the people had no substance. The streets seemed empty – a vast concrete desert of a place with neither heart nor soul. She hated it. She couldn't wait to be free of it. Over and over again she thanked God for her release. She had been sinking into the hopelessness of the place herself but God in his infinite mercy had saved her before depression had irrevocably weighed her down.

On her knees she thanked Him.

Several times a day she phoned Andrina to eulogise about the house, the shops, the churches, the people. She organised the removal with a hymn in her heart. Getting the house in Bearsden was her salvation. She didn't care that McPherson did very little to help. She enjoyed being given a free hand. He wouldn't have done anything to her complete satisfaction. He was too easygoing. Sometimes he nearly drove her mad with his attitude.

'What do you need to do that for?' he'd say. 'It's perfectly clean as it is. Sit down and relax.'

But to sit down and relax and do nothing was impossible. The sight of a picture not quite straight could trap her into deep anxiety. Even if she didn't see anything she would have a nameless fear of something being wrong, of something being unclean.

She worried about Andrina's house, and meticulously questioned her each time she phoned about what housework she'd done and how thoroughly she'd done it. She worried about Andrina's neighbour, the filthy Slater woman, coming into the house and contaminating the chairs with her fat thighs. Once Sophie had been visiting Andrina and on reaching Andrina's landing, she'd noticed the Slater woman's door open. The windowless lobby was a dark tunnel, but she could make out a chair with clothes flung carelessly over it. Under-clothes too, shameless black satin. Some magazines lay on the floor and the whole place had an immoral, dirty look.

The woman had come hurrying breathlessly up the stairs clutching an oversized basket. 'Oh, hello, hen,' she called out. 'I just ran down to the back to hang out some washing. I don't get that much time with me being out working. Is Andrina not in?'

Sophie had stabbed at the bell. She was glad to turn away from the woman. The dyed hair, the painted face, the flashy earrings, the obscene cleavage. The smell of cheap perfume made her feel sick.

The moment Andrina opened the door she'd pushed inside and shut it behind her. 'That woman's out there.'

'Josie? She's harmless, Mummy.' Then Andrina had laughed. 'She's not going to bite you.'

She'd hated Andrina then. Hated her for her stupidity, her lack of understanding, and her laughter. 'I can still smell the dirt from her house. That woman is a bad influence on you in more ways than one. I got a glimpse of her hall just now. She'd left her door wide open. I shudder to think what her rooms are like if that's the way she keeps her hall. An untidy house is a sign of an untidy mind. A dirty house is a sign of a dirty mind.'

Andrina was wearing a modest black dress with a neat white collar high at her neck. No make-up was visible on her face, which was startlingly pale and creamy against her deep flame of hair.

'You ought to tie that hair of yours back,' Sophie told her. 'It looks positively indecent hanging loose about your shoulders like that. Pin it back like mine.'

'It's difficult to keep it back, Mummy, with it being so thick and wavy and curly. It's easier with your hair. Yours is straight and smooth as glass.'

'Get it cut short then.'

'Remember I did that once and it curled up more than ever?'

'Well, give it a good hard brush and pin it back as tight as you can.'

'Yes, Mummy.'

Sophie was suspicious of Andrina and her 'Yes, Mummy's', and her evasive eyes when she uttered the words. There was an aura of wicked sensuality about the girl. She couldn't hide it by averting her gaze or by fixing Sophie with one of those wide-eyed innocent looks. The way she was dressed and her unmade-up face didn't fool her either. Sophie thought, 'This is for my benefit. What does she wear when I'm not here? That's what I'd like to know.'

The intensity of her worry about Andrina however was

161

swamped by the excitement and the amount of time and attention she needed to devote to the house in Bearsden.

Oh, happy removal day. She'd arranged that McPherson would drive her over so that they would be in Drumchapel to check that all their belongings were safely packed on to the removal van. Then they would be at the house in Bearsden to see that everything was properly unpacked and the furniture placed exactly where she wanted it.

McPherson had bought his first car, a modest little Mini. It didn't compare with the Corporation limousine in which he was in the habit of travelling when attending to council business. Nevertheless, Minis were very popular and fashionable. She was perfectly happy with their smart little car. Perhaps one day she would learn to drive. Although McPherson jokingly said that a public safety warning would have to be given each time she went on the road.

'You don't have the nature to be a good driver, Sophie,' he explained. 'You're too quick and impatient. You function on too short a fuse.'

She had become what McPherson called 'a back seat driver' instead. Although in fact she sat in the front beside him, she'd keep a running commentary while he sat in heavy silence, leather gloved hands loose on the wheel, staring determinedly ahead.

'Watch that child. He might dash out . . . Remember it's left turn here. Talk about me being quick. You're racing along, Andrew. Watch these lights, they're going to change. What's he doing in front?'

Sometimes she'd thump at the horn. This at least elicited a response from McPherson.

'*Don't do that, Sophie!* If you touch the horn again I'm stopping the car and putting you out. You can wait for a bus.'

Of course, he wouldn't dare. Oh, happy, happy removal day.

She took a last look around the Drumchapel house. She had scrubbed every inch of it, of course. Nobody would be able to accuse her of leaving a dirty house. But it looked so small, so seedy, so pathetic. The word formed like a sneer in her mind.

Pathetic. Outside, some shabby looking youths were hanging about at the street corner. Waiting to see what trouble they could get up to, no doubt. It wouldn't matter what kind of houses, what size of houses, they built here, the people who lived in them would bring the place down to their level, making a slum of it.

Goodbye, Drumchapel. Good riddance to you all.

As the van and the car moved away, her heart and head were reverberating joyously with the song, 'Onward Christian soldiers, going as to war, with the cross of Jesus, going on before . . .'

Once in the house in Bearsden, she bustled about giving orders and making cups of tea for the men. McPherson said, 'Do you need me to stay any longer, Sophie? I've a couple of people to see at the Chambers.'

'No, no, on you go.' She hardly noticed him.

'Right, I'll see you later.'

'No, no.' She rushed after one of the removal men. 'Not in there. Upstairs. That's to go upstairs.'

'But you said . . .'

'I've changed my mind. Put it in the big bedroom, the one at the front. I'll show you *exactly* where it's to go.'

She hurried upstairs in front of the man. McPherson escaped. He hadn't to see anyone in particular but he thought it best to get out of the way and leave Sophie to it. She was in her element. As happy as a dog with two tails. At first he thought he'd go to the club. Then he remembered he hadn't had a decent meal all day. Instead of his usual cooked breakfast, Sophie had put a few slices of toast and a pot of marmalade on the table and he'd had to make do with that. A cup of tea and a sandwich had passed for lunch. He decided to make for the Corn Exchange. He could relax there, have a good meal, enjoy a brandy and a cigar.

He had barely settled at his favourite table, hadn't even given his order, when a voice said, 'Do you mind if I join you, Bailie McPherson?'

It was Bernard O'Maley.

163

'Bernard! Sit down. I haven't seen you in here before. How are you getting on? You certainly look prosperous enough.'

'I come here now and again. I've been doing fine – building up a good-going business and a reputation along with it.'

'Splendid. Still in the same line, are you?'

The waiter came to take their order. After he'd gone, Bernard said, 'I've got some good men working for me and I'm making contacts for more work.'

'Oh yes, I believe Robert mentioned you had quite a few pubs and clubs on your books now.'

'I'm ambitious, Bailie McPherson. I intend my business to keep expanding. I was thinking of going into other areas. Crowd control at outdoor or indoor events for sport or entertainment. Personal security for visiting dignitaries, pop groups, you name it.'

They finished their prawn cocktail, then Bernard continued, 'The Corporation organises quite a few events or gives licences for events as well as premises.'

'Yes.' McPherson was beginning to get the drift. 'That's true. There's always something going on in Glasgow, and indeed, in the City Chambers.'

'Here's my card,' Bernard said.

McPherson studied it. 'The Trongate?'

'Yes, I've rented a small office there. It suits me for the moment. If you put any work my way I would, of course, show my appreciation with a commission for your trouble – a generous percentage of the fee.'

McPherson tapped the card against the tips of his fingers. He was a good man, Bernard. He'd always liked him.

They talked in more detail until the Entrecôte Steak Belgrade arrived. It looked delicious. 'Let's have a bottle of their best wine,' Bernard said. 'This is on me,' he added with a careless wave of the hand to indicate whatever was on the table. They ordered a Châteauneuf-du-pape. Bailie McPherson leaned back in his seat and hooked his thumbs in his waistcoat. He felt pleased with himself, and the world, and Bernard O'Maley.

A decent big man, Bernard. One of the best.

Chapter Twenty-Four

Frank could hardly believe his eyes. Although why he should be so surprised he didn't know. There was surely a naïvety about him. Like a child, he always expected the best in people; he seldom foresaw the worst scenario. As a result he kept being surprised, disappointed, let down – although he valued, indeed treasured in retrospect, the process of learning about life and people. People were endlessly interesting to him.

His brother Michael was sitting on the pavement outside his boxing club in Garngad Road, cropped bullet of a head thrown back, drinking a bottle of beer. He knew Michael liked a drink but surely never during training.

'Michael, I thought you were training.'

'So?'

'You won't get fit with drinking in the middle of it.'

'If I'm lucky I'll get blotto.' Michael's bruised and broken-nosed face was a picture of misery.

'What's wrong? I thought you were doing so well. You're making a steady wage and a good bit extra with your boxing. And you've your nice wee house to yourself and your lovely wife.'

'The trouble is, Frank, I've got a not so lovely mother-in-law.'

'Och, ignore her.'

'Easy enough for you to say that. She's not your mother-in-law. I'm living in the next street to the Stoddarts. Caroline runs to Big Martha with the slightest complaint about me or a problem in our marriage, and round Big Martha comes to sort me out. She even barged into the pub the other night and laid one on me. See this black eye? That was her. Then she punched and pummelled me all the way out on to the street. What could I do, Frank? If it had been a man, I would have felled him with one blow. But I can't hit a woman. Especially a woman old enough to be my mother. But, by Christ, she can throw a hammer of a punch.'

Frank didn't know what to say. It seemed an insoluble problem. There was no use suggesting Michael tried to stop Caroline from running to her mother every time she had some complaint or grudge. Everyone knew that Caroline, as an only child, had been spoiled and babied all her life. In Frank's opinion, however, any baby would have more brains. Talk about a dumb blonde! He had always thought that Bridie's sister, Doris, came into that category (although according to Bridie, Doris's hair was dyed and Caroline's was not), but Caroline was ridiculous. It always fascinated him to observe people – what made them tick, and he mulled endlessly over both his brothers' choice of wives. There was Bernard, so tough no one would ever dare say 'boo' to him, so hard-eyed and to all appearances completely insensitive that one would have thought he wouldn't have cared less about any woman becoming pregnant by him. Frank wouldn't have been surprised if Bernard had told Doris to go to hell. Yet he'd married her. Hard-faced intelligent Bernard – there could be no denying that Bernard had brains – had chosen a silly, empty-headed wee snob like Doris Gallacher for his life's partner. Admittedly, once you got to know Doris and looked past her surface silliness, she was harmless enough. Frank wasn't so sure about Bernard.

Then there was Michael. Another tough guy in his own way – and he had married a silly, empty-headed wee girl as well.

There was nothing so strange as folk. They fascinated Frank so much he was finding more and more that only through drama could he fully explore the relationships and conflicts they sparked off. Although poetry was still his first step in exploration and communication. But it had become only a first step.

He had started on a play as soon as he'd moved into Bridie's house – or rather, Scobie and Carragh's house. Everything seemed to be working out quite well at first. He and Bridie had

166

everything in common. It was wonderful to be so close to her, lying with his arm around her in the recessed bed in the Gallachers' front room. After they made love, they'd lie like that, discussing the latest book they'd read or play they'd seen. More and more they were spending their precious savings on theatre tickets, but as Frank said, 'It's really an investment, Bridie. An investment in my career and our future. I've got to study drama – and as you know, I read as much as I can about it – but there's nothing to beat seeing plays brought to life on the stage.'

Bridie agreed. The only thing they had disagreed about was his decision to come and live with her in Turner Street. Of course, as it turned out, she had been right. It had been fine at first. In fact, it had been sheer heaven compared with sharing a room with Tony. He much preferred Garngad to Blackhill too. This might seem strange to some people because Garngad was made up of old cobbled streets, ancient black tenements, and constant crowds of people milling about, especially on the busy Garngad Road. Women having a 'hing' leaning, arms folded on the sills of open windows, and watching the teeming life underneath them: the children playing; the men going in and out of the pub; the street buskers; women shouting across to each other and enjoying a gossip; children racketing around on the cobbles that lead off Garngad Road; the streets that Frank and Bridie were so familiar with – Turner Street, Villiers Street, Bright Street, Cobden Street.

In comparison, Blackhill had relatively new houses. Many of them had patches of earth at the front that had once been tidy gardens. They boasted bathrooms and sculleries and gas cookers and tiled fireplaces. When his mother and father had got their house in Blackhill, their old friends and neighbours had come to visit and be proudly shown round the house. Many of them came especially to enjoy a bath as well.

Yet to Frank – despite all the disadvantages of outside lavatories and unhygienic kitchens, coal bunkers spreading coal dust over everything including kitchen beds, and pots of food simmering on old black ranges – he preferred Garngad.

167

Of course, as Bridie said, the reason everything went well at first was due to the fact that Scobie had disappeared for one of his sojourns in Barlinnie. He had been caught breaking into a pub and stealing bottles of whisky. He had actually been caught in the pub drinking the whisky. Moreover, he had refused to leave. Indeed, he had become violent and hit the beat constable over the head with one of the bottles. The bottle broke, the constable continued his struggle with Scobie, and he ended up having his face lacerated with the jagged glass of the bottle.

Scobie, when sober, was perfectly good-humoured with the police, and they with him. Scobie always greeted the local bobbies by their first names and wished them a friendly good morning. When drunk, he cared about nobody and he had no friends. When drunk, he was a different person altogether. The scarring of the local bobby meant Scobie had lost the benefit of any good humour any members of the Glasgow police force ever had towards him.

The house in Turner Street without Scobie was quite bearable. There were no physical comforts, not even a rug or a piece of linoleum to cover the floor, but at least there was peace and quiet. A rhythm or pattern became established. After work, Frank and Bridie and Carragh would have their tea. Then he would go through to the room and write for at least a couple of hours. Bridie stayed in the kitchen with Carragh. She didn't mind. The quicker he got on with his writing and made some money the better, as far as she was concerned. He wouldn't get much chance once Scobie came out again, she warned.

On Sundays, the three of them went to Mass. Usually they met Maureen and Patrick and Doris there. Sometimes they went over to Blackhill to have what Doris called 'lunch' with the O'Maleys. Sometimes Michael appeared in the chapel. At first, Caroline had come with him. Her father and mother had soon put a stop to that. Apparently there was a running battle with the priest over this. According to Michael, Father Riley and Father Monachan had been giving him hell on one side, and Big Martha Stoddart and Orangeman Jimmy Stoddart had been giving him hell on the other.

Then one day, on his way home from work, Frank met Michael again and found him in a worse state than ever. He had obviously been at the pub and was still clutching a bottle of beer.

'Don't you start on me, Frank,' Michael warned. 'I've had it up to here with the lot of them.'

'I don't know what to say, Michael.' Frank felt upset on behalf of his brother. 'I wish I could help in some way. Do you think if I had a word with Martha . . . ?'

'What?' Michael gave a mirthless laugh. 'Thanks, pal, but no thanks. I've enough on my plate without worrying about you being flattened.'

Frank sighed. 'Well, try and keep off the drink, Michael. You don't want to become like Scobie.'

'That reminds me,' Michael said. 'Scobie's out.'

'He can't be. He has months to go yet.'

'He'll have had his sentence reduced for good behaviour. How's that for a laugh?'

'I hope to goodness he behaves himself in the house.'

'Forever an optimist, that's you, Frank. He was roaring drunk the last I saw of him. Challenging all comers to a fight, silly wee nyaff.'

'Oh God,' Frank groaned. 'I'd better run in case he's in the house.'

'He was making in that direction.'

'Oh God. Be seeing you, Michael.'

'The best of luck, pal.' Michael raised his bottle of beer.

By the time Frank reached Turner Street and climbed the stairs of the Gallacher close, he was gasping for breath. He'd never had much time for exercise and he was definitely out of condition. In his haste the key stuck in the door and it took him a long minute to get it to turn properly. He could hear Carragh screaming and he thanked God that Bridie had said she would be calling in at the library on her way home from work.

'Scobie!' he shouted when he burst into the kitchen. 'What do you think you're doing, man?'

169

'None of your fuckin' business,' Scobie sneered round at him.

Frank had never before realised how revolting Scobie could look. It wasn't the bald head with its collar of grey hair. It wasn't the nose like a misshapen potato or the pocked skin. It was the bleary, sneery, ugly expression.

'Leave her alone.'

'Piss off.'

'Get your hands off Carragh right now or I'll call the police and get you put away for another stretch.'

'This is what the busies call "a domestic",' Scobie sneered. 'They don't care a fuck about domestics.'

'Then, if need be, I'll deal with you myself.'

Scobie let out a roar of laughter. 'You? You big leek. You couldn't deal a pack of cards.' And with that he gave Carragh such a blow in the face it sent her reeling back to crash against a chair and clatter with it on to the floor.

Frank was horrified and sick to his soul. He hated any kind of violence at any time, but witnessing brutal violence against a frail elderly woman was too much to bear. He rushed at Scobie, but before he could even aim a punch, Scobie had thumped him below the belt and he'd doubled up, breathless with pain.

The pain made him lose his temper and he quickly made another lunge at the smaller man, only to be felled again. Once on the floor Scobie put the boot in to Frank's head and body, making Carragh scream again.

As Frank lay huddled on the floor in a haze of pain, he realised that Scobie was capable of kicking him to death in his drunken rage. Frank's fingers fumbled round the heavy poker, and with a desperate lunge he swung it in a scything arc across Scobie's legs. As Scobie crashed forward on to his hands and knees bawling murderous obscenities at him, Frank wielded the poker in a clumsy back-handed swipe across the older man's head.

170

Chapter Twenty-Five

'Is that Bernard's car down there?' Robert's voice held a note of surprise.

Andrina's spine hardened into a stiff icicle. She kept her back to Robert. 'I didn't know he had a car.'

'Yes, a Ford Anglia.'

'Well, if it is his car, either he and Doris are about to pay us a visit, or they're having a day out in the Green. It's Fair Friday, don't forget.'

'The car's across the road. I can't see who's in it for the trees. Or if anybody's in it.'

'We'll be late for Mummy, if we don't get a move on. You know what a stickler she is for everyone keeping exact time.'

'Right.' Robert moved away from the window. 'If the O'Maleys had been coming here, they would have parked at the close.'

'So it can't be them. There's a tram due at the end of the road in five minutes, Robert. If we run we'll just make it.'

They caught the tram by the skin of their teeth. It took them to near where they'd get a bus for Bearsden. Robert said, 'This is your mum's big day. Showing off her new house for the first time. She'll be in her element.'

Andrina barely murmured a reply. Her mind was filled with Bernard. And the fear of him. She didn't know if he *had* been in the car, yet all the time, in her heart, in her bones, she did know. Earlier in the day, she had been out doing some local shopping. Had he been there then – watching her, following her? She trembled inside at the thought. It was something impossible to cope with. Beyond understanding. Crazy.

'I offered to help, you know,' Robert continued. 'In any way I could. Painting, decorating. But she would have none of it.'

'She never trusts anyone to do anything properly,' Andrina

managed. 'She's obsessional about getting everything perfect – or what's perfect in her eyes.'

'She'll wear herself into an early grave if she doesn't slow down a bit.'

'There's no telling her. I've tried. Dad's tried. Sometimes I think she's getting worse as she gets older. It's just her nature, I suppose.'

'Obsessive behaviour can be a symptom of something serious, some hidden problem.'

Andrina smiled, but she felt far from happy. 'When are you going to put up your shingle? Doctor Anderson, psychiatrist, specialist in obsessional behaviour?'

'Just something I was reading the other day. An article in the *Sunday Times*. Didn't you see it?'

'It takes me a week to read that paper, plus the daily *Glasgow Herald*.'

'Your mother came into my mind while I was reading it. I felt quite worried about her.'

She touched his hand. 'That was kind of you. But she probably just needs a few tranquillisers. Something to slow her down.'

To Andrina, obsessional behaviour didn't have anything to do with the speed and thoroughness with which her mother worked. Obsessional behaviour was the slow determination, the patient pursuit of her by Bernard O'Maley. She wished now she'd read the article. Although she suspected it might only have made her more frightened.

Sometimes she wondered if she ought to tell Robert about Bernard. Each time she immediately shrank from the terrible consequences such a revelation might bring. Bernard was Robert's best friend. It would ruin not only their friendship, but their helpful association at the club. Worse, Robert might attack Bernard, and Bernard would be likely to seriously hurt him. It would cause bad feeling and terrible distress all round, including distress for Doris. And at the end of it all, would Bernard change his obsessional behaviour towards her? Andrina doubted it. There was also more to it than all these

172

considerations: deep down she was rather flattered and excited by having such an ardent (and attractive) pursuer. The danger of it had an edge of excitement, a secret thrill. It was just her over-active imagination, of course, like how she used to feel when she read romantic novels in secret. (Her mother banned them as wicked.) She suffered with the heroine. She fell in love with the handsome, brooding and often brutal hero. Of course, the books always had a happy ending and the hero always turned out to be a really nice man after all. And safe.

Drymen Road was tree-lined and quiet. The terraced houses were tall and imposing, in good quality silver-grey stone.

'Nice place,' Robert said. 'Though the danger of being here too long might be that you'd forget how the other half lives.'

'Sometimes I wonder how Daddy can afford to live the way he does.'

'He got a real bargain of this place.'

Robert rang the bell and the door was immediately opened by Sophie, who must have been watching for them coming off the bus. Her silver hair was pulled so tightly back, it seemed to pull her eyes wide. It looked painful. She was wearing a dark wool dress with a cameo at her throat.

'Come in. Come in. I've put another mat just inside the door here so that you can give your feet an extra wipe. That's the worst of light coloured tiles and self-coloured carpets. They show every spot of dirt or dust. What do you think of it?' She waved an arm around the hall.

'Beautiful, Mummy, absolutely beautiful.' Andrina was genuinely amazed and overcome with admiration for the sparkling white woodwork, the outsize royal blue and cream tiles on the hall floor and the royal blue carpet on the stairs. The royal blue carpet also covered the floors in the sitting room and dining room. The kitchen and scullery had cream linoleum.

'You'll have a terrible job keeping all this linoleum clean,' Andrina said. 'Especially in a kitchen and scullery.'

'Oh, I'll manage,' Sophie said happily, although her sharp eyes and thin face betrayed a feverish flush.

'Where's Andrew?' Robert asked.

'Come on through to the sitting room.' Sophie hustled them before her.

Not a thing was out of place and, as Robert and Andrina admitted to each other and laughed about afterwards, they wondered if Sophie had tidied McPherson away. However, he'd just been upstairs at the bathroom.

'Him and his filthy old pipe,' Sophie had complained after they'd enjoyed a wonderful meal of poached fresh salmon with cucumber sauce, followed by Scotch trifle.

McPherson calmly ignored his wife and continued to puff away. Sophie watched him in agony. As soon as he knocked some ash into the ashtray, she grabbed it and dashed to the kitchen to empty it and wash it.

After coffee they were shown the back garden which consisted of a drying green and a patch of earth at either side of the path the length of the green.

'It was an overgrown mess,' Sophie told them. 'A right jungle. I dug up the side and planted some flowers.'

'I had the job of mowing the lawn,' McPherson said. 'One of these days, I must get a new mower. All we've got just now is an old rusty thing left by the previous owner.'

'We've joined the local branch of the Church of Jesus. The minister's very nice, isn't he Andrew? Very gentlemanly. The manse is a beautiful big villa. Most of the houses here are big villas of course. There's a really good class of people here.'

Robert couldn't help smiling at this. 'What does it feel like to be a Labour man in a Tory stronghold, Andrew?'

'Oh, I don't hold their politics against them. Anyway, it's not them I represent. I do my best for the ordinary working man. They're the ones who voted me into office. That's where my first loyalties lie.'

'But for health reasons,' Sophie interrupted, 'he needed to live as far away from his work as possible. He needed a bit of peace. Remember how people were never off our doorstep, Andrina?'

Andrina began to say 'Yes, but that was when you lived in Dumbarton Road, not Drumchapel', but her mother rushed on, ignoring her.

174

'All the time, every minute of the day and night, they were after your daddy for help and advice. He was being completely drained. I was too. We both needed a bit of peace and relaxation.'

'It's certainly a lovely place,' Andrina said.

'Yes. And it's so easy to get out into the country from here. Especially now that we've got our wee car. Isn't it, Andrew?'

'When I can manage to persuade her to lay down her duster or scrubbing brush and take off her apron and come with me.'

Sophie ignored him too. 'Now that we've got the place more or less organised I thought I'd invite a couple of the neighbours in for tea one day soon. Get to know them. Next door have a grown-up daughter. I peeped out the back bedroom window the other day and saw them – mother and daughter – sunbathing on deck-chairs. They looked very relaxed and elegant in good quality cotton sundresses and dark sunglasses. I went to the local library to find out the husband's profession. He's a headmaster.'

'Oh?' Robert was interested. 'What's his name?'

'Maurice Pemberton.'

'Pemberton? Unusual name. I think I met him at a conference last year. I believe he was about due for retirement.' He turned to Andrina. 'Remember that thing I went to on Standards in Modern Education?'

'Good.' Sophie clasped her hands together and shook them with pleasurable anticipation. 'That'll give me another point of contact, something to talk to them about.'

'Do you think that's a good idea, Sophie?' Robert gave one of his amused little smiles. 'As headmaster of an exclusive private school in Bearsden, he might not be all that impressed with a teacher in Blackhill Secondary.'

'Maybe not.' Sophie had obviously taken him seriously. 'Yes, you're quite right, Robert. Safer not to mention it.'

Robert and Andrina had laughed about this on the way home, and later, over their evening cup of Ovaltine, Andrina said, 'Poor Mummy, she's so excited about living in Bearsden. It's almost as if she's been blessed and arrived in heaven. I hope

175

it lasts. I mean, I hope the people of Bearsden don't disillusion her. I don't think she could bear it.'

'I suppose once she finds her niche she'll be all right. No doubt she'll join the Women's Guild at the church and become involved in all sorts of good works and local events.'

'Did you hear Daddy talking about joining the golf club?'

'I heard what it cost. I was a bit surprised your mother didn't draw the line at that.'

'I know. But what puzzles me is where is he getting all the money? They've bought all that extra furniture as well.'

Robert shrugged. 'God knows what these big firms pay for consultants. And he's got more than one consultancy now, hasn't he?'

'I've no idea.'

'I hope . . .' Robert hesitated, worriedly.

'What?'

Robert shook his head. 'Nothing. Let's go to bed. I'm very fond of Sophie, but I must confess she exhausts me more than a class full of kids. And, believe me, coming from where I teach, that's saying something!'

'She has the same effect on me. I'm sorry for Daddy. At least we can get away on our own.'

'Oh, I think he manages that too.'

In bed, she cuddled towards him and he made love to her, gently, as usual, and with his usual restraint. He was a most self-disciplined and considerate man. She'd never seen him lose his temper although he could express anger at injustices.

She could imagine him controlling a class full of Blackhill rowdies with good humour, as well as his authoritative voice and manner. His reputation as a karate black belt would help, of course.

She loved and admired and trusted him. She kept assuring herself of this as she lay, long after he'd fallen into a deep sleep, and she was left, round-eyed in the darkness, in a strange, disturbing limbo.

Chapter Twenty-Six

The Gallacher kitchen looked even more like a tip than usual. Wooden chairs with spars missing wobbled on their sides on the uneven floor. The table had also been knocked over. A milk bottle had gushed out a white river. Sugar crunched underfoot and mixed with mince and mashed potatoes. It was a late summer evening and sunshine, beginning to fade, abandoned the room in dusty shadow. There was a smell of onion and cabbage, sour sweat, and blood.

Bridie had arrived home while Frank was out phoning for an ambulance. Carragh was whimpering in the corner between the sink and the press. Scobie was lying on the floor with his head near the metal fender. There was blood on the fender and on the floor. It looked as if he'd fallen and struck his head on the fender's sharp metal edge.

Before Bridie noticed the bloodstained poker, she knew instinctively that there had been a fight and Frank was in danger. She felt no concern for her father. He'd been asking to be cut down for years.

'Where's Frank?' she yelled at her mother.

'Away phoning for an ambulance, hen,' Carragh sobbed. 'Is your da all right?'

'Fuck him,' Bridie shouted with uncharacteristic coarseness. 'If the police see this they'll think Frank done it and they'll arrest him.' She rushed at the poker, snatched it up and, pushing her mother away from the sink, proceeded to scrub at the poker and wash off the blood.

'Frank didn't mean it, hen. He was trying to protect me. But your da didn't mean it either. It was the drink. See if he's all right. Please, hen. I don't feel able. I'm in such a state. I think I need an ambulance myself.'

Bridie thoroughly dried the poker and laid it in the

fireplace. Only then did she kneel down beside her father.

'Da?'

A groan and a mumble told her at least he wasn't dead.

'Da, you listen to me. My Frank never touched you. Never touched you. You were steaming drunk and you staggered about and tripped and fell and knocked your head against the fender. You did this to yourself, do you hear? My Frank never touched you.'

Another groan seemed to indicate compliance.

'Right,' said Bridie, struggling to her feet. She rushed around putting the room to rights. The table was lifted. Chairs were tidied around it. Milk was mopped up, mince and potatoes scraped off the floor. She was in the middle of doing this when an ashen-faced Frank appeared.

'The ambulance is on its way. Christ, I'm sorry, Bridie. I haven't killed him, have I?'

'Now, you listen to me.' Bridie came over to him and stared close as if her glasses weren't functioning properly. 'Whether he lives or dies, you never touched him. He was drunk and he fell and hit his head against the fender.'

'But . . .'

'Damn it, Frank,' she shouted at him, 'there's no buts about it. If he lives you could get a long jail sentence. If he dies they could hang you. Our lives would be ruined, finished. I'm not going to allow that, Frank. I'm not going to allow that drunken bum to finish us, Frank.'

'Good God.' Frank pushed back his hair. 'The man must be in pain. He could be dying. How can you just stand there calling him names? Get out of my way.' He knocked her aside and went over to kneel beside Scobie. 'Are you all right, Scobie?'

'Of course I'm not fuckin' all right,' Scobie managed. 'You've bashed my fuckin' skull in.'

'You heard me, da,' Bridie warned. 'You heard what I said. If the doctors or the police ask what happened, Frank never touched you. If you say anything against Frank, I'll be the next one to bash your skull in. I'm telling you, da. I mean it.'

'Aye, aye,' Scobie groaned.

'Right. How about you, ma?'

'Anything you say, hen.'

'How do you feel?' Bridie asked Carragh, still in an uncharacteristically aggressive voice. 'Are you in pain? Do you need to go in the ambulance?'

'I'll have to go with your da, hen. It's my place.'

As it turned out, nothing was needed to be said – not to the ambulance men, at least. They had collected Scobie before – from street pavements, from pubs, from closes, even from railway lines.

'At it again, was he?' they greeted the family. Then to the patient, 'See you, old man, one of these days we'll not be able to patch you up.'

As they lifted him on to the stretcher, Scobie mumbled something that the others couldn't catch. One of the ambulance men obviously heard, because he replied, 'Up yours as well!'

Afterwards, alone in the house, all Bridie's aggression suddenly evaporated. She began to sob and moan. Frank grabbed her into his arms and they clung tightly to each other.

'I warned you, Frank. I warned you what it was like and what it would do to us.'

'He's not always been as violent as this, surely?'

'Maybe he's got worse, but he's always been violent. If it wasn't to my ma, it was to the boys or to me and Doris, or to someone outside – some local gangster. I suppose he's got worse because the drinking's got worse. It's the drink, right enough. Da's good natured when he's sober. He likes a laugh. Sometimes he plays practical jokes. I don't go along with that kind of thing, but you've got to laugh at him sometimes. You've just got to laugh.' She was still helplessly weeping as she spoke, and Frank had to keep hushing her and comforting her.

'The thing is,' Frank said later as they were both drinking a cup of tea, one on each side of the fire, 'he'll have to stop drinking.'

'And pigs'll have to learn to fly.'

179

'No, I mean it, Bridie.'

'So do I. He's over sixty and he's been drinking all his days.'

'It's never too late.'

'How do you know, Frank? I don't suppose you've ever been drunk in your life. One or two pints of beer and you're quite happy. You don't want to, you don't need to drink more than that. Once my da starts he can't stop.'

'He's an alcoholic.'

'Of course he's an alcoholic. We've known that for years.'

'Alcoholics have been known to stop drinking,' Frank said thoughtfully. 'If I can get him to Alcoholics Anonymous.'

'If you can get him to AA, you're a worker of miracles, Frank.'

'It's worth a try.'

Bridie sighed but said nothing. Frank visibly stiffened with resolve.

'When Scobie comes out of hospital, I'm going to do it, Bridie. I'll get your da to AA or die in the attempt.'

'Don't say things like that even in a joke, Frank.'

'I'll have to get him there, Bridie.'

For a long minute Bridie stared across at her husband.

'What are you thinking,' he asked eventually.

'I was just remembering how you persevered all these years – ever since you were a wee boy – to get a poem published. And how, against all odds, you succeeded. And I was just thinking, if anyone can persevere and get my da to change his ways, you can, Frank. You just never give up, do you?'

'I'll get my play accepted next. You wait and see.'

'I believe you.'

'And I'll get your da to go on the wagon.'

Bridie sighed. 'Oh, he's always doing that. He never stays on it, that's the problem.'

'This time, he will. I promise you.'

'Try not to be too optimistic, Frank. I don't want you to be hurt and let down.'

'Trust me.'

She smiled. Her glasses were steaming up with the heat of her

180

tea, but she could still make out his thin, eager face and the clothes that hung on him so inelegantly.

'I trust you. I love you as well.'

'One of these days . . .' Frank began, and she knew and loved what was coming, 'I'm going to take you out of all this. You're going to have a lovely roomy house with high carved ceilings and deep-pile luxurious carpets on the floor. The fireplace will be tiled, and there'll be beautiful paintings on the walls. The furniture will be solid and elegant and carved from beautiful wood. In the kitchen you'll have every modern gadget. The cupboard will be full of the best linen. The wardrobe will be packed with expensive and fashionable clothes. Everything your heart desires, Bridie, you will have. I promise you.'

'I know, Frank.'

'It'll be wonderful.'

'I know.'

His eyes had dreamed over. 'And I'll be a famous play-wright. And you'll be proud of me.'

'I'm proud of you now.' She took off her glasses and rubbed at them with the corner of her skirt. 'And I know you know best about writing and what you want to say, only . . .' Her words hung in the air, held up with worry and uncertainty.

'Only what?'

'I can recognise people in what you've written of the play so far, and I'm a bit worried . . .'

'Oh, I don't think anybody will recognise themselves. People seldom do. As Rabbie said, "O Wad the Power the Gift tae gie us, to see ourselves as others see us." '

'Still, do you not think . . .'

'And when a friend of D. H. Lawrence expressed her concern about how Lawrence was using things about her, he said he was not falsifying her "truth", he was erecting a work of fiction on a frame of actual experience. The thing that matters, you see, Bridie, is that it should be my presentation of what I see as the truth – and it should also, if possible, be a work of art.'

'The scenes with the priest especially,' Bridie persisted. 'I'm afraid the Church isn't going to like that.'

181

'No,' Frank admitted, 'I don't expect it will. But an inhibited writer goes nowhere, Bridie, unless his very inhibitions are his subject matter. I believe that to write is to indulge in an intentionally promiscuous communication.'

She loved him when he talked like this. He was the dearest, the cleverest, the most talented man in the world. And to think he'd developed his talents and his brain and his decent nature against a background of places like Garngad and Blackhill. To her, he was a walking, talking miracle and every day she thanked God for him. But it was because she believed in God and His goodness and mercy towards both her and Frank that she wanted to protect Frank from the wrath of the Church, and maybe even the turning of God against them.

'I know that, dear,' she agreed gently and replaced her spectacles. 'It's just that our church and priests have their good side, don't you think? They do quite a lot of good around here. I mean there are two sides to everything, don't you think?'

Frank sighed. 'I know. I know. But they go about so many things in the wrong way. Beating up Scobie for instance. That's never helped or cured him. And they've no right to do it. I'd no right to touch Scobie either, but at least I've the excuse of self-defence.'

'Well, I suppose they probably look on themselves like an ordinary father chastising a son.'

Frank shook his head. 'In too many areas of life they go too far. So often they're wrong, Bridie. So terribly wrong!'

'Maybe it's the way you feel just now, dear. Just the way you're seeing things at the moment. Things haven't been easy for you.'

He'd written a poem about how he felt at the moment:

> 'I did not doubt before, but now
> I feel unsure of all my past
> Of self and faith; I know somehow
> I must be free,
> I must be me,
> To find a surer way at last.'

182

He didn't tell Bridie about the poem. Instead he said, 'It's my duty as a writer to express things as I see them as honestly as I can.'

'Yes, but to take on the Church, Frank. I'm afraid . . .'

'Exactly! That's one of the things that's wrong with it. So much of their teaching is based on fear. For instance, you're afraid I'll be damned and burn in Hell for questioning and making other people question, aren't you?'

'No, no, dear,' she said. But she was. Apprehension was tightening its grip on her. She tried to tell herself that the recent violence in the house, and the terrible business of Frank's involvement, was what had really unnerved her.

She didn't know. She couldn't think. She had been talking to Frank about his play in her usual quiet and gentle voice, as if Frank hadn't nearly committed murder. Maybe only now the shock of it was catching up on her. She was shaking, collapsing inside.

She smiled and blinked over at Frank. 'I wonder if Da's got any whisky hidden in the house. I wouldn't mind a wee drop in my tea.'

Chapter Twenty-Seven

'You can't go out and leave me like this. Where are you going? Why are you getting all done up? What's going on, Bernard? For pity's sake, tell me.' Doris had to shout because of Tony's drums racketing through from the next room.

Bernard was going out again without her. He had told her he was going out on a job and it was true that he worked most nights, but he was taking far too much care about his appearance to be just going to work. He looked like a hundred dollars in his smart, lightweight suit and fashionable silk shirt. He was bending a little at the knees so that he could see in the mirror to smooth a palm over his hair. She felt a real mess in comparison. Her dark hair was showing at the roots. Her belly bulged. Her skirt drooped. She was tormented with a varicose vein, and she was wearing horrible flat-heeled shoes.

'Bernard!' She tugged at his sleeve. 'Don't just ignore me.'

He flicked at his jacket as if she'd contaminated it. 'I'm going to work. And my work needs total concentration, Doris. I've explained all this to you before.'

She immediately began to howl and cry and swear. She howled and cried and swore a lot these days. 'You bloody selfish pig. You don't care about anybody but yourself.'

'You're just getting yourself into a state.'

'Is it any wonder? If you're not out at work, you're in bed asleep and if you're not asleep, you ignore me.'

'What is there to say?'

'It's not fuckin' good enough,' she shouted broken-heartedly.

He looked at her then – a cold, distasteful look that made her weep all the more. She knew he didn't like coarseness in a woman. He never swore himself. At least, she'd never heard him. She would rather he had shouted and sworn at her, even

184

hit her, like her da used to hit her ma. At least it would have shown some emotion, some feelings towards her.

She felt helpless, childlike. She wanted him to hold her and comfort her and love her. She knew she was doing everything all wrong. She didn't know what to do to make things right. She kept making things worse. Shouting at him, swearing at him, trying to force him to stay in with her, pay attention to her – nothing was any good.

He was polite, always so bloody polite, never an unkind word. She bloody hated him. If she'd been a man, she would have battered him with her bare fists. 'I'm going to tell your mammy on you,' she sobbed.

After he'd gone without another word, she trailed miserably through to the living room to find Maureen wasn't in. She had just dried her eyes on her smock when Tony came clomping and whistling through from his room.

'Jesus, Doris, you look like something the cat dragged in.'

It was too much. Howling louder than ever she ran past him and out of the house. She had a vague idea of going to Garngad to be with her own mother. She was so upset she didn't pay attention to where she was putting her feet. She remembered an initial feeling of surprise when she suddenly lost her balance and went hurtling down the stone stairs, bouncing, crashing, crunching against them. She lay at the bottom for what seemed like forever. She felt in pain literally from head to toe. Her head had cracked against one of the stairs and she'd twisted her foot under her when she landed.

'Tony.' She tried to call out but her chest hurt and the word came out as a faint moan. She tried the names of some of the neighbours. Nobody came. Most of them would be in their living rooms at the back watching television. Or they'd be out. She tried to help herself and had just managed to crawl on all fours up a few steps when Tony came whistling and clattering into view.

He gave one of his big, buck-toothed laughs. 'What's the game?'

'Help me up to the house,' she managed. 'I've hurt myself.'

185

None too gently, he heaved her up and she howled with pain.

'I told you I've hurt myself, you eejit. I fell down all these stairs.'

'I'll carry you if you like.' He was still grinning.

'OK. But take it easy. I'm in agony.'

Once in the house he propped her into a chair.

'Will I get Bernard? I know where he'll be.'

She hesitated. She needed her husband more than she'd ever needed him before, but she knew he would be scant comfort – if any comfort at all. He would do his duty by her but there would be no love with it. That was the terrible thing. The ultimate loneliness. There could be no hiding the fact any more. Bernard didn't care about her. She began to moan and weep.

'Stay there,' Tony said. 'I'll get him.'

After Tony had gone, she tried not to faint or be sick. She couldn't move out of the chair. Never in her whole life had she experienced such pain, had felt so ill. When she heard the key turn in the outside door, she prayed that it would be Maureen. From her, at least, she would get some love and sympathy. But it was Bernard who strode into the room. He was saying, 'I hope this isn't just another of your . . .' Seeing her, he stopped.

She didn't say anything. What was the use?

'What happened? Tony just called out something was wrong with you and disappeared before I could ask him anything.'

'I fell down the stairs.'

He took a few steps towards her. 'It'll be all right.' He'd said that before but it hadn't been all right. 'I'll go and phone for an ambulance. That's what Tony should have done right away. I'll tell one of the neighbours to come in and wait with you. I'll be lucky if I get a phone box working within a mile of here. Can I get you anything first? A brandy or something?'

She shook her head.

'I'll be back as soon as I can.'

In a few minutes Mrs Hennessy appeared. 'Is this no terrible, hen? And you carrying the wean. It was with you being so heavy at the front. It would knock you off balance. Poor wee soul. Is it awful sore, hen? Will I make you a wee cup of tea?'

'Ta,' Doris managed, and Mrs Hennessy bustled away through to the scullery.

Years seemed to pass before Bernard returned, quickly followed by the ambulance men.

Bernard came with her in the ambulance. He sat talking to the ambulance men. It was the ambulance man who patted her and held her hand. She desperately clung to him as the pain increased.

Andrina went to see Doris in the hospital and was shocked at the sight of the grey face and lank hair. There was a look of Carragh about her – except that Carragh never had the bitter look that Doris had now.

'I was so sorry to hear about the baby.' Andrina took Doris's limp hand and squeezed it sympathetically.

'It was a wee girl. I called her Carragh after my mammy.'

Andrina didn't know what to say. At last she managed, 'You'll have lots more children, Doris.'

'Do you think so?'

'Of course. Why not?'

Doris's lips twisted. 'Oh aye. Why not?'

'Has Bernard been in to see you?'

'He came with Maureen last night.'

'Is he coming again tonight?'

'I hope not.'

Andrina was shocked. 'Doris! I'm sure Bernard must be very upset.'

'What? Him?'

'He won't be able to show his feelings. You know what men are like.'

'I know what he's like. A right cold-hearted bastard.'

Andrina patted Doris's hand. 'He's got a very tough, stressful job. That probably has a lot to do with what he's like. It won't have anything to do with you, Doris.'

'No?'

'No.'

'As soon as I get out of here, I'm going to try to get my old job back.'

'What will Bernard think about that?'

'I don't care a f . . .' she caught herself in time and struggled to find some of her old ladylike restraint. 'I don't care a fig what Bernard will think. Anyway, knowing him, he won't be in the slightest interested in what I do. All he's interested in is himself, and his business. I've never known anyone in my whole life so single-minded.'

'I know how you feel about going back to Daly's. I often miss Copland's: the company of the other girls, some of the laughs we used to have.'

'I know.' Doris's eyes saddened, remembering. 'I miss it terribly.'

'And the interest of all the different customers, and the smart clothes. I asked Robert only the other day what he would think if I went back to work. I've never seen him look so offended. He's a bit touchy and old-fashioned about that sort of thing. "I'm perfectly capable of keeping my wife," he said. "If you're short of anything all you have to do is tell me." I couldn't make him understand it wasn't the money. He clammed up. Didn't want to know anything about it.'

'Why don't you just do it?' Doris said. 'Like I'm going to do it, and to hell with him.'

'Well, Robert's really very good to me. I don't want to hurt or upset him. And of course, there's my mother. She would hit the roof.'

'What's it got to do with her?'

Andrina gave a dazed little laugh. 'Well, I . . . Mummy's very fond of Robert, and she'd think I was neglecting him by going out to work. You don't know her, Doris. She can make me feel so guilty. It really upsets me.'

'I know enough about her. She hates Bernard, doesn't she? That's why Robert didn't invite him to your wedding. I wondered at the time what she had against him. Mr Wonderful, I thought he was at the time. Your mother obviously was better at judging him than me.' Doris's mouth

188

twisted. 'A very clever woman, your mother.'

Andrina felt uneasy in the silence that fell between them. To break the awkwardness of it she said, 'As soon as you're better we must meet and have a nice meal together somewhere. And we could call in at Daly's and Copland's and see all the girls. You won't be starting work right away, will you?'

'As soon as I can fix it up.'

'You'll have to get your strength back first, Doris.'

Doris smiled and her hand tightened on to Andrina's. 'You're a good friend, Andrina. I'm terribly grateful. Yes, we'll have our day out. I'll look forward to it. What I'm not looking forward to is going back to live in that house in Blackhill. I used to think it would be so much better than Garngad and my da. But you know Patrick is just as awful in his own way. He's a right thieving git, so he is. You'll pardon the expression. And there's never a bit of peace inside the house, what with him and Tony. Nobody seems to mind except me. They switch the wireless on for music at mealtimes and Tony batters away at the rhythm on the table with his big paws and makes all the dishes rattle about. They just laugh. Maureen thinks he's a lovely boy. Can you beat it? Him with his mouth always hanging open in a silly grin showing those big horsy teeth of his. Our Francie wasn't right in the head, but at least he was quiet and harmless. I never thought they should have put Francie away. I was terribly upset about poor wee Francie.'

Andrina patted her hand. 'We'll meet regularly. Have a good time. Forget all our troubles.'

Doris nodded. 'Ta.'

'Is there anything else you need brought in? How about some peroxide for your hair? You'd feel better if you got it back to normal.'

'Would you, Andrina?'

'Of course.'

'You're a real pal.'

'I'll bring in some make-up as well. It can do wonders for the morale.'

Doris nodded, but tears had sprung to her eyes.

'Oh, Doris, please don't cry.'

'I thought there might just be a chance . . .' The tears overflowed and poured unchecked down Doris's cheeks. '. . . that the baby would bring Bernard and me closer together. It was a wee girl. I called her Carragh after my mammy.'

'I know. You told me.'

Doris looked so lost and helpless in her misery that Andrina stretched over and pulled her into her arms. Patting her back as she would have comforted a child, she tried to hush the distraught woman.

'Sh . . . Doris . . . Sh. Will I call the nurse? Maybe she could give you something to calm you.'

'I'm a terrible nuisance.'

'No, you're not. Of course you're not. You just lie back. I'll fetch the nurse. It's no trouble.'

'Ta.'

The nurse gave Doris something that soon made her appear not only calm but sleepy. Her eyes kept closing and the hand that clung to Andrina's became limp again.

'I'd better go and let you have a good sleep,' Andrina whispered close to the colourless face. 'I'll come again tomorrow with all the things I promised.'

Doris didn't answer and Andrina slipped her hand gently away. Outside, she caught a tram back to Monteith Row. She hardly dared think, she felt so upset. Words kept chasing each other round and round in her mind.

'Oh God, poor Doris. Oh God, poor Doris. Oh, dear God!'

Once home she made herself a cup of tea and sat nursing it beside the empty fireplace.

It was nothing to do with her, she assured herself. Bernard was mad. She had told him he was mad. She had done nothing to encourage Bernard's attention. She had refused to listen to him. She was happily married to a dear, good man. She had made that perfectly clear to Bernard. It was really shocking the way he had treated Doris.

'Oh God, poor Doris. Oh God, poor Doris. Oh, dear God!'

She was still sitting nursing her cup when Robert arrived

190

home from taking his class for a sketching lesson in the Campsies.

'Darling, what's wrong? You look like a ghost sitting there. Your tea's stone cold. I'll put a match to the fire, then I'll make you a fresh cup.'

'I was in visiting Doris.'

'I see. How is she?'

'In an awful state.'

'No wonder. But she'd be glad to see you, I'm sure.'

'Yes, she was. But I wished I could have done more to help her.'

'Losing a child must be the worst thing in the world. I don't suppose there's anything that can be done to make anyone feel better in such circumstances.'

'I suppose not.'

'You're doing your best, Andrina. Try not to get too upset. Once Doris is on her feet again, we must have her and Bernard over for a meal.'

'I've promised we'll meet in town and have a meal. Just her and me.'

'You can do that too. But it would be nice for the four of us to get together more often.'

Andrina made no comment. Robert soon had the fire creaking and crackling in the hearth. They'd had the old range and high mantelpiece taken out, and a modern tiled fireplace and gas cooker put in place. The coal bunker had been removed and hidden in a cupboard in the hall. With the dining recess where normally a bed would have been, the room was now a kitchen cum dining room, and a very cosy and pleasant place either to work or to relax in.

More often than not, they used it as a living room, especially in the winter. They only used the front sitting room when they'd company, or on a nice summer evening they'd sit at the window and look out at the Green in between reading or listening to the wireless. They had two wirelesses (or what were now called transistor radios) – one in the front room and one in the kitchen. One had been a wedding present from the girls in

191

Copland's. The other had been from Robert's uncle Jimmy, who had since died.

This evening the summer sun had cooled and the kitchen had turned chilly and dull.

'I'm sorry, I forgot the time.' Andrina roused herself, got up and rinsed out her cup at the sink. 'I've some of that pie left that I made yesterday. Will that do with chips? It won't take me long to peel the potatoes. And I can soon make some custard.'

'Let's go out,' Robert said. 'You need cheering up. Come on, get your coat. It's not often we treat ourselves. Bernard was telling me about a new place that's got the best food in town – and he should know.'

'Should he?'

'Of course. It's his job. It takes him to all sorts of places. He's become quite a connoisseur. He's a strange mixture, isn't he?'

'Yes,' she said, avoiding his eyes. 'Very strange.'

Chapter Twenty-Eight

Sophie was thrilled at being invited next door to Mrs Pemberton's for afternoon tea. As she said to McPherson, 'Fancy! I didn't need to make the first approach. She did. She put a little card through the door. On one side there was their name and address and telephone number. On the other was the invitation to afternoon tea.' (She'd learned afterwards that Mrs Pemberton hadn't telephoned because she didn't know if their phone had yet been installed.) 'Andrew! Andrew, are you listening?'

'Yes, dear.' McPherson was sucking absently at his pipe, his eyes above their pouches of dark lizard skin were dreamy. He was thinking of a very lucrative deal he'd managed to put Bernard's way. He also would gain much benefit from it. One of these new pop groups was coming to Glasgow. Youngsters went mad about them apparently. Bodyguards and also very strict crowd control were needed. It was to be an outdoor event on the Green. Television cameras were going to be there. It was going to put Glasgow on the map – hopefully in a good way for a change. There mustn't be any trouble. For too long Glasgow had suffered from a bad reputation, especially for violence, although nowadays at events like this a lot of what was called flower people turned up and drug taking was the problem with them. He'd said to Bernard that drug-taking hippies and Glasgow neds didn't seem a good mix. Bernard had assured him that everything would go well. Security and crowd control would be – to use Bernard's words – as tight as a badger's arse.

'You'll notice,' Sophie was saying, 'that she didn't come knocking at the door. They don't do that here like they do in the tenements. There's no running in and out of each other's houses. They show a bit of respect for privacy. I'm really looking forward to it. Andrew! Andrew!'

'Yes, dear.'

'I wonder what I should wear.'

'Your brown dress with your cameo. That's a good cameo. A real family heirloom.'

'I know.'

'There you are then.'

'Yes, and my brown dress is plain but good quality. Yes, you're quite right, Andrew. I'll look perfectly respectable in that.'

She couldn't sleep the night before the visit, and the next morning she took a bath and put on clean underwear and brushed her hair and pinned it so tightly back her eyes took on an oriental look. She had already polished her shoes until she could see her face in them. She pressed her dress. She even washed her cameo and polished it up with a soft duster, and did the same with her spectacles. She worried about whether or not to take a gift to Mrs Pemberton. It was the custom in working class districts always to take a gift if it was the first visit to anyone's house. Indeed, it was quite usual to take a packet of biscuits or a cake or some small offering any time you visited anyone. But would that be proper in Bearsden? She didn't want to appear common or insult the woman by taking something. On the other hand she did not want to risk looking ignorant or mean. Eventually she decided on her home-baked butter shortbread, packed prettily in tissue paper, in a little cardboard gift box in a discreet fawn colour, and neatly tied with a gold-coloured ribbon.

Mrs Pemberton seemed delighted. 'We must exchange recipes, my dear. I've never quite mastered shortbread. I have quite a good Madeira cake recipe you might like to try. I never divulge any of my recipes as a rule. One gets known for one's special little treats. Each one to his own, I always say. But as a little gesture of good will to a new neighbour, I'll make an exception with my Madeira cake.'

Already Sophie was enjoying herself. As Mrs Pemberton went to fetch the tea tray her eyes rapidly took in the comfortable room, the white Adam fireplace, the heavy lined

194

curtains, the chintz chair covers. There was a trolley nicely set with fine china cups and saucers and tea plates and a three tiered cake stand. The cake stand boasted a plate of tiny scones, a plate of buttered fruit bread, and a plate of dainty sponge cakes. Then, to top all these delights, Mrs Pemberton returned with a silver tray on which sat a silver teapot, sugar bowl and milk jug.

Sophie couldn't contain herself. 'A silver tea service! Mrs Pemberton!'

'It is beautiful, isn't it? It's a family heirloom. It belonged to my husband's mother.'

'Like my cameo.' Sophie fingered it with pride. 'It belonged to my husband's mother too.'

'I noticed it right away, Mrs McPherson. I always recognise and appreciate quality.'

'Yes, so do I. Your tea service is so . . . so elegant.'

'Yes, isn't it?'

Mrs Pemberton too was elegant in a matronly kind of way. Sophie guessed she could be anywhere between fifty and sixty. Her hair was light brown and beautifully permed. Not one grey hair was to be seen. She went into town every week to have it shampooed and set. She also had a special rinse to cover the odd grey hair or two.

But that was another of her little secrets. Her dress was well cut and in pretty shades of turquoise. Sophie was fascinated to learn that Mrs Pemberton had made the dress herself.

'I'm interested in dressmaking too,' she confessed in between delicious sips of Earl Grey tea, 'but altering is about my stretch. You know – taking up hems, letting out or taking in a tuck here and there.'

'Oh, you must allow me to help you make something for yourself.'

'I couldn't put you to all that trouble, Mrs Pemberton.'

'No trouble at all. It'll be a pleasure. Now, can I be honest with you, my dear?'

'Yes, of course.'

'Well, I don't think brown is your colour. I can see the

material is good quality. But brown doesn't flatter you, Mrs McPherson. You need something to brighten you up.'

Sophie began to feel uncomfortable, began to shrink protectively inside. 'Oh, I'm not one for bright colours. Not for myself.'

'Something just a *little* softer – lavender perhaps?'

'Well, I don't know.'

'You have such a lovely fair skin and slim figure, my dear. I envy you. I'm afraid I'm too fond of these.' She offered Sophie a sponge cake and selected one herself. 'Your husband's a Glasgow bailie, I believe.'

'Yes.'

'We must make a four for bridge some evening.'

'I'm afraid I've never played bridge.'

'Oh, my dear, you must learn. *Everybody* plays bridge. We go to *so* many bridge parties. My husband is a *very* accomplished player. We'll get together as a foursome first to break you in, so to speak. You'll soon pick it up.'

Sophie began to relax again with the prospect of many happy evenings with new friends and neighbours. Church membership was discussed next. The Women's Guild and the flower arranging club were recommended. Golf was another must.

'For me?' Sophie had to laugh. The idea of her out on a golf course was too much. 'I can't imagine playing golf. I've never been one for sports of any kind. My husband is keen, though. He's already applied for membership of your local club. I must admit I was rather shaken at the cost of the subscription.'

'Oh, my dear, it's worth it. You meet so many important people. People who would be a help to you and your husband in so many ways. And why shouldn't you play golf? Lots of ladies do. I do. It's also good for helping to keep fit. By the way, there's a very good keep fit class in the town hall.'

It was all working out beautifully. Better even than Sophie had ever dared hope. Perhaps some of the ways of keeping busy weren't exactly as she'd expected – she'd been thinking more in terms of 'good works', but no doubt she'd learn about that too in time. After all, she'd hardly settled in the place yet.

196

She could hardly wait to tell McPherson all about the visit. 'She already knew you were a bailie. She never mentioned you being Labour, of course. She was too well-bred.'

'I'm not ashamed of being a Labour man,' McPherson protested. Although in fact he had been wondering recently if he wasn't developing more towards Liberalism. There was something so well-balanced about the Liberal Party. There was nothing too extreme about it. It had a proud history. He had been reading quite a bit about it recently. Of course he couldn't rush into anything like that. Glasgow was a red-hot Labour place, and it was Glaswegians who had elected him. He wasn't a fool. He knew that it paid him to remember that.

He had no doubts about his move to Bearsden. He liked the house. There was space to move, to breathe in it. Room to get away from Sophie. He had commandeered the bedroom on the half landing next to the bathroom as his study. In it he had a desk and swivel chair, bookshelves, a carpet and a comfortable easy chair beside the fire. There he could sit enjoying a pipe and a bit of peace after telling Sophie that he'd paperwork to attend to.

Although, in actual fact, he and Sophie had been getting on surprisingly well since the move to Bearsden. She was so much happier for one thing, which made life a lot easier. Quite often they went for a walk together in the evening, he with his black walking umbrella and she with her coat and pull-on hat and brogues – the proper thing for week-day walking. Although it was September the air was still balmy and pleasant. They explored around, getting to know the place, absorbing the solid, prosperous, secure atmosphere.

Sophie walked apart from him as usual, but he could sense her happy excitement. 'It's magic, isn't it, Andrew? You feel it too, don't you?'

He had to agree with her. He had never felt so happy and content in years. 'Will you never learn to relax?' But he laughed as he said it. He knew that would be expecting too much. Sophie was like an overwound alarm clock or a time-bomb waiting to go off. She was – always had been – a

197

hysterical type. At least now she was hysterical with happiness.

She looked better too. The first time they'd been to Bearsden church she had worn a new, very smart costume in navy blue, instead of her usual shapeless muddy brown things. With it she teamed a white blouse which tied with a bow at the neck. This, for Sophie, seemed outrageously frivolous. Not as frivolous, however, as the tiny pearl stud earrings she'd taken to wearing. He'd never in all the years he'd known her seen her wear any jewellery whatsoever, except the cameo he'd given her.

He said to her, 'You look very nice.'

She'd flushed with pleasure and looked quite pretty. He felt proud of her too when the next week they'd attended church. He wore his trilby hat and best pinstripe suit with his heavy gold watch and chain over his ample girth, Sophie wore a dress in soft lavender shades she'd made herself. Her hat and gloves and shoes and handbag were navy blue. They went with Mr and Mrs Pemberton and their daughter, Samantha. He and Sophie didn't of course walk arm in arm like Mr and Mrs Pemberton. Sophie never touched him in public.

Samantha was a charming girl whose hobbies were riding and skiing. She was in her late twenties and unmarried. There was no hurry, Mr and Mrs Pemberton explained. It was so important to find the *right* partner. He and Sophie had been in no doubt that the Pembertons meant somebody with money.

'And why not?' Sophie had said.

Why not indeed? They were both beginning to regret their own daughter's hasty choice of a husband. Robert was a nice enough man but – a schoolmaster in Blackhill of all places! And to make matters worse he showed no signs of having any ambition whatsoever. McPherson often thought that Andrina would have been far better off married to Bernard O'Maley, Catholic or not. But of course that was something he knew better never to even hint at to Sophie. Sophie had been thinking of the respectable young men in the Bearsden church. Professional men from good homes (large villas), like Doctor James Honeyman, who was building up a very lucrative private practice, Mrs Pemberton said. Or the lawyer Blair Matheson, who was in partnership with his father – a very lucrative partnership, Mrs Pemberton said.

'What elegant young gentlemen,' Sophie remarked. 'Isn't it a pity Andrina didn't meet someone like them?' Not, of course, that I've got anything against poor Robert,' she added hastily. 'Poor Robert is a good Christian man.'

It was the 'poor' that was the trouble.

Sophie discovered that it was *the* thing to have an 'At Home', and so she invited several of the neighbours and one or two of the other ladies from the church. For days beforehand she cleaned and baked and polished until she was in a near frenzy. But everything went superbly. She was complimented on the lightness of her French Fancies and the crispness of her almond biscuits. Mrs Hawthorn from further along the terrace (her husband was a bank manager) said they were all so glad to have such a *suitable* newcomer to the terrace. One never knew these days. With young people taking over so much and standards being not only eroded but tossed to the winds. My dear, have you seen those Beatle young men's long hair? They had all seen even worse. There had been pictures and stories of Elvis Presley and the disgustingly sexual gyration of his hips while he sang. There were scenes of nakedness and debauchery when hordes of so-called flower people got together. There were Mods and Rockers and motorbikes and drug taking. There were pictures of young people dressed like absolute tramps on CND marches. What was the world coming to?

It was all most enjoyable.

Andrew was pleased to hear that Sophie's 'At Home' had been such a success. He was able to share the pleasures he had experienced at the golf club. Sophie was always keenly interested in who he had met and always asked, 'What does he do?' He was pleased to be able to tell her that he'd got on so well with old Hawthorn, the bank manager, or Sanderson of Sanderson and Galbraith, the well known firm of architects, or the Reverend Dinwoodie, who lived in such a beautiful manse surrounded by trees beside the loch.

It was a great source of pride when he and Sophie were invited to a dinner party at the manse.

'Dinwoodie and I have been getting on really well at the club. Did I tell you I showed him round the City Chambers the other day and gave him lunch there? He was impressed, I could see.'

'Yes, dear.'

Sophie was thrilled at the invitation. She had, so far, only admired Bearsden's beautifully proportioned villas from a distance. It would be fascinating to see what one of them was like inside. Mrs Pemberton was delighted for her, and accompanied her into town to help choose a new outfit for the occasion. Mrs Pemberton was already a dear friend; a wonderfully kind woman, a perfect lady. They had tea in the Willow Tearoom; Mrs Pemberton said it was *the* place to go. They chose a spotted shantung dress with a black velvet belt and back fastening. It was, as Mrs Pemberton said, smart, sophisticated, but discreet. It was also rather expensive but as McPherson said, it was important to make a good impression, and anyway he could afford it. He said he was making quite a bit of extra money these days, and who better to spend it on than his wife? McPherson was a different man since he'd come to Bearsden. He spent much more time at home. They'd never, in all the years they'd been married, got on so well.

Just before they left for the manse he said, 'Just a minute, Sophie. I've a present for you.' And, to her surprise and delight, he fastened a strand of pearls round her neck. They were such a good match for her pearl studs.

'Oh Andrew! Thank you. They're just perfect. In such good taste. You're really a very generous man.'

He could sense that if she had been a demonstrative, affectionate type of woman, she would have thrown her arms around him and kissed him. She was teetering very near to it. But of course she didn't. Instead she turned away, fingering the pearls with that strange, furtive sensuality of hers.

There was another couple at the dinner party, a Professor Brodie and his wife. Charming fellow. Of course, the university was hoping for a higher grant from the council. A lot of people

200

tried to be as charming as possible to influential men like Andrew McPherson from the City Chambers. Everyone knew that he was in the running to be Senior Bailie next year, and from there the natural progression was Lord Provost.

The Reverend Dinwoodie was talking about his elderly parishioners and a concert that he was organising for their entertainment. Some of the elderly ladies and gentlemen would need transport to bring them from their homes to the church hall on the evening of the concert, although most of them were still able to drive their own cars.

'I was just talking to old Noble the other day – he must be nearly eighty now – and I offered to pick him and his good lady up myself – but no, he's a game old bird, he would have none of it.'

Andrew said, 'Noble? An unusual name. It was my wife's maiden name.'

The Reverend Dinwoodie smiled over at Sophie. 'Really? Do you think our Nobles would be any relation, my dear?'

'No. I have no living relations.'

McPherson said, 'Sophie was an only child and her parents died when she was young. I never met them.'

All in all it was a delightful evening. McPherson remarked on this to Sophie on the way home in the car. 'A most successful evening,' he said with satisfaction. 'An evening to remember.'

Sophie didn't answer. She seemed lost in thought, miles away. It wasn't like her to be so quiet. She must be exhausted. She tried so hard. She always flung her heart and soul into everything. He retreated into his own pleasurable thoughts.

Chapter Twenty-Nine

'Are you sure you're doing the right thing, Michael?' Frank asked worriedly. He'd sought his brother out at the boxing club in Garngad Road as soon as he'd heard.

'Sure, I'm sure. And I'll tell you why. It's not just the money. It's the chance of getting away as often as I can from Big Martha Stoddart. But there's quite good money to be made fighting at the booths all the same. And there's plenty of them –there's booths in Edinburgh and Falkirk, nearly every town of any size. Then there's all the travelling with the fairs in the summer time. I'm told you can get a fight a day there, if you're game. And I'm game, Frank. I'm game for anything that'll give me a wee break away from here.'

'Some wee break,' Frank said. 'A fight a day at travelling booths. You'll be punch drunk before you're thirty.'

'But there's always the chance of a real improver. I could hit the big time, Frank. Then, if I'm good enough, I could make hundreds, maybe thousands, just for one fight. I'd better get back up. Be a pal and stay and watch. It won't take too long. Then you can tell me what you think.'

'OK, OK.'

Frank regarded it as a measure of Michael's desperation that he would in the least value his opinion. Michael had been one of those who had seen Frank's practice of writing poetry as being 'weak' and 'pouffie'. Michael knew that Frank had an equally low opinion of boxing. However, to please his brother, he stayed in the club and watched as Michael climbed back into the ring and continued with his training.

It wasn't in any way a pleasant place, as far as Frank was concerned. It was bleak and grimy and cold. Broken windows were boarded up. Knots of gangsters crouched around the ring playing pontoon and smoking. Smoke continuously thickened the air, new smoke adding to ancient smoke. Smoke that had stained the ceiling and walls a muddy brown. Smoke that mixed with the stale odour of sweat and sickness in Frank's nostrils. And there was a coarse yet empty echo about the place that saddened him.

Michael was shadow boxing, head down, his dark crop of hair glistening with sweat: southpawing forward, upper-cutting, jabbing, counter punching, weaving and swaying, checking and reaching, giving fist flurries at an imaginary opponent. Despite the cold air, sweat was beginning to steam off him. Eventually he dropped his hands to his sides and did a shuffle on the spot, shaking his head from side to side, before climbing out of the ring and returning to Frank.

'How did I look, Frank?'

'You looked great, Michael. First class.'

'Thanks, Frank. How're you doing yourself?'

Frank glanced at his watch. 'I'll tell you after I've been to the hospital.'

'Och aye, the word's been going around that you were collecting old Scobie today.'

'They've promised to hang on to him till five. Even if it hadn't been my half day off work, I would have taken the time off.'

Michael laughed. 'To stop him doing a pub crawl? I wouldn't bet on it.'

'I'm aiming to do more than stop him doing a pub crawl today. I'm going to stop him drinking altogether.'

'Poor old Scobie.'

'What do you mean – poor old Scobie?'

'Well, I know how it feels to *need* a drink. *And* how it feels when you get one.'

'I know how it feels when Scobie gets more than one. He nearly kicked the stuffing out of me. Not to mention Carragh's black eye and other bruises.'

Michael shrugged. 'Oh well, best of luck to you, pal.'

Scobie was waiting for Frank in a shabby, baggy-trousered suit and big cloth cap jerked to one side of his head.

203

'By Christ, son,' he greeted Frank, 'I'll never look at another drink as long as I live. I swear to you. I've had my last drink. I'll never touch another drop as long as I live, so help me.'

'I'll help you all right, wee man,' Frank said, gripping Scobie by the elbow and manoeuvring him outside. 'As soon as we get back to Turner Street, you and I are going to have a long talk.'

'Aye, right you are, son. Anything you say.'

They took a tram to Garngad Road and after they got off, Frank took a grip of Scobie's elbow again as they passed the pub at the corner of Garngad Road and Turner Street. Already the gas-lamps were lit, softening the grimy black tenements, sparkling the cobbles.

'You don't need to worry, son,' Scobie assured him as they turned into their close. 'I'm a reformed man.'

'I wonder how many times you've said that, Scobie.'

'A few, son. A few. But this time I mean it.'

Carragh had the door open for them when they got up the stairs.

'Hello there, hen,' Scobie greeted her. 'How's my favourite wee woman?'

'Fine, fine.' Carragh stirred a pot on the range. 'I've a nice plate of mince and tatties for you.' She dished Scobie's up first.

He smacked his hands together and gave them a vigorous rub. 'My favourite! You're a wee stoater, so you are. And how's my other wee girl?' He turned to Bridie who was sitting at the table, her head bowed over a book. Bridie was depressed about Scobie's return, and when Bridie was depressed she always retreated into a book. Both she and Frank ate their meal in silence. Scobie and Carragh chatted away quite happily. It was as if nothing had happened. After the mince and potatoes, Carragh proudly produced some apple tarts from the City Bakeries.

'My favourite again,' Scobie cried. 'By God, it's good to be home.'

'Right then,' Frank said, once the apple tarts had been demolished and they were on their second cup of tea, 'can I talk to you, Scobie? Can we have a serious talk? It's important to both of us, all of us.'

204

'Fire away, son. Fire away.'

Carragh hastily began clearing the table. Then, as she washed the dishes at the sink, she tried to be as small as possible and pretend she wasn't there. Bridie took her book through to the room.

'Is this the way you want to go on with your life?' Frank asked. 'You're losing your self-respect and the respect of your family and friends. You're ruining not only your own life but all of our lives. Is this how you want to go on?'

'No, son, I do not. I know it's like wee Carragh says – it's the drink, and I've given it up.'

'Yes, you've told all of us that – over and over and over again. But you never give it up, Scobie. Look at you, man. Look at you!'

'OK, OK. I'm fed up fuckin' looking at myself. But what else can I do?'

'You could try the League of the Cross. You can sign the pledge there and Father Shannon is very supportive, I've heard. He has a lot going on. There's card schools – solo and pontoon – you'd enjoy that . . .'

'I can enjoy a card school or a game of pitch and toss at any street corner. I don't need to join the League of the Cross.'

'Well, I've heard that the AA can work wonders.'

'For fuck's sake . . .'

'No, for your good wee wife's sake. You regularly batter her silly. Last time you would have killed her if I hadn't stopped you. You nearly killed me. You're getting worse, Scobie. You know you are.' Frank leaned eagerly forward, one hand pushing back his hair. 'Now listen, there's a man in my office who's an alcoholic. He doesn't make any secret of the fact that he's a member of Alcoholics Anonymous. It's worked for him. Maybe it could work for you, Scobie.'

Scobie sighed. 'I know you mean well, son, and I know I should give up and I will give up. I promise you.'

Frank banged back on his chair again. 'Oh shut up, Scobie. We're all sick of your stupid promises.'

'No. This time I mean it, Frank.'

'OK. It's up to you, Scobie. But as I say, I hope you realise you're not only harming yourself but your family. *And* you're losing friends. *And* things are going to get tougher. After what you did to Constable MacLean's face the police are more likely to kick you down the stairs, down the whole length of Turner Street and Garngad Road, the next time they come to arrest you.'

'This is one hell of a way to speak to a man when he's just come out of hospital. It's not Christian.'

'And don't get it into your head,' Frank went on, 'that Father Riley will believe you either. You've had a beating from him before, Scobie, and you're very likely to get one again.'

'OK. OK. First thing after Mass tomorrow I'll go and see Father Shannon. Just to see what he has to say about the League of the Cross. I'm not promising any more than that.'

'How about the AA? I could go with you.'

'Let me sleep on that, son. I mean – it's such a terrible disgrace.'

'What?' Frank rolled his eyes and smacked a palm to his brow. 'You that's beaten your wife? You that's fought with all your friends? You that's vomited all over the place, been scraped up from the gutter – you think going to the AA is a disgrace?'

'Well, you know what I mean.'

'No, I don't know what you mean, Scobie.'

After a few seconds Scobie half-laughed and said, 'A lot of us used to think – I mean, not just me, even your own da – that you were a bit of a weak-kneed jessy with all that poetry and stuff. But you're not, are you, son?'

'Scobie, you can be tough inside without looking tough on the outside, or by taking part in violence. Anyway, toughness of any kind isn't the be-all and end-all of everything.'

'It is in Glasgow, son.'

'You only know one part of the city, Scobie.'

'It's where I live.'

'Your life could change – but it's up to you.'

Scobie sighed. 'OK. We'll give it a whirl.'

206

'The AA. Good man!' Then, seeing the worried apprehension in Scobie's eyes, Frank added, 'Don't worry, I'll come with you. We'll just look in and see what goes on. As I say, it's entirely up to you.'

Bridie's curiosity had got the better of her feelings of hopelessness. She'd been listening at the kitchen door. Frank found her when he was on his way through to the room. Once they'd shut the door behind them, she said, 'Oh Frank, do you think it'll work this time?'

Frank flung himself on to the bed and shielded his eyes with one hand for a few seconds. 'I don't know. I can't be by his side watching him all the time. If I can just get him to the AA, I think that's his best chance. This man in my office says it worked for him. Of course it's alcoholics helping one another. They know what it can be like. No doubt they'll keep an eye on him when I can't. I've my work to go to.'

'You've done wonders already. By the way, did you see Michael?'

'Yes, it's true enough. He's packed in his job. He's going to do the rounds of the booths. He reckons that way he'll make some money and escape from You-Know-Who.'

'Talking about jobs – Doris has gone back to work in Daly's. You wouldn't have thought she needed to, would you? I mean they're not like us. I need to go out for the money because we're saving up.'

'I expect she couldn't stand being cooped up in Blackhill all day and every day. I don't blame her.'

'Come to think of it, Frank, I wouldn't like to be cooped up here all day and every day. Especially if you weren't with me. I could stand anything just as long as we're together.'

He smiled over at her, his eyes becoming dreamy. 'I love you. And one day I'm going to take you out of all this. You're going to have a lovely roomy house with high carved ceilings and deep pile luxurious carpets on the floor.'

She'd heard it all before so many times – word for word.

'Everything your heart desires, Bridie, you will have. I promise you.'

'Yes, dear,' Bridie said, but her heart was heavy. Frank had little enough time for his writing after he came home from a hard day's work. Now some of that precious time was going to be taken up by struggling to keep Scobie on the straight and narrow. If anyone could sort Scobie out, Frank could. But even so, she feared it was a hopeless task. They were on a slippery slope, her and Frank. They were being dragged down. Frank wasn't getting the chance he deserved. More and more she feared nothing but a black pit awaited them. Frank couldn't see it. Part of his life, part of his mind, was separate from her – lost in the images of his fiction. He had another world in his head to which he could withdraw, escape. It was a world that gave him enormous pleasure and satisfaction, despite the hard work involved. In his world he could give life a unity, a meaning, a shape to suit the purpose of his fiction.

Maybe the getting away from Turner Street, maybe the dream house, the carpets, the furniture, the clothes – maybe all of that was no more than fiction.

She picked up her book, adjusted her spectacles, and began reading.

Chapter Thirty

They were sitting, one on either side of the kitchen fire. The fire was burning cheerily, but its brightness was not reflected in the faces of either Doris or Andrina.

'Talk about golf widows,' Andrina said. 'We're karate widows.'

Doris sighed. 'When it's not karate it's work with Bernard.'

'Robert's the same.'

'He doesn't work at nights, does he? Teaching's a day job.'

'It's supposed to be. But he's always bringing work home at night – to mark things, give assessments, write lectures, prepare future projects, things like that. Then there's Parent- Teacher Association nights at the school. At weekends he often takes pupils for painting and sketching trips. He says his workload is nothing compared with the English and Maths teachers. Like a lot of people, I used to think teachers had a right cushy job with such short hours, nine to four. I thought, what a walk-over. Nothing of the kind. It's the most stressful, demanding occupation. They need all the holidays they can get. Especially a conscientious teacher like Robert. He really cares about his pupils, worries about them.' It was her turn to sigh. 'They take up more of Robert's time and thoughts than I do.'

'Knowing how you feel makes me feel a wee bit better. I keep wondering if there's something terribly wrong with me.' Doris patted her lacquered confection of hair and tried to give a light-hearted laugh. 'I can't think what, but there you are.'

'There's nothing wrong with you, Doris. You're a very pretty girl.'

'Right enough he still wants me for love-making.' Despite her efforts to keep her voice light, it dropped into bitterness. 'If you can call it that.'

'It's different with men. They don't understand.'

'You're only a year older than me. What makes you an expert on men?' Immediately the words were out, Doris's face crumpled with distress. 'I'm terribly sorry, Andrina. I didn't mean to be nasty.'

'It's all right. It's just that Scotsmen are supposed to be notoriously bad at showing their emotions. They think it's being soft; they have to have this "hard man" image. But I suppose I was meaning how it is with Robert and me. I've no other personal experience. All I had before was romantic stories, and we shouldn't go by them. They're just a big con.'

'Definitely. Not one of them that I've ever read described the quick in-out-and-Bob's-your-uncle that Scotsmen call love-making.'

Both women suddenly hunched forward, overcome by a fit of the giggles. At last Doris managed, 'Sorry for being so terribly coarse and unladylike, Andrina. But some men drive you to it, don't they?' She lit up a Woodbine. 'I take it you still don't smoke.'

'My mother would have a fit.'

'She certainly knows how to lay down the law. A terribly strong character, is she?'

Andrina hesitated. 'She has very strong views.'

'Same thing.'

'I don't know. I worry about her a lot. She's so . . . so intense, so highly strung. She cares too much, I think. Especially about me. She phones me a couple of times every day. And I see her at least a couple of times a week.'

'You're an only child. I suppose that explains it. My ma always had too much on her plate – too many problems with my da, for a start – to have any time to bother about me. Or any of us, for that matter.'

'She would care about you just the same.'

Doris shrugged. 'God alone knows. It's the same with Bernard.' She avoided Andrina's eyes. Pride wouldn't allow her to admit to being totally unloved. 'I don't know if he cares much about me.' She blew smoke out and tossed her head back as if it didn't really matter.

210

'Oh Doris,' Andrina murmured, 'I'm sure he does.'

'You don't know him. He's Mister Charming when he's here. The perfect gent.'

Andrina didn't know what to say. The last time they'd all been having dinner together, Bernard had indeed been the perfect gentleman, although she'd found his reaction to certain innocent things she said a bit confusing and disturbing. When, for instance, she'd been trying her best to be a good hostess and asking each of them if they wanted second portions of anything or more wine, she'd said to Bernard, 'What can I do for you, Bernard?' His only reply was to raise an eyebrow and slide her one of his slightly amused sideways looks. Doris and Robert had been chatting to each other and hadn't noticed. It was nothing really. Yet it made her flush and quickly divert her attention away from him.

There had been one or two other little incidents like that – subtle, fleeting, and dangerous. She had not been able to relax until he and Doris had left.

Tonight, the four of them would be having dinner together again, after the men returned from the karate club.

'Did he mind you starting work again?' Andrina asked.

Doris puffed at her cigarette and shook her head as if not trusting herself to speak.

Andrina rose. 'They'll be back soon. I'd better put the potatoes on. How about an aperitif?'

'That would be terribly nice, I'm sure.'

They were still in the kitchen sipping their Martinis when the men returned, filling the small room, dominating it with bouncy swaggers, as if barely able to contain their enormous energy.

'What's for dinner?' Robert asked, rubbing his hands together. 'We're starving.'

Andrina went over to peer into pots and examine the contents of the oven. 'Robert, give Bernard a drink. Oh, and open the wine, please. I'll just get all this organised and on to the table. I've got baked ham with pineapple to start with, and apple pie with custard.'

'Sounds good. What'll you have, Bernard?'

'If you're opening the wine, a glass of that'll do.'

'Just plonk by your standards, Bernard. I can't afford champagne on a teacher's wages.'

'I've told you. You can get a job with me any day.'

Robert laughed. 'I've certainly got plenty of experience with crowd control for a start. When the kids get out at so-called playtime, it's like releasing a crowd of wild animals. My mother tells me it was never like that in her day. According to her they were too afraid of the teachers even to make a noise in the playground. Not that I believe her. At least not to that extent.'

'I was afraid of you when I was a kid,' Bernard said.

'Never! You've never been afraid of anybody in your life, Bernard. You were a right tearaway when you were a kid. I'm not that old, mate. I remember.'

Bernard grinned. 'Well, let's say all the kids, myself included, respected you.'

'That's better.' Robert raised his glass. 'Here's to your continuing success.'

Bernard took a sip of wine. 'Thanks. It's not all plain sailing, but I'm getting there.'

'Where?' Doris suddenly butted into the conversation. 'Getting where?'

'Where I want to go.'

'Oh? And where's that, Bernard? I'd be terribly interested to know.'

'Soup's out,' Andrina announced. 'Sit in, everyone. Have a glass of wine, Doris. Doris and I were having a lovely chat while we were on our own, weren't we, Doris?' She hastily filled Doris's glass, knowing from past experience that drink put Doris into a more happy and relaxed mood.

'This is delicious,' Bernard said. 'I know I've told you before but you really are an excellent cook, Andrina.'

'Thank you.' Andrina felt pleased. She was proud of her talent in the kitchen. She had her mother to thank for that. Sophie was up to cordon bleu standard, really first class. She'd never formally taught Andrina, but Andrina had watched her mother's culinary efforts with great interest. She had picked up a lot of tips just by watching and admiring.

The sweet (one of Robert's favourites) was another triumph for which everyone congratulated her. By the time it was consumed much wine had flowed. Robert had very quickly had to open another bottle. And then another. Everyone was getting very merry.

They had brandy with the coffee. Robert and Bernard had two brandies. Eventually Bernard said, 'My God, Robert. I forgot I was driving. I hope there's no cops about. I can't afford to lose my licence or get into any trouble with the police in my line of business.'

'What the hell,' Robert said with a somewhat drunken wave of his hand. 'Stay overnight. We've a spare room.'

Doris giggled. 'Great. But there's only one teeny wee problem. I haven't brought a nightie.'

'Andrina can lend you one, can't you, darling?'

'Yes, of course,' Andrina murmured. She suddenly felt stone cold sober.

Doris said, 'I'd have to leave here not later than eight-thirty in the morning. Daly's like their young ladies to be ready to start work a wee bit before nine.'

'I'll give you a lift in,' Robert said. 'We'll let Bernard have a long lie, seeing he's a night bird. Unless you've any early jobs on tomorrow, have you, Bernard?'

'I'll stay on one condition.' Bernard winked at Robert. 'And that's if Andrina gives me breakfast in bed.'

'Sure, sure,' Robert laughed. 'Nothing but the best of service in this house.'

Andrina felt herself flush. She desperately fought to appear calm. 'I'll do nothing of the kind. What do you think I am?'

'Darling, we were only joking.' Robert was obviously enjoying the joke. He was drunk. She felt annoyed with him for being so stupid.

Doris too – equally blind, equally stupid – was laughing. 'Quite right, Andrina. Don't encourage him.'

'Encourage him?' Caution smoothed out Andrina's voice.

213

Doris said, 'He doesn't need any encouragement to be the typical Scotsman who thinks the little woman is just there for his convenience – to serve him hand and foot, to use when and as he pleases. Just part of his goods and chattels. It's terribly old-fashioned, but there you are . . .'

'Andrina doesn't know anything about that type of man, Doris,' Robert said. 'She's married to me, remember?'

'Ooh.' Doris widened her mascaraed eyes. 'Modest with it, isn't he?'

'I'd better start the washing up.' Andrina began stacking the dishes.

'Oh, leave those till the morning,' Robert said. 'You'll have all day tomorrow to wash them. It's late. Let's all get to bed.'

Andrina rolled her eyes. 'I've nothing else to do all day tomorrow, of course.'

'I'll give you a hand with them tomorrow before I leave,' Bernard said.

Robert put his arm around her waist. 'Go on. Take Doris through and fix her up with a nightie and whatever else she needs. I'll lock up and be through in a minute.'

In the spare room with Doris, Andrina could hear the two men laughing together in the kitchen. Deep, rumbling male sounds. She imagined she detected a coarseness. She wondered if they were telling each other vulgar jokes. The mood Robert was in, she wouldn't put it past him. He was always different in Bernard's company – rougher, tougher – not the quiet, artistic, sensitive Robert she knew. She experienced a violent spasm of hatred towards Bernard. Then fear at the thought of being alone in the house with him next day. It seemed impossible to face such a prospect. Utterly impossible. Doris was chatting away to her but she wasn't listening. Her mind was darting desperately about. At last a solution occurred to her. First thing in the morning she'd slip next door and ask Josie to come in and stay with her until Bernard left.

She was so relieved at the thought, as soon as she went to bed and her head hit the pillow, she sank into a deep sleep. Too deep.

214

When she woke up, Robert had gone from her side. She lay listening, totally alert now, and apprehensive. She heard Doris and Robert call out to Bernard, 'See you later'. She heard the outside door close. She was alone in the house with Bernard. The realisation made her heart race in alarm. The whole bed seemed to reverberate with the beat of her pulse.

She heard his footsteps cross the hall and fade. Into the other bedroom? Or the kitchen? She strained to listen. The footsteps grew nearer again. The bedroom door opened and Bernard came in. He stood over her, holding a cup of tea. 'Morning, sleepy-head. I've brought you some tea.' He wore nothing but a pair of white cotton underpants. His tanned, muscular body was acutely disconcerting and frightening.

She was suddenly aware too of how she must look – her tousled hair, her lack of make-up. Embarrassment added to her other emotions. As she pushed herself further up on her pillow in order to drink the tea, he sat down on top of the covers. She shivered, unsure whether it was caused by the cold air on her bare shoulders and arms, or if it was her apprehension.

'Cold?' He reached out to rub her arms and shoulders.

'I'm all right.' She shrank back into the pillows and tried to concentrate on finishing the cup of tea. But she couldn't stop herself from babbling in between sips. 'I don't usually bother with tea. I'm an early riser, as a rule. I don't know what went wrong this morning . . . I'm usually up and making Robert's breakfast long before he's up. He should have wakened me. It's most unlike him to rush out like this without any breakfast . . . He must have slept in too. Of course, we were very late last night and we all had more than the usual to drink . . .' She couldn't stop.

Eventually he took the cup and saucer from her and laid it on the bedside table. Then he just sat staring silently down at her until her skin prickled with heat under his careful scrutiny. Then, with one easy movement, his mouth was on her with a tender passion she had never experienced before. Through his lips she called out, 'No . . . no, this is wrong . . .'

215

All she could picture in her mind's eye was her mother's face looking down at her in horror.

Her mother and God.

Chapter Thirty-One

As Bernard eased back from her, she saw that his face had changed. His features, normally hard-edged, had softened. His eyes had lost their cold menace. Instead, from them waves of tenderness washed over her. She knew then, despite her protestations, that she already belonged to him. Nevertheless, as soon as his lips covered hers again, she struggled and tried to move away. But suddenly, without any apparent fumbling or movement, his big frame engulfed her. He was pushing inside her. She was stunned, yet at the same time physically aroused. Mind and body became a mad merry-go-round of conflicting, confusing thoughts, emotions and sensations. She was horrified and panic-stricken. At the same time her body opened and revelled in hysterical ecstasy. As his thrustings grew faster and deeper, she heard herself make coarse, uninhibited animal noises.

Eventually they both cried out in unison. Then he withdrew and began gently kissing her eyes, her cheeks, her nose, her neck, while whispering over and over again, 'I love you . . . I love you . . . I've always loved you . . . You're so soft and feminine and adorable . . . You hold me like a velvet vice . . . My adorable little velvet . . .'

Shock and horror returned and she began to struggle to free herself of him. 'Please let me go. Please go away. This is so wrong.'

'No. We love each other. That can't be wrong.'

Somehow she got out of the bed, fled to the bathroom and locked herself in. She slumped against the door. Unable to bear the guilt, she tried to pretend to herself, despite the ecstasy still pulsing inside her, that nothing had happened. Eventually she persuaded herself that what had happened hadn't been her fault. She had nothing to blame herself for. She would not be the recipient of God's wrath for condoning the sin of adultery. She had been raped. Admittedly it had been a loving rape, but a rape nevertheless.

'Andrina, darling, are you all right?' Bernard shook the door handle.

'Please go away, Bernard.' Then, to make sure he'd go, she lied with feeling, 'My mother said she was coming for coffee this morning. I'd die if she arrived and found you here. Even the thought makes me feel sick. But I'll be all right as long as you go away.'

She heard him sigh through the door. 'All right, for your sake. But I'll be in touch soon.'

She listened to his heavy tread across the hall. Then the outside door shut. Still she felt apprehensive. Very gently she creaked the bathroom door open. The silence in the shadowy hall reassured her. She hurried across to the kitchen, praying as she passed the phone that it wouldn't ring. She made herself a cup of strong coffee and sat hunched over it, nursing it, trying to sort out her thoughts. But her thoughts had become a dark whirlpool of guilt and fear.

She was illogically certain that her mother would know. The certainty tightened her into a tense ball, waiting for the phone to ring. When it did suddenly jangle into life, it sent her rushing to the sink to violently retch and vomit. At the same time the phone kept exploding in harsh bursts of sound, filling the house with its relentless insistence.

She went to answer it eventually but had to lean against the wall, she felt so weak and faint.

'Darling, are you all right? I'm phoning from the box in Garngad Road. I was worried.'

'Just leave me alone.'

'Darling Andrina, I love you.'

She replaced the receiver as if it was burning her fingers.

Hurrying through to the bathroom she ran a bath and threw in plenty of perfumed bath salts. Her mother might arrive at any moment and smell sex on her. She realised she was being ridiculous. It was Friday, her mother's turn of having the daily coffee morning shared by the ladies of the Guild in Bearsden.

218

Her mother couldn't possibly arrive on the doorstep this morning. It didn't matter.

Perfume rose with clouds of steam from the bath, thickening and sickening the air. Andrina lay in the hot water, trying to purify herself physically and mentally.

Beginning to relax, despite herself, she remembered the smooth flowing, then quick ecstasy of Bernard inside her, and marvelled at it. It was something she had never felt with Robert. She closed her eyes, remembering Robert and Doris, but they were only a passing thought. Her mother was by far the most overpowering concern. It was as if her mother was there in the flesh, her flinty eyes narrow with disgust and hatred. And behind her, a dark ominous shadow of a vengeful God. Nothing could blot out that face, those eyes. After bathing and dressing, Andrina tried to keep herself as busy as possible, to concentrate on other things. She was grateful for the debris of the night before: the dirty dishes cluttering the round table in the dining alcove in the kitchen; the pots and oven dishes lying on top of the cooker and on the draining-board at the side of the sink, food hardening round the edges; the crushed table napkins; the crumbs on the floor.

She set about clearing up and washing the dishes at breathless speed. Instead of just sweeping and mopping the floor, she got down on her knees as a sort of penance and thoroughly scrubbed every corner of it. Then she went through to the two bedrooms and forced herself to strip off the beds and remake them with clean sheets and pillow-cases. She stuffed the other sheets into the washing machine, convinced that they smelled of sex.

By lunchtime the house was immaculate, the sheets were folded over the clothes horse in front of the fire, and she couldn't think what else to do. She didn't feel like anything to eat, but forced herself to heat some soup left over from the night before. While she was absent-mindedly eating it the phone rang, making her nerves jangle into life again. She went through to the hall and stood staring in anguish at the instrument before gingerly lifting the receiver to her ear.

'Hello?'

'You took your time answering.'

'Oh, it's you, Mummy.'

'Who did you think it would be? Were you expecting someone else to call?'

'No, I wasn't thinking. I've been doing a bit of spring cleaning.'

'It'll soon be Christmas.'

'You know what I mean.'

'You and Robert will be coming here for Christmas lunch, I hope.'

'Oh yes, thanks, Mummy.'

'I'm inviting Robert's mother as well.'

'That's kind of you.'

'She'd be on her own otherwise.'

'Yes.'

'Are you all right?'

'Of course.'

'You sound as if you're not all there.'

Andrina affected a laugh. 'What a thing to say.'

'How did last night go?'

'Last night?' Her voice tightened warily.

'You had people to dinner – you said.'

'Oh, but I told you when you phoned last night. They enjoyed the meal, everything went well. I told you what I made. For starters we had . . .'

'Who were these people?'

'Mummy, I told you – a friend of Robert's from the school, and his wife.' In a way it wasn't a lie and so she could say the words with some conviction. 'How are you, Mummy? How did your coffee morning go?'

'Fine. Fine.'

It was Andrina's turn to detect something wrong, something subtle she couldn't place. 'Are you all right, Mummy?'

'Why shouldn't I be all right?'

'You always go to such extremes. I hope you aren't overdoing things. Did you bake for the coffee morning ladies?'

'I certainly wouldn't dream of offering anyone shop cakes and I hope you never do either. You never know what's in bought stuff.'

A silence followed. Unusual for her mother. 'Are you still there, Mummy?'

'Yes.'

'Are you sure you're all right?'

'A bit over-strained, that's all. There are very high standards to live up to in a place like Bearsden. I have to be extra careful.'

'Nobody could have higher standards than you, Mummy. You've nothing whatsoever to worry about on that score. You're a wonderful housekeeper, a superb cook, a conscientious Christian . . .' Andrina gave a short laugh. 'If anyone needed character references for the place, yours would be absolutely impeccable.'

'I've always done my best,' her mother said, and there was another silence.

'Do you want me to come over and see you today?' Andrina asked.

'No. I'll see you and Robert on Monday. I'll have to go now. I'll phone again tonight.'

'Take care, Mummy.'

'Why do you say that?' The usual edge of suspicion returned to Sophie's voice.

Andrina sighed. 'Just because I love you and want you to keep safe and well.'

'Come straight after you've been to church. Our church here is just along the road, so I'll be home long before you get here and have everything ready before you and Robert arrive.'

'I'll look forward to it, Mummy.'

The phone clicked. For a few seconds, Andrina stood looking at it. There was this almost psychic thing between her mother and herself. Usually it only worked the one way. That is, Sophie seemed to immediately tune in to the worried wavelengths of her daughter. This time it was the other way around. Something was worrying her mother and, Andrina felt certain, it wasn't just about her.

221

In a way she was glad of the distraction, to take her mind off herself and the enormity of what had happened. It helped too to pay a visit to Josie next door and have a cup of tea and a chat before going out to buy something for Robert's tea. At least she could feel safe for half an hour or so in Josie's, knowing that her mother couldn't burst in and discover her, although it occurred to her that her life – certainly her relationship with her mother –was becoming more and more based on deceit. Deceit had taken root, and was growing like a pernicious weed, more and more out of her control.

She longed to confide in Josie about Bernard, but she felt sick at the thought. Later, when she was travelling into town, or while she was strolling around the shops, there were times when her spirits lightened and she began to forget about what had happened. For brief moments she actually felt happy. Then the memory would suddenly flood back and she would feel sick again. It hadn't been a dream. Yet it was impossible to believe. And all the time her body betrayed her by aching for Bernard to hold her, to engulf her again.

'Oh God, please forgive me,' she kept thinking. 'Oh God, don't let my mother find out.'

She had a meal of the best fillet steak waiting for Robert, and she greeted him with unusual warmth. They had never been all that demonstrative with each other.

He laughed. 'To what do I owe this special treatment?'

'What do you mean? Can't I just make you a nice meal and kiss you hello without being questioned?'

'Calm down. I was only joking.'

'Sorry. For a minute I thought you sounded like my mother.'

'Your mother?' Robert echoed incredulously.

'Suspicious – you know how she's always questioning me.'

'She cares about you. Dotes on you. I suppose you could say we have that in common.'

'She phoned earlier. I thought she sounded . . . I don't know . . . a bit worried.'

'Tell me something new. Your mother's a worrier, especially about you.'

'No, this time I thought it wasn't just me.'

'What made you think that? What did she say?'

Andrina shrugged. 'Probably it was just my imagination.'

She was glad of the diversion. Glad that Robert enjoyed the steak and had two helpings of chocolate mousse.

Later, in bed, they made love and she tried to be as affectionate as possible. Making love with Robert had never been in any way unpleasant. On the contrary, she had always believed it to be perfectly adequate. She realised now that this was only because she'd had no other experience to compare it with. She kept thinking about the other experience as Robert made love to her, kept struggling to purge the image of Bernard from her mind.

'I must never, never, allow such a thing to happen again.' She repeated the words to herself like a mantra. 'Never, never, never.' She would never even wear that nightdress again. It was made of green silk, low cut to show her cleavage, and trimmed with lace. It had a split up each side to the top of her thighs, the slits also trimmed with lace. She loved beautiful, sensual underwear. It was something her mother no longer could see and in which she felt free to indulge. She always kept her underwear in a locked drawer just in case her mother ever decided to poke about in the bedroom. If her mother found a locked drawer Andrina could always pretend that it contained Robert's papers for the school.

Lies. Lies. Lies. They were the eggs she had to continually walk on.

'I love you,' she said to Robert. But he was already sound asleep.

Chapter Thirty-Two

Even going along the few yards to the shops, the respectable Bearsden shops where she met respectable Bearsden people, was spoiled. Sophie hurried along like a criminal, eyes furtively, apprehensively darting around. In the shops she was absent-minded, forgot what she'd come for, didn't hear the assistant speaking to her, jumped when someone said hello.

She kept struggling to quell her panic, kept telling herself that her filth of parents weren't the only ones in the world with Noble for a second name. How ironic the name was, how totally inept. Noble. Noble, of all things! Of all things, noble they were not. She was afraid to make any enquiries. Afraid of what she might find. Yet she was obsessed with finding, ferreting out. She had to know. She couldn't live with the fear, the disgrace, of suddenly being confronted, being claimed by them in public. She had to know from where to hide.

She kept urging herself to have some common sense. Her fears were illogical. They had last set eyes on each other when she was a small child, a lifetime ago. How could they recognise her? How could she recognise them?

Oh, she would recognise them all right. Their disgusting behaviour had been carved with a red hot poker on her mind. She burned with hate at the thought of them. The fire of her hatred had never been quenched.

She had prayed a thousand times that they were dead, and now she prayed for their death with even more fervour. Going to church had become an agony almost beyond endurance, in case she would suddenly come upon them in the congregation. Especially the service on Christmas Day.

'Are you feeling all right, Sophie?' McPherson asked. As usual they were walking along a little apart, he with a leather-gloved hand holding his bible, she clutching her handbag.

Sophie was so abstracted she didn't hear him. He did not speak louder, but injected his voice with more urgency.

'Sophie!'

'What?'

'Is there something wrong? You look so tense and anxious.'

'Do I?'

'I thought you were looking forward to Andrina and Robert and Jean coming for Christmas lunch.'

Christmas had gone right out of her head. Spoiled. Forgotten. Irrelevant. Oh, she'd prepared the lunch. The Christmas pudding and the cake had been made ages ago, in another, happier world. The soup, the turkey and all the trimmings she'd prepared yesterday. It all had been done automatically, as if in a dream.

'I am looking forward to them coming. Everything's ready. I told them to come after church.'

'You haven't seemed well for some time. I think you should see Doctor Manders. He seems a nice chap. Remember we met him at the Allisons' bridge party?'

Doctor. Doctor. Take a few minutes from your bridge party with the Reverend Dinwoodie and his genteel little wife, and cure me of my putrid, perverted parents. 'It's my nerves,' she said. 'I haven't been sleeping too well recently. Once all the excitement of Christmas and New Year's over, I'll be able to relax.'

'Old Manders might be able to give you something.'

A couple of doses of Belladonna poison to help Duncan and Agnes Noble die in the agony they deserve? 'I'll see. But I'll have to wait until after the holidays now. I expect his surgery will be closed over Christmas and New Year.'

'Phone and ask.'

'On Christmas Day?'

'Well, as soon as you can. You look like death, Sophie, and you seemed absolutely radiant with good health for a while. Something's gone wrong.'

'All right. All right,' she hissed at him. They were approaching the church now and she was obsessed with her private

225

agony. People were streaming through the gates from all directions, stylishly dressed, carefully coiffured, dignified, smiling people. People content with their lot. The sound of car doors shutting made an orchestra with the chiming of the church bells. From inside the church the organ added its richer, deeper notes.

Happy, happy day, the whole orchestra proclaimed.

God, oh God, don't let it be them, Sophie kept praying. Have mercy. Help me. Let them be dead.

The church was packed; the pews in the middle, at the sides, up on the balcony were all full. They sat downstairs near the back. The front pews were all private, booked and paid for. Sophie's eyes scannned all the heads. She couldn't see them. Unless they were upstairs. Unless it wasn't them at all. All during the service she prayed it wasn't them at all.

Later, after she'd arrived safely home, she was able to relax with relief. Putting the last touches to the lunch kept her busy. She was able to greet Andrina and Robert and Robert's mother in a bright and cheerful manner.

'Happy Christmas, Mummy.'

'Happy Christmas, Andrina. Happy Christmas, Robert. Happy Christmas, Jean. Come away in.'

She hurried her greetings. McPherson was the one to do the kissing and back-slapping on such occasions, not her. Any physical display in public she regarded as embarrassingly indecent, worryingly unchristian.

Once coats and hats had been put away and the guests settled beside the fire, McPherson offered them what they had both come to call 'a little refreshment'. Sophie had always been against drink and had often in the past nagged McPherson about his indulgence in it. In Bearsden, however, it seemed one of the civilised things to do: to have 'a little refreshment'. After all, it said in the bible, 'a little wine for the stomach's sake'. An aperitif was the thing before lunch or dinner, wine with a main meal, a brandy or a liqueur afterwards. At least, when one had guests.

Andrina and Robert had a Martini. McPherson had a

whisky and lemonade and Sophie and Jean sipped at sherries. There were two bottles of wine to have with the meal, a claret and a chardonnay. The white was chilling in the fridge. The red had been opened to breathe at room temperature.

There were crimson and gold crackers and yellow and orange and green and blue paper hats. It was a merry and enjoyable meal. Everyone complimented Sophie on it. The only complaint was that they'd eaten too much. Afterwards, they opened all the presents.

Robert gave McPherson a box of cigars which he much appreciated. He had acquired a taste for a good cigar, although he still smoked his pipe when relaxing at home. The cigars were normally kept for special occasions, either when visiting in Bearsden or after business meals in the city or elsewhere.

Sophie gave Andrina a leather-bound, gilt-edged copy of *A Life of Christian Self-Denial* by Lady Jessica Ford-Smythe.

Robert, Andrina and Jean Anderson stayed for a late-afternoon tea – Earl Grey tea, turkey sandwiches, Chistmas cake and chocolate peppermint creams. A lovely time was had by all.

'You must all come to me at New Year,' Jean Anderson said.

'No, no. Please come to me,' Andrina pleaded. 'We had New Year lunch at Adelphi Street last time. It's our turn, isn't it Robert?'

'Definitely,' Robert agreed. 'We insist. New Year's lunch at Monteith Row.' They always made it lunch rather than an evening meal for Sophie and Jean's sake. They didn't like to be out late.

The invitation was accepted and goodbyes were said. Another kissing, back-slapping, hand-shaking performance from McPherson, and another hasty wave and shrinking away from Sophie. She waved again from the window as Robert and Andrina and Jean walked along Drymen Road to the bus stop.

'I should have run them home,' McPherson said.

'You did offer.'

'I know, but I should have insisted.'

'Too late now. There's the bus.'

227

'You'd think Robert could afford a car by now. Even a second-hand one.'

'You know how poor a teacher's wages are. He dresses well, thank goodness. Both of them do.'

'Yes, he's a decent chap. But Andrina could have done better. She's a fine-looking girl.'

Except for the Noble red hair and green eyes. The words were a bitter sneer in Sophie's mind. 'Yes, she could have been the wife of Doctor James Honeyman. Such an elegant gentleman with that carnation he always wears in his lapel. Or the wife of that wealthy lawyer, Blair Matheson. Think of it. She could have been mistress of one of those lovely big villas on Roman Road.'

McPherson sighed his regret along with hers. 'Pity. Yes, a great pity. Such a lovely girl, she could have had the very best.'

Before she'd left, Jean had insisted on washing up all the lunch and tea dishes. Andrina had dried them while Sophie put everything away in its proper place.

After they left, however, and McPherson had settled himself in front of the television (a new acquisition and much enjoyed), Sophie went through to the kitchen and washed all the dishes over again. She trusted no one to clean anything really thoroughly and conscientiously but herself. Then she hoovered the dining room carpet, examining under the table and chairs and sideboard and in every corner for any stray crumbs.

McPherson felt like calling out, 'Do you need to do that today – Christmas Day – a holiday?' But he saved his breath. He knew Sophie well enough to realise she *did* need to do it. No, she had more than a need to scour and clean and scrub and wash and hoover. It was an obsession. She was the same with her personal hygiene. He often said, if she could have steeped herself in bleach or disinfectant and boiled herself to sterilise herself, she would. She bathed and washed her hair every day – more than once a day, he suspected. And she had developed an absolute compulsion to keep scrubbing at her nails and hands.

He decided just to relax and enjoy a pipe and watch the Christmas variety programme. Sophie would come through and sit down when she felt she could. Even then, of course, her fingers would be busy, knitting or sewing or darning or mending. This time she came through and, much to his chagrin, seemed to want to talk.

'Remember the Reverend Dinwoodie mentioned the Nobles?'

'Yes.'

'Did he say anything else to you?'

'You were there.'

'You've played golf with him since then.'

'Yes, but . . .'

'Well, did he mention them then?'

'I don't think so.'

'Think, think, think now.'

'For goodness sake, Sophie, there's surely no need to get so worked up.'

'Did he mention their first names?'

'Why do you want to know? You don't believe they could be relations of yours, do you? You told me . . .'

'Never mind what I told you. Did he mention their first names?'

McPherson puffed at his pipe in silence for a few seconds. Then he said, 'No. The Nobles have never been mentioned since that night of the dinner.'

'I wonder how I could find out. I've *got* to find out. I can't stand it any longer.'

'Can't stand what any longer? Sophie, is there something I ought to know?' He felt suddenly uneasy, apprehensive.

She hesitated, wringing at her hands, her eyes twitching vaguely about.

'Sophie!' He had known there was something wrong. He could only hope it was nothing that might affect his good reputation.

'All right. All right. Maybe I should have told you. But I never thought there would be any need. As far as I was concerned, my parents were dead. But in fact they might not be.'

'What the hell is that supposed to mean? They're either dead or they're alive – there can't be any "might" about it.'

'I was taken from them because they . . . they were not fit to be parents. I was taken into care, put in an institution. I never saw them again. I never wanted to see them again. They're dreadful people. Cruel, vulgar, common, wicked . . .'

'Good God! And you've not only lied to me – you've told the Pembertons, the Brodies, the Dinwoodies, and God knows who else in Bearsden, that your parents were dead.'

'Maybe they are,' she cried out wretchedly. 'I don't know.'

'But you think the Nobles. . . ? Good God, Sophie.'

'How can I find out? You'll have to help me, Andrew.'

'Calm down. I'll find out.'

'How? What will you do?'

'There's the electoral roll for a start. That'll give their full names.'

'Duncan and Agnes Noble.'

'Duncan and Agnes Noble,' he repeated after her. 'I'll find out. But what we're going to do if it is them, Sophie – God alone knows.'

Chapter Thirty-Three

The Alcoholics Anonymous office was up a dark and dirty stair in West Nile Street. Scobie promised he'd meet Frank there straight from work – straight from Frank's work, that is. Scobie finished work earlier than Frank.

Frank had to do a tax return or some sort of extra work this week, and he didn't get out of his office until after seven. He would just be able to grab a sandwich somewhere and reach Scobie in West Nile Street in time for quarter to eight.

The AA meeting started at eight, but when Frank had phoned they'd told him to come at about quarter to, so that he could have a cup of tea and meet everyone.

The AA office was round the corner from the Bay Horse pub, and Scobie decided he'd nip in for a pint before Frank arrived. He hadn't let on to Frank but he was up to high doh about the meeting. He really needed a drink. At first, arriving at the close in West Nile Street, he'd paced back and forth trying to work up courage. He'd cursed Frank for putting him into this agonising situation. At the same time he knew it wasn't Frank. Frank had left it to him.

Frank had said, 'Look at you, man. Look at you.' And that was enough. He knew how he looked. He knew what he was doing to himself. It hadn't mattered enough when he thought of what he was doing to Frank or to Carragh or to his family. It had been bad enough to know that he was hurting them physically, but it was his personal hurt that was really getting to him. He was hurting deep inside. He was lost. He was lonely. Even in a crowd, he was lonely. Even in bed with his wife he was lost and alone.

For the first time he could see, and he could accept in his own mind, that he needed help. He wanted help. But first of all he needed just one pint to give him the courage to go and get it.

He was still in the pub when Frank arrived.

'I thought I'd find you in here,' Frank said. 'OK, what's it to be, Scobie? Are you coming with me to the AA, or do I leave you here and let you end up in that gutter outside? It's up to you, wee man.'

Scobie nodded. For once the drink wasn't making him feel a big man with a swagger. He was still a wee man, and he was hell of a frightened one. He hadn't a clue why. But he growled, 'What the fuck are we standing here for? I said I was going, didn't I?'

They went along West Nile Street, in the close and up the stairs in silence. Both of them were afraid to say a wrong word.

In the office – which consisted of a biggish room with brown linoleum on the floor and some folding chairs – men and women were standing or sitting around in groups drinking tea and talking. A man at a small side table was pouring mugs of tea, only half filling them out of consideration for the recipients, so that they wouldn't spill the tea and draw attention to their shaking hands.

The man said to Frank as he handed him the mug, 'Hello there, my name's Jimmy. Have I met you? Have you been here before?'

'No, I'm Frank. I'm with Scobie, my father-in-law here.'

'Right, Scobie, havin' trouble with your bevvy, eh?'

'I suppose you could say that.'

'Well, you're in the right place. There's none of us will tell you you're an alcoholic. That's something you'll need to decide for yourself, but if you hang about with us, hear what we've got to say, and if you want what we've got to offer, it's there for you.'

'Fair enough.'

'I'm an alcoholic, but we'll see. You can come to this decision yourself. The meeting will be starting in ten or fifteen minutes. Do you want a cup of tea?'

'Aye, thanks, Jimmy.'

'Sit down, the pair of you.' Whilst pouring the tea, Jimmy turned his head and called across to a group nearby. 'Peter, do you want to come and talk? Here's Scobie. It's his first time.'

And as Peter came towards them he added, 'He's having a lot of trouble with the old booze.'

'It's sore, isn't it?' Peter said, sitting down beside Scobie. 'Well, up here you'll hear talk about it like you've never heard before in the pub. I suppose you've tried to stop drinking yourself, Scobie?'

'Aye,' Scobie said. 'Thousands of times.'

'I know, I know. You get up in the morning and you've made a right arse of it and you say – never again.'

Scobie shook his head. 'Oh, the times I've said that. Never again. I'll never touch another drop for the rest of my life.'

'We don't say that here, Scobie. We just stop drinking for a day at a time. You just say – I'm not going to take a drink today. I'm not going to ask you to stay away from a bottle of whisky, or a barrel of beer. I'm going to ask you to stay away from one drink for one day. It's as simple as that.' He looked round at Frank. 'Is this your boy?'

'No, it's Frank, my son-in-law.'

'Are you all right, Frank?'

'Yes, I can take it or leave it.'

'That's fine. Well, we're not interested in people who can take it or leave it. We're not even interested in people that should be stopping the drink. We're only interested in people that *want* to. You've got to *want* to stop.'

'I want to,' Scobie said. 'Christ, I want to. And that's the truth.'

'OK. But another thing to keep in mind, Scobie. It's no use stopping for the wife, or the boss, or for anybody else. You have to stop drinking for yourself. But don't worry, the wife'll benefit. Here, the meeting's going to start. We'll just turn our chairs round and face the front. That's Sam at the table. He's the chair. The man next to him is Tommy, he's tonight's speaker.'

Sam rose and gazed at the audience. He was a mild looking man in a well-cut suit and a waistcoat with a gold watch chain strung across it. He looked as though he'd never taken a drink in his life.

233

'Good evening, friends. My name's Sam and I'm an alcoholic. I want to welcome you all to this Monday night group of Alcoholics Anonymous, here in West Nile Street. I'd like to welcome anybody that's new, anybody that's struggling, anybody that's just come back. I don't want to take up much time because Tommy here is going to share his experience, strength and hope with us.' He picked up a piece of paper from the table. 'I want to read the preamble first. It tells us what Alcoholics Anonymous is and, just as important, it tells us what it isn't.'

Frank was impressed by the man's sincerity and the directness.

'The preamble goes like this,' Sam went on. 'Alcoholics Anonymous is a fellowship of men and women who share their experience, strength and hope with each other that they may solve their common problem. There are no dues or fees for AA. We are self-supporting through our own contributions. AA is not allied with any sect, denomination, political organisation or institution. It does not wish to engage in any controversy. Our primary purpose is to stay sober and help other alcoholics to achieve sobriety.'

Sam replaced the paper and waited for a few seconds to allow everyone to digest it. Then he said, 'Now, when you listen to Tommy's story, it is advisable to look for the similarities, not the differences. If Tommy was in the jail and you weren't, don't be saying to yourself – oh I'm not an alcoholic because I wasn't in the jail. If Tommy's *not* been in the jail, don't you be saying – oh I've been in the jail so I'm different from him.' Sam leaned forward, palms down on the table. 'Where you drink, what you drink, how much you drink isn't important. *It's alcohol.* This is the last card in the pack for us. We've tried the churches, psychiatrists, hospitals, signing the pledge, not signing the pledge, going to the pub half an hour before shutting time, going out with only a pound in our pocket. We've tried the lot. Nothing works. Nothing works except what you'll learn here. One last thing before I hand you over to Tommy – sit back and relax. Any worries you've got, lay them at the door. Any

234

religious concepts or any bigotries you've got, just lay them at the door – pick them up on your way out. All right, Tommy?'

Tommy lumbered to his feet. He must have been at least eighteen stones with an orange peel skin and a liberal sprinkling of dandruff on his navy blue duffle jacket.

'My name's Tommy and I'm an alcoholic . . .'

Afterwards, when Scobie and Frank were going down the stairs, Scobie said, 'You marked my card there, Frank.'

'How do you mean?'

'You told that Tommy bloke all the things that I've said and done. Don't try to deny it. That bloke wasn't talking about himself, he was talking about me.'

'But I didn't, Scobie. I swear it. I've never spoken to Tommy in my life. All I did was phone the AA number and ask what time the meeting was and if we could go along. That was all.'

'Aye, sure.'

'Scobie, as soon as we get home, I'll swear on the Holy Bible, on my Granny's grave – anything you like.'

Scobie lapsed into a worried silence. He was still silent and somewhat subdued when they arrived home. His mind was in turmoil. He was amazed. He had believed he was the only person in the world that said and did the things Tommy had admitted to. But there had been other things Tommy had been speaking about that Frank couldn't have known of – the hidden fears. Being afraid and not knowing what you're afraid of. Being lonely in a crowd. The hopelessness and despair.

Carragh was hovering about offering cups of tea, her eyes anxious yet hopeful. It was pathetic. He had no hope. He had stopped drinking before, for a day, for a week, even for as long as a month. A lot of good it had done him.

'How did you get on, Da?' Bridie asked.

Frank answered for Scobie. 'He's promised to go back tomorrow night. Haven't you, Scobie?'

'A lot of shit,' Scobie said.

Frank sighed. 'So you're not going to go. OK. Nobody's going to twist your arm.'

235

But he did go. Just to see how he'd get on without Frank at his elbow. Jimmy and Peter greeted him like old pals.

'There you are, Scobie. Just in time for a cup of tea. On your own tonight?'

'Aye. Just thought I'd drop in.'

'You're always welcome, Scobie.'

'I thought Frank had marked my card yesterday. There was that much Tommy was saying . . .'

'It sounded as if he was talking about you?' Jimmy interrupted.

'Aye.'

'And me,' Jimmy said.

Peter added, 'And me. And, Scobie, if you do hear anything that hasn't happened to you, add the wee word – "yet".'

Jimmy passed him a steaming mug of tea. 'You'll often find, Scobie, we all go down more or less the same road. The slide down into alcohol is like being on a bus. You can go to the terminus – and the terminus is premature death and a wet brain. But you can get off the bus whenever you choose.'

'That's right,' Peter agreed. 'You can sit here and listen to all the horror stories and say to yourself, I've never done that, but just add that wee word – "yet". That's *the* most important word to remember.'

Scobie took a slurp of tea. 'I don't remember what I've done half the time.'

'I used to be the very same,' Peter said. 'Many a night I went to bed with a Rita Hayworth and woke up beside an old witch. I've never gone to bed with an ugly woman, Scobie, but by Christ I've woken up with a few.'

Scobie couldn't contain a cackle of laughter, and Jimmy and Peter laughed along with him.

Then Peter turned serious again. 'But all the same, it's humiliating, Scobie, and it's even worse for a woman alcoholic. A woman was telling me at the meeting the other night how she used to wake up and have to search for her knickers and bra while a man lay snoring in the bed – a man she didn't know. As far as she was concerned, she'd never seen him in her life before.

Didn't even know where she was. Terrible for a woman, that. A terrible humiliation.'

'Aye,' Scobie agreed.

Then the meeting began and Scobie heard more stories. This time, after he got home, he told Carragh something about it.

'There was one man,' he said, 'told some story. My God, Carragh, you should have heard him. He's been in jail fifty-six times for drunkenness. I'm not as bad as that.'

'Aye, Scobie, but there's many a time you should've been in the jail and you weren't.'

It was then he remembered the times that Doris or Bridie wanted to send for the police and Carragh wouldn't let them.

He also remembered the wee word he'd been told that was so important. He should have said, 'I'm not as bad as that – *yet*.'

Chapter Thirty-Four

Bernard and Doris had come for a game of Scrabble and a bite of supper. They'd been enjoying the game. Bernard kept trying to get away with rude swear words that triggered off noisy but hilarious arguments and had them all checking the dictionary. Andrina kept trying not to blush. She marvelled at the nerve of Bernard accepting Robert's invitation to come again. It was awful to think what he'd done, and yet there he was – Robert's best friend, Doris's normal husband – just as if nothing had happened. Every time she looked at him, she felt truly shocked, absolutely appalled.

Despite this, she found herself being coquettish, giving him arch sideways glances. She was ultra-conscious of herself every time she moved. Walking over to the fridge to get Robert another beer, or to fill up the bowl of crisps, became an art form, a symphony of sensuality. Fear made her heart falter, yet still the sensuality remained. It was the way she turned her head, the slow movement of her fingers, the inward, caressing attention she gave to her breasts and hips when she walked, the leisurely way she crossed her long legs. Every part of her told him, told her, she had been awakened again.

They had their game of Scrabble at the table in the dining alcove in the kitchen. Then after the game, when they were clearing it away in readiness for supper, she went over to the cupboard for cups and saucers. Bernard followed her.

'Let me help you,' he said as she reached for the dishes. As he lifted them from the shelf he pressed his body against hers. She immediately drew away, shocked, frightened, heart thumping with the danger of it. And the excitement. They were all helping to set the table, laughing and bumping into one another, but when Bernard's body came against hers, there was a slowness to the movement. Every touch was a caress. Even passing the

238

salt during supper when his fingers brushed against hers – it was flesh to flesh, warm and suggestive. She tried not to look at him, to avoid him, head held high to purposely ignore him. Doris became the centre of her bright, polite attention. She laughed encouragingly at Doris's chatter about all the so-called amusing happenings in Daly's.

Doris would precede her stories with a flap of her scarlet-nailed hand and, 'I had to laugh. It was so terribly amusing . . .'

Andrina laughed, not knowing or caring what she was laughing about. She was amazed that neither Doris nor Robert seemed to be aware of the electricity sizzling in the space between her and Bernard.

Just before he and Doris left, Doris announced, 'Must pop into the little girls' room.' Robert went through to the bedroom to fetch the coats.

'We've got to meet,' Bernard said, coming towards Andrina. She pushed him away. 'Don't, please. This is awful. You mustn't.'

Yet only a few minutes previously, when she had been putting pots away in the cupboard under the sink, she had not kneeled down as she normally would. She had kept her legs straight and bent over, knowing that she was revealing herself up to her thighs, and lingering that second or two longer than was necessary.

Even when she was pushing him away and hissing at him in shocked tones, her body was still moving with sensual provocation.

'I'll call here tomorrow,' he said. 'Ten-thirty in the morning.' She just managed an anguished 'No' before Robert appeared with the coats.

That night she was in a fever of restlessness and apprehension. Previously she had gained some comfort from assuring herself that she hadn't really committed the sin of adultery. She had said no. She had struggled. She had fought to resist giving in to any feelings of pleasure.

She said her prayers, pleading yet again for God to forgive her.

Next morning, after Robert left, she bathed and perfumed her body. She brushed out all the tangles from her curls and applied her make-up with extra care because her hands were shaking so much.

Bernard arrived exactly on time, and for a few seconds of panic she thought she couldn't go and open the door. She simply wanted him to go away. She couldn't cope with such a dreadful situation. He knocked again, loudly, insistently. He wasn't going to go away. Somehow her legs carried her through the hall.

Every time she saw him now, she experienced a shock. It was like plugging into the electricity of life. Sharing her heightened sense of urgency, he led her straight to the bedroom, laid her across the bed and immediately lay on top of her. He kept repeating 'I love you, I love you', as he plunged inside her over and over again. She tried to remain passive, unmoved. In some strange twisted sense of morality, she didn't feel so guilty if she was denying herself pleasure from him.

He had reached a climax and was still on top of her when the doorbell jangled through the house.

'Dear God. Don't let it be my mother!'

Panic-stricken, she punched at him and fought herself free of his smothering weight. The bell jangled again as she jerked and tidied at her clothes. She ran out to the hall, then stopped to take a deep breath before opening the door.

'Hello, hen.' It was Josie. 'Can I come in a wee minute?' Josie always preceded her visits with this request. It heralded a normally enjoyable gossip about Josie's bar customers of the night before over a cup of tea or coffee and an Ayton Sandwich. Sometimes Josie appeared with a pot of tea or coffee. Today she was proffering a bag of biscuits.

'Oh, Josie, it's you.' Andrina nearly burst into tears of relief and, taking Andrina's pleasure at seeing her as an invitation, Josie came in and made straight for the kitchen.

'Here, you've slipped up today, hen.'

'How do you mean?'

'You haven't even the kettle on.'

Andrina's tremors of panic had not quite died away. She was confused. 'Did we arrange for this morning?'

'Did we arrange for this morning . . .' Josie echoed in disbelief. 'What's up? Lost your marbles or something? Last night, when you were seeing your visitors out and I came home from work, I said, "Tomorrow morning?" And you said, "Yes".'

Probably she did. Although she had no recollection of it. When Bernard was anywhere near her, she couldn't concentrate on anything or anyone else.

'Could you put the kettle on, Josie? I won't be a minute.' She shut the kitchen door behind her and hurried back to the bedroom. Bernard was standing staring out of the window.

'You'd better go,' Andrina whispered. 'It's my neighbour.'

Turning towards her he said, 'I'm going to move heaven and earth to snatch every moment I can to be alone with you.'

'Please, just go. And as quietly as you can.' Hastily she retreated back to the kitchen and shut the door again. Josie was putting the Ayton Sandwiches out on a plate. Ayton Sandwiches were their favourite biscuits.

'What happened then?' Josie asked. 'How did it go?'

'What do you mean?'

'No need to snap my nose off. What's up with you today?'

'Nothing. I don't know why, but I thought it was my mother at the door.' She had to laugh. 'It quite unnerved me.'

'Oh aye. With me due as well. That would have been a turn-up for the book, right enough. See them born-again Christians!'

'I'm afraid my mother thinks everyone who isn't is destined for hell – is half-way there already, in fact. If you decided to be saved, she'd probably accept you with open arms.'

'No thanks, hen. That would be like being pals with a piranha. I'll just take my chances and keep on my job at the pub.'

'How did you get on last night?'

'I didnae meet the man of my dreams, if that's what you mean. I wouldn't mind the Big Man, him that was visiting you last night.'

'Bernard?' Andrina feigned innocent unconcern. 'I told you, he's a friend of Robert's.'

'I know him and his brothers. Well, when I say I know them I mean they sometimes come into the pub. Occasionally he's come in with them. I haven't seen the Big Man for a while, though. I suppose with him being married and going up in the world as well. Although I haven't seen Frank or Michael or Tony either for a wee while. And Michael – that's the boxer one, Bernard's twin – he certainly likes his tipple.' She gave a hoot of laughter. 'His mother-in-law's Big Martha Stoddart. The last time he was enjoying a few drinks at the bar, she marched in and hauled him out. He's terrified of her. And him a champion boxer as well, and every bit as big as Martha. See us behind the bar, we nearly had a fit, we laughed that much!'

Andrina thought she heard the front door click shut. It helped her to relax. She made a pot of tea and put out the cups. 'I've never met any of Bernard's family, except his young brother Frank. I've heard about all of them from Robert. Bernard mentioned last night that Michael was fighting in fairground booths. Loves it, apparently. Can you imagine?'

'No. Getting punched about every day is no my idea of making a living. Funny both him and Michael being in violent kind of jobs. They don't look much like each other, but obviously they've some things in common.'

'I suppose. Help yourself to milk and sugar, Josie.' Andrina kept her eyes averted.

'Thanks, hen. That's a nice looking wee wife Bernard has. A bit too wee for him, I'd have said. But everybody to their own taste, I suppose.'

'Her sister Bridie married Bernard's young brother, Frank. It was quite an unusual wedding. Robert and I were the only other ones there.'

'Fancy! They're Papes as well. That's what Big Martha's got against Michael, I suppose. Poor sod. No wonder he loves travelling about with the booths. Gets him away from here. See mothers and mother-in-laws. A right torment, so they are!'

'My mother-in-law's really nice.' As she said the words,

Andrina's heart suddenly gave a flutter of fear. Jean Anderson lived just over the other side of the Green and the river. It didn't take her long to come across the bridge and along Monteith Row. It could have been her at the door this morning. 'She doesn't visit me very often.' She said the words out loud, trying to gain extra comfort from the sound of them. 'Even though she's just across in Adelphi Street.'

No extra comfort came. Guilt, fear, danger did a mad dance inside her.

The feverish heat of excitement was also awakened.

Chapter Thirty-Five

The age of miracles was not past. Scobie had not had a drink for over six months.

Every night he'd gone to the AA meetings. 'Ah've never missed one night,' was his regular boast now. The AA had become the most important thing in his life.

Patrick O'Maley had once said, 'You don't need to go to the AA, Scobie. Can you not use a bit of will-power?'

Scobie's reply to that was, 'Have you ever tried stopping diarrhoea with will-power?'

He had thought a lot about his drinking, and talked a lot about it at the AA. He'd come to the conclusion that he'd been obsessed with drink before he started drinking. He didn't know why.

His father took a drink, but only a few pints on a Saturday night. He had been a labourer in the gasworks. A muscly wee man he'd been, with a big walrus moustache and a laugh to match. Scobie remembered his father enjoying the parties they used to have in the house. His father's party piece, which he boomed out with great gusto, was a song about a model lodging-house. Why these doss-houses for down-and-outs were called models, no-one knew.

'When it's springtime in the model,
The model in Carrick Street,
The bugs begin to yodel and
Ye cannae get to sleep.
You get up to read the paper,
Or wash your dirty feet,
When it's springtime in the model,
The model in Carrick Street.'

Scobie remembered being loved by both parents. He looked back on his childhood as a happy one. They were poor, but then so was everybody else. He had never felt deprived.

But right from the start he'd had this obsession with the drink. He'd started at about fifteen. From then until his late twenties had been a honeymoon time. He could take it and hold it. Of course, during that time, he'd never taken too much. Not compared with his more recent years. Or at least, as far as he could remember. The trouble was, he could remember very little. He couldn't even remember the year he got married.

Nowadays, he could go into his old haunts, mostly the pub in Castle Street. He felt more at home there because it was the favourite of both his Garngad and his Blackhill pals. He could go in now and drink a glass of Irn Bru or any kind of ginger. He knew he had to keep off that first alcoholic drink, that one drink for just that one day. That was all he had to worry about.

Patrick was now saying to Michael, 'Can you no use a bit of will-power? Why can't you just take a few pints of beer or a few whiskies and leave it at that?'

Michael was in danger of careering down the same slippery slope that Scobie knew so well. He was going to end up punch drunk into the bargain if he went on with so many fights. Scobie had gone with Patrick on the road for a few days to watch Michael fight at the booths. He had been surprised at the size of the crowds that were always attracted by the barker's 'Hurrah, hurrah, hurrah . . . Who's going to challenge these great men?'

On the platform stood the line-up of pugs, including Michael, arms folded across his chest. In their colourful dressing-gowns they stood, crooked noses, torn and misshapen ears, daring anyone to challenge them.

'What Michael needs,' Patrick said, 'is a good manager and a really hard training session to get him fit enough for the big time.'

'What Michael needs,' Scobie said, 'is to get off the drink.'

'I keep telling him . . .'

'And I keep telling you, Patrick. Michael's like me. He can't just take a few pints or a few halfs. He mustn't touch it at all.'

Patrick sighed. 'Oh, I don't know. Would it do any good if you had a word with him, Scobie?'

Scobie thought this a bit of a joke. He could do damn-all with his own sons. Admittedly, thank God, they weren't all alcoholics. 'Sure, sure, no harm in trying.'

'The thing I can't understand,' Patrick scratched his thick bush of curly hair, 'why is he like that? I can take a good drink and leave it. So can Frank. So can Tony. So can Bernard. All good, sensible boys.'

Scobie thought that to include Tony, and even Frank, into this description was somewhat of an exaggeration. But Patrick was prone to get carried away at times. Out loud Scobie said, 'Did you know Frank's had another book of poems published and another story in some high-brow magazine.'

'Don't embarrass me. I've enough on my plate with Michael without worrying about Frank.'

'I'd better go.' Scobie rose in an energetic bouncing movement that matched the swagger of his walk. Since he'd stopped drinking he was aggressively fit. Even at his sixty years he could have taken on any of the pugs at the booths and given them a good go for their money. 'I'll see Michael as soon as I can.'

Out in Acrehill Street he took a deep breath of spring air – a somewhat risky thing to do in Blackhill with the gasworks, the railway, the dust and the litter floating about the place, to mention but a few hazards.

As it happened, Frank was coming in the opposite direction, thinking along similar lines. He'd heard his mother wasn't keeping well and had come over to pay a quick visit. He and Scobie met in the lane that cut in to the far end of Acrehill Street near the distillery. This was the way into Blackhill from Garngad.

'Hello there, son,' Scobie greeted him.

'Did you see Ma?' Frank's thin face was anxious.

'Naw. She was having a wee lie down. Your da and me were having a blether about Michael.'

'I'd better go and see how she is.'

'Aye, OK son. See you later.'

246

Frank raised a hand in agreement, turned off the lane and went loping along Acrehill Street. The place had got worse. He wondered if the changes were affecting his mother's health. Usually good-humoured if somewhat melodramatic, she had become tense and anxious and her voluptuous plumpness had melted away. She now had a slim figure. It wasn't normal for her. Even her thick mop of grey hair had thinned and hung limp and straggly about her face. Only her big, dramatic eyes were still the same.

She worried about Michael, who was making a real cock-up of his life. Big Martha had developed phlebitis and could no longer get out and around, so she wasn't the main problem in Michael's marriage now – as far as coming round to Bright Street or the pub and bullying Michael was concerned. Caroline and Michael had twins, a boy and a girl, Sean and Sally. Michael was apparently leading Caroline a terrible life – at least when he was the worse of drink, which according to Caroline was happening more and more often.

But Frank felt sure it wasn't just worry about Michael that was affecting his mother so much. After all, she'd had her share of worries with Bernard and Tony and indeed with himself. She'd come through all that, to all appearances unscathed. He believed that the biggest part of his mother's problem was her present environment. Blackhill had always depressed him, but at least at first it had been comparatively peaceful. Now all tranquillity that had ever been there had gone. Aggression had taken its place. The first post-war generation were in their teens now and sweeping aside all the old accepted values. Pop groups like the Beatles and, more aggressively, the Rolling Stones epitomised the radical changes in outlook of this new generation.

People now 'did their own thing'. They wore outlandish clothes, they did things and said things hoping to shock. They joined extremist cults in their efforts to find their 'inner selves'.

In Glasgow, gang warfare, violence and vandalism were becoming rife. And nowhere more so than in Blackhill. In the 1920s and 1930s the razor gangs fought one another. They were

247

never really a threat to the general public. Hard-core slum dwellers of that time, of which these gangs were a part, were the product of unhealthy, overcrowded houses, unemployment and undernourishment. As a result, they included debilitated people, low in energy and initiative. The problem since the fifties had become centred round youths who at least were reasonably well-fed. They had become vigorous, and were able to express their alienation and frustration at their bleak future through violence and vandalism, although they didn't consciously realise why they acted as they did. They had become a threat to a wider society.

Cars were stolen, brought into Blackhill, stripped of their valuables and set on fire. The streets were littered with burnt-out shells. Or they were driven into back courts off Acrehill Street and left to burn or rust away.

Despair and ruination hadn't been helped by the Glasgow Corporation, who'd crowded the area by building even more houses in Blackhill, using up any green spaces with no thought to the quality of life of the inhabitants. Also, no decent maintenance or repairs had been done to the older houses.

Frank wasn't sure who or what was most to blame. New houses fell into disrepair and neglect as soon as they were built. Gardens were left as pieces of dirt ground. Children dug holes in them. An old lady in the bottom flat had allowed Patrick to have her bit of garden and Patrick had managed to grow a few roses. He'd been really proud of them, but had thrown in the towel in disgust the day he'd found somebody had broken all their heads off. Now dogs urinated on every piece of ground fronting the tenements. Stairhead windows were smashed and left unrepaired. Wind howled through them and sent rain battering over landings and against doors. Closes were daubed with graffiti, a new phenomenon that was desecrating walls, bus shelters and even the walls of schools, and becoming more and more aggressive, more obscene. Stairhead coal cellar doors were smashed through and used as toilets by young delinquents. Back court middens were smashed into piles of rubble. The houses themselves had broken windows and flaking paint.

His mother had done her best to keep her house clean and decent but surrounded by such neglect in such a depressing desert of a place, was it any wonder that her health and her spirits had become affected?

His father opened the door to him. 'Scobie's not long away, son.'

'Yes, I met him in the lane. How's Ma?'

'A bit tired. She's having a lie down.'

'Is that you, Frank?' His mother's voice agitated through from the bedroom. 'I'm just coming, son.'

'Don't get up, Ma. I'll come through.'

'No, it's all right.' Panting for breath, she appeared in the doorway. 'I was just lying on top of the covers.' She was fully clothed, but her clothes hung loosely on her and looked crushed and shabby. At one time she'd had quite a flair for clothes. She never settled for dark colours, as so many women did, to give a slimmer silhouette. The vivid colours she favoured shouted to the world, 'To hell with it!'

'How are you, son? I'll make you a nice wee cup of tea.'

'Sit down, Ma. I'm fine.' He put his arm round her shoulders and led her through to the living room. 'More to the point, how are you?'

'I get a bit tired these days. Old age creeping on, I suppose.'

'Don't be daft. You're not old. You're in your prime. Isn't she, Da?'

'I keep telling her. There's not a finer looking woman in the whole of Blackhill and Garngad put together than my Maureen O'Maley.'

'Away with you,' Maureen laughed. 'I know you're dying to meet up with your pals. I'll be all right now Frank's here.'

'And Doris'll soon be in from the shop,' Frank added.

'Away you go, I said.'

Patrick did as he was told and left.

'He worries about me,' she explained after he had gone, 'but there's no need. I just get a bit of a headache now and again.'

'I worry about you, Ma. I wish you could get out of this place.'

'Where to, son? No use thinking of going back to Garngad. They're knocking it down. Anyway, I'd miss having a scullery and a bathroom. Although, mind you, I had many a happy day in my wee house in Garngad. Which is more than Michael and Caroline are having, it seems. Not that Caroline ever complains to me, but your da tells me Michael's drinking too much.'

'Any place would be better than here,' Frank said, his mind still haunted by the bleak surroundings. 'Even taxi drivers are refusing to take fares to Blackhill. And I'm sorry for the train drivers at the back there.'

It must have been a nerve-racking journey for the drivers passing along the back of Acrehill Street. They were under constant attack by all sorts of missiles and obstacles. Sometimes the track was blocked altogether and of course the cargoes were never safe.

'I keep telling your da,' Maureen sighed, 'but there's no stopping him and Tony when they get together. They gallop along like cowboys after these trains. The other night it was a whole crate of whisky they came back with. Your da never used to be like that. Honest as the day is long, my Patrick used to be.'

'Is Tony at home?'

'No, he's off again. To Newcastle, I think he said. He's with this new group.'

'I hope to God he doesn't still bang away at his drums when he's here. It's enough to give anybody a headache.'

'Och, there's no harm in him, Frank. He's a lovely boy. And so is Bernard. Only, I'm awful worried about how Doris and him are getting on.'

'How do you mean?'

'Most of the time he seems to ignore the poor lassie. I can't help feeling sorry for her. I worry in case it was all my fault.'

'Don't be daft, Ma. How could Bernard's marriage problems be your fault?'

'Well, I . . . I was the one that persuaded him to marry Doris. She was expecting his wean and I thought it was the right thing to do. That's what I thought at the time.'

'It was the right thing to do. If Bernard was responsible for

250

getting Doris pregnant, then he had to face up to his responsibilities.'

'I suppose so, son. But the awful thing is neither of them is happy. I thought they'd settle down. Doris thought that too, poor wee lassie. She had visions of her and Bernard settling down eventually like a right old Derby and Joan.'

There was a moment's silence as both of them tried, and failed, to visualise the picture.

'Well,' Frank said eventually, 'they'll just have to make the best of it.'

'There's such a cloud of misery over the place when they're both in the house. Bernard has never blamed me. He's never once cast anything up to me. He seems to love me just the same. In a way that makes me feel worse, he's that good to me. Always bringing me things to tempt my appetite. He even has flowers delivered to the door for me, all done up fancy in cellophane and ribbons. And not even on my birthday. He says it's just to cheer me up. But Holy Mother of God, I wish he'd do something to cheer Doris up. She's the one that needs it.'

'Surely Bernard could afford to get a place of his own. It's not fair on Doris or you, especially when Tony keeps coming home. It's too much of a crush here.'

Maureen sighed. 'I doubt if it would make any difference, son. He's up to something, though. I know Bernard.'

'How do you mean?'

'Remember when he used to go after something he wanted? He always used to clam up. Remember even that first paper-round? We didn't find out about that until he started getting up earlier in the morning and disappearing. It was the same with that SAS thing. We would never have known about that if it hadn't been for Gordon Dougalston getting into the same line of business and *his* mother knowing about it.'

'He's working for Bernard now.'

'I know. Mrs Dougalston told me. She's got a mouth the size of Loch Lomond, that woman.'

'What's all this got to do with Bernard and Doris?'

'I'm not sure. I just feel it in my bones that Bernard's up to

251

something. I've tried to get it out of him. But as I say, he's always been good at clamming up and shutting people out when he wants to. I'm that sorry for poor wee Doris. But don't get me wrong, Frank,' she added hastily, 'Bernard's a lovely boy.'

Chapter Thirty-Six

Duncan and Agnes Noble. It was them. Duncan and Agnes Noble, The Cottages, Bearsden Lane, off Drymen Road.

'What age were you,' McPherson asked, 'when you were taken from them?'

Sophie was wringing her hands, clinging to herself, shivering. 'I don't know. Four, I think. Four or five. Or maybe six. I can't remember.'

'The chances are they won't recognise you. I mean, how *could* they recognise you?'

Just when everything was going so well. Everything was so wonderful.

'Sophie, are you listening to me?'

'Look at Andrina.' Her voice was monotonous, inward looking. 'We've got photographs of her at that age. Look at her now. If we'd never seen her in between, we'd recognise her. I'd recognise her.' Her with her round baby eyes and red hair.

'That's different.' McPherson didn't sound too sure.

'If *they* ever saw Andrina that would banish any doubt. She's the image of my so-called mother as I remember her. Red hair. Chubby face. Cupid's bow mouth. Curved body that she flaunted, just like Andrina flaunts hers.'

'She'll be an old woman now.'

'What's that got to do with anything?'

'Don't pick on me, Sophie. This is all your fault.'

'All my fault?'

'You know what I mean. You shouldn't have lied.'

'What was I supposed to say?'

'If you'd told me the truth in the first place, we could have discussed the situation and thought of something that would have prevented this complication from arising.'

'I never thought there would be any need.'

'So you keep saying. The only way I can think of is for one of us, or both of us, to have a private word with the Reverend Dinwoodie, and probably everyone else you've lied to.'

'Tell them?'

'As diplomatically as possible.'

'We're not talking about one of your political deals.'

'No, this is more important. It's about our credibility and our reputation and standing in this community.'

'I know. I know.'

'All we need to say is that you were taken into care as a young child and you'd assumed your parents were dead.'

'No details?'

'What *are* the details?'

'No details,' she repeated, half to herself. 'I suppose it's the only way?'

'Who have you told? About them being dead, I mean.'

'At the Dinwoodies' dinner party, somebody asked me about my parents.'

'So that's the Dinwoodies and Professor Brodie and his wife, for a start.'

'It was the same at my At Home.'

McPherson groaned. 'You'd better have a coffee morning or something and mention it there. I'll be meeting Dinwoodie and Brodie at the Golf Club this afternoon. I'll have a quiet word with them. Nobody might ever find out. The Nobles, even if they did recognise you, might never say anything. But just to be on the safe side . . .'

'They'll recognise me,' Sophie interrupted. 'They'll know me. They'll make no secret of it. They won't be ashamed. They were never ashamed. Absolutely shameless.'

'All right. All right. We'll prepare the ground. Don't worry. Handled properly, people will sympathise with you. Just calm down. Yes, they're bound to sympathise.' He was assuring himself as well as her. 'Yes, it'll be all right, don't worry.'

Afterwards Sophie phoned Andrina. 'Are you all right?'

'Of course I'm all right, Mummy.'

'Have you been to church?'

'I told you when you phoned this morning.'

'That was the morning service. It's time for the evening service now. Are you going?'

'Yes.'

Sophie's tormented mind detected the minutest hesitation. 'You're lying.'

'No, Mummy.' Andrina's voice heightened with anxiety. She had arranged for Bernard to visit her while Robert was at evening service. 'It's just that I've a bit of a headache. I was just thinking how nice it would be to take a rest.'

'What have you been doing to give yourself a headache?'

'I don't know. Nothing.'

'You must have been doing something.'

'I haven't been doing anything.'

'You're singing in the choir. How can you not go to church? How can you let people down? What will they think?'

'I never said I wasn't going to church, Mummy.'

'What will people think?'

'I will go to church, Mummy. I promise.'

'What will you wear?'

'I don't know.'

'What did you wear this morning?'

'I . . . I can't remember.'

'You don't change on Sundays for evening service. What are you wearing now?'

'My black suit,' she lied.

'You told me yesterday that suit was at the cleaner's. You've been tarting yourself up, giving yourself a showing up at the church. Giving us all a showing up. What'll people think? Have you no shame?'

Now Andrina really did have a headache, and the enormity of what she'd planned with Bernard was draining all strength from her legs. They could no longer support her. She groped for the hall chair. To commit adultery was sinful enough. To commit it with Bernard was a thousand times worse. To commit it while she should be in God's house was unforgivable.

'I'm sorry, Mummy. I got mixed up. It's my headache. I forget. I meant to wear my black suit.'

'You didn't wear that disgustingly short green dress to provoke men?' Sophie's voice dropped to quiet menace. 'Not in the church. Not that disgusting dress that shows your thighs and your breasts. Not in the church. If you wore that disgusting dress in God's house, I'll never speak to you again.'

'No, Mummy. Honestly I didn't. I swear I didn't. I wore my . . . I wore my . . .' The fact she was wearing the green dress now unnerved her, but she hadn't worn it to church that morning; '. . . new navy coat and cream straw hat with navy ribbons,' she babbled with relief, remembering.

Then she started worrying about how to get word to Bernard if she did go to church now. She was so distracted with the idea of Bernard coming to the door and finding she had gone, she hardly heard the rest of what her mother said.

She replaced the receiver and sat staring at the door.

Robert had already gone to collect his mother who always accompanied them to morning and evening service. She had promised him she would take a couple of painkillers and have a quiet rest. She couldn't just turn up at the church now, she told herself. Surely Robert would think it odd after the act she'd put on for his benefit less than half an hour ago. Anyway, by the time she'd changed back to more 'churchy' clothes, she would be far too late for the service.

All the time in the back of her mind was a tremor of fear. She was afraid of what Bernard might think or say or do if she wasn't waiting for him. She could never feel sure about Bernard. He could do such strange, unusual, sometimes delightful, often dangerous things. He could tell her exactly what she'd been wearing, down to the last detail, on exact days, years before they'd got together. It was unnerving and a little frightening to realise she had been under such close scrutiny yet had been completely unaware of it at the time.

He was so different from Robert in this respect. Although physically tough, there was an old-fashioned gentlemanliness about Robert, and at times he could be absent-minded.

Sometimes, Robert forgot her birthday or their anniversary. Bernard forgot nothing. Recently he'd sent a beautiful bunch of long-stemmed red roses – one rose for each year that they'd known each other, right back from when they'd both been at school. She'd had to pretend to Robert that she'd bought them herself because they'd been going so cheap in a sale in a flower shop in town. It never seemed to occur to Robert that a sale in a flower shop was highly improbable. She'd certainly never heard of such a thing.

Bernard had fingered them and smelled them and admired them that evening when he and Doris had come for supper. He and Doris visited quite often, and the visits were fraught with danger. Indeed, each minute was a knife-edge of potential insanity, crazed excitement. If they were left alone together for even a few minutes – when perhaps Robert had to answer the telephone in the hall and Doris had to go to the bathroom – Bernard would come rapidly over to her, plunge into her, have sex with her while she was nearly fainting with the physical thrill, mixed with the terror of being discovered.

But they never were discovered. When Doris or Robert returned to the room it was always to find Andrina and Bernard sitting, calmly chatting, exactly as they'd been before.

Every time they made love she tried not to respond, to lessen the pleasure and with it the guilt. Every time, in her imagination, she felt her mother's eyes upon her, heard her mother calling her 'filthy adulteress'. Every time, she shrank back at the thought.

She was still sitting in the hall when the doorbell shrilled through the quietness. Weak with anxiety she went to open it.

Bernard was wearing a light grey Armani suit and a dark blue shirt the colour of his eyes. He came in without a word. Then after the door closed, he said, 'No one has ever made love to you. Your husband has had sex with you many times, no doubt – but tonight I'm going to love you.'

The bathroom was large and had mirrored walls and a thick, deep carpet. With casual ease Bernard picked her up and carried her through the doorway, kicking the door shut behind him. Then he laid her gently down on the floor. Swiftly he unbuttoned her clothing until her entire body was naked before him as he crouched over her. Then he began at the tips of her fingers and kissed, rubbed, sucked, stroked and made his way into the palm of her hand. She was amazed at how highly erogenous her palms were. He continued up her arms, shoulders, neck, face, eyebrows, earlobes – not one inch of her was neglected. He continued down the entire length of her body, down each leg to the tips of her toes. An hour passed without a word being exchanged. The still summer evening was silent except for her tiny moans and sighs. Finally his mouth rested on her private mound, by this time swollen with desire. Once again she felt about him the odd juxtaposition of power and gentleness, and it sent pleasure burning into the core of her being. It was then, as usual, she became aware of her mother, aware of God, aware of the seventh commandment.

Bernard, sensing her withdrawal, said softly but with authority, 'Not this time. Lie back. Switch off. Let the physical overtake the emotional. Enjoy my love. Come, my velvet. Let yourself come.'

She relaxed, forgot everything except him and the ecstasy he was creating inside her.

She cried out his name.

Afterwards she knew she would never be the same again. After that evening she made up for lost time. She realised the highly sensual side of herself that she had suppressed to some degree or another for all of her adult life. Now she really became aware of her body, aware of the pert shape of her breasts, the fullness of her nipples, the voluptuous curves of her hips, the long slim shapeliness of her legs.

She became aware of men – their eyes, their mouths, their broad shoulders, their male mannerisms. But she desired only one. His approval, his opinions, became the yardstick for dressing, for shopping for clothes and underwear. He was fastidious. Nothing but the best pleased him. Lingerie, night-wear, everything had to be luxurious, sensual, but never crude or tacky. Hands obsessed him. Every female who came his way was first judged on her hands. As a result, she became fastidious about manicuring her nails and giving her hands a massage with cream. It became a nightly ritual that she never failed to perform. Red varnish was not permitted. He only liked soft colours on long, elegantly shaped nails. She had to wear gloves and take great care while doing housework.

She became as obsessed with him as he was with her. It seemed as they became more and more daring a miracle that neither Robert nor Doris had ever found out.

Although Doris knew that something was wrong. Or, to be more accurate – that everything was wrong.

Often she'd come to Monteith Row on her own when Bernard and Robert were at the karate club. She'd sit neatly on the edge of a chair in her short, tight skirt and sip a G & T. She thought it terribly smart and upper-class to call gin and tonics 'G & Ts'.

'I'm sure there's another woman. He doesn't want me any more, he doesn't need me any more, not even for sex.' Suddenly tears flooded from her eyes. 'The terrible thing is I still love him. Oh Andrina, I'm so terribly unhappy. What am I going to do?'

And Andrina hushed her and patted her and then went to make her a comforting cup of tea.

Chapter Thirty-Seven

Frank whispered to Patrick, 'I'll sit with her now. You'd better go home and get some rest.'

Maureen had been brought into hospital, and was now drifting in and out of sleep. She looked more relaxed and peaceful than she'd done for years. Happier too, yet apparently she was dying of cancer. Tony had been sent for; Michael too. Bernard had looked in earlier on his way to work, and had promised to come back first thing in the morning.

The next day, true to his word, Bernard arrived exactly on the hour he'd promised, filling the screened-off area with vibrant health. It made Frank exhausted and depressed just to look at him.

Patrick came trailing in behind Bernard. 'How is she?'

'Much the same. Heavily sedated.'

'I might as well have sat here all night along with you, Frank. I've just tossed and turned at home. I'll take over now, son. You'd better go and have a wash to freshen yourself up and then get off to your work.'

Bernard was standing at the foot of the bed staring at his mother. He said, 'Did the doctor see her again last night?'

Frank nodded.

'What did he say?'

'It's just a matter of time.' Frank turned to Patrick. 'I can't go to work today, Da. I can't leave her. I promised I'd stay. Anyway, I'm not fit to work. I couldn't concentrate. And I'd never forgive myself if she . . . if it happened . . . They said it could . . .'

Patrick sank down on to the chair and buried his head in his hands. 'What am I going to do? I'm no use without her.'

Bernard said, 'Pull yourself together, Da. You're no use to anyone if you let yourself go to pieces.'

'You don't understand,' Patrick began to sob. 'I love her.'

'You think I don't?' Bernard said.

'It's different for you. It's a different kind of feeling altogether. We've been together since we were younger than you. Before any of you came on the scene.'

Frank patted his father's shoulder. 'I know. I know, Da. But you don't want her to see you like this. If she wakens and sees you like this, she'll be upset.'

Bernard said, 'I'll go and have another word with the doctor or whoever is on duty. Then I'd better phone Tony and Michael again. They might not have realised how urgent it is that they get here right away.'

'OK, son.' Patrick wiped his eyes with a grubby-looking handkerchief. 'And thanks.'

Michael had already left the booth where he'd been working and was on his way to Glasgow when Bernard phoned, but Tony was still in Newcastle. After a late gig he was sprawled in bed, completely given up to sleep. His thunderous snoring filled the house and seemed to shake it to its foundations. His landlady battered wildly at the door, even kicked it in her desperation not only to get him up, but also to shut him up. Eventually, scratching and yawning and showing every one of his tombstone teeth, he reached the phone in the lobby. He wore nothing but a vest and Y-fronts, neither of which was all that clean.

'An absolute disgrace,' the landlady called him, and not for the first time.

'Oh it's you, Bernard. Yeah, I was coming today. How is Ma? Jesus, as bad as that? Aye, right Bernard. Pronto.'

It was a terrible carry-on. Poor old Ma. Pity he'd miss tonight's gig. But if the old girl wasn't going to last out . . . Anyway, Bernard would kill him. Scratching and yawning again, he wandered back to his room to pull on a pair of frayed denims and a T-shirt, then left to catch the first train back to Glasgow.

It was just as well the train didn't go any further than Glasgow's Central Station because he'd fallen asleep again. A cleaner had to punch him awake. 'Here you, ur ye gonnae get aff here, or ur ye no?'

'I had a rough night, hen. Didnae stop till three o'clock this mornin'.'

'You'll have a rough mornin' as well if you don't get oot ma way.'

'Keep your hair on, hen.' He picked up his case and plodded off to find a taxi.

'Where to?' the driver asked.

'Acrehill Road, Blackhill.'

'Just ma luck,' the driver groaned. 'Ah felt in ma bones it was gonnae be wan o' them days.'

'Here wait a minute, Jimmy. I've no tae go home. I've to go straight to the hospital. The Western. It's ma Ma. She's dyin'. My brother Bernard says I'll be lucky if I see her before she goes.'

'Oh, I'm sorry, son.' The driver was immediately contrite. 'I'll put the foot down.'

They'd only gone a few yards when Tony spotted a couple of his mother's old neighbours.

'Here, stop a minute, Jimmy.'

He opened the door and called out, 'Hey, Mrs Donnelly, Mrs O'Hearn.'

'Oh, hello son. Is this you going to see your mammy?' Mrs O'Hearn spoke in a hushed tone instead of her usual bellow.

'Aye. Can I drop you off anywhere?'

'Well, it's on your way right enough. Our Jessy's. You know Jessy? Our other sister.'

'Oh aye. Hop in then.'

'How is she, son?' Mrs Donnelly enquired in an equally low, respectful tone.

'Bernard sent for Father O'Rourke.'

'It's any minute then?'

'That's what Bernard said.'

They commiserated at some length, and when they reached their sister Jessy's corner they waved Tony a sad farewell. The taxi continued on its way to the Western Infirmary but just before it reached its destination, Tony suddenly leaned forward.

'Here Jimmy, stop here will you?'

The driver gazed in the direction indicated. He could not believe that his passenger was meaning either the Caledonian pub or Harry Tate's, the bookies.

'Here?'

'Aye,' Tony said, 'I just want to have a wee half and put on a line first.'

The driver was dumbfounded. But of course he hadn't been on the job for very long.

When Tony eventually did arrive at the infirmary, his mother had, the nurse informed him, quietly passed away. He was stunned. He had never really believed that his mother would ever go away anywhere. He was the one who went away. She was always there waiting for him when he came back. She always had been there. He had taken it for granted she always would be.

Bernard had to lead him home like a child. Bernard took them all home. Bernard saw to everything – the funeral arrangements, including booking a restaurant for the funeral tea. Doris wept as if it had been her own mother who'd gone. She told Andrina later, 'I feel I've nobody now. At least nobody in that house who understands or cares about me. She was Bernard's mother and she loved him, but she knew what I was going through. She was kind to me. I'll miss her terribly.' She gazed at Andrina with tragic, mascara-smeared eyes. 'Thank God I've still got you.'

After the funeral Bernard had called for Robert and they both went to the club and did a hard session of karate. Doris told Andrina, 'The sweat was pouring off him when he got back. He had a bath and went straight to bed without a word. It's terribly hurtful when he does that – ignores me. I mean I'd rather he hit me. Much rather. I could just die when he ignores me like that. It's just terrible, Andrina.'

Doris was in a pitiful state. She had obviously lost weight. She looked scraggy and miserable. Robert said she looked as if she might go the same way as Maureen. Andrina felt furtive and fearful with guilt. And the guilt about Doris sharpened the fearful guilt about Sophie. When she was with Bernard, she said, 'I'm so sorry about your mother,' and she put her arms around him, wanting to comfort him. But soon everything was forgotten in the insanity of their passion. They had both become insatiable; their behaviour was nothing short of madness. It brought her out in a cold sweat just to think about some of the things they'd done. They were simply asking to be found out.

They physically linked at every possible opportunity, however short a time, however awkward a spot or position. If they had only two or three minutes they climaxed with incredible speed and urgency. No corner of her home was left undiscovered. They made love squeezed in cupboards, in the bath, over the kitchen table. Her particular penchant was for making love in unusual and risky places. And they took incredible risks – out on the landing, over the bannister, in the back close.

Her heart was constantly racing with the danger of it all.

She phoned Bernard at his office and told him it would have to stop. Doris was not only incredibly unhappy, Doris was suspicious. Doris had become convinced there was another woman. It was surely only a matter of time until Doris found out who the other woman was.

Bernard said maybe that was the best thing that could happen – bring everything out into the open, once and for all. Let Doris know. Let Robert know. Let everybody know. Then they could both get a divorce. 'We could get married, Andrina. We must get married. I've wanted to marry you from the first moment I saw you.'

'Everybody' meant her mother. Even the thought made Andrina panic. 'No. Doris trusts me. It would be terrible. I couldn't bear it. I couldn't do that to her. I feel bad enough as it is.'

'I'll see that I get a divorce then. It'll be a first step.'

'I don't want her to know about me. I'll never speak to you again if you tell her about us. I'll never forgive you.'

If Doris knew, Doris would stop at nothing to reek spiteful revenge. Doris would broadcast it from the rooftops. *Sophie would be sure to find out.*

'The rotten two-faced shite,' Doris had once thrown all ladylike pretensions to the wind and yelled in anger and disgust about a colleague at work who had once let her down. Andrina could imagine Doris adding, if she ever found out about her, 'and her supposed to be a goody-goody Christian. She even sings in the bloody choir!'

'She won't know about you,' Bernard assured her. 'Leave it to me.'

'It's no use. I can't see you again, Bernard. I mean it this time. It's all getting far too complicated.'

'Then I'll uncomplicate things. One step at a time. Leave it to me.'

'You don't understand. I can't marry you and it's not only because of Doris and Robert. There's my mother. It would kill her, Bernard. I just couldn't do it to her.' She couldn't explain to him how her mother needed the image of perfection in her daughter. It had become worse since Sophie had moved to Bearsden. She'd never stopped boasting to everybody about her. It was 'my Andrina can do this', and 'my Andrina can do that'. The extremes of her mother's behaviour, the apparent desperation and anxiety behind everything she said or did, locked Andrina into her mother's neurosis. There was nothing more infectious than anxiety.

'You're not a child,' Bernard said. 'You can do what you like.'

'If only it was that simple.'

'It can be that simple.'

'Not for me. Never.' She was bound to her mother by invisible chains that grew ever tighter and more painful. She would never be free as long as her mother was alive.

'One step at a time,' Bernard repeated. He was a dreadfully obsessive man. It frightened her that he did not understand about her mother.

'I'll always love you,' she told him, 'but I can't go on this way.

We've both been acting crazy. It's impossible to go on like that. Please don't phone me again. Don't be alone with me again.'

She hung up. Then she stood, shivering with relief that it was finished – all the madness, all the wickedness, all the guilt. It had been getting so much worse. Absolute madness. She couldn't stop shivering. She'd made such a narrow escape.

Chapter Thirty-Eight

'Why can't you just face the truth?' Bernard said. 'It isn't working out. It never will work out. We've no child to consider. The only sensible thing is for you to divorce me.'

Doris smoked in silence.

'I'll be straight with you, Doris . . .'

She gave a sarcastic hoot at that but Bernard continued.

'There's someone else.'

Doris's mouth twisted. 'I knew it.'

'Look, we've been friends for most of our lives. Why don't we part on good terms?'

'We've never been friends.'

'All right, have it your own way. We've known each other for . . .'

'We haven't even known each other.'

'I'm trying to be civilised about this.'

Doris made another sarcastic, derisive sound.

'OK,' Bernard said. 'If you don't want it the easy way, you can have it the hard way. I've never loved you. Never for one second, and I never will. I don't just love this other woman, I adore her. Now I may never be able to marry her but whatever happens, we'll keep on loving each other.'

Doris looked away so that he could not see the pain in her eyes.

'As far as our divorce is concerned,' Bernard went on, 'I can arrange to be caught and photographed with a woman who won't mind her name or her picture being used. It's the quickest way out for both of us. You'll be free to get somebody else as well.'

But she only wanted him. 'You're forgetting one important thing.'

'What?'

'We're Catholics.'

'So?'

'I don't need to spell it out.'

'Look, Doris, I wouldn't care if I was the Pope and you were Mother Theresa. Has it not sunk in what I've just said?'

It had sunk in all right. She had known from the beginning that he'd never loved her. But still, she'd hoped against hope. Now, with him actually saying the words. And worse, telling her that he loved someone else . . .

'Who is the lucky lady then?' she sneered. 'Have you broken your golden rule of not mixing business with pleasure after all? I knew you didn't get all dressed up like a tailor's dummy every night just to deal with drunks and trouble-makers. Not the kind of trouble-maker you were trying to make out.'

'Are you or are you not going to divorce me?'

'Why should I?'

'Why shouldn't you? Our marriage, such as it is, is well and truly over – finished, Doris. Caput. Understand? Now, either you walk out that door, or I do. If you co-operate, I'll see that you never go short of money. If you don't, you'll find that one way or another, and to put it mildly, your life will grow more difficult by the day. Depend on it.'

Her heart had started to thump. She suddenly feared all her vague suspicions about Bernard could become a reality.

'All right,' she said, puffing at her cigarette and sending a jet of smoke towards his face. 'Have your fuckin' divorce. I'll be a lot better without you.'

'A lot better,' he agreed.

But she was broken-hearted. She couldn't rest in peace. She ran to Andrina for comfort.

'I'm just pole-axed, Andrina. Absolutely gutted. I knew he just married me to give the baby a name but still . . . to toss me aside and be so cold and dead-pan. It was terrible.'

'You'll be better without a marriage like that,' Andrina soothed. 'You hadn't been happy for ages. You're a very pretty girl. You'll easily find somebody else.'

'I can't think of anybody else. He's like a dark shadow over my life. I'll never feel free of him.'

'Now you're just being melodramatic – letting morbid feelings get the better of you.'

'I've felt so depressed . . .'

'It's only natural.'

'Such a failure . . .'

'Well, when a marriage breaks up, I suppose . . .'

'So terribly inadequate, any self-confidence I ever had has gone.'

'It'll come back if you give it a chance. You'll build a new life, you'll see. You have your job at Daly's. You're an excellent saleswoman. The floor manager once remarked on that to me.'

'Did he?' Doris brightened slightly.

'Yes, I just came in to have a word with you about our lunch arrangement, remember, and you showed me some new stock that had just come in and I ended up buying that lovely little black dress with the deep, plunging neckline.'

'Oh yes!'

'On my way out of the department I mentioned to the manager that I hadn't really come in to buy anything. And he said, "Ah, but our Mrs O'Maley is an excellent saleswoman. We value her services very highly." '

'Did he?'

'Honestly.'

'I like my job right enough.'

'And everybody there likes you. Including all your customers.'

Doris gave a helpless laugh. 'You certainly work hard at trying to cheer me up.'

'Well, you deserve to be happy.'

'Oh, Andrina, what would I do without you? I feel better already.'

And so she did. But much later, when she was back in her mother and father's house in Garngad, and lying on the 'hurley bed' that was now dragged out from under the kitchen bed, the shadow returned to haunt her. She listened in the darkness to the snores of her mother and father and felt lonely and bitter. She determined to find out who Bernard's fancy woman was.

269

She'd find out even if it was the last thing she did. What good it would do her she didn't know. But the mountain of hatred and resentment growing inside her had to have a focus. They might have worked out, her and Bernard, if this rotten, scheming bitch hadn't wormed her way between them. The rotten bitch had lured Bernard away. This happened often in the serial stories in the Red Star Weekly, Secrets, and Family Star. Doris was an avid reader of melodramatic serials and it was easy for her, especially now in her unhappy state, to get fact and fiction confused.

It turned out that Vera Thomson who worked in Haberdashery had a boyfriend who worked for Bernard, and in the canteen over every meal or tea break Doris sought Vera's friendship, co-operation and advice. Vera enjoyed being a part of a conspiracy and promised she'd use all her wiles to try and get any information she could out of George, her boyfriend, about any woman in Bernard's life.

'Mind you, it won't be easy,' Vera warned. 'Impossible, in fact, if George thinks I'm trying in any way to be critical of his boss. He admires your Bernard, he really does. I think they all do.'

'Oh, he's a great tough guy, you see,' Doris said. 'Men like that. That's the be-all and end-all for most men.'

'I must admit I go for tough guys myself,' Vera giggled. 'That's why I go for George in a big way.'

'If you're fly about it,' Doris urged, 'you know – use a bit of tact, be real crafty, do you think you can do it?'

'I can but try.' Then something suddenly occurred to Vera. 'Oh but here, why do you want to know? I mean, you're not going to do anything to her, are you? That would give the game away, put me right in it. I want none of that.'

'No, no. I swear it's just curiosity. I just can't rest until I know. Wouldn't you feel the same yourself? I'm just dying to know, that's all. What's she got that I haven't got? That's all I want to know.'

Vera giggled again. 'OK, then.'

It turned out to be money – which was a comfort in a way.

This was something that George admired about Bernard as well. Bernard knew how to get on in life. Bernard always had an eye on the main chance. A man – Mungo Ford – who owned God knows how many dance-halls all over the country, was putting a lucrative amount of jobs Bernard's way. So much so that Bernard had to take on more men. Part of the reason Bernard was the chosen one out of all the other security firms was the fact, according to George, that Mr Ford's daughter, Jane, had fallen hook, line and sinker for Bernard. They'd met when her father had invited Bernard home to dinner one evening.

Apparently Jane and Bernard had a lot in common.

'She does karate, would you believe?' Vera giggled. 'A right keep fit fanatic. A great gymnast, apparently. She's even picked up prizes for that. And of course she's got oodles of money. Or at least her father has, and she's an only child. A late one as well. George says it's common knowledge her mother was middle-aged and her father quite elderly when they had her. Now her mother's dead and she'll inherit everything when the old guy snuffs it. She was married but it didn't work out. She's divorced now.'

Doris treated Vera to sausage and mash in the canteen and two caramel wafers for her tea. She also gave her a present of a Max Factor foundation. Vera was delighted.

Jane Ford. Jane Ford. The name kept going round and round in Doris's head. Sometimes, in bed at night, she'd imagine herself tracking Jane Ford down, confronting her, scratching her eyes out. Sometimes she thought – to hell with both her and Bernard – she didn't care.

Sometimes she just hid her head under the blankets and wept until she was exhausted.

Chapter Thirty-Nine

Scobie felt sorry for Patrick. His family was breaking up around him. Michael had been in hospital with delirium tremems and was a wreck of the man he'd once been. Despite this, he still could put up a decent show at the booths and he'd never stopped saying (without being asked) that he could control his drinking. Patrick said he didn't know how Caroline put up with him. Because of shortages of money they'd moved from their two apartment to a one apartment, or 'single end' as it was known in Glasgow.

Scobie could imagine what Caroline was suffering, cramped in that tiny room with not only Michael and the two children, but as often as not Michael's drunken pals as well. Carragh had put up with the very same when he'd been drunk.

The O'Maley single end was upstairs from Scobie and Carragh's room and kitchen, and they could often hear the rabble of fighting and singing. The kind of songs bawled out depended who had brought the bevvy. If the bringers of the booze happened to be Catholic, they'd all bellow out Catholic songs:

> 'Take it down from the mast, Irish traitors,
> 'Tis the flag we Republicans claim,
> It can never be owned by Free Staters
> Who shed nothing on it but shame . . .'

If the ones who'd brought the bevvy another night happened to be Protestants, the shout was 'Fuck the Pope' and 'The Old Orange Flute'.

> 'A married a Fenian, her name was McGuire,
> She picked up my flute and she flung it in the fire

272

But as it was burning she heard a strange noise,
Twas the Old Orange Flute playing The Protestant
Boys . . .'

Michael joined in no matter what the song happened to be. The important thing was getting the alcohol. That was what had once ruled Scobie's life, and now it ruled Michael's. Scobie had spoken to Michael as he'd promised Patrick, but the boy didn't want to know.

'There's no problem, Scobie,' he'd insisted. 'I can control my drinking.'

Michael hadn't yet reached his rock bottom, the level at which enough shame, humiliation and fear took over and made you accept the fact that you were an alcoholic and that you wanted help.

Scobie had managed to help others, though. At first he'd gone round with another guy from AA to visit alcoholics in their homes. The other guy, Scott Manderson from Bearsden, had insisted he'd do the talking. Scott was a nice chap in his own way but when it came down to brass tacks, he wasn't the best one to talk to hard men (or women) from places like Garngad, the Gorbals or Blackhill. He very soon saw this for himself and agreed that Scobie was the man for these areas. So Scobie spent much of his time in dangerous excursions into the toughest areas of Glasgow talking to some of the dregs of humanity who had hit rock bottom. To a lesser man, this could have been overwhelmingly depressing, but Scobie could usually manage to see a funny side to even the worst situation.

'Sometimes ah've got to laugh . . .' he'd confide to Scott, or Jimmy, or Alec at the AA. 'No to their faces, but afterwards. Ah cannae help it.'

Only a few days previously he'd visited a single end in the Gorbals. It was the pits. Every penny had long since gone on drink. Everything pawnable had been pawned. Not even a piece of linoleum covered the floor. There was evidence of much violence. Whitewashed walls were streaked with missiles of food and drink that had missed their intended target. The backs were broken off wooden spar chairs. No coal warmed the rusty grate. The window was broken and covered by a piece of old cardboard. In the hole-in-the-wall bed lay a pathetic specimen of a man covered by an old coat instead of blankets. His equally afflicted looking wife hovered helplessly at Scobie's elbow. Her hair hung in lank strands around a sunken-cheeked face. A cardigan with holes in the sleeves drooped over her skinny body and she was wearing a pair of men's socks. Scobie found it difficult to judge by appearance who was the alcoholic in such a situation, because the partners of an alcoholic had also gone through hell.

'What's your name, hen?' he asked the wife.

'Nellie,' she quavered.

'Right, Nellie. You make us a cup of tea, hen.'

'Aye. OK.'

'Now then, Tommy.' He turned his attention to the twitching, unshaven, red-eyed figure on the bed. 'You're having a wee bit of a problem with the drink, eh?'

'Aye,' Tommy agreed, 'you could say that.'

'Right.' Scobie launched into his usual spiel. 'Now I'm no going to ask you to give up a bottle of whisky or a barrel of beer, Tommy. And I'm no going to ask you to give up drinking for the rest of your life. All I'm asking you to do is to keep off the drink for one day . . .'

At first Tommy seemed to be listening, but soon his eyes glazed; his attention had wandered. Scobie knew he'd lost him.

'Tommy!' He raised his voice. 'Tommy, where are you? What are you thinking about?'

Slowly Tommy returned. 'Ah was just thinking, Scobie – if I stopped drinking, what would happen to ma social life?'

Scobie's eyes rolled around the pit of a room. 'What bloody social life?'

'Well.' Tommy thought for a minute. 'For instance, when I take Nellie out for a meal for a wee treat.'

Nellie had been shuffling towards Scobie clutching a lidless teapot and a cracked cup. She suddenly let out a howl of

274

derision. 'Whit? Oot for a meal? We've never been ower that door thegither for twenty bloody years!'

Scobie knew that Tommy was only trying to find excuses for not stopping drinking. It was the same with Michael. Caroline would become another Nellie. She should leave Michael – but of course, where would she go except back to Big Martha? And she'd vowed she'd never do that.

But Doris had left Bernard. Apparently Bernard had been having it off with some woman whose father owned a string of dance-halls. Bernard's firm did regular work for the father. Jane Ford, her name was. Worth quite a bit of money, apparently. She owned a big villa in Pollokshields.

'I can't understand it,' Patrick said. 'I've given these boys such a good example. I was happily married to my Maureen for all these years. Yet would you look at the mess they're making of their lives. Michael's made a right cock-up of everything. Bernard's wife's divorced him. No lassy'll have Tony. And Frank writes poetry.'

Scobie shook his head in sympathy. Secretly he was glad his Doris was shot of Bernard, although it had upset Carragh from a religious point of view. It upset him as well that Doris had been excommunicated. Poor Doris was pole-axed about it. Shattered to the core. Nevertheless, she'd never been happy since the day she'd married Bernard. Bridie had got a far better deal with Frank, poetry or not. And wee Carragh thought the world of him. It was a bit awkward though since Doris had moved back to Turner Street. Now Frank and Bridie were never away from the Corporation Offices, pestering everybody in sight about getting a council house allocated to them. The latest development was Frank thinking of going to plead his case to Bailie McPherson.

'Use Bernard's name,' Bridie urged. 'Doris says McPherson often does business with Bernard.' In her desperation, she had been all for asking Bernard to make the approach to the Bailie, but Frank said that Bernard had plenty on his plate with his business, which seemed to take up more and more of his time – not to mention Jane Ford. Then they learned that Bernard was moving away from Acrehill Street and Blackhill. No Corporation house for him, however. He'd acquired a flat in Sauchiehall Mansions. A beautiful place it was, a spacious two-room and kitchen and bathroom with a square hall you could have a dance in.

Bridie was quite bitter about it, and could hardly bring herself to be polite when Bernard showed them round.

'What's he needing a big house like that for now that he's on his own? It would have fitted him better to have provided a place like that for his wife.'

Frank had to agree.

Bridie said, 'What does he think he's playing at?'

Frank didn't know. He often had a vague feeling that there was something shady, not quite above-board in what Bernard did.

Nevertheless, he'd been surprised when Bernard said, 'If you're expecting Bailie McPherson to do you any favours you'd better be ready to give him a good bung.'

'Bailie McPherson takes bribes?'

Bernard laughed. 'You always tended to live in cloud-cuckoo land, Frank. But I wouldn't use the word "bribe". Have a bit of tact. Slip him a hundred quid in a large brown envelope, and say you'd like to treat him and his wife to a nice night out – for any trouble he might go to on your behalf.'

'A hundred quid!' Frank echoed.

'I'll lend you the money.'

Bridie said stiffly, 'We don't want anything from you, Bernard. We've got all we need.'

Bernard shrugged. 'Suit yourself.'

Afterwards Frank repeated incredulously to Bridie, 'A hundred pounds. A fortune! And him sitting up there on the bench like a saint dealing out justice to other people. Could you beat it?'

'Nothing surprises me any more, Frank. Or shocks me. Bernard's no saint either. I know he's your brother, but the less we have to do with him the better.'

'Oh, hang on Bridie . . .' Frank began worriedly.

'He's going to end up in serious trouble and we don't want to get involved.'

'He seems to be doing very well. You just need to look at the way he dresses. And that flat . . .'

'He's violent – and so far he's got away with it.'

'But that's his job – to deal with violent situations, I mean.'

'That's the kind of man who gets on in the world and gets a house in Sauchiehall Mansions.' Bitterly she added, 'It's not fair.'

'Don't worry, we'll have a nice house too, Bridie.'

Bridie sighed. 'I know we vowed we wouldn't be affected by anything around us, we'd keep our own standards, we wouldn't be dragged down, but I'm so desperate to get a place of our own, Frank . . .'

'You think we should offer the bribe?'

'We've got over a hundred saved, and if it's the only way, Frank . . . Even with my da being sober, it's terrible in that wee dump of a place. Never any peace or privacy inside the house. Always a queue for the lavatory outside. The whole building's a cesspool. It's depressing me so much I can't stand it any longer. Remember I've had to suffer it longer than you. I've been stuck in that place ever since I was born.'

The thought of offering a bribe went completely against Frank's grain, but he felt for Bridie's sake he had to do it. Resentment and hatred flared inside him. He hated the saintly, socialist, Christian Bailie more than he'd ever hated anyone in his life. One day he'd show him up. He'd write a play about the Glasgow Corporation and all the graft and corruption involved. Already he'd had plays published by Samuel French which were being performed here and there by amateur companies. The one about the priests hadn't been accepted yet though, and he was planning to have another go at rewriting it. He could understand why local companies wouldn't have the nerve for that one. But one day a television or a film company would. He was determined they would. One day they would also snap up the one he was going to write about a bent Bailie.

277

Feeling even more bitter than his wife now, he kept thinking, 'One day . . . one day.'

Chapter Forty

'It's like something out of a book,' Mrs Pemberton said. Although in fact she'd read very few books.

'Why were you taken into care?' asked Mrs Hawthorn.

Sophie shook her head. 'It's such a long time ago. A lifetime ago. I was only a small child. I really don't know.'

Mrs Jones from the other end of the terrace leaned forward and dramatically lowered her voice. 'And you're sure it's them?'

'Duncan and Agnes Noble,' Sophie said. 'It would be too much of a coincidence for both to have the same name. And I gather from Mrs Dinwoodie that they're the right age.'

'How fascinating!' Mrs Jones was a dedicated member of the local drama group. She thoroughly enjoyed any 'heightened life experience', to quote her own words. As a rule, however, not many heightened life experiences came her way. 'What are you going to do?'

'I don't know,' Sophie answered honestly. 'But I feel very strongly that I don't want anything to do with them. They must have neglected me or done something wrong to warrant me being taken from them. They can't be very nice people.'

Mrs Pemberton said, 'People grow older and wiser, my dear. They've always seemed a charming, elderly couple to me.'

'Yes,' Mrs Dinwoodie said, 'the Christian thing is to forgive them, Mrs McPherson. They're in their twilight years. Perhaps this is God's way of giving them a chance to make up for any unkindness they might have done to you when they were young and foolish.'

Mrs Hawthorn agreed. 'Yes, after all these years it would be such a happy reunion.'

Mrs Jones was ecstatic. She clasped her hands and gazed

heavenwards. 'How lovely! I can just see it. Child and parents re-united after a lifetime of being lost to each other . . .'

Sophie was thinking behind her tight, polite expression. What did they know about anything? Everything had been lovely for them, all right. 'I'm afraid I don't have your generous, forgiving hearts . . .' she said.

Mrs Pemberton smiled. 'You've a very nice nature, dear.'

'And you're a good Christian,' Mrs Dinwoodie said. 'That is why you will be able to forgive your mother and father.'

'Forgive and forget, they say.' Mrs Jones pronounced the words with a dramatically raised hand as if she was reciting 'To be or not to be'. 'But you have already forgotten. So all that remains is for you to forgive.'

'Yes, you must get together as soon as possible,' Mrs Dinwoodie decided. 'And I think the manse would be an appropriate place, with the Minister and myself at hand, to make sure the reunion is smooth and happy, and has God's blessing.'

Sophie was beginning to feel sick. 'I really don't think . . .'

'Mrs McPherson.' Mrs Dinwoodie was determined. 'You'll have to meet them sometime. It's a wonder you haven't come face to face already. Far better a proper Christian reunion in the manse than an unexpected confrontation in the street where you might be flustered enough to say the wrong thing. Do remember that they are an elderly couple and the Minister is responsible for their welfare as well as yours.'

Sophie was so choked with hatred at the mere thought of the 'elderly couple' that she couldn't speak.

Mrs Dinwoodie took the silence as capitulation, and proceeded to arrange the exact day and time of the meeting.

Afterwards Sophie told McPherson that she didn't know how she could possibly go.

'You'll have to go. We don't want to get on the wrong side of people like the Dinwoodies. Their friends are our friends now. You don't want to alienate yourself from some of the most influential people in the district.'

She didn't.

The meeting was set for the next day. The minister had arranged for the couple to arrive at the manse earlier than Sophie so that he 'could gently prepare them . . .'

'If we're not very careful,' Mrs Dinwoodie said, 'the shock could kill the old souls.'

It was the only cheering thought Sophie had to cling to. She couldn't eat any breakfast, and because she felt faint by lunchtime she forced herself to eat a sandwich. It turned to acid in her stomach and churned and burned with her hatred.

McPherson said he'd take the afternoon off and go with her. She was grateful for this. He could, as he said, divert some of the attention away from her.

They drove to the manse in silence, along the tree-lined main road, down the leafy side-street towards the loch, up the winding drive to the imposing villa with its peaceful view over the dark mirror of water. McPherson stopped the car and sat for a moment, leather-gloved hand on the wheel.

'Now remember, we've to go on living here. The best you can do at the moment is to force yourself to be polite.'

'All right. All right.'

'You don't look all right. You look demented. For pity's sake try and relax.'

She took a deep breath.

Mrs Dinwoodie opened the door. Smiling, eyes shining, obviously enjoying herself. 'Come in. Come in. Mr and Mrs Noble are so looking forward to meeting you.' She laughed. 'That sounds strange – as if they've never met you before. Seeing you again, I mean.'

In the drawing room sat an old woman with a dried-up, wrinkled face and wispy grey hair. But the eyes were still round and slightly protruding, like a child's. Like Andrina's. They were strained with anxiety and apprehension. The old man stood up, brazening it out. She remembered the slight, rocking swagger, the shoulders twitched back. Still the cocky bastard.

'Well, could you beat it?' he said.

She couldn't.

'After all these years. It's great to see you. Isn't it, mother?'

281

'I've thought about you so often,' the old woman quavered. And oh, how often I've thought about you.

'Well,' Mrs Dinwoodie said archly, 'aren't you going to give your old mum and dad a nice kiss?'

'I'm not a kissing kind of person.'

McPherson said, 'That's right. The more emotion Sophie feels, the less she's able to show it. I'm Andrew, Sophie's husband.' He strode across the room and gave both Duncan and Agnes Noble a hearty handshake. 'Fancy us all ending up living in the same place. Nice area, isn't it? Sophie and I are very happy here.'

Mrs Dinwoodie said to Sophie, 'Do sit down, Mrs McPherson. I was just about to pour the tea. Now isn't this nice?'

Somehow the afternoon passed. McPherson dominated most of the conversation, except when the Reverend Dinwoodie solemnly spoke about the wonderful reunion, which he blessed as if he was performing a marriage ceremony. Sophie hardly uttered a word, but when she was forced to speak she managed to be polite. Even to bring a small, cold smile to her lips.

Eventually, the Reverend Dinwoodie said, 'I collected Mr and Mrs Noble in my car and brought them here, but I'm sure you'll want to give them a lift back home . . .'

'Of course, of course,' McPherson immediately agreed.

The Dinwoodies came to stand at the front door of the house to wave them off. McPherson packed the Nobles into the back seat. Sophie sat stiffly beside her husband at the front. She managed a smile and a wave for the minister and his wife.

The car crunched over the gravel of the drive, then out on to the street.

'It was so nice to see you again,' Agnes Noble said.

'Well, it wasn't nice to see you,' Sophie replied.

'Sophie!' McPherson sounded shocked.

Sophie ignored him and went on, 'And I hope I don't see you again. I suppose it's bound to happen in passing because we live in the same place. Or some other well-meaning person like Mrs Dinwoodie will try and get us together socially. But I just want you to know that I don't want anything to do with either of you. I hate the sight of you.'

'Sophie!' McPherson really was shocked.

In the back seat Agnes Noble began to cry. Her husband put a comforting arm around her.

'It's one thing,' Sophie continued, addressing McPherson now, 'pretending to our friends, but I see no point in pretending to that pair. It'll save a lot of complication and difficulties if they know exactly where they stand. As far as I'm concerned, that's nowhere near me.'

McPherson said, 'Sophie, we're supposed to be committed Christians, and because of that if nothing else . . .'

'I'm just being honest. If I'm forced to meet them again socially as I was today, it's better that they're under no illusions about me wanting to see them. I'll never come near them of my own free will.'

McPherson didn't say any more. The car was filled with the old woman's heartbroken sobs and the misery of the old man's silence.

As soon as they reached the cottages, McPherson opened the car door and assisted the couple out. The old man and woman were tottering, clinging to one another for support. McPherson saw them to their cottage, helped them find their key and opened the door for them. 'Will you be all right? Do you want me to come in with you?'

Duncan Noble shook his head.

Back in the car, McPherson said, 'That was shockingly cruel, Sophie. Especially to two old people.'

'What's being old got to do with it?'

'Being old like that means being helpless.'

'I was helpless as a child. They didn't care about being cruel to me.'

'So you do remember what happened, then?'

'Yes, but I don't want to talk about it. I can't.'

'Don't worry. I'm not going to force you.'

By the time she got home she was absolutely drained of energy. She collapsed back in a chair and closed her eyes.

283

'I'll make you a cup of tea,' McPherson said.

After sipping the tea she felt a little better, happier, safer. The Nobles would avoid her now. There would be no repetition of today's afternoon tea party. She could begin to pick up the threads of her life. Everything was going to be all right. She tried to keep assuring herself of this. Everything would go back to normal. Life in Bearsden, the good life, would return to being exactly as it was. She had been enjoying it so much. Yet now, no matter how she tried to cheer herself, the joy had gone. A thousand uncertainties, a thousand fears, gnawed at the dark edges of her mind.

The Dinwoodies wouldn't let the matter rest. They would keep visiting the Nobles. It had always been considered part of both the minister's and his wife's duties to visit the elderly of the parish. They would question the Nobles. When would they be seeing their daughter again? They were not seeing their daughter again? Why not? Would the Nobles be eventually pressed into confessing? Surely not. Yet she could no longer be sure of anything. Except the fact that if they did confess the truth, that would be where the interest, all the sympathy, would end. All the influential, solid citizens they knew in this most decent and respectable of places would draw their skirts away from the dirty puddle of such a truth. They would avert their faces in disgust from the Nobles, and from her.

She could only be really safe if Duncan and Agnes Noble were wiped from the face of the earth. If she could think of any way of doing it without being found out, she would do it. That was one thing she was *absolutely* sure of.

Chapter Forty-One

Bernard didn't phone very often because he was away so much. When he did phone, however, sometimes from England, once from Ireland, Andrina hung up on him. She missed him, yet at the same time there was the enormous relief from worry and anxiety. She might have succumbed to temptation again when Bernard returned to Scotland, however – but she was saved by the fact that she became pregnant with Robert's child. For a panic-stricken few minutes she'd wondered if it could be Bernard's, but in quickly counting back she realised it couldn't. It made the relief, the escape from worry and anxiety, all the more wonderful. She thanked God for it. She couldn't bear to think of what might have happened if the child had been Bernard's. Horrifying scenarios of her mother looking at the child as soon as it was born and seeing a resemblance to Bernard kept rearing up in her mind to make her sweat with fear. She had to keep reminding herself, reassuring herself. It was all right. She was safe. The next time Bernard phoned she briefly told him about her pregnancy before hanging up again.

Gradually she relaxed. She enjoyed being fussed over by everyone. Needless to say, Robert was especially delighted. So was Josie, and they had lots of chats over the coffee cups about knitting patterns and names. She couldn't bring herself to tell her mother, and so sent a brief little note instead. Sophie never mentioned it. Attending the church with Robert either in Bearsden or Rose Street, Andrina felt good and pure. And safe. In the choir she sang like an angel.

Josie said, 'Pregnancy suits you. You look not only beautiful, but serene.'

'I feel so well. I suppose I'm lucky I'm so healthy.'

Quite often, especially as the birth drew near, Sophie insisted that Andrina stayed at Bearsden for a few days at a time, so that she could look after her. It was wonderful to lie back and have her mother put cushions behind her to make sure she was properly supported. Sophie would also put a footstool under her feet. She would ply her with her favourite chocolates, and cups of tea and tasty meals. Surely her mother must love her?

The actual pregnancy or birth was not discussed. Her mother had never spoken about such things. It was just as if Andrina had some sort of debilitating illness and had to be properly looked after. And properly looked after she was.

McPherson always maintained that Sophie was at her best when someone was ill. She never spared herself. 'She'd keep going all night and all day; she'd run herself into the ground looking after any of us,' he would say.

And he was right.

Andrina had the baby at home in Monteith Row. The midwife and doctor were there with a gas-and-air machine, and all went well. She gave birth to a little girl. Robert had been anxiously waiting in the kitchen and when he was called through, Andrina was propped up in bed, washed and powdered and in her white satin nightdress, her auburn hair brushed out over the pillow. The midwife was holding the baby. Robert rushed over and gazed at his new daughter admiringly, incredulously, before turning to Andrina.

'She looks beautiful, darling, absolutely perfect.'

Trust him, Andrina thought with an inward pout, to do the wrong thing: it should have been her he looked at first, her he admired first; and he should have congratulated her. However, he sat on the bed and held her hand and asked her how she was feeling. Then the midwife placed the baby in her arms and he went into raptures again, gently touching and tracing its sleeping face with his finger, holding and kissing its tiny hand.

Andrina was thinking how strange it was that here they were with their child, her and her husband, and she had no love for him. She had thought she loved him once – so long ago, it seemed – now she knew that love was being with Bernard. Love was the stirring passion that could fill her heart and mind to the exclusion of everything else. Too late she realised how little

286

Robert meant to her. She lay back on her pillows and closed her eyes. She hadn't really anything against him. He was a good husband. He was kind, he cared about her, he could be depended on to provide for her. She just didn't feel anything for him. Nothing at all.

'You must be exhausted,' he said. 'I'll leave you to have a good sleep.'

She smiled without opening her eyes. She felt the midwife lift the baby from her.

After a few days, once she got up and around, she was happy showing off the baby to Josie and Doris and Robert's mother, and anyone else who cared to come. Some of the girls she used to work with in Copland's arrived one night, all bringing presents. They had a real fun night. They congratulated her on producing such a beautiful, placid baby. They also enthused about what a wonderful supper she produced. She was a marvellously creative person, they said.

She kept the baby beautifully too. She took pride in that. She carefully, conscientiously, bathed her every day, and powdered her and dressed and fed her. She enjoyed putting her to the breast. It gave her a thrill that was almost sexual. When Doris visited her they'd both take the pram out for a walk around the Green. Doris would get a turn of pushing the pram; she'd keep gazing longingly at it.

'You're so terribly lucky, Andrina,' she'd sigh. 'A good husband, a nice home, a lovely baby. God's even blessed you with looks. You've got everything.'

'Do you ever hear from Bernard these days?' Andrina asked casually.

'Not *from* him,' Doris replied. 'I hear *about* him from Bridie because of course Frank's in touch. Not all that often because Bernard's away so much, but they do get together occasionally.'

'Has he married again?'

'Bernard? No. That woman – Jane Ford – probably chucked him because of his work. He turns night into day. It's not natural.'

Andrina couldn't help feeling glad that Bernard was not with anyone else. Although she daren't see him again it helped to imagine him still carrying a torch for her. 'Have you got over all that now?' she asked Doris. 'You were so bitter for a while, especially about the woman, weren't you?'

Doris shrugged. 'I suppose so. Although what I'd feel or do if we ever came face to face, I don't know. I still think if it hadn't been for her . . .' She shrugged again. 'Oh well, that's life.' Then something occurred to her. 'Robert used to be friendly with Bernard. Doesn't he ever see him now? Bernard used to help Robert in his karate club, didn't he?'

'Robert used to be his teacher in the school as well as the karate club,' Andrina said, 'so they've known each other for ages. But with Bernard being away, I suppose – I don't know – Robert hasn't mentioned him for a while.'

Then one day, out of the blue, Robert said, 'Oh, by the way, Bernard was at the club last night. I forgot to tell you. We had a good session. I've invited him to come for a bite of supper tomorrow night and to see Jennifer.' Robert laughed. 'He told me she just cannot be as beautiful and as perfect as I was making out.'

She had to go and make a cup of tea and potter about with her back to Robert in case he detected her confused and heightened emotions. Or saw the violent pulsing of her heart. Suddenly, from drifting pleasantly along on a calm surface, she was plunged into a highly dangerous, totally exciting, wild current of life again. She struggled to hold on to the safety of the calm shore.

'I might go over to Mummy's tomorrow night.'

'What?' Robert was incredulous.

'I'd leave Jennifer with you.'

'Don't be daft. We've not seen Bernard for ages. How do you think it would look if your purposely went out? You can see your mother at any time. He'd know that.'

She couldn't think of anything else to say without arousing suspicion. 'Oh, all right.'

She couldn't sleep. Next day her mind and emotions were in

a turmoil as she cleaned every corner of the house. She forgot to feed Jennifer, and was only reminded by the child's indignant crying.

'Darling, I'm sorry. I'm sorry.' She soothed and kissed the child's warm head as she suckled her. It occurred to her that it was time Jennifer was off the breast altogether. Her mother had long since presented her with a couple of bottles and teats and tins of powdered baby milk. Although she'd never actually mentioned the word breast-feeding, Andrina suspected her mother thought it was too disgusting for words.

She took a long time bathing and dressing, then making the supper. Robert said he and Bernard were having a karate session then coming home together. The moment her eyes met Bernard's, she knew nothing had changed. The electricity between them frightened her. She knew only too well all the complications and difficulties it could lead to in her life.

Bernard said, 'As beautiful as ever, Andrina. I've told you before, Robert, and I don't mind repeating it, you're a lucky man. I'd change places with you any day.'

Robert laughed. 'Just you keep your eyes off my wife. You're here to admire the baby, not her.'

'OK, OK,' Bernard said. 'I'll come back when you're not in.'

'Not if you value your life, mate.'

They had always joked like that. Bernard seemed to enjoy tempting fate. He had the most wicked, devilish, nerve-racking courage. It terrified and exhausted her. She never knew what he'd say or do next.

He'd brought a bottle of wine to have with the supper and a solid silver teething-ring with a little silver bell on it for Jennifer. Jennifer grabbed it in her tiny fist and shook it about and giggled with delight.

'She's absolutely gorgeous,' Bernard said. 'Just like her mother.' And he put an arm round Andrina's waist and squeezed her. Andrina pushed him away. Fool that he was, Robert laughed.

For supper she'd made shepherd's pie, with treacle sponge to follow. Fortunately she and Bernard were never alone, and eventually Robert saw Bernard to the door. When he returned to the kitchen to begin helping Andrina clear the table and do the dishes, Robert said, 'It's good to see Bernard again. I'm glad to hear he's doing so well. I always knew he would be successful, of course. I always said, didn't I?'

Andrina kept her head averted as she worked. 'Yes.'

'I've never understood what your mother had against him.'

'He's a Catholic.'

'Well, OK, he's a Catholic. But the strength of her dislike seemed to go far beyond the religious thing. It was downright hatred. I expect if she saw him today she'd still be the same despite the fact he's done so well for himself.' He shook his head. 'I'm very fond of your mother. She's been good to us. But she is a woman of rather worrying extremes.'

Oh, didn't she know it. Didn't she know it.

Leaning over the sink, conscientiously, religiously cleaning the dishes, Andrina began to sweat.

Chapter Forty-Two

'Will you marry me?' Bernard persisted on the phone next day. It was as if her original conversation with Bernard, far less her relationship with him, had never been interrupted.

'I've told you – no. I can't.'

'I love you and you love me.'

'Yes,' she agreed. Her feelings for him had not changed. They had only retreated into her dream world. She made love to him in her mind while she was suckling her baby. He plunged inside her as she lay in bed with Robert. Sometimes she longed so much for the reality of him that she wept, but quietly so that Robert wouldn't hear. Never a day, never a night passed that she didn't think of him and long for him.

Jennifer kept her busy, of course. Her mother adored the child. Sometimes she thought the baby was Sophie's saving. Sophie had been heading for a nervous breakdown. Her father confided to her that it all stemmed from the terrible childhood she'd had. Apparently her parents weren't dead as she'd always pretended, they were actually living in Bearsden. Seeing them again had stirred up all the trauma of Sophie's childhood, McPherson said, and he had to force her to go to the doctor and get tranquillisers. She'd worked herself into a dreadful state.

What a strange world it was, Andrina thought, that could repeat patterns like that. She couldn't bear to look back at her own childhood. Sometimes though, when she felt overtired or stressed, memories would come unbidden. She would feel helpless, terrified, alone in the darkness listening to strange menacing sounds. Sometimes she'd see fearsome shapes and shadows on the walls, not knowing then that it was the flickering reflection of the fire. Then the fire would die and there would be stillness. And pitch blackness. And freezing cold. Oh, the terror of those long hours. The indescribable relief on seeing her mother again. The desperate clinging to her.

She didn't want to know what childish traumas her mother had suffered. It was enough to try to cope with her own, and yet their unspoken terrors bound them together. Not that her mother ever gave any demonstration of affection – even to baby Jennifer. Andrina felt inhibited, almost ashamed to show any affection for the child herself when her mother was there. While her mother was under the same roof, Andrina gave Jennifer furtive, secret kisses. But Sophie showed a keen interest in Jennifer. She bought her clothes. When she visited Monteith Row she insisted on bumping the pram down the stairs and going outside for a brisk walk with the baby in the Green. She changed her nappy and bathed her and tucked her into her cot. She encouraged visits to Bearsden. She insisted that Andrina and Robert had nights out. She'd attend to Jennifer. She was terribly efficient with the child. It was as if she didn't trust Andrina to do anything properly for the baby. Just as years ago, she'd never trusted her to scrub the floor clean enough, or empty the bin without spilling ash.

'Try and come as often as you can,' McPherson said. 'It keeps her busy. Keeps her mind off other things.'

And of course Sophie never tired of showing the baby off to all her Bearsden neighbours and friends.

She'd become a regular sight now – earnestly, busily pushing the pram down Drymen Road, spectacles glinting in the sun, hands locked over the handle. Andrina spent nearly every weekend at Bearsden. Sometimes Robert couldn't come because he had a karate class or he was away on some outing he'd promised his pupils. On these occasions she'd sit around the house fantasising about Bernard, or walk alone around Bearsden dreaming about him. Or she'd just feel resentment against her mother for taking over yet another part of her life. Her mother always pounced on Jennifer the minute she saw her and did everything for her. It left an empty ache in Andrina's heart.

If she dared to object, her mother withdrew into that dark silence that she feared so much.

When she spoke to Bernard about it, he laughed and said, 'Why the hell are you so afraid of her? What can she do to you? You're a grown woman. Do you think she'll strike you or something? It's ridiculous.'

She didn't care what Bernard thought about her relationship with her mother. In encouraging or threatening confrontation with her mother, he triggered off blind panic. That was all that mattered.

'Well then,' Bernard insisted, 'why can't we get married?'

'We've been through all this before. Nothing's changed.'

'Of course things have changed. I'm divorced, for one thing.'

'Yes, I heard all about that.' She couldn't keep a note of bitterness from her voice at the thought of Jane Ford.

He ignored the hurt tone. 'And for another thing, I've got a flat. Look, it's no use trying to talk over the phone. Why don't you come to the flat and we can talk properly? There's a few things I want to explain. And I'd like you to see the place. You could advise me about decoration and furnishings. Whatever way you'd like the flat to be – that's how I want it to be.'

He told her the address and she couldn't resist the temptation to meet him there the following afternoon. She threw all caution to the winds. Now she was feverish with excitement. She had no difficulty in persuading herself that as long as the relationship was kept secret, everything would be all right. Now that Bernard had a place of his own, it would be more than all right – it would be perfect. It would be so much safer, more discreet – their secret love nest. She'd have to take Jennifer, of course, but that wouldn't matter. The child could be put in another room with a toy or something. She began dreaming and planning about how she would furnish the flat, exactly to her taste. She was so excited she had an orgasm just thinking about Bernard making love to her again. She knew perfectly well that once alone in the privacy of his flat they wouldn't just talk. Previously, apart from anything else, it had become difficult to be alone – especially during the long school holidays when Robert was at home so much. More importantly, there

293

was always the danger of her mother arriving. Doris had always kept in touch, of course. Hungry for any news of Bernard's private life, Andrina had encouraged these visits. From time to time, she also heard snippets from Robert. He had told her that Bernard was getting more and more caught up with work. He'd had several jobs not only in different parts of Scotland, but in England as well. Well-known groups were employing him and his men to accompany them on tours of clubs and theatres, which kept him away from home often for months at a time.

Robert blamed Bernard's job for the divorce – being away so much, and also meeting so many glamorous women. Andrina had suffered at the thought of the glamorous women, but long ago Bernard had assured her that no one could match her in looks and other women meant nothing to him. His thoughts of love were for no one else but her.

The next day she bathed and shampooed her hair and brushed it until it gleamed like burnished metal. She slipped into the silky sensual underwear that Bernard admired. On top she wore a strapless white cotton dress with golden polka dots. It fitted closely at the bust and waist but had a wide circular skirt. On her feet she wore soft white leather pumps.

She used very little make-up, just mascara and pink lip-gloss. Happy with herself she did a twirl of admiration in front of the wardrobe mirror. She looked healthy and full of life – eyes, hair, teeth, lips shining.

Then she went to put on the baby's coat. Jennifer sat sucking a dummy teat, looking very pretty with her sky-blue eyes and silvery blonde coxcomb of hair. Andrina felt a wavering, an uncertainty. She had a sudden disturbing vision of Bernard's attention and admiration fixing on the child, as so many people's did. She felt ashamed of the thought and the feeling of jealousy that accompanied it. She quickly kissed the child's forehead. 'Mummy's darling little girl,' she said.

Yet she was unable to shake off the shameful jealousy. She didn't want to take Jennifer with her. She wanted Bernard's flat to be a special place only for Bernard and herself. She wondered about leaving the baby behind. It wouldn't be in any way like when Sophie had left her. It wouldn't be cold and dark. She wouldn't be neglected and hungry. It was a beautiful summer's day. Jennifer was dry, adequately dressed and well fed. Andrina hesitated, wanting to leave her, unsure if she could cope with the guilt. Eventually she ran next door to Josie.

'Josie, could you do me a really big favour?'

'If I can, hen.'

'Could you look after Jennifer for a couple of hours? I'll be back in plenty of time for you to get to work, I promise.'

'As a matter of fact, I'm not working tonight. A pal and me have got tickets for a show in the Pavilion. As long as you're back in plenty of time for letting me away for that.'

'Oh thanks, Josie.'

She ran back to fetch Jennifer. She hugged her and showered her with kisses. 'You're going to be all right, darling. Everything's going to be all right, I promise.' Then, feeling free as the wind, she joyously hurried to Sauchiehall Mansions.

He opened the door to her and, without a word of greeting, moved aside to allow her to enter. In the hall, he stood gazing at her in silence for a time, before taking her hand and leading her into the bedroom. He laid her on the bed, spread out the circular skirt of her dress, extending it from one side of the bed to the other. Then he stood watching her. Long ago she had come to accept this habit of his, and could now relax under his long silent scrutiny. She knew he was admiring the sight of her, eating her with his eyes, and as the sun streaming in through the bay window warmed her skin, she almost purred with pleasure. She felt sensuous under his gaze. To her it was a kind of foreplay and it had just as powerful an effect. Eventually he fell on top of her, just as she was, complete with dress and stockings and shoes. She cried out in delight and soon they were both groaning and moaning and making uninhibited animal sounds of pleasure.

Afterwards his hands gently caressed her breasts and her abdomen and he said, 'You're so soft and feminine, Andrina, and when we make love, you hold me like a velvet vice. I love you and I want to marry you.'

295

Talk of marriage agitated her again. She struggled away from him into a sitting position. 'Why can't we just go on like this? It'll be perfect now that you've got a place of your own.'

He sighed. 'My darling velvet. You have a husband and a child to go home to when you leave here. You forget I'll be on my own.'

'I can't imagine you living like a monk, Bernard.'

'Darling, I swear to you, you are the one love of my life.'

'All right, I'll come as often as I can. But no more talk of marriage. We'll have wonderful times here together.' She swung her legs off the bed. 'Now, *please* show me your flat.'

He took her hand again and led her around while she suggested colours and furnishings and furniture with all the excited eagerness of a child.

'You'll notice,' he said, 'that I already have a few basic essentials.'

'Yes,' she laughed, 'the bed.'

'First things first.'

Time flew as they made their plans. Bernard gave her a credit card so that she could order whatever was needed for the flat. It seemed to her that it was just like getting married. In fact, Bernard's flat was far more 'hers' than the one in Monteith Row. In Monteith Row many things were to Robert's taste. There had been the presents too, from Robert's mother and her mother and other friends and relations, so that in fact the place reflected a mixtures of tastes. In Sauchiehall Mansions Bernard gave her an absolutely free hand. Everything, down to the style of the last teaspoon, was exactly what she liked. She had chosen the ornaments, the furniture, the carpets. It felt more like her flat than Bernard's. She loved the place (as he did too), but she also felt keenly possessive towards it.

When she went shopping for the flat, she took Jennifer with her. When she visited Bernard at the flat, she left Jennifer with Josie. Or, more and more often, she managed to leave her in Bearsden with her mother on some trumped-up excuse. It had always to have some kind of twisted truth to it, because her mother was like a bloodhound in sniffing out lies. For instance she told Sophie, 'I'm helping a friend settle in to a new flat. I've already helped choose the colour scheme . . .' She chattered on, making sure first of all that her mother's attention was mostly taken up with Jennifer. She'd always plop the child on to Sophie's lap before she began to reel off her excuses. It helped of course that Sophie was always so eager for the chance of being left with Jennifer. Andrina escaped gleefully from these encounters, shivering with success and excitement but also with fear and vastly-increased guilt.

She also felt the fear, to a lesser degree, when Bernard phoned her. Often he'd phone and she'd be standing in the hall listening to his words of love and sexual passion, while in the kitchen her mother and father and husband would be sitting talking, or enjoying a meal.

Robert never asked who was on the phone, but her mother always did. It was her mother's habit to pry into everything. Eyes would narrow to hard slits behind steel-rimmed glasses. Her voice would sharpen.

'Who was that?'

Andrina went over to the cupboard so that her face could be hidden. 'That friend I told you about – you know, the one who's got a new flat. Who wants pudding and who wants cheese and biscuits? Or you can have both if you want.' Then she popped her head round the cupboard door, all wide-eyed and innocent. 'What about you, Mummy? It's bread and butter pudding – your favourite.'

Or she'd just say, 'Is that Jennifer crying?' And her mother would forget about the phone call and rush through to the bedroom to see if there was something wrong or if Jennifer needed anything.

One evening, not long after the work on the flat was finished, Bernard called her from work and asked her to be in the flat waiting for him dressed in the lingerie, the wedding dress – everything that she'd worn on her wedding day. She agreed, but with a fast-beating heart and a feeling of danger of a different kind than usual. Surely this request was very strange. But then, Bernard was a strange person – quite different from

297

anyone else she'd ever known. It was Josie's day off, and she was going on a trip to Rothesay with one of the other girls from the pub. Andrina persuaded her to pretend to Robert that she was going along too.

'I'll explain later,' she told Josie.

Josie was mystified, but agreed. And so it was that Robert was left to look after Jennifer for the whole day and most of the evening.

Andrina spent hours in the Sauchiehall Mansions bath, perfuming her body in preparation, then paying great attention to her hair and make-up just as she'd done on her wedding day.

She had bought a record of classical music. She watched out of the window, and put the record on as soon as she saw Bernard's car come into view down the street. Then she stood waiting for him, in her silvery white crinoline dress and her sparkling tiara and veil. But he went first of all into the other room to change into a morning suit – striped trousers, morning coat, and starched shirt complete with grey silk tie. When he entered the bedroom he stood staring at her for what seemed like hours. Tears began trickling down his features and blurred their hardness. He took her arm and led her over to the mirrored wall. On the fourth finger of her left hand, after discarding her original wedding ring, he placed a gold band.

'I love you, Andrina, and now I feel you're really mine.'

Then he lifted the skirt of the dress and hooped crinoline undergarments and entered her with a force that was quite frightening. His erection was throbbing with power inside her. His thrusts were perfectly timed, long and gentle at first, then building until eventually he seemed to plunge his wonderful, muscular body, his entire being, into her. Their love-making went on for most of the evening. He climaxed again and again but could not content himself. Time and again he entered her, remaining hard for hours. She thought him a truly remarkable man.

And he was hers.

Chapter Forty-Three

'I'd rather give key money to a private factor than encourage that two-faced bastard,' Frank said. He had thought he could approach Bailie McPherson – now *Senior* Bailie of the City of Glasgow, no less. In his desperation for a decent house for Bridie and himself, he had said he would do it. In the end, though, it went too much against the grain. At least it was well known about key money. One could almost say it was honest and above board. It had become so common it was accepted as the normal channel and practice to go through in order to get a house in the private sector – if and when there was one available.

'I'm past caring about how we get a place,' Bridie said. 'Just so long as we get out of here. I'd even go to Blackhill if it meant being on our own.'

The Council were knocking down the old Garngad bit by bit and rehousing people in Blackhill.

'No way,' said Frank, 'anywhere but Blackhill.'

They were both speaking in undertones in case anyone heard them. They had got into the habit of this desperate whisper. It had been bad enough with Scobie and Carragh always moving about in the kitchen (which was within hearing distance), or in the tiny windowless space between the kitchen and the front room, or one of them coming into the room for something, like using the pail in the cupboard. (If there was a queue waiting for the lavatory on the downstairs landing, or if it was during the night and it was too cold and dark for Carragh to go out to the lavatory, she would creep through to the room and use the pail.) She was always awfully apologetic about these disturbances but, as she said, 'When you get older, son, ye cannae wait.' The smell of urine constantly pervaded the room, even though Carragh religiously emptied the pail every day.

299

Now, to add to Frank and Bridie's miseries, Doris was mooning about all the time. It was beginning to seem as if she'd never get over Bernard.

'To think,' she kept saying, 'that he kept me stuck in that dump in Blackhill, and then as soon as we're divorced he gets a posh flat in Sauchiehall Mansions for his fancy woman.'

'Oh, I don't think he's living with anybody, Doris,' Frank tried to comfort.

'What's he needing a big flat like that for, then?'

'You know Bernard. He's always had big ideas.'

'I know Bernard all right,' Doris said bitterly. 'There'll be another woman. There's always a woman with him.'

'I'm not so sure about that . . . He spends so much time in physical training. And then with his job . . .'

Doris's mouth twisted. 'Aye, well, now we all know what he was training for.'

'I'm sorry it didn't work out for you and Bernard, Doris. If there was anything I could do . . .'

'Thanks, Frank. It's over now. It's just . . .' Tears welled up and messed mascara down her face. 'I don't seem to be able to forget . . . I mean, he hurt me something terrible, Frank.'

Frank felt even more sorry for Doris than Bridie did. Perhaps because he had lived under the same roof as Bernard, he had more of an idea what Bernard might be capable of.

Bridie tried to be patient and sympathetic to Doris, but alone in the front room, she whispered to Frank, 'She's driving me up the wall with going on about Bernard so much. Why doesn't she at least make some effort to forget him and get on with her life? Honestly, Frank, if we don't get out of here we'll both go mad. You're not getting any peace to do your writing. I can't even get a minute's quiet to read. If it's not Doris, it's Carragh, and if it's not them, it's Scobie. Sometimes I think it's worse living with him now that he's sober.'

Scobie liked to have a blether. Or a game of cards. Or dominoes. During the day while Frank and Bridie and Doris were at work, and as often as not Carragh was out for her messages, or at the steamie, or just blethering with a neighbour,

Scobie joined the corner boys. They weren't all boys of course. Some were elderly like himself. Some were too old to work. Some were young but couldn't find any work. Some were ex-servicemen who had fought for their country and had once again been let down. They'd returned to nothing else but signing on at the 'broo', as the labour exchange was called. Some of them had come back to bombed shells that had once been their homes.

Young or old, employed or unemployed, they met and hung about the street corner and talked about football and female conquests and the state of the nation. Sometimes they'd hunker down and have a game of pitch and toss. At other times, especially in the evenings, Scobie was glad of a change of company and welcomed a blether or a game of dominoes with Frank. Or he'd pester Frank and Bridie and Doris to make a foursome in a game of cards. Scobie had always to be either talking or doing something, or both. And he enjoyed a good laugh. Bridie couldn't stand it when he either told jokes or played jokes on anyone – especially on her or Frank. Bridie had not inherited her father's sense of humour.

In the end, Frank went to a factor's office in town, paid him key money, and eventually was informed that he could have a flat that had become vacant. It was in the Gorbals; not a place they would have chosen. However, they were assured that much redevelopment was planned there too – indeed was already in progress – and they would be rehoused into one of the brand new houses in the area as soon as they were built. The new Waddell Court in the Gorbals had been opened by the Queen in 1959. A high-rise block of flats was already being built and was due to be ready for the first occupants in just over a year, in 1965. Each of the new flats had every modern convenience – beautifully equipped kitchen, bathroom, central heating throughout.

Frank and Bridie were in seventh heaven at the thought of eventually having such a place. 'It's worth putting up with an old house for a wee while in order to qualify for a place like that,' Bridie said. Frank agreed. 'And we'd be on our own,' Bridie said. 'We'd have privacy.'

301

Shangri-La.

Bridle warmed to the subject. 'I bet you're just meant to be there, Frank. The Gorbals has produced lots of famous people. Thomas Lipton became the world's richest grocer. Allan Pinkerton, the founder of the world's biggest private detection agency.'

Frank caught her enthusiasm. 'John Buchan, novelist and Governor General of Canada.'

'Isaac Wolfsen, founder of one of the biggest store groups in the country.'

Frank laughed with excitement. 'Michael would include Benny Lynch, world Champion boxer, on the list.'

'One day everyone will include Frank O'Maley, world famous writer.'

'Oh Bridie,' Frank sighed, and they clung to each other in happiness and hope.

The house was a room and kitchen, with an outside lavatory, in Cumberland Street, one of the main shopping areas of the Gorbals. It was just under half a mile long and had a continuous row of shops on both sides of the street. As well as the shops there were traders with barrows selling fish and fruit and coal briquettes. It was a crowded, bustling, noisy street, but it had a warmth and friendliness. Frank enjoyed studying it from the quiet privacy of his own room window.

'After all,' as he told Bridie, 'people are my raw material.'

They made the room and kitchen as nice as they could afford. Helped by an upstairs neighbour, Mr Menzies, they took down the long high shelf in the kitchen and put in a free-standing kitchen cabinet. The cabinet was Bridie's pride and joy. It had frosted stained-glass doors in a sunburst pattern on the top part, and cream doors, then a pull-out enamel work surface, two drawers, and then two more doors.

'Wonderful amount of shelf space for everything,' Bridie boasted to everybody.

They had a kitchen table with an enamel top ('So easy to keep clean – just a wipe over'). The floor was covered with linoleum tiles the same colour as the sunburst glass of the cabinet, and there was a pretty autumn coloured rug in front of the fire. They hadn't been able to afford the old range being taken out.

Frank said, 'It's not worth the bother if we'll be moving to a new place soon.'

They hadn't got rid of the high hole-in-the-wall bed either, preferring to sleep in the cosy kitchen, keeping the front room as their best place and always looking nice to receive visitors. Despite this, it actually worked out that when any of the family came to visit, they automatically walked into the kitchen. The front room was seldom used except by Frank who enjoyed watching the world go by from the window.

'I'll have to move that wee table from the window,' he told Bridie eventually. 'I'm so interested in watching everybody down on the street I'm not getting on with my writing.'

The Gorbals had a fascinating mixture of people. Down through the years it had welcomed the Irish, the Jews, the Poles, the Lithuanians, the Highlanders, and the Lowland Scots from rural areas. From this international mix a new type of Scottish character had emerged. It had the devil-may-care of the Irish, the shrewdness of the Jewish people, the solidarity of the Eastern Europeans, plus the natural wit and industry of the Scot. Wonderful people – just asking to be written about!

As often as not now, Frank wrote at the kitchen table while Bridie was washing dishes at the sink, or preparing a pot of soup for the next day's dinner, or just sitting by the fire and reading. Sometimes he found himself nodding off to sleep over his papers. After a hard day's work and a good meal of Bridie's soup and mince and potatoes, or toad-in-the-hole, it wasn't easy to work for another few hours – even if it was at his writing.

Frank and Bridie talked about it, and it was decided that he'd get up at five-thirty every morning and write for a couple of hours before he went to the office. So that's what he did. After doing his writing stint he insisted on giving Bridie a cup of tea in bed and then, while she was drinking it, he made the breakfast.

'You've a day's work ahead of you too, Bridie,' he told her. 'Why should you do all the cooking and housework as well as your ordinary job? No, it's only fair that we share it.'

Nevertheless Bridie always hurried home from the bookshop and did as much as she could before Frank arrived. 'You're already doing two jobs with the office and your writing,' she said.

With both of them working so hard, they didn't have much energy left for entertaining, apart from the family who visited sometimes – more often than Bridie and Frank might have wished. Scobie especially liked to drop in. Doris and Carragh too.

Their immediate neighbours in Cumberland Street were cheery and friendly, and said they'd 'fairly enjoyed the wee night' when Bridie and Frank had invited them in for supper – 'so that we can all get to know each other,' as Frank had explained.

Nevertheless, despite all the eager preparation Bridie and Frank had made to ensure the evening's success (their first formal supper party), a slight reserve had developed among their guests. There had even been a few awkward periods of silence, especially after Frank had spoken about his writing. Everybody had been very nice and polite when saying goodnight. But Frank, ever sensitive to nuances of mood, caught in their voices and their lack of lingering an element of relief.

Later, lying cuddled together in the kitchen bed, he and Bridie discussed the evening. 'Let's face it, Bridie. It's always been the same – I embarrass people.'

'I wouldn't put it as strongly as that, Frank. I think they had a good night. I mean, they enjoyed the meal and everything. And I'm sure they liked us. It's just that we haven't much in common with them.'

'It's not you, Bridie. It's me. It's me and my writing. But I don't care. One day they'll boast about knowing me.' They laughed together and cuddled each other closer. 'One day they'll say, "Here, I used to live up the same close as that famous guy. Believe it or not, he once had me into his house for supper." '

They clung to each other, feeling blessed that they had each other, and truly grateful for their love. Bridie thanked the Blessed Mary, Mother of God, every night for her good fortune in having Frank, and their wee room and kitchen in the Gorbals. As they made tender love to each other they were oblivious to the sounds of drunken songs outside on the stairs, or the cats howling in unison in the back yard, or the faint echoes of a domestic battle in one of the other flats, or the weeping and wailing of a baby.

It was a cold night outside. A bitter wind was raging down through the black caverns of the tenements and sending gusts of rain battering against the kitchen window. Every now and again the window rattled and the cream paper blind puffed out. But the kitchen fire filled the small room with a rosy glow, and the storm outside only made Bridie and Frank feel more grateful for the warmth of their love and the safe haven of their own home.

Bridie no longer felt envious of Bernard's flat; Frank never had. He was truly sorry for 'poor wee Doris', as he was now in the habit of referring to her. After he and Bridie made love they lay in each other's arms in the cosy hole-in-the-wall bed and chatted about this and that – including Doris and Bernard.

'I never thought she seemed right for him,' Bridie said.

Frank agreed. 'It's funny, though,' he said. 'As far as I know, he's never been all that much of a womanizer. But of course he never used to speak about that side of his life – still doesn't.'

'There's definitely been that woman – Jane Ford.'

'The thing is, with Doris being a good Catholic, I suppose she still feels married to him. In the eyes of the church she still *is* married to him.'

'I know.'

'Poor wee Doris. I saw her the other day. I was up near the Charing Cross end of Sauchiehall Street in my lunch hour to buy some typing paper. It must have been her lunch hour too. She was standing across from the Sauchiehall Mansions gazing up at Bernard's flat.'

'That's pathetic,' Bridie said. 'No good can come of her doing things like that.'

Frank agreed.

Chapter Forty-Four

The strain was tying Sophie in knots. But the more she felt over-strained, the harder she worked. As well as attending church services three times on Sunday, she rushed out to every other service that was held during the week. She was a member of the Women's Guild, and helped run whist drives and jumble sales and coffee mornings for various church charities. She was forever beavering away in the church kitchen or hall. Her total commitment and her capacity for hard work made her a natural choice for innumerable committees. The only area she firmly declined to have anything to do with was the care of the aged in the community.

'I'm sorry, Mrs Dinwoodie,' she told the minister's wife, 'but it would upset me if I had to have contact with the Nobles again. I did try, as you know. But it was no use. I just feel now that I don't want to take part in anything that might bring me into contact with them.'

'I understand, my dear. I and all your friends feel for you. One would think at their age they would know better. They don't even come to church now. They say they're not able to get out and about, but several people have offered them a lift. I'm sure you must have done so yourself.'

'They just don't want anything to do with me. They never have. It upsets me even to talk about them, Mrs Dinwoodie. I would be grateful if you would try not to mention them in my presence.'

'Of course, my dear. I'm sorry if I've upset you.'

McPherson expressed the view to Sophie that she might regret not making it up with her parents while she still had the chance. 'After all,' he reminded her, 'they might not last much longer.'

'What do you know about how I'd feel?' she raged at him. 'It would fit you better to attend to your relationship with your own mother. How often do you go and see her? She's a widow living on her own in that wee dump of a place, and you hardly ever go near her.'

McPherson went stiff with annoyance. 'I'm a busy man. I visit her when I can.'

'I'm a busy woman but I visit her more often than you do. And I keep in close touch with Andrina both by phone and by visiting her. When did you last speak to your daughter or go to see her? And you work in the City Chambers, not ten minutes in the car from her place. Don't you dare lecture me about how to treat family.'

'You go to extremes, that's your trouble,' he accused. 'You're never off that phone to Andrina – and it's not just for a motherly chat. You give her the third degree. You've missed your vocation. You should have been in Hitler's Gestapo. Don't imagine she'll enjoy hearing from you or seeing you. All you'll do for her, if you go on the way you're doing, is make her as bad a nervous wreck as yourself.'

'You don't know what you're talking about,' Sophie said. 'No mother could be more attentive and caring, and she knows it. That girl couldn't do without me. Look at how she depends on me to help her with Jennifer.'

'By God, you weren't always caring or attentive, Sophie. As I said, it's always one extreme to another with you. And if you ask me, it doesn't seem right that Andrina's always so keen to dump that child on you.'

'What a way to talk! She doesn't *dump* her. She knows that Jennifer will be well looked after while she does her shopping or cleaning or sees to her friend.'

'It would fit her better to see to her child. Maybe it's like mother, like daughter with her and you. Is that why you're always giving her the third degree? You're afraid of her becoming like you used to be?'

'Don't talk rubbish. Andrina's had a good Christian up-bringing, which was more than I ever had.' She felt worried and suspicious. Andrina *was* leaving Jennifer with her rather often.

Not that she personally objected to having the child. She would happily keep her all the time – forever, if it were possible. The child meant so much to her, was so necessary to her. She felt she could devour her; she felt fiercely possessive towards Jennifer.

But why was Andrina leaving the child with her so often? She made plenty of excuses. Too many excuses. Was Andrina trying to avoid responsibility for Jennifer? Or was there some other reason? Suspicion and fear became worms in her brain, poisoning it, rotting it. She couldn't bear any thoughts of Andrina bringing disgrace or shame of any kind on her good name in Bearsden. She'd worked hard to make a place for herself in the community. She was accepted as one of them now. No one knew the whole truth about her background, and she prayed that no one ever would. The Nobles had not tainted her reputation here after all.

Life had been going on the way she wanted it to – needed it to – frenetically busy, with gratitude and praise being showered on her for all her good works. Now she kept taking off her spectacles, vigorously polishing them, hooking them back on again and peering through them as if to catch and pin down anything suspicious.

She dialled Andrina's number. There was no reply.

Andrina hadn't seen her neighbour for some time – not since the day Josie had looked after Jennifer and she'd gone to see Bernard's flat. There had been a friend of Josie's in when she'd arrived (much later than she'd promised) to collect her daughter. Josie had been waiting to go out. They'd tickets booked for a show and they rushed from the house the moment Andrina arrived. Andrina called her apologies after them as they clattered away down the stairs, but she wasn't really bothered. She was too happy, too elated.

Since then she'd managed to persuade her mother to have Jennifer – sometimes for a whole day at a time – and as a result she'd not needed Josie as a babysitter again, until Josie's day out to Rothesay, when she agreed to pretend that Andrina had gone with her. On that occasion Robert had looked after

Jennifer. She promised to explain to Josie later, but again it was some time before she'd seen her neighbour or at least had the opportunity to speak alone with her. Either Josie wasn't in, or had somebody in with her, or was at work, or on her holidays. She'd gone for two weeks to Dunoon. Apparently, the place was packed with American sailors – and Josie liked sailors.

Eventually they did get together for a cup of coffee. Andrina had decided to confide in her friend. She felt so happy, she had to tell someone. Anyway Josie, she felt sure, was unshockable – working in a pub, and such a rough one at that, and going out with sailors . . . She listened with some impatience to Josie's giggling stories about her dates with an American called Dwain from the deep South. Eventually she got her turn.

'Oh, Josie, I've got the most wonderful lover. You know who I mean. He used to go into your pub with his brothers. Bernard – one of the O'Maleys. Remember he and his wife visited here? I've known him off and on since I was about fifteen – but we didn't really get together until comparatively recently. He's really tough and very ambitious. He's getting on so well and he's got a flat of his own now.' Her large round eyes shone with joy, remembering. 'It's a beautiful place. That's where I was that day of your outing to Rothesay. Bernard and I spent the whole day together, and I dressed up in my wedding dress, and I did my hair in the special way I had on my wedding day, and I took extra care with my make-up, and I wore my wedding tiara and veil, and he made love to me like that . . .'

'That's bloody obscene!'

'What?' For a moment Andrina was confused. She had been so happily carried away with her memories of the day. She stared at Josie with blank eyes and sagging mouth.

'Do you mean to tell me,' Josie's voice climbed a ladder of incredulity, 'that you got me to lie for you? You got your husband to look after your baby, while you dressed up in the clothes you married Robert in, and allowed some other guy to fuck you?'

Andrina began to tremble like a frightened child. 'It wasn't like that.'

310

'What do you mean it wasn't like that? You've just told me it *was* like that. It's bloody obscene,' Josie repeated. 'And here was me thinking you were such a lady, and a goody-goody one at that. Here was me thinking – God, I've got to laugh – here was me looking up to you. Such a great one for cleaning the house, such a great cook and baker, such a great church-goer. You even sing in the bloody church choir!'

'You don't understand – Bernard and I love each other. And he's so romantic. There was nothing obscene or vulgar about it. There never is with him. Everything is so romantic. So . . . so perfect.'

'My God,' Josie groaned. 'Well, it's really none of my business, hen. And I don't want it to have anything to do with me. So don't you ever again ask me to look after that innocent wee wean again. Because, much as I like having her, the answer'll be no way – no chance.' She shook her head. 'And to think I'd been wondering if I should confess to you about my giggle and slap and tickle with Dwain. And him and I free agents, not married or anything. God, I feel a right fool.'

Andrina was upset for the rest of the morning, but after preparing lunch for Jennifer and having a glass of sherry and a light but nourishing meal herself, she began to feel better. After all, what did Josie know about love? Love changed everything. Love was the most important thing in life. It even said so in the Bible.

Thinking of the Bible made her remember the filthy word 'adultery'. It made her stomach cave in. But she quickly turned her mind to what it said in Proverbs: '. . . love covereth all sins', and gradually she felt better again. She did love him – totally, passionately. At the beginning she had been shy, easily shocked, inhibited by guilt. As time passed, she became more aware of the strength of her own sensuality. Her pouting mouth, her full up-tilted breasts, her softly rounded hips. She became more and more aware of Bernard's sexuality. But he was romantic too. He made everything different and beautiful. They had been spending a great deal of time together, but the poignancy of the situation was that the times they specially

311

wanted to be together, they had to be with their families. Now that his mother was dead, Bernard felt his father needed his family, and him more than ever, at Christmas and New Year. They spent Christmas Day at Frank's place. On Boxing Day, they all gathered together with Bridie's mother and father and the rest of the Gallacher family in Blackhill.

However, at times like Christmas and New Year and birthdays and Valentine's Day, Andrina and Bernard coped by celebrating these occasions on special dates of their own.

Their Christmas Day, for instance, was on 22 December. The planning began in their minds weeks before, however. Much consideration was given to what she would wear. After trailing round Argyle Street and Sauchiehall Street and Buchanan Street many times she settled on a burgundy velvet dress. She knew Bernard loved the soft sensuousness of velvet and she always thrilled when he called her 'my beautiful velvet'. The dress had a sweetheart plunging neckline. The sleeves were very narrow taffeta of the same dark colour, and a ruffled tail at the bottom of the skirt was in a matching fabric. She thought it classic because of the cut and shape and the richness of the fabric. Admiring herself in the mirror, turning this way and that, she also decided it was terrifically sensual because of its figure-hugging fit and the way it accentuated every curve. Also, to make the most of her curves, she wore underneath the dress a black satin basque which laced up the front and had black suspenders. To add to the effect her legs were provokingly sexy in sheer black lace-topped stockings. Black satin court shoes completed the alluring picture.

On the more mundane side she had shopped in plenty of time for a small frozen turkey, cranberries and all the trimmings. She carefully stored them at the back of her freezer. If Robert saw the turkey he would just take it for granted that she would be going to cook it for him and Jennifer and herself. If he asked her about it – after all, they were all going to her mother's for Christmas again this year – she would be ready with some lie or other. It had become quite easy to lie to Robert.

312

The most exciting purchase was a magnificent spruce Christmas tree, and she enjoyed searching around for all-white decorations with which to adorn it. Gradually, during the month of December, all these things were sneaked out and taken to Bernard's flat in preparation for their Christmas on the twenty-second.

The night before the big day she took Jennifer to Bearsden and asked her mother to keep her overnight and all next day on the pretext of doing the Christmas shopping.

On the morning of the twenty-second, she let herself into Bernard's flat with her key and set to work decorating the place and doing all the cooking. Then she set a small table at the bottom of the bed and draped it in a white damask cloth trailing down on to the carpet. The centrepiece was an extravagant display of red roses and fresh holly, finished with three red candles. Two fine-stemmed crystal glasses and silver cutlery completed the picture. A beautiful Christmas music record was ready to play on the machine. After everything was under control in the kitchen, she set to work on the tree. It stood in the corner of the bedroom shimmering with the white baubles, angel hair and white lights.

Finally, she showered and carefully dressed and made up in time for Bernard arriving home from work. He also showered and, still in the bathroom, changed into a smart suit and white wing-collared shirt she'd left ready for him.

On entering the bedroom he stood, quite mystified. The only light came from the tree and the candles on the table. Wafting in the warm air was the heartwarming smell of turkey and bread sauce. In the background the old familiar carols chimed out. He took her in his arms and they danced wordlessly round the room, round the Christmas tree and the Christmas table. They seemed to be silently floating in a sea of love. Then, standing by the tree, they gently made love as they gazed and feasted on each other.

Eventually she managed to pry herself away to serve dinner. They chatted happily over the various courses, and sipped champagne and laughed with the sheer delight of it all. Then, after exchanging gifts, they lay down in front of the tree and made passionate love under the twinkling lights.

Three days later, she went through the motions of a family Christmas.

Chapter Forty-Five

Michael was ashamed. He was ashamed of being beaten in one booth too many. He was ashamed of his flattened nose and cauliflower ear. He was ashamed of losing the sight in one eye and not being allowed to box again. But most of all he was ashamed of his fears. He didn't know why he was filled with fear. He'd open the door, meaning to go out, and he'd hear Mrs McAllister on the stairs and he'd feel afraid and hastily shut the door again. Why was he afraid of Mrs McAllister? He didn't know. There was no sense to it. Nothing in his life made sense any more. He loved his wife, but when he was sober he'd look at her and be shocked at the difference in her appearance from when they were first married.

Caroline had been such a pretty girl with her fair Shirley Temple curls and rosy cheeks. Now she looked like a bent old woman. Her face was grey and gaunt, her hair a dry frizz, and there was a frightened, apprehensive look in her eyes. What Caroline was afraid of was him.

Time and time again he tried to make it up to her. He'd swear he'd stop drinking. He'd get his old job back as a brickie. He'd give her most of his wages. He'd keep away from the pub – he kept trying. He played snooker. Or he went on Sunday to watch the street team from Garngad playing the Blackhill boys on the football pitch between Barlinnie and Hogganfield Loch. Football, especially in Garngad, was more than a sport – it was a disease. Locals or pals could forgive a man for committing adultery, but they couldn't forgive him for not playing football. They'd say, 'Och, she must have been a slag anyway'. Sunday kick-abouts could reach a really high standard. The teams were often made up with young men waiting to go to Celtic, Rangers, Partick Thistle, etc. Or else it was guys who were finished with the senior teams and had stepped down to juniors. So you often

315

had guys playing football who were juniors, but they were bald and fat and maybe thirty.

Sometimes violence erupted among the spectators. Players were knifed and the referee had to be very tough not to be intimidated. Michael felt the sport was a poor second-best to boxing. At first he'd gone to the boxing clubs and hung about watching young up-and-coming fighters in training. But he'd had to take a few drinks to get him there. It hurt him so much to know that he was no longer part of what he regarded as 'The Noble Art'. He'd been flung out of the clubs on several occasions because he'd been so drunk he'd tried to climb into the ring and show the boys how it should be done. Now the clubs had banned him.

Men who used to ask for his autograph when he was champion of Scotland had looked at him as if he was dirt and sneered, 'I wouldn't give you a job if you were the last brickie on earth.'

He'd got a job eventually with a firm over on the north side of the city. The boss who engaged him didn't know about his drinking, or didn't care. After all, most building site workers took a drink, needed and deserved a drink after running up and down ramps all day carrying heavy hods of bricks.

He'd told Caroline, 'This is our new start, pet. We'll be able to buy some nice things for the kids and a few comforts for the house. Not to mention something for yourself. You deserve a wee treat.'

That first pay-day he'd hurried straight home, avoiding his workmates who were all hanging about the corner waiting for the pub to open. He handed over most of his pay to Caroline, and she was so pleased and hopeful. The kids were delighted too with the sweeties he'd bought for them.

They'd all enjoyed a good tea, and then he said he was just going out for a game of dominoes. The happiness and the hope once more died in Caroline's face. Dominoes were played in the pub.

'I'll just have one pint while I'm having a game.'

'Oh Michael, how many times have you said that? You must

316

have said it about as many times now as you've promised to give up the drink altogether.'

'No, but this time I mean it, pet.'

The fact was he always meant it.

'You always say that too.' Suddenly Caroline began to sob and weep broken-heartedly. This had set the kids off as well. He couldn't bear it. After a struggle with himself he said, 'All right, all right, I won't go. I'll stay in.'

And he did. And he stayed sober all week.

The next week he meant to do the same. But on pay-day he thought he'd just have one pint before going home. Instead of hanging about with the lads waiting for the pub to open, however, he hid in the Co-op. Why did he do that? He didn't know. He had the same furtiveness when buying a bottle of whisky to take home. He slipped it into his jacket pocket and slunk out as if he was stealing the thing. At home he hid it under the bed.

After that he went into the pub every pay-night. He stood at the bar or sat in his corner drinking and feeling guilty and listening to all the lads talk the most awful shit. They talked about Celtic and Rangers and he had no interest in Celtic or Rangers. (He often went to Celtic Park, but that was because there was always plenty of booze on the bus.) They talked about horse-racing and he'd no interest in horse-racing. He knew every fight they'd been in, every woman they'd made love to, or every woman they claimed to have made love to. Until he was bored out of his skull.

He got to the stage beyond guilt. He *wanted* to be in his own house. He *wanted* to be home. And he couldn't go. It was a terrible dilemma. For an unknown reason he couldn't go. It was inexplicable.

Time after time, knowing that Caroline was waiting, desperate for his wages, he spent them all. Long ago he'd sold his Crombie coat to get money for drink. All successful boxers wore Crombie coats – it was like what a fur coat meant to a woman. In his case it had hidden cigarette burns on his suit. He smoked when he drank and fell asleep. He used to say, 'I only smoke when I have a wee refreshment.'

317

Sometimes, as well as drinking in the pub near his work, he'd go on to the pub in Castle Street where he'd meet the Garngad and Blackhill crowd. There he was liable to get into serious trouble. Men like the coalman he owed money to would be there. They'd say to their pals if they had to leave, 'Watch him – and if he goes on to the whisky, nail him.'

Going on to the whisky from beer meant he must have more money than he'd been letting on. He was ashamed of the fact that on more than one occasion he – the ex-champion of Scotland – had been beaten up by some small-time gangster.

Caroline had wept on these occasions too. It was an added worry that some of the regulars at the Castle Street pub weren't just small-time gangsters. Some of the bigger boys had guns. All of the men, gangsters or not, took their sport and their hobbies very seriously. One of these hobbies was pigeon-keeping. He'd seen one of the gangsters put a gun to the back of a man's head and say, 'Are you going to give our Bobby back his fuckin' hen?'

He'd seen the day when, guns or not, he would have seen any gangster off, such was his contempt for them. Because he was drunk, however, he'd done nothing. He never had fought when he was drunk.

'That's one thing about Michael,' people would say, 'he never fights when he's drunk.'

What they didn't know was that he *couldn't* fight when he was drunk.

His father used to say he made a virtue out of necessity. That was the truth. Now his father would have little if anything to do with him. 'It's a disgrace how you treat your wife,' Patrick would rage. 'You're a disgrace to the whole family and to yourself. Pull yourself together, man. Have a bit of will power. Take a leaf out of Bernard's book. Look how well he's doing. He's never come snivelling to me for money for drink, or anything else. He gives *me* money. He's a good lad, our Bernard.'

Bernard, who had never stuck to any rules of the Noble Art. Bernard, who was as quick to use his feet as his fists. He could call it karate or whatever he liked, there was nothing noble nor even fair about it. What Bernard did was fast and sharp and jerky and vicious. There was nothing graceful about it. To Michael, boxing had always contained an element of dance. To him it was like ballet. Not the latter-day slugging in the booths, but the real art in the ring he'd once been so proud to take part in.

He was ashamed that, after trying everyone else, he had been forced to go to Bernard for a loan of money. His wages had gone on drink. There was no food in the house and the children were both ill with asthma. It was terrible to see them and Caroline suffer. He felt shattered by the sight of them. So much so he could have killed for a drink as he made his way up Sauchiehall Street to the Sauchiehall Mansions. He hated the prospect of asking Bernard for help. He knew Bernard thought no better of him than Patrick did. Everybody seemed to have turned against him. He felt he was dying with thirst inside. Surely Bernard would help him. Bernard was his twin.

His brother's close was tiled and clean and quiet. In fact, unlike the closes in Garngad and Blackhill, it had a cathedral-like hush. Michael's legs – once able to spring up the Campsie Hills – trembled weakly on each stair.

Bernard took a long time in coming to the door. Once inside, Michael had a good idea why. The smell of sex was thick and hot in the air. Bernard showed him into the kitchen, but as they passed the bedroom Michael sensed someone else's presence. An aura of waiting, of suspended animation, hung about the place.

'You're sober, I see,' Bernard said. 'I suppose that means you're skint.'

'I really need your help, Bernard.'

'No way,' Bernard interrupted. 'You're even more stupid than I thought you were if you actually believe I'd give you money for booze.'

'No, not for booze. It's for Caroline. She's worried sick about the kids. They're both ill and there's nothing in the house . . .' He had never before felt so ashamed as he did under Bernard's look of disgust.

'Who's to blame for that? You've got a job. You get wages.'

'I swear,' Michael said, 'I'll never again spend a penny on booze. I've had my last drink . . .'

'Aw, shut up,' Bernard said. 'I can't even give Caroline any money because you'd get it out of her. You'd even steal money off your own kids to get a drink.'

To his eternal shame, Michael began to weep. 'Bernard, I swear . . .'

'Get out, you drunken bum.'

He had no alternative but to shuffle miserably back along the hall. He hadn't even his bus fare back to Garngad. It was a long walk, and waiting for him was not only a distraught Caroline and two ill children in a fireless room, but an outraged Father Riley.

'Talking and preaching's obviously no good to you,' the priest shouted, taking off his black jacket and dog collar. 'You rotten, selfish bastard. This'll maybe teach you to think of your poor wife and children in future.'

Michael took the beating gratefully. He knew he deserved it. And nothing could hurt him more than he was already hurting inside.

Chapter Forty-Six

Michael shuffled fearfully, furtively back and forward past the close in West Nile Street for what seemed hours, but still couldn't muster enough courage to go in. Eventually he gave up and returned to Garngad. But on his way upstairs he stopped at Scobie's door.

'Jesus, Mary and Joseph,' Scobie cried out. 'What a state you're in, man!' He stood aside to allow Michael to shamble into the house. 'You get worse looking every time I see you.'

Carragh and Doris were in the kitchen drinking tea. It was Saturday afternoon and Doris, who'd had a dose of flu, wasn't due to restart work until Monday.

'Holy Mother of God,' Carragh said. 'Sit down, son. I'll pour another cup.'

Michael's good eye was swollen and half-shut. His lips were contorted with bruising. His whole face was so puffy and discoloured he was unrecognisable.

Nobody asked what had happened.

'I'll pour his tea,' Scobie said. 'You sit where you are, Carragh.'

He passed Michael a half-filled cup. Even so, Michael had to concentrate very hard and use both of his hands to lift the cup without allowing its contents to slop wildly over the top.

Carragh said, 'I took a bowl of soup up for Caroline and the weans. They were all wiring into it before I came back down. It'll put some strength into them. I made it with good beef stock.'

'Thanks Carragh,' Michael mumbled. 'You know I drank all my wages last night.'

'Many a time I've done the same,' Scobie said.

'Aye, many a time,' Carragh echoed.

'I tried to get a loan from Bernard but he sent me packing.'

Doris stiffened. 'Hard-hearted bastard. To his own brother too. I'll give you a loan, Michael.'

Michael shook his head. 'No. He was right. I'd only have spent it on drink. Caroline or the weans wouldn't have seen a penny of it.' Tears welled up from his grotesque face and lost their way back down it. 'He said I'd steal from my own weans if they had any money, and he was right.' He turned to Scobie. 'I went to West Nile Street this morning.'

'You did the right thing, Michael. You'll get help at the AA. Look how they helped me.'

'But I didn't go in the close. I didn't have the courage. Me!' The words 'Champion of Scotland' hung in the air.

'Don't worry, son. Drink up your tea. I'll go back with you. I would never have got there in the first place if it hadn't been for Frank.'

Michael was visibly trembling all over. Even his head was nodding out of control, making it all the more difficult to bring his cup to his mouth. 'Aye, Frank's OK. But I can understand how Doris feels. Our Bernard's a hard-hearted bastard. He's always got his own way. He could twist Ma round his little finger. It didn't matter what he did, he was always Ma's "lovely boy", her favourite. She used to stick up for Frank, but underneath Bernard was the one she admired. He was always her "lovely boy". I didn't stand a look in, of course.'

There was a bitter ring to his voice and Carragh said, 'Och, don't be such a self-pitying slob, Michael. You're talking nonsense and you know it. Your ma loved all of her boys. She loved each of you in a different way, that's all.'

'Drink up your tea, son,' Scobie said, 'and we'll be away.'

'Aye, OK Scobie.'

The bitterness about Bernard still hung about his mind like a fog on the way back to town. It was as if all the frustration, guilt, shame and hurt he had previously been suffering had found a focus.

'He *is* a rotten bastard.'

'Who?' Scobie asked.

'Bernard.'

'Well, I have to admit, son, he didn't do right by my Doris. And she didn't want to divorce him, you know. She's a good Catholic, our Doris. But he persuaded her or talked her into it. I don't know how he managed it, but he did. It was him that wanted the divorce.'

'And he always gets what he wants, just as I said. And he doesn't care how he manages it, or who gets hurt in the process.'

'Well, it does look as if you're right there, son.'

'All my life I've fought fair and square, and look where it's got me.'

'Aw, now haud on there, Michael, haud on. You've nobody to blame but yourself for what's happened to you. Make no mistake about that. You've literally drunk yourself into the gutter. I know what it's like. I've been there myself. Take it from me, it's no use blaming anybody else. Who's fault was it that I nearly drank myself to death, eh?' Helplessly Michael shook his head and Scobie went on, 'I had a mother and father that showed me more love than most. I had a sister and two brothers – all dead now, God rest their souls – and none of them were alcoholics. God forbid that I should blame Carrragh. Her that's stuck by me all these years. Or my two wee lassies.' He grinned. 'Mind you, sometimes I think my boys would drive anybody to drink. But they got off their mark as quick as they could and I don't blame them. I was making their life a misery. I was making everybody's life a misery – just like you are, son. It's got nothing to do with Bernard.'

They were nearing the AA close, and Michael's steps began to falter.

'You'll remember,' Scobie said, 'how I used to treat poor wee Carragh. God, I was so ashamed but I went on and on. If I hadn't eventually admitted to myself that I had a drink problem and gone with your Frank to the AA, I would have been the death of Carragh – and I love my wife, always have loved her.'

'I love Caroline.' Michael made an effort to straighten his

shoulders. 'I'll do it for her. I'll go up there and I'll take the pledge. For Caroline's sake . . .'

'No, no, son,' Scobie interrupted. 'It's nothing like that. You've got the wrong idea. In the first place you've not to do it for your wife, or your da, or your boss, or your pal, or anybody else. You've just to do it for yourself.'

Michael felt frightened again and he suffered another humiliating attack of the shakes. He felt like an old man, older than Scobie who had taken his arm and was helping him up the dark, quiet stairs. He needed a drink more than he'd ever needed one in his life. Just one drink.

Bernard could down drinks whenever it took his fancy, and he never needed to face the humiliation of God knows what in a place like this.

Michael wanted to run away. Yet to turn and run now would be an even greater humiliation. He despised himself enough as it was. Yet at the same time he believed he was a better man than Bernard. Hadn't he been champion of Scotland? Bernard was probably no better than a gangster.

And Bernard had not been faithful to Doris. Bernard never spoke about his conquests, but he had a look of sexual self-confidence and experience about him that spoke volumes. It was in the relaxed, open-legged way he sat, in the easy swagger of his walk, in the narrow knowing look in his eyes.

'I've always been faithful to Caroline,' Michael told himself. Yet even as he thought this, he knew that physically it was not true. When he was sober he had been faithful, and always in his head he had been faithful. But there had been times after a night of boozing when he'd wakened up in a strange bed beside a dirty wee scrubber.

He groaned in anguish at the memory. He felt ill with the shame of it.

'You're going to be OK, son,' Scobie comforted. 'You're just going to go up here and have a wee cup of tea and a blether with other guys like yourself and like me. We're all in the same boat.'

'Aw Scobie,' Michael managed brokenly, 'you don't know some of the things I've done. You don't understand.'

'Try me,' Scobie said.

'I love Caroline. Yet when I've been drunk, I've gone to bed with other women.'

'Same here,' Scobie said.

'You're not just saying that?'

'Why should I lie, Michael?'

Michael's head twitched about helplessly, the floodgate of memory draining him. 'I've given Caroline a terrible life. I've brought the scum of the neighbourhood into her house. And still I've turned on her, blamed her. I remember once blaming her for a crowd of drinking buddies going away early. I said they'd gone home because they were too embarrassed to ask her for the lavvy key. They'd just gone home because the booze had run out, of course. And anyway, one of them was big Danny Malloy and if he was game enough to shoot a policeman and axe a police dog, he was game enough to ask for a lavvy key. But that's how ridiculous and stupid I've been, Scobie. Fancy blaming Caroline . . .'

'OK. OK. So you were bloody stupid and ridiculous. But that's all in the past. Just like all the stupid, ridiculous and downright wicked things I've done are in the past. Oh aye, son. I could top any of your stories any day. I've been a right wicked bugger in drink and that's the truth. You just ask Carragh for a start. But first you'll hear plenty stories from guys in this AA office that'll match yours. Believe me, son.' He opened the door and ushered Michael into the windowless hall. Through another door was a biggish room with brown linoleum on the floor, some folding chairs stacked against the wall, and men and women standing or sitting around in groups talking. A man at a small side-table was pouring mugs of tea.

The man said to Michael as he handed him a mug, 'Hello there, my name's Jimmy. Have I met you? Have you been here before?'

Scobie said, 'This is Michael. He's a pal of mine.'

'Right, Michael,' said Jimmy. 'So you're having a wee bit of trouble with your bevvy, son?'

Chapter Forty-Seven

'Bridie! Bridie!' Frank was beside himself, frantic, gone mad, dancing, leaping about the kitchen waving a piece of paper high in the air.

Bridie scrambled up in bed. 'What's wrong? Frank, what is it?'

'Nothing's wrong. Everything's wonderful. Wonderful! They've accepted my play. Television! Hallelujah!'

Bridie paled. 'The one about the priests?'

'No, the bent Bailie. Don't look so worried. This is the answer to all our prayers. People kept telling me there was this "Magic Circle" – a few writers got all the work. A newcomer like me didn't stand a chance.' His thin face was feverish, his eyes protruding. 'But I've done it, Bridie. I've done it!'

Bridie climbed down from the hole-in-the-wall bed and searched about for spectacles and slippers.

'Aren't you going to congratulate me?' Frank yelled.

'Of course, dear. You've worked hard and you deserve every success. I just hope this doesn't get you into any trouble, that's all. Cause any unpleasantness for us. We've been so happy here in our nice wee house. I don't even care any more about getting one of the new flats. And the neighbours are really kind. Mrs Gormley offered to take my washing with hers to the steamie the other day . . .'

'Bridie, what on earth's Mrs Gormley and the steamie got to do with me getting a play accepted for television?'

Bridie found her spectacles and pushed them up the bridge of her nose. 'Now, Frank, don't act the innocent. You know perfectly well what I mean. Some of the things you write are liable to offend people. The bailie in your play is based on Senior Bailie McPherson, and he's a friend of your father's. And Bernard's got a lot of work through Bailie McPherson. That's enough potential trouble for a start.'

'I'm sure Bernard is well able to handle any trouble that comes his way.'

'And so soon as the newspapers get a whiff of scandal, or any suspicion of graft and corruption – and that's what your play's all about – it's going to hit the headlines. You know what the papers are like, the tabloids especially.'

'Great publicity.' Frank's eyes misted with joy. 'With that kind of publicity it's bound to be a success.'

'But Frank, success isn't everything. Think of the repercussions for everybody. Think what it might do to Bailie McPherson and his family. *They* won't think publicity like that's very great, will they?'

'I don't care what he thinks. He deserves all he gets. But you're forgetting something, Bridie. My play's a work of fiction, not a documentary. Only you and I know that I based the main character on Bailie McPherson.'

'It's about a Glasgow Bailie.'

'There's more than one Glasgow Bailie, and none of them are called John Munroe.'

'But Frank . . .'

Frank laughed. Nothing could spoil this wondrous moment for him. 'Stop worrying. John Munroe is younger than Bailie McPherson. He lives in Newton Mearns, not Bearsden. He has a handsome son, not a beautiful daughter.'

'All the same . . .'

'Be happy for me, Bridie. *Please.*'

Bridie blinked and tried to smile.

'They want me to go to the BBC to discuss it. Look! Read the letter. They're most impressed, they say. Most impressed.' He savoured the words. 'The BBC.'

'And so they should be,' Bridie said. 'You're a wonderful, talented man. I'll put the kettle on.' She couldn't altogether understand why she wasn't as joyously happy as Frank. She struggled valiantly to hide the fact, but the truth was she felt inexplicably depressed. She tried to tell herself she was just worried about what Frank's play might stir up, the uncertainty, not knowing what effect it might have. At the same time, she knew it was more than that. A different fear had taken root. 'Do you think you should warn your da and Bernard about it?'

'Oh, I expect it'll be ages before it actually reaches the screen. I'll tell them about the acceptance, of course. My God, I feel like running around the Gorbals and Garngad and Blackhill broadcasting the news through a megaphone.'

Bridie managed to feebly laugh along with him. Frank was such a child at times with his high hopes, his optimistic dreams, his wild enthusiasms. He had such an open-faced guilelessness too. She loved that about him. She loved his pale, pinched face and lank hair that he kept forgetting to get cut. She loved the way he never looked tidy and she had to keep straightening his tie and flicking dandruff from the shoulders of his jacket.

Frank didn't forget to get his hair cut before he went to the BBC, though. He laboriously pressed his suit. She starched his shirt. (Shirts always looked so crumpled on him.) He bought a new tie in Woolworths. He was feverish with excitement when the great day came, so much so that Bridie thought he was actually coming down with flu. He couldn't eat any lunch.

'Wish me luck,' he said before he set off. And she did. He'd wanted her to go with him but she was much too shy. Even in the shop she preferred working in the back rather than out front, dealing with the public.

Frank was walking on air when he returned. Everything had gone well. She became confused with all the people he'd met and what their jobs were. But as far as Frank was concerned, it had been no trouble. No trouble at all. He'd enjoyed it. He'd got on well with everybody. Everybody had been excited about the play. There had to be other meetings. Lots of meetings.

He ate a huge dinner. Afterwards he was much too restless to settle down to write, or even just to watch TV.

Despite her protests about it being too late and him having to get up early for his work in the morning, he insisted on going to visit his father to tell him the good news. He would have gone the day he'd first received the letter, but Patrick had not been in. He'd phoned Bernard but there was no reply. He'd gone to Michael's house in Garngad and never managed to find him either.

'I told you you were wasting your time there,' Bridie said. 'Michael's as bad as Da now. He's never out of the AA offices. Anyway, you know what your family's like.'

But of course Frank, forever the optimist, imagined they'd all be delighted for him. She reminded him about how his father had received his first poem.

'Och, that was years ago and the poem was rotten. Da loves his telly. He'll be thrilled about this.'

She groaned inwardly. No way could she see Patrick O'Maley being thrilled about anything Frank did, especially anything he'd written. However, she said no more and went quietly along with her husband.

'Da,' Frank cried out immediately he burst into the house in Blackhill. 'You'll never guess. The BBC has accepted one of my plays. They're going to put it on television.'

Patrick's eyes narrowed suspiciously beneath their bushy grey brows. 'You're pulling my leg.'

'No, Da. Honestly.'

'How did you con them into that?'

'They liked the play. They're really excited about it. They think it'll cause quite a stir.'

'What've you been saying? I hope you haven't been saying anything about Blackhill.'

'No,' Frank's face lit up. 'But what a good idea!' He suddenly saw a scene in which his father and Tony were galloping along beside a moving train armed with meat-axes, ready to hack open stolen crates. 'That's a great idea,' he enthused.

'You just watch it,' his father warned. 'Watch it, do you hear?'

'It's so much more atmospheric than the City Chambers,' Frank said out loud to himself.

'What've you been saying about the City Chambers? Here . . .' Patrick heaved up from his chair with a sudden rise of indignation. 'You haven't been saying anything about Bailie McPherson, have you?'

'Not as such,' Frank murmured absently. He had already written the first page of his Blackhill play in his mind.

'What do you mean – not as such?' Patrick's bloodshot, bulging eyes demanded an answer. He was skint and hadn't been able to go to the pub. He was in no mood for Frank. He never was in the mood for Frank, at the best of times.

'What Frank means,' Bridie blurted out, 'is that it's about a *type* of Bailie. A fictitious character. It's not about any *real* person.'

'It's one thing making a bloody fool of yourself,' Patrick shouted. 'It's another thing altogether making a fool of other folk.'

The sudden loudness of his father's voice snatched back Frank's attention. 'What's up with you?' he asked in astonishment. 'All I said was I've had a play accepted by the BBC. I thought you'd be pleased.'

'Well, I'm not fuckin' pleased.'

'OK, OK,' Frank said. 'There's no need to bawl your head off, Da.'

'We'd better go.' Bridie tugged at Frank's arm, adding apologetically to Patrick, 'We just popped in for a minute.'

'Aye, well, you can just pop out again.'

After they left the house, and were walking down the dark dusty street with its old newspapers and tin cans careening aimlessly about in the wind, Frank said, 'Could you beat that? He's getting worse in his old age. But here, Bridie, he set me thinking. Blackhill could be a very dramatic setting for a play. So would Garngad. I've been using other districts as backgrounds but why should I? Write about what you know. I read that somewhere. It's good advice.'

Bridie now felt not only worried but ashamed. It would be dreadful if Frank started writing about good friends and neighbours. It was going to be bad enough when the play about the Bailie and the City Chambers came out. If Frank started writing about people nearer home, how could she face them? She imagined herself slinking about, avoiding people. Patrick's fury would be multiplied a thousandfold. She began to sweat.

Frank hugged her arm through his as they passed the dark corners of closes and ghostly walls desecrated by graffiti. 'Come

330

to think of it, Bridie, Garngad and Blackhill and the Gorbals are hotching with characters – real characters.' He was happy and excited again. 'My God, I don't need to look any further than our own families. That's where real originality lies.'

Bridie, far from being original, was thinking entirely in clichés. She was thinking of hornets' nests being stirred up, and cats among pigeons, and thorns in sides. She felt quite distracted and wished Frank had never had anything accepted. She had always been proud of him being a writer. It made him different from the rest, different amd special. Now for the first time she wished he'd just stick to his safe nine-to-five job in the office of Messrs Goldmayer Ltd – Wholesale Warehousemen, and forget about all his other carry-on. It was different enough being a 'collar and tie man', as Carragh proudly referred to her son-in-law. The more she thought about it the more she became convinced that Frank was being selfish and insensitive. Another thing, she disliked the sound of the television people and the actors and actresses. They seemed to inhabit a different world altogether from the one to which she and Frank belonged. She didn't want Frank to have anything to do with these people. No good would come of it.

All the time she struggled to be happy for him. 'I'm really proud of you, Frank. I really am,' she kept assuring him and herself. She felt furtive, guilty and disloyal about her thoughts. She also felt apprehensive, insecure. She had a sudden vision of Frank mixing with glamorous strangers. Normally she never gave her appearance a thought, but now she became conscious of her plain, bespectacled face, her straight mousy hair, her dowdy clothes. For days afterwards, alone in the kitchen or in the lavatory, she nursed her rosary beads for comfort. Over and over again, she rapidly repeated, 'Hail Mary full of grace, the Lord is with thee, Blessed art thou among woman and blessed is the fruit of thy womb, Jesus. Holy Mary Mother of God, pray for us sinners now and at the hour of our death. Amen.'

Chapter Forty-Eight

There were times of tenderness, romantic music in the background, gentle words of endearment. At other times there would be shouts and screams and groans and grunts of utter abandonment, and the smells of sex and sweat. All self-consciousness had long since been thrown to the winds. Bernard and Andrina had invented their own Kama Sutra. Everything was in the merciless pursuit of orgasm.

They made it their business to take every opportunity to be physically linked together, he inside her, she enveloping him.

He called her his velvet vice. There was nothing she wouldn't do to please him and therefore please herself. He would telephone and tell her what to wear the next time she came to him, and what he wanted her to do. Even the call excited her. He liked her to look very smart and sophisticated, and especially to wear hats. He had a 'thing' about hats.

He called her and told her he'd bought her this fuchsia-pink wide-brimmed straw hat to match a dress she had of that colour. He'd been fantasising about her in high heels and wearing this hat. He wanted her to be sitting on the edge of the bed wearing it that evening. As usual, she looked forward to carrying out his directions. She made an excuse to Robert about going to some extra-mural class, and in a shopping bag carried out everything she needed for Bernard's flat. There she bathed and made up extra carefully. She washed her hair and styled it to perfection. She donned her fuchsia pink silk taffeta cross-over dress and wore nothing underneath it. She slipped her feet into elegant high-heeled shoes of matching soft leather. Then she placed the huge-brimmed hat to sit low over her eyes to create that mysterious smouldering look she knew he loved. Previously she'd prepared a supper of tiger prawns in a champagne sauce over wild rice. She'd set a small round table at the foot of the bed with pretty glasses and pink candles. Strawberries with a hot chocolate dip were to follow. Even the food had to match the colour theme of the evening. They always paid scrupulous attention to detail.

At his estimated time of arrival she perched herself, perfectly prepared, on the edge of the bed. She crossed her legs, revealing a long seductive stretch of smooth golden-brown skin, lotioned, glistening. Her heart raced wildly as she heard Bernard's key in the door, then his slow deliberate tread across the hall.

Once inside the bedroom he closed the door behind him and stood for a long time staring at her in silence. He always obtained great pleasure just by looking at her, knowing she was prepared for him. She found his stare highly flattering, and it spurred her to desire him with an even greater longing. But first he asked her to walk around the room for him. At one time, she'd found this embarrassing. He'd persisted, however, with gentle words, assuring her it was his love for her that created his desire to watch her move before him. Eventually, after many occasions, she had become skilled at parading provocatively around and enjoyed the sensation of his eyes boring holes in her ankles, her legs, her hands, her breasts.

She always looked forward to what he had in store for her next. The next time, in fact, he had instructed her to be in the shower on his return. She didn't hear him come home or lock the front door behind him. She didn't hear his footsteps cross the hall or enter the bedroom. It startled her when the shower door was opened. Then his tall muscular body towered behind her. Already the warm, steamy atmosphere was mildly sensual. His hands held her shoulders, then slid caressingly down over her back as the warm drops of water soaked their hair and skin. Taking the soap, he picked up each of her feet in turn and pulled the soap between every toe, then round the sole, then with gentle rubbing motion up the calves of her legs, stopping short of her bottom. From the ankles again, he went up the front and the insides of her calves and thighs, just leaving off before he reached her most secret, exciting place.

Again he turned her round. He reached down, and taking

each buttock firmly in each hand, soaped them, rotating them together. Lust and heat fevered her. She felt light-headed with excitement and desire as he eased her round to face him. Regardless of the water cascading down over them both, he kept her at arm's length, staring at her, before beginning to sculpt her breasts in lather. As he moved the breasts together, a beating, a madness, an exquisite shuddering desire took possession of her. He drew her closer and pressed himself against her breasts. By this time she was frenzied with the need to feel him inside her. Tantalisingly, he pressed his penis against her, rubbed it softly against her groin, teasing her to distraction until she begged him to enter her. As he did, he gripped her tightly and she cried out his name, over and over again.

More and more now, when they made love, it was a kind of madness. It was something they craved all the time, like an addiction. But they were not able to get together nearly as often as they wanted. Sometimes Bernard would be away on business, but more often than not it would be because Andrina, for one reason or another, couldn't get away. There was no longer any use asking Josie to babysit, and Sophie was becoming too suspicious and difficult.

Weeks, sometimes months, would pass without them seeing each other. When they did, it was like going home. She loved the flat as well as Bernard, and she was proud of it. Although her name was not on the door, she felt it belonged to her. Just as Bernard belonged to her. It gave her a wonderful, luxurious, supremely satisfied feeling – like a cat with a bowl of delicious cream.

Lying in the comfortable bed in the flat, happily exhausted after making love for an hour, she was unprepared for Bernard spoiling her euphoria by talking about marriage – although she should have known that Bernard's obsessiveness meant he would never give up trying to completely possess her.

'Darling velvet, we can't go on like this. I know we've gone over it all before, but you must try to think from my point of view. It's not natural for me to remain celibate for most of the time – for weeks and months when you say you can't see me. I love you. I'm proud of you. I want you to be constantly by my side. I want you to accompany me when I go on tours. I want to show you off as my beautiful wife. I want everybody to know you're mine. No, please don't run away,' he added hastily as she stiffened from him and made to rise. 'Why do you always panic like this? What is there to be afraid of?'

She shook her head, hugging herself. 'I don't know. Please, don't make me think about it. I'm happy going on just as we are.'

'Well, damn it, I'm not!'

She was shocked at the venom in his voice. Suddenly, for a second or two, she caught a glimpse of another person, a stranger. She began to weep and immediately he was Bernard again, gathering her gently into his arms, whispering tender endearments.

'My darling, my dearest beautiful Andrina. I love you, but I'm only human. It's not natural for a normal healthy man to be such a loner.'

'Well.' Her large, childish eyes desperately searched for an escape from the immediate situation. 'Don't be a loner. Get a girlfriend to go around with you. Live a normal life.'

'Without you?'

'We could go on seeing each other like we do now – just as often as we can. I've got Robert, so why shouldn't you have somebody for when we can't be together?'

He sighed. 'Nobody can compare with you. How could any woman match the perfection of my lovely little velvet?'

She laughed with relief, gave him a quick kiss and swung her legs off the bed. 'I'll have to run.'

The truth was she'd left Jennifer alone in the house and sleeping. Love-making with Bernard had blotted out all thoughts of anybody else, but now she'd begun to feel agitated and apprehensive. What if Jennifer woke up and began to cry? What if she'd hurt herself? What if one of the neighbours heard Jennifer? What if one of the neighbours had seen Jennifer's mother going out? What if they sent for the police? What if it got into the papers? *What if Sophie found out?*

Once outside she began to run and, far too agitated and impatient to wait for a bus, she hailed a taxi. She sat on the edge of the seat, bent forward, tense, hands twisting together. In her posture at least she looked exactly like her mother.

'My God.' Her thoughts flayed her with anguish and regret. 'How could I have done this? How could I have left my little girl on her own?'

Josie met her in the hall. She was nursing a tear-stained Jennifer. 'It's a bloody good job I had your spare set of keys.' She was pale-faced and bug-eyed with anger. 'You're a bloody disgrace.'

'Oh Josie, I'm so sorry.' Andrina grabbed Jennifer from her neighbour, and showered the child with kisses. 'Darling, I'm sorry. Mummy's sorry. It's all right. You're all right now.' To Josie she cried out, 'It'll never happen again. I promise. Please don't tell anybody, oh, *please!*'

'That wean could have choked, or anything could have happened. I just don't know how you could have left her like that.'

'I shouldn't have left her. I realise that now, but she was sound asleep and I only meant to be a few minutes.'

'You're a bloody liar. You've been away well over an hour.'

'I didn't think I'd be away all that time.'

'He took longer than usual, did he?' Josie sneered. 'You made sure you were back in time for Robert, though. That'll be him coming up the stairs now. Timed exactly.'

'Oh Josie,' Andrina began to weep. '*Please. Please!*'

'Don't worry, I won't say anything to anybody. If I ever find out you've left that wean again though . . .'

'Never again. Never again.' Hastily she wiped at her eyes. By the time Robert reached the door she was quite composed.

'Hello Josie,' he greeted her. 'Are you coming or going?'

'Just going.' Josie passed him at the door. 'Time I was getting ready for my work. No rest for the wicked.'

'Darling,' Andrina said to Robert after Josie had left. 'Take Jennifer for a minute, will you? I made a steak pie earlier. I've just to pop it in the oven and do the potatoes.'

'Sure. Come to daddy, love. Have you been crying, pet? What's the matter, eh?'

Jennifer clung close to him, still hiccoughing with sobs.

'I think she fell or banged herself,' Andrina said. 'You know how she's beginning to get into everything.'

'Och, poor wee pet,' Robert soothed. 'Show Daddy the sore bit and I'll kiss it better.'

Andrina busied herself at the oven and the sink. She felt shaken with relief. No harm had been done. No harm at all. Josie wouldn't say anything. It was as if nothing had happened. Nothing had happened. She kept trying to reassure herself, but every now and again a wave of horror would engulf her. She must have been mad to leave Jennifer. What had she been thinking of to do such a dreadful thing? Yet all the time she knew.

She made a bread and butter pudding for Robert. He liked solid, unimaginative things like bread and butter pudding. There was delicious home-baked apple pie afterwards to enjoy with his coffee. Andrina was a good wife – Robert was always saying so.

So was his mother. 'You're a wonderful cook and baker,' Jean Anderson often said admiringly. 'And you keep this wee house beautiful – absolutely spotless.'

And she was a good mother. Robert and Jean said that too. Dear little Jennifer. Andrina didn't want to do anything that would put her at risk. She wondered if she dared ask Robert's mother to babysit. But Jean was now troubled with arthritis and hadn't been keeping well for some time; her hands had become quite deformed and swollen. She'd probably say she wasn't able to look after the baby.

Andrina sighed over her apple pie and Robert said, 'Anything wrong?'

'Wrong?' Eyes wide and innocent, she smiled across the table at him. 'Of course not!'

337

Chapter Forty-Nine

'But why?' Bridie was near to tears. 'We've got a lovely wee house here, and anyway we're liable to get allocated one of the new flats any time now. And we both *like* the Gorbals. It's such a *friendly* place.'

She thought of all the times that Mrs McLachlan next door had let the coalman in when she and Frank were at work. Or the gas man. All the keys fitted all the doors in the building, and as often as not people just left their keys in their doors.

Everything was moving too fast. Even the screening of Frank's play had been quicker than either of them expected. It had slotted, all too conveniently as far as she was concerned, into a series already in production.

'The West End is where the BBC is.' Frank struggled to be patient. 'It would be so much more convenient. And it's where they all stay. The BBC people and the actors and actresses, everybody. It's a wonderful district, Bridie. It's so *interesting*. There are so many different types of people.'

'You said there were interesting people here. You're always watching them out the front room window. You said a fascinating panorama of life passed by that window.'

'I know. I know. The whole of Glasgow is a fascinating panorama of life.'

'We're perfectly happy here.'

'And we'll be perfectly happy in the West End. At least come and look at the place, Bridie. It means so much to me. Steve Martin's got a job with Grampian and he's moving up to Aberdeen. He and his wife want somebody to buy their marvellous flat in Botanic Crescent. They're really sorry to leave it.'

'Anyway, Frank, we can't afford to buy a flat.'

'I can get a mortgage. I've been making enquiries. One of

these days I'm going to give up my job in the office – and write full time.'

'Oh, Frank . . .'

'I didn't tell them that. Apparently, they're not so keen on giving mortgages to full-time writers. Unless you're making a fortune, I suppose. I would never have had the nerve even to ask about such a thing before. But now I have real prospects, Bridie. I'm going places, and I don't mean just to live in the West End. I was just waiting to see how the play was received and look at the reviews.' He tossed a pile of papers into the air. 'Look at them!'

'I've seen them, Frank.' She had read each review several times. So had Frank. Astonishingly flattering words leapt from the page of each newspaper: 'wonderful . . . gripping . . . hard-hitting . . . honest . . . revealing . . . brilliant.'

'Well?' Frank said.

'They're very good.'

'They're rave reviews. *Rave* reviews. That's what the producer said on the phone.'

'But we can't plunge ourselves into a huge amount of debt – thousands of pounds, Frank, we'd have to get a mortgage for all that money – just on the strength of one play. It's madness. I think you should try to calm down. Calm right down, Frank. Get back down to earth.'

'But they've accepted my other play. That's the piece of good news I was keeping till last. I knew you'd be worried about the mortgage but there's no need, pet. They've taken *another* play. They want more hard-hitting stuff, they say. Apparently they can't get enough of it. I could give up the office now. It would give me so much more time to write.'

'Oh Frank . . .' Bridie wailed.

'But I won't. I won't. I'll stay for a wee while yet. Just to please you. Just to set your mind at rest. But oh, Bridie, Bridie, please come and see the flat in Botanic Crescent. It's so beautiful, overlooking the park – you'll love it. And it's so handy for the BBC. And the BBC Club is where everybody from the BBC meets for a drink and a talk. It's in Botanic Crescent, just a few doors along from the flat.'

Bridie's heart sank.

'Say you'll come, Bridie, for my sake, pet. Please!'

Reluctantly she nodded. 'If you're that keen.'

'Aren't you going to congratulate me?'

'What about?'

He laughed. 'You get more dozy every day. The play, of course. They've accepted another play.'

'The one you've been working on? I thought you weren't going to be finished with that one before Christmas.'

'No, no. The one about the priest.'

'Oh, Frank . . .'

'Don't worry.' He laughed again. 'What can they do? Except excommunicate me.'

'Holy Mother of God. It was bad enough with Doris . . .'

'Just joking. Just joking. All it will do is raise a bit of controversy. That's a healthy thing, Bridie. Nothing for anyone to be afraid of.'

That was what decided her about moving to the West End. At least no one there knew her, and there wouldn't be such a concentration of chapels and priests. It would be impossible to hold up her head on the Gorbals, impossible to go to Mass there, after Frank's play about the priest came out. She hardly spoke a word on the way over to see the house, she was so devastated. Frank didn't notice. He talked excitedly and non-stop until they reached Botanic Crescent.

'Look at it! Didn't I tell you it was a lovely place? Just look at it, Bridie.'

A low road ran off Queen Margaret Drive (where the BBC was situated) and alongside the leafy, tree-lined Botanic Gardens. Arching up to the right of this road, and separated by a grassy belt and more trees, was Botanic Crescent. As they walked up the Crescent, they passed large three-storeyed terraced houses, one of which housed the BBC Club. Then there were four-storeyed red sandstone buildings with big bay windows and gardens in front.

'Aren't they beautiful? Isn't everything absolutely beautiful?' Frank enthused.

Bridie couldn't deny it. Yet even before she entered the beautiful tiled close and climbed the quiet stairs, and saw the beautiful stained glass door of the flat, she felt homesick for her own wee house in the Gorbals. Her first impression, when Steve Martin opened the door and ushered them into the house, was of a cavernous space filled with rows of doors. A huge cheeseplant, lit from beneath, cast a giant jigsaw shadow over the walls and roof. Bridie and Frank walked forward, feet sinking deep into the soft mulberry carpet. Bold, colourful paintings sat with quiet authority on the walls, softly picked out in the glow of brass downlighters.

'I think Samantha's in the kitchen. Come on through,' Steve said.

The kitchen was huge, bigger than their front room in the Gorbals. Terracotta tiles gave a warm but practical flooring. Mellow timber units contrasted with the Mediterranean lilac blue of the walls. A collection of Majollica plates clustered in a friendly huddle on one wall. Their bright colours made a vivid splash against the subtle background.

There was no Samantha.

'Through here, darling,' a voice called.

Steve laughed. 'Through to the sitting room, folks. Sorry about that. I was in the study when the doorbell went.'

They followed him across the hall and into an even more impressive room. Bridie was first stunned by the imposing bay window, carefully stripped back to its original wood, the soft honeyed oak. The curtains were pale cream as was the carpet. The whole room seemed a symphony of ivory and cream except for the huge scarlet abstract painting above the fire. Like a splash of carmine blood it brought strength to the subtlety of the room.

There was nothing subtle, however, about the woman who rose, arms outstretched, to greet them. 'Darlings!'

Samantha made Bridie feel like a colourless mouse. Blonde hair was pinned haphazardly on top of her head with tendrils hanging like rivulets of pure gold. Mexican shell earrings dangled noisily from her ears as she spoke. A dramatic scarlet and turquoise kaftan billowed around her. She swooped towards Bridie on bare feet flashing scarlet toenails that matched fingernails so long that Bridie marvelled at anyone being able to function with them. How did Samantha manage to peel potatoes or do any normal household chores?

It turned out Samantha had a 'treasure', in the form of Mrs Hennessy who lived in Maryhill. Mrs Hennessy came every morning to 'do' for Samantha. It was Mrs Hennessy who peeled the potatoes and did all the normal household chores.

'You can inherit her, darling,' Samantha said, gaily flicking cigarette ash all over the place, 'unless of course you have your own staff.'

Bridie stared down at her feet and murmured something incoherent.

Frank laughed. 'We come from a room and kitchen in the Gorbals. Your Mrs Hennessy has probably been used to more than us.'

'Frank!' Bridie muttered, glaring furtively round at him.

Steve joined in the laughter. 'Samantha hasn't a clue. Her daddy's in merchant banking. She thinks this . . .' he flung his hand around, 'is poverty and hardship.'

'You have a beautiful home,' Bridie forced the words out, hating Samantha for her careless self-confidence.

'Thank you, darling.'

Afterwards Bridie told Frank, 'If she'd called me darling one more time, I would have throttled her with her own beads.'

'Och, Samantha's all right. It's just the way they talk.' Frank hadn't been a bit shy. He'd taken everything happily in his stride. He never ceased to amaze Bridie. 'What do you think? About the house – wasn't it wonderful? Did you see the view from the window – a sea of green – did you ever see so much lush greenery?'

'I'm surprised at you, Frank. I really am.'

'How do you mean?'

'I thought it was people you liked to see from your window. You've never been in the slightest interested in trees or any kind of greenery before. You've never been interested in going for holidays or even a day out in the country.'

'This is different. We'd have the best of both worlds – all worlds – there. There's the lovely view, there's the park. But two minutes away, there's the BBC Club – always packed with creative people.' He sighed with pleasure. 'I could enjoy talking shop to them to my heart's content. Then, less than two minutes beyond that, there's Queen Margaret Drive and the BBC. Five minutes from the flat, at the end of Queen Margaret Drive, there's the main Great Western Road, and off that there's Byres Road.' He hugged Bridie in his enthusiasm. 'You'll love Byres Road, Bridie. There's a library and all sorts of interesting shops there. Lots of fascinating people. The West End's the university area too, so there are students and academics as well as BBC people. What do you think, Bridie? About the house?'

She thought of Mrs McLachlan next door, and the Gordons and the Menzies upstairs. Mr Menzies was a godsend – a more eager-to-help neighbour you couldn't meet. He'd fixed their rattling windows. He'd replaced a doorknob that had fallen off. He'd even fixed the television. Frank was absolutely useless with his hands. As he admitted himself he wouldn't know one end of a screwdriver from another.

Mrs McLachlan had always insisted on taking Bridie's turn to wash the stairs. 'Och, you're out working every day, hen. I'm at home all the time. And I've time on my hands now that the weans are at school.'

When both Bridie and Frank had gone down with the flu, all the neighbours rallied round. Their key would turn in the door, and there would be a shout of, 'It's only me, hen.' And in would come Mrs Gordon or Mrs Menzies or Mrs McLachlan, or Mrs Sinclair, or Mrs Webster from downstairs. They would bring a bowl of soup or pudding. They'd make pots of tea and hot lemon drinks and straighten up the bed.

Bridie's throat tightened at the thought of all her good neighbours. She'd never appreciated them more than she did now.

'Bridie, what do you think?' Frank repeated.

'If it's what you want, Frank.'

'But I want you to want it too.'

She felt a stab of bitterness and resentment. She fought to ignore it. 'Whatever makes you happy makes me happy, Frank. But I'll miss the Gorbals and my neighbours here. They've been good to us.'

'We're not going to the other end of the world, pet. You can still come back here and visit them.'

But visiting wouldn't be the same.

She smiled. 'Yes, all right, dear.'

'Oh, Bridie, Bridie.' Frank's eyes gazed rapturously beyond her into the future. 'Didn't I always say that one day all our dreams would come true?'

Yes, she thought sadly. But when did our dreams separate and become different?

Chapter Fifty

Michael and Caroline were delighted to get Frank and Bridie's flat in the Gorbals. Garngad was becoming a derelict area. Buildings were being torn down all around them.

Dereliction was going on in the Gorbals too, of course. Plaster dust thickened the air, and everywhere mud squelched underfoot. But the flat in the Gorbals was a room and kitchen. Michael and Caroline's single end had become chaotic with the twins and the new baby.

'What with the pram, and the twins' bed, and the table and chairs, there wasn't an inch of space for us to move in that room,' Caroline said. 'It was driving us mad.'

Nevertheless, Caroline looked a changed woman. Her fair hair had a healthy bounce. Her eyes were bright and happy. She looked comfortably plump. She and Michael were having a housewarming party and all the family were crowding in to what had once been Frank and Bridie's front room.

'We hadn't to do a thing to this place,' Caroline enthused. 'Frank and Bridie had it so nice.'

Hearing her, Bridie felt like weeping. It was an agony to see someone else lay proud claim to her room. The Gorbals flat still felt like home to her. This was where she belonged. Already she hated the West End.

'Oh, there you are, Bridie,' Caroline greeted her. 'I was just saying to everybody how nice you and Frank had kept this place.'

Drowning in a sea of misery, Bridie's gaze dropped. 'Thanks.'

'How you doing, Michael?' Frank said cheerily. 'Still keeping off the booze?'

'Of course. But we've got beer for anybody that wants it. And gin for the girls.'

'Just a soft drink for me,' Bridie murmured.

Doris, trying not to totter on her stilts of heels, joined them. She was on her second gin and tonic. Alcohol was proving no comfort. She wished she'd never come. She had known Bernard would be there, and she'd bought a new scarlet minidress to make sure he noticed her. She'd hoped against hope that a miracle would happen and he'd turn to her again. She'd picked over every minute of their relationship a thousand times, trying to understand it, trying to find out where she'd gone wrong. In moments of terrible despair she'd stare at herself in the mirror and tell herself it was simply because she looked too small, too fat and too common. The whole family, including Bridie, were too small. It was terrible. The only consolation was she and Bridie hadn't inherited Carragh's bandy legs. She'd moan and sob broken-heartedly against the mirror, and feel that no amount of back-combing and piled-up hair, no amount of make-up or false eyelashes, would change what she was. It didn't matter how tight her pantie girdle was, or how high her heels – nothing made any difference.

Yet Bernard had wanted her once. He had made love to her. He had asked her to marry him. How had it all gone wrong?

At other times she'd assure herself that maybe she was a bit on the small side, but actually she wasn't a bad looker. Other men had told her so. (Eddy McGuire in despatch was always trying to get off with her and telling her what a smasher she was.) She was definitely better looking than Bridie. Bridie had always been plain and had never been in the slightest interested in making the best of herself. Yet she'd got (and kept) Frank. All the same, Bridie had better watch out – Frank was mixing with glamorous actresses now. How long would it be before some bitch got her claws into Frank? And Bridie would be left in the same boat as her.

Because that's what it came down to in the end: some cruel, selfish bitch had taken Bernard away from her. She'd been afraid that he'd bring Jane Ford with him to Michael and Caroline's housewarming party, though she had no idea if he was still seeing her. She'd hyped herself up, ready to scratch the bitch's eyes out. But there he was – as cool, as self-confident, as uncaring as ever. He'd given her a nod of recognition that didn't disturb the flow of his conversation with Scobie. She felt a stab of hurt and resentment at her father for having anything to do with Bernard. She'd expected him to show more loyalty, and she said so under her breath to Bridie.

'Och, what is he supposed to do?' Bridie asked, somewhat impatiently Doris thought – making her even more hurt. 'He's Michael's best friend, so he had to come. And Bernard's family, so he had to come.'

'Nobody *had* to come!' Doris said.

'Why did *you* come then?' Bridie snapped.

'Charming!' Doris downed her gin and tonic. 'That's all I need, you to bite my nose off.'

Bridie sighed. 'I'm sorry, Doris. I just wish I was back here, that's all. I hate where I am now.'

'How can you hate a place like Botanic Crescent? It's terribly posh. I'd give my eye teeth to live there, so I would.'

'I've got a horrible neighbour. Every time I go out or come in, her door opens a crack. Either she or her husband watches me all the time. It's really horrible.'

'Just shout, "Mind your own business, you nosey old bag." '

'I wish I had the nerve.'

'Next time I come to see you, I'll do it. Now that you mention it, the last time I visited you somebody opened that door and pretended they were polishing the door knob.'

'That would be her husband. He seems to do all the housework, while she just floats about with a frilly gauze cap over her curlers and a frilly négligé.'

'Don't let a couple of arseholes like that get you down, Bridie. Just think yourself lucky you've got a good man and a lovely house.'

'I suppose I am.'

'Of course you are. But Holy Mother of God, Bridie, try to do something with yourself.'

'What do you mean?'

'Well, look at you – not a scrap of make-up, and you never

put a curler near your hair, and your clothes just hang on you. It's bad enough being short-sighted and stuck with glasses, but there's lots you could do. Buy more fashionably-shaped glasses for a start.'

'Och, Doris, you know me . . .'

'More important, Bridie, I know men. They're suckers for a pretty face and an offer of a good shag, and Frank's a man, and now he's mixing with . . .'

'I know. I know,' Bridie interrupted miserably. 'But I can't possibly compete with actresses. It's not just actresses either – he meets all sorts of women, including women writers. I can't do anything about them. He just loves to talk about writing. He always has. He's in his element meeting other writers. He's joined a writers' society now and goes to their meetings. Oh Doris, what am I going to do?'

'I told you, you'll have to make a bit more effort with yourself.'

Bridie blinked and pushed at her glasses. She was blinking a lot these days. It had become a nervous habit. 'People would just laugh at me if I suddenly started painting my face and curling my hair. I'm sure Frank would. It's just not me.'

Doris reluctantly agreed. She couldn't honestly see make-up or curling performing any miracles for Bridie. 'Well, treat yourself to some sexy black underwear and a black lacy nighty.' She didn't have much hope for sexy underwear making Bridie attractive either. What Frank had ever seen in her, God alone knew.

She went over to the sideboard to get herself another drink but Carragh stopped her with a hand on her arm. 'I think you've had enough, hen. You don't want the big man,' she jerked her head in Bernard's direction, 'to see you making a fool of yourself.'

'Bastard,' Doris said brokenly.

'Now, now.'

'I'll never get over the way he humiliated me, Ma. He was terribly cruel to me, so he was.'

Carragh tutted. 'Your da's been cruel to me in his day, by

348

God he has. And well you know it. Bernard was never as bad to you as your da was to me.'

Doris sighed. 'I don't know how you stood it.'

'I didn't see I'd much choice, hen. I couldn't have done what you did.'

'Oh, Ma, don't start.'

'I don't know what the world's coming to,' Carragh said. Her face, under her squashed black felt hat, acquired an aggrieved expression. She kept her hat on when out visiting because she had become self-conscious about the fuzz barely covering her scalp. It was one thing for Scobie to have gone bald on top, but for her to go the same was a hard cross to bear. 'What with you divorcing your man. And Bridie's man writing a play about a priest. That's the next one that's to come on the telly, Bridie told me. Talk about being upset – and no wonder, by all accounts. That's why she agreed to move. What Father Riley will say, I dread to think. And what's possessed Frank to make an attack on the church – because that's what Bridie thinks it is – I just don't know. He's such a nice chap, you know how fond of him I am. And he's always gone to Mass, and the church has never done him any harm. I just can't understand young folks any more.'

'Attacking the church?' Doris squealed. 'That's terrible, so it is. What next? I'll feel humiliated all over again. We'll probably *all* have to move.'

Carragh sighed. 'We will all be moving again, hen, by the looks of things. I'll be sorry to leave Garngad.'

'We'll get a nice new house.' A flicker of hope widened Doris's eyes for a second or two. 'With a bathroom.'

'Aye, they look nice enough,' Carragh said without much enthusiasm. 'But I've heard folks in the new flats have been complaining about dampness. I just wonder how long these places will last. Our building in Garngad must be over a hundred years old. I wonder if them new flats'll still be standing in a hundred years' time.'

'They'll surely see us out,' Doris said.

But no optimism could raise Carragh's spirits. She was

seeing not only the old familiar buildings being torn down, but the break up of the close-knit communities within them.

Michael came across then. 'What are you drinking, Carragh? Can I get you something?'

'No, I'm fine, son. I'm surprised you have any hard stuff in your house.'

Michael grinned. 'I'm hoping you lot'll finish it all off so's I won't be left with any temptation. My da's doing his best at the moment. Him and Tony.'

'Aye, I can see that. Any moment now Patrick's going to give us a song.'

Sure enough, minutes later, Patrick suddenly threw back his head and belted out:

'In Mountjoy Jail one Monday morning,
High upon the Gallows Tree,
Kevin Barry gave his young life for the cause of liberty.
Just a lad of 18 summers and there's no-one can deny,
As he walked to death that morning,
Barry held his head on high.
"Won't you shoot me like a soldier,
Do not hang me like a dog,
For I fought to free old Ireland,
On a still September morn . . ." '

Laughing, Frank came over to Bridie's side. 'Da's well away.'

Doris suddenly looked as if she was about to burst into tears. 'Holy Mother of God, it's supposed to be a happy occasion. What's he singing a sad song like that for and depressing everybody? Your da's about as bad as Bernard. He doesn't care a damn about other folks' feelings.'

Bridie stiffened as Frank put an arm around her shoulders. He was happy all right. He didn't care a damn about *her* feelings. All the O'Maleys were the same.

Chapter Fifty-One

'Bailie McPherson?'

McPherson nodded, then accepted the outstretched hand.

'I'm Tom Gordon of Gordon Construction. I've been told through a mutual friend, Bailie McPherson, that I could approach you. You're a man I could speak to.' In other words, he knew Bailie McPherson was a man who would take a bung. 'John Douglas . . .' Gordon went on, 'from the Church of Jesus in Rose Street.'

'A good man, John,' McPherson said. 'Gives a lot of support to the church.'

'As you do yourself, Bailie, as you do yourself.' In other words, friends that pray together stay together. 'What are you drinking?'

'Whisky.'

Gordon ordered a good malt. 'I'd like to tender for the Northern Road flats. Any chance, do you think?'

Bailie McPherson took his time, savouring the whisky before answering. 'I could use my considerable influence with the planning department.'

'I would be grateful if you could, Bailie McPherson.'

'After all, you are an old established construction firm.'

'We are indeed, and if we got this contract . . .'

'I will certainly argue your case to the best of my ability . . .'

'You won't regret it, Bailie McPherson.' In other words, it was going to be a really good bung.

McPherson felt pleased with himself. He enjoyed several more whiskies and a splendid meal at Tom Gordon's expense. On the way home in his silver grey Mercedes, he savoured a Havana cigar. The Merc was a new acquisition of which McPherson was extremely proud. A real bargain from someone for whom he'd done a few favours. A present of Havanas had been given to him at Christmas by a hotelier who had been grateful for receiving yet another licence. Pub owners too had showered him with bottles of Glenmorangie or Famous Grouse. He'd had gifts of vintage port and 'sherry for your good wife'.

He leaned well back in the driving seat, mostly because he felt so pleasantly relaxed, but also because he had grown more portly. Sophie had begun to nag at him about losing weight. His cheeks and nose had become mottled with fine red veins, giving his skin a brightly coloured hue. Sophie warned, 'If you don't cut down on all this rich food and drink, and lose a bit of weight, you're going to take a stroke or a heart attack.'

It was all very well for her. She'd always been built like a greyhound. Her nature helped keep her thin. Always worrying and ferreting suspiciously about. He just wasn't like her. He was generously built, and it was good that it was so. It made him look more imposing – a man of substance. He no longer worried about what his father would think or what his father would do. His father had lived in a different world. His father was one of the old school of socialists. His father had been willing to die for the working man that he represented. Andrew McPherson had decided to *live* for them, and live as well as he could into the bargain. This meant learning a thing or two from what went on in big business and among Tory colleagues. He knew about quite a few businessmen's tax fiddles and ruthless practices, some of which were on a criminal scale that was breathtaking in their scope and audacity. He often suspected they only got away with it because they made enormous donations to the Tory party. He felt saintly in comparison. He helped ordinary folks get houses. He helped small guys with wee corner pubs get licences. He listened sympathetically to problems of all kinds from the poorest section of society – and he did what he could for them. He'd even done a few police officers a good turn when it was needed.

He was a very popular man.

He'd phoned Sophie to tell her he was working very late and would snatch something to eat in town. This was in case she'd kept a meal hot for him as she often did. Sophie was a good wife

– too good sometimes. He just wished she could relax a bit. Tonight she'd be waiting for him in a house in which never a speck of dust would dare descend. His slippers would be waiting for him inside the front door. The back door was only for tradespeople. She always gave him his place. The cushions on his favourite armchair by the fire facing the television would be plumped, ready for him to sink thankfully into. His pipe and tobacco pouch (the soft leather one she'd given him at Christmas) would be lying on the small table beside his elbow. He still enjoyed a pipe in the privacy and comfort of his own home.

When he did arrive in time for dinner, Sophie would present him with a wonderful meal. Indeed, more and more he was insisting on business lunches instead of later meals. Not even the best cordon bleu chef in town could compete with Sophie's dinners. He had never been tempted with other women. He was a strict believer in the sanctity of marriage and was genuinely shocked to learn of the extra marital adventures of colleagues or friends. A committed Christian, as he always had been, and Sophie now was, could not and certainly should not ever contemplate anything that might endanger the marriage vows.

When he had said 'Until death do us part,' he had meant it.

'You know the latest news?' Sophie asked once he had donned his slippers, loosened his tie and settled in his chair to concentrate on the business of filling a pipe.

'No. What?'

'Agnes and Duncan Noble have committed suicide. They were both prescribed sleeping pills and tranquillisers, and apparently they saved them up and took them all at once.'

'My God, Sophie,' he cried out, his pipe forgotten in the shock of such a revelation. 'That's terrible. I'm so sorry.'

'Why? I'm not.'

It was then he noticed how feverish her face was, and how unnaturally bright were her eyes. She looked quite demented. Insane almost.

'My dear, they were your mother and father. Whatever happened in the past, they were still your own flesh and blood.

353

Here, let me pour you a glass of whisky. It'll help calm you down.'

'They robbed me of my childhood. They made a nightmare of most of my life.'

'Sophie, that was all years ago. You've been harming yourself ever since – harbouring such black emotions, being so bitter and unforgiving.'

'You don't know. You don't know about them or about the so-called "home" they caused me to put into. For years I couldn't bear to think about them – it was too painful. I still can't think about the institution and what I suffered there.' She put her hands to her head. 'My mind blacks out.'

'My dear . . .' was all he could say. He felt for her. He wanted to put his arms around her to comfort her, to show her some loving tenderness. But he knew sadly it would be no use. They didn't have that sort of relationship. In the silent darkness of their bedroom she would cling to him with furtive passion and she'd have rapid, desperate sex with him before turning away into her cold, closed world once more.

'We'll have to go to the funeral,' he said. 'Everybody will expect it. It would look bad if we didn't.'

'One more ordeal,' Sophie said, half to herself. 'One more ordeal, and then it'll be finished for good. I'll be free of them.'

'That's right. Just cling to that thought. Everything's going to be all right.' But secretly he doubted it. Sophie was Sophie. He couldn't see anything ever making her any different. Who was it who said, 'Give me a child for his first five years and you can do what you like with him afterwards'? Sophie's character had been long since formed. It wouldn't matter what happened now. He suspected the only way Sophie could change, if she changed at all, would be to get worse. No matter what she was trying to make out, she must feel the most awful guilt.

Suddenly he felt anxious. 'It's just occurred to me. There'll be an inquest. I hope to God nothing is dug up that will damage our reputation.'

Sophie began agitatedly pacing about the room. 'Even

354

beyond the grave they won't leave me in peace. Even beyond the grave they'll try to ruin my life.'

'Now wait a minute,' McPherson said. 'Let me think . . .'

Sophie was wringing her hands. 'If the newspapers got a hold of the story behind this . . .'

'No, wait a minute, Sophie. A lot of people owe me favours. I should be able to use my influence to hush anything up. Leave it to me. Try not to worry. I'll make a few phone calls. I'll see a few people tomorrow.'

'The phone's hardly stopped all afternoon. I've had to leave it off the hook. You'd wonder how the news got around so quickly. They were only found this morning when their home help went in.'

'I hope to God they didn't leave a note.'

'Apparently it just said they were sorry.'

'Oh God!' Surely Sophie *must* feel guilty. After all, most people even felt guilty at any normal death of people they loved.

'Sorry!' Sophie laughed bitterly. 'I hope they burn in hell.'

'Sophie, you're upset. You don't mean that.'

She laughed again. 'What would you know? Brought up by a mother who always thought you were marvellous. No doubt your father doted on you as well.'

Now *he* felt guilty. He hadn't visited his mother for some time. They'd had her for Christmas dinner, but he'd only popped in to see her a couple of times since then and it was now June. Certainly Sophie had visited on separate occasions and had had her over to Bearsden for afternoon tea. But he seldom managed any spare time during the day and so he hadn't seen her then. Andrina visited her too, although the old girl must be getting senile because she denied ever seeing Andrina for months.

'She's been to see you several times, Mother,' he'd patiently persisted. 'Robert told me.'

'Well, if she's been telling Robert she's been coming to see me, she must be up to something. She must be sneaking off to see a fancy man because she certainly hasn't come to see me.'

'Mother!' He was horrified that there should be such ideas in

355

her head. 'You mustn't ever think such things. Our Andrina's a good girl and a perfect wife to Robert. Indeed, Sophie and I often say she's too good for him. He's not as committed a Christian as we once thought he was. Andrina never misses a service, and to see and hear that girl sing in the choir is like watching and listening to an angel. Sophie and I are really proud of her. But we know from friends who still go to Rose Street that Robert is a very poor attender. Andrina is too loyal, of course, to ever say a word against her husband.'

'That may be so,' Mrs McPherson insisted, 'but she never comes to see me.'

McPherson sighed. That was one of the reasons he avoided going to see his mother too often. Her mind was beginning to go and it saddened him.

'She's still never appeared on that doorstep,' she'd said, as if simply carrying on their previous conversation from where it left off.

'Mother,' he had said gently, 'Andrina said she saw you only a couple of nights ago. She tucked Jennifer up in bed and left Robert to babysit while she came and checked that you were all right. She worries about you being lonely since we've moved away to Bearsden.'

'Think I'm daft?' his mother jeered.

In actual fact he did. After all, she was in her eighties and had acquired some disgusting habits, like taking out her false teeth to eat – something she would never have done ten years before when she was in her right senses.

'They hurt my gums when I eat,' she explained, but it was no excuse.

'Think I'm daft?' she repeated. 'Well, think again. I'm telling you, there's more to that girl than meets the eye.'

Chapter Fifty-Two

Andrina had been admiring the new négligé she'd bought when she heard the doorbell ring. It was eleven in the morning; coffee time. But she knew it wasn't likely to be Josie popping in. They were on speaking terms, but no longer as close as they had once been. Andrina wished she'd lied to Josie. It had been a mistake to tell her about Bernard. She hoped Josie wouldn't see him coming up the stairs this lunch time. Bernard was due to arrive within the hour.

The doorbell gave a longer, more aggressive buzz. It was definitely too early for him. He always came exactly on time. She felt apprehensive as she hurried to answer the door.

'Mummy!'

'Well,' Sophie snapped, 'aren't you going to ask me in?'

Mind and heart racing in panic, Andrina opened the door wider and stood aside. She followed the older woman into the kitchen. 'Is there anything wrong?'

'I had to come to town to buy a black coat and hat. There's a funeral I've to attend in Bearsden.'

'Is it anyone I know?'

'No.'

'A cup of coffee?'

'Yes.'

'Would you put the kettle on, Mummy? I was just on my way to the toilet when you rang the bell. I won't be a minute.' She shut the kitchen door behind her and flew across to the bedroom. The négligé must be hidden in case her mother came through. She stuffed the froth of satin and black lace under the mattress, then with shaking hands tried to smooth the coverlet back down. The thought of Bernard coming to the door while her mother was in made her sweat. There was nowhere she could hide him. By the time she returned to the kitchen she felt sick and faint.

357

Her mother said, 'I never heard the chain being pulled.'

'Gosh,' Andrina turned back into the hall. 'I get more forgetful every day.' In the bathroom she pulled the chain, then returned to the kitchen, anxiously glancing at her watch. 'I thought you had a black coat, Mummy.'

'An ancient, shabby old thing. Your daddy insisted I get something really smart.'

'So this is you on your way to Sauchiehall Street, is it?'

'Your daddy said I should pay you a visit.'

'Oh? I tell you what. Why don't you have a very quick coffee just now, go and do your shopping, then come back here – say about four o'clock – for a nice leisurely afternoon tea, and you can show me what you've bought?'

'Where's Jennifer?'

'She's through in her room having a little nap.'

'At eleven o'clock in the morning?'

'She was up very early. She gets tired running about. She's a very active two-year-old.' Two years, five months. Another one year, seven months before she could be accepted into the local day nursery. It would be good for Jennifer. Everyone said how the little ones loved the nursery and how it made them so clever. Actually Jennifer wasn't all that active but now that she could get around (and she could talk), she could pose problems when Bernard came to the house. If she were kept up late, however, and awakened early, and kept amused to keep her awake, she was usually ready for a nap at about midday. Although at the moment she was simply lying, clutching her teddy and sucking her thumb. She was really a very good little girl. But maybe she was bored at times, not having any other children to play with. She'd enjoy the nursery, Andrina kept assuring herself.

For no apparent reason, she remembered how, when she was much older than Jennifer and she'd been naughty, her mother made her lie across the bed. Then she'd slapped her legs, slap, slap, slap, until her skin burned, and there seemed more hatred in every blow. It was the only physical punishment her mother had ever meted out to her.

All of the other children were going to the swimming baths,

and she was desperate to go too. Instinctively – knowing her mother would never allow this – she'd not told a lie but omitted part of the truth. She said she was going to Mary Ferguson's house and they were going to do their homework together. But before the homework, Mary loaned Andrina her sister's bathing costume and they'd joined a crowd of girls and boys in a noisy splash and a lot of laughs in the local baths.

Her mother (she should have known) had checked up on her and found out the whole truth.

'Half naked, and with boys!' she quietly accused. 'You wicked, wicked girl.'

She had never smacked Andrina again after that, maybe because she was getting too big a girl to be smacked. She had simply shut her out in icy disgust – completely ignored her. This was a thousand times worse than any physical attack. It had taken a long time of desperately trying to please her mother, and being perfect enough in every way, before Andrina regained the slightest attention.

'It's a disgrace. You ought to be ashamed of yourself.'

Andrina's eyes flew wide. 'Disgrace?'

'You should be out with that child in the Green. She should be getting some sunshine and fresh air. A park right across the road and you've got that poor child shut up in her room.'

Andrina sank down on to the chair. Her legs had literally given way. 'I've pulled a back muscle. I'm not able to get the push-chair up and down the stair. I'm sorry, Mummy. I know she needs to get out, but my back hurts even when I lift her. She hasn't been out for ages.' This was true. All she'd omitted to say was how she had strained her back. She prayed her mother wouldn't ask.

'Forget the coffee,' Sophie fussed to her feet. 'I'll take Jennifer for a walk right now.'

'Will she need her coat?' Andrina's voice was anxious. She was still unable to relax.

'No. It's lovely and warm outside. I'll take it just in case though.'

In a matter of minutes Sophie had the child in the push-chair and was bumping her down the stairs. Andrina ran through to watch out of the front room window.

'Don't let Bernard appear. Dear God, don't let her see Bernard.' She felt she'd have a nervous breakdown, completely collapse, if her mother saw him coming to the house. If her mother saw Bernard, she'd immediately know everything. It was at times like this that she didn't want to see Bernard ever again. No one or nothing else mattered but the anguish she was in.

I can't stand this, she thought, running to the phone to dial the number of Bernard's flat.

'Bernard?' She thanked God he was still there.

'Darling, what's wrong?'

'Don't come. Mummy is here.'

'How long before she leaves?'

'For pity's sake, don't come.'

'Darling, I hardly ever see you when it's Robert's school holidays. Taking his class out sketching today is our only chance. Then there's my tour. I'll be away for over a month. Where is she now?'

'Across in the Green with Jennifer.'

'Persuade her to take Jennifer for the rest of the day. Overnight if possible.'

'She's supposed to be going shopping.'

'Your mother is a very capable woman. She'll manage. And you know how possessive she is with Jennifer. She'll be easily persuaded.'

'I couldn't relax here with you now. Not today. I'm too shaken. I don't think I could even make it over to your flat.'

'Phone me once you've made the arrangements with your mother. Then I'll call for you and take you to Loch Lomond for a picnic. That'll help you to relax. I'll bring the champagne if you can put some food together. And darling . . .'

'What?'

'Wear something accessible.'

As Bernard had predicted, there were no problems persuading Sophie to take Jennifer back with her to Bearsden, although there had been a few unexpected questions about Granny McPherson.

'Granny McPherson says you've never been to see her.'

'Oh, Mummy, you know how forgetful she is.'

'I know she forgets where she puts her purse and her doorkeys and her spectacles, but she always remembers when I've been to see her.'

'She complained to me about you and Daddy not going to see her.' The one occasion when Andrina had visited Granny McPherson in the past year the old woman had indeed made this complaint.

Sophie stared hard at her daughter and then, apparently deciding she was telling the truth, she busied herself with manoeuvring the push-chair out of the door. 'You don't need to come for her tonight. I can manage for a few days.'

'No, I'd better. Robert misses her. I'll come at about seven.' That would give her plenty of time to get home before Robert. Or to phone him from Bearsden.

As soon as her mother was safely away, she phoned Bernard. Then she rushed out to the shops to buy the necessary food. Family picnics meant sandwiches of corned beef, sausage rolls, iced cookies (Robert's favourite), and chocolate biscuits (Jennifer's favourite). Picnics with Bernard were always sumptuous affairs, with smoked salmon, half chickens, strawberries, Belgian chocolates, and a bottle of champagne. Andrina took care to pack a white damask starched cloth to spread out, and two fine crystal glasses. After the meal they would savour sex. It always seemed even more thrilling out of doors, and as usual she looked forward to it with breathless excitement.

The drive to Loch Lomond was picturesque. It never ceased to amaze strangers to Glasgow how easily and quickly such beauty spots could be reached from the city. They stopped at the quaint little hamlet of Luss, right on the shores of the Loch. It had become Andrina's favourite place in the whole world. On a grassy spot they set out the picnic. They both loved to eat alfresco and take in the sights and sounds and smells of the natural surroundings. They fed each other erotically and sipped champagne from each other's glasses. They lazed and chatted. Entwined in each other's arms, they strolled along the shingle. Then they stopped to lean against a huge old tree. Bernard lifted her up in his arms and, supported by the tree trunk at her back, she wrapped her legs around his waist. Each time he plunged inside her he called out, louder and louder, how much he loved her, adored her, as if he wanted the whole world to hear.

And all the time she groaned and moaned in abandonment and delight. The breeze caressed her face and hair. She felt its coolness on her bare legs and bottom. Waves softly lapped against the shore. The pungent aroma of pine tantalised her nostrils. She opened herself to her lover, relishing him and the wondrous sensuousness of nature. Beyond caring about anything or anyone, she wanted the flame inside her to burn forever.

Chapter Fifty-Three

McPherson had not seen the play. He had been far too taken up with the council and other business. At home, the trauma of the funeral engulfed his attention. He only became aware of the impact of the play when newspapermen began sniffing around. Soon he realised that a dangerous situation could arise if care was not taken.

Fortunately, he'd always been a careful man. He had always been a calm, easygoing man as well. This play by Frank O'Maley, however, made him angry. He phoned Bernard O'Maley's office, only to be told he was away on a tour with some famous pop singer and his group. He wouldn't be back for another week or two. This inconvenience gave fuel to McPherson's anger. How dare an O'Maley, of all people, stir up trouble like this? Through a contact in the BBC, he managed to get a copy of the script of the play. Reading it, fear overshadowed his anger. No wonder the newspapermen were on the hunt. Here was a dramatised account of his political and Council experience. He realised of course that what happened to the man in the play and how he functioned could apply to other politicians, local or national – and councillors and bailies. He believed it was how the system worked. It was just the way of the world; it was life. It was simply being practical and realistic. It was being mutually helpful and co-operative.

This play, however, was taking a different view of it, using ugly, unacceptable words like 'graft' and 'corruption'. Frank O'Maley seemed to have an uncanny knowledge of exactly what went on. How could this be? He was only a clerk in the office of some back-street warehouse. Emotions chased around inside McPherson: confusion, uncertainty, suspicion, fear. Surely Bernard hadn't been the source of his brother's information? Bernard wasn't a stupid man. Nor was he indiscreet. At least, McPherson had never thought of him as an untrustworthy, indiscreet man. Anyway, Bernard had slipped him many a long brown envelope – if there were to be accusations of guilt flung around, Bernard would be as guilty as anybody.

On the other hand, Bernard or anyone else in a similar position could argue that they had been forced into offering 'sweeteners'. They could claim, quite wrongly of course, that they had been held to ransom and had no choice. But why should Bernard put him on a spot like this? Anyone else in a similar position, who had experience of giving so-called 'sweeteners', wasn't Frank O'Maley's brother. It had to be Bernard who'd spoken to Frank and, purposely or not, given him the idea for such a dangerous and scurrilous piece of work.

He could hardly wait until Bernard came back. The waiting was an agony.

Sophie's sharp eyes noticed the change in him, the barely concealed anxiety. 'Is there something wrong?'

McPherson hesitated, puffing at his pipe in a futile effort to draw comfort from it. 'You remember the O'Maleys?'

Sophie's eyes narrowed and her sleek grey head pushed forward, suspiciously, aggressively. 'What about them?'

'You only met Bernard. But there's four brothers. One of them, Frank, does a bit of writing. He's recently had a play put on the BBC about graft and corruption in the City Chambers. A tissue of lies, of course, but a lot of people – especially newspaper people – are thinking where there's smoke there's fire.'

Sophie sat down. 'Surely they're not believing a silly play? It was a story, wasn't it? It wasn't put over as a documentary.'

'No. It was supposed to be fiction. Unfortunately, there's a widespread belief that most writers get their ideas from real life, and base their characters on real life people.' Worries scurried about his brain like ants. Who else in the City Chambers had as many 'consultancies' – especially on the payroll of building firms – as he had? Who else had done as much work over the years in persuading fellow committee members that such and such a firm most deserved their vote? (Some of the firms he now had shares in.) Who else had as much influence and used it on so many occasions, indeed at every opportunity, and in so many ways? Once the lid was lifted on the day-to-day workings in the committee rooms and boardrooms, once questions began to be asked, there was no telling what picture might emerge. He suddenly saw the intricate web of people involved, the paid officials and civil servants who put people his way, and who also received gifts. He had learned that everyone had his price. But he was at the top of the pile; the buck stopped with him.

He felt shaken to the very foundations of his being. He was in terror of losing his good reputation, his respected place on the bench, his trusted position as a representative of the people of Glasgow, his Christian character in the church, his respectable standing in Bearsden. Even his marriage could be in jeopardy. His chest tightened. It was all so damned unfair.

'I always knew that family were trouble makers,' Sophie said.

'I've heard a rumour that one of the papers is thinking of running a series on what they claim goes on – how people get contracts, etc. Once these things start . . .' He puffed resolutely at his pipe. He mustn't allow his imagination to run away with him. Keep calm, that was the thing. He'd have a word with Bernard as soon as possible.

'And no doubt,' Sophie said, 'that Bernard has never forgiven us for stopping him having anything to do with Andrina. This could be a way of getting back at us – of blackening your character.'

'It's not Bernard who's written the play. It was his brother.'

'Comes to the same thing. They were as thick as thieves, that crowd. They *were* thieves. I heard all about them. They've all been in jail . . .'

'Not Bernard.'

'Why do you always stick up for that Pape?'

'I don't always stick up for him. I've never even mentioned his name to you for years.'

'He'll do us harm, Andrew. I know it.' She twisted her hands in her lap. 'Have I never to have any peace? Every time I think everything's all right, and I can relax, something else blows up.'

He nearly said, 'You've never relaxed in your life. You wouldn't know how,' but he contained himself. Instead he murmured, 'It might not come to anything. Even the newspaper thing – even if the rumour was true, it would just be another story to them. They would soon lose interest and find something else.'

He didn't sound convincing. Nor did he convince her.

'No good will come of this. I know it. I just know it.'

'Now calm yourself, Sophie. It'll certainly be no good to anyone if you get yourself into a state.'

'All these expensive gifts at Christmas from all these firms.' She spoke worriedly out loud to herself. 'And that huge donation to the church – just because I mentioned that we needed money for the restoration fund. It'll look bad.'

'We'll just have to wait and see what happens.'

'Just wait and see? Just wait and see? Can't you do better than that?'

'It wouldn't be wise for me to contact Frank O'Maley direct. But I'll go and see Bernard. He might be able to influence his brother – perhaps into making a public statement that the play had no connection whatever with any real character or situation. Bernard has influence in other directions as well, and plenty of useful contacts. He might have people in the newspaper world . . .'

'How do you know where he is?'

'I heard he has a flat in Sauchiehall Mansions. He sometimes does work for the Council – protecting visiting dignitaries, etc.'

Sophie's eyes darkened murderously. Her mouth set with hatred. 'That filthy Pape's the one to blame for all this. He'll have put his brother up to it.'

'I'll have to think,' McPherson said. 'Just let me think.' His thoughts soon turned bitter. It was all very well for aspiring local Tory politicians. They were practically all businessmen; monied men in the first place. Most Labour councillors were ordinary working men with only their pay packet at the end of the week. Colleagues like Will Chalmers was employed as a labourer. Tommy Hayes was a plumber. Joe Donnelly was a brickie like himself. All of these men and more, including himself, had been brought up on conditions of scarcity. Was it any wonder that in dealing with, and having unheard amounts of money under their control, they became somewhat overwhelmed? That they accepted a few gifts to smooth their path along the way? Although, of course, monied Tories or not, he knew of a few of them who were into more than taking gifts. But he, and most of his colleagues on the Council, including the Tories, had done their best for the people they represented. He had also fought for his country. Surely his countrymen could not throw him to the wolves?

He and Sophie hardly spoke at all for the rest of the night, but the atmosphere in the house was taut with anxiety. She made them both a hot toddy with plenty of honey in it to help make them sleep. They knelt side by side by the bed and silently said their prayers, knowing that both were desperately praying for the same thing. Except that Sophie was also praying that Bernard O'Maley would be banished to hell to burn there forever.

After they both climbed into bed they lay side by side, minds busily ferreting away for answers and escape routes.

McPherson thought again about tackling Bernard – not in his office, that would be too public, too risky. No, he'd go to the flat as soon as he confirmed that Bernard had returned. Despite what Sophie had said, he still didn't think that Bernard had purposely set out to do him any harm. Why should he? They had been getting along so well. Many a good meal they'd had together. Many a gift Sophie had enjoyed without knowing where it had come from.

Sophie had always been a woman of extremes, and her feelings for Bernard were only a symptom of her own nature. Bernard had been in love with Andrina in his youth but he'd taken defeat with good grace. Perhaps he'd married Doris Gallacher in a kind of extended rebound, who knows. That and the pressure of a doting mother whom Bernard adored.

No wonder the marriage hadn't worked out.

One comfort out of all McPherson's present problems, he assured himself, was the fact that his marriage would stand firm through anything that life might fling at him. Sophie had faults aplenty but she knew that he had always stood by her in her darkest hours. She would do the same for him.

A tremor went through him as he thought of how his darkest hour might soon be approaching.

'Oh God,' he prayed again, 'please help me.'

Then he resolved again to go and see Bernard.

Chapter Fifty-Four

'My dearest, darling velvet,' Bernard wrote, 'I have just put down the telephone and your voice is still in my ears, your vision is still in my mind, reinforced by your picture; and my love for you fills my heart.

'There are other parts of my body that show signs of love for you but poets don't write about those much. These past few months without you have been bad enough, but when I look back at earlier times, it is terrible to think there have been not only weeks and months, but years between our kisses and caresses – even our sight of each other. But the flame of love, passion and devotion never flickered. Something fed it and kept it burning.

'I look at your picture now and I want so much to touch your face with my fingertips, trace your lips with my tongue, bury my face in your neck and whisper my love for you as I gently kiss you. To feel your wonderful body in my arms, to smell and taste you, but above all, to be near you.

'To hear you talk is one of the great luxuries of my life, and to see you is a prize I value so highly. To kiss and caress you makes me as rich as kings, and when our bodies smooth and fuse and thrill together, I am in the realm of the gods.

'I long for you so much. You are my last thought at night and the first in the morning and my day-long delight. We shall enjoy each other's company for days – yes – even longer than we've had before. We shall love, laugh and live together for longer periods. We shall walk, eat and listen to music together. We shall hold hands in a quiet peace. We shall move our naked bodies together in a beautiful exciting fashion, and our lips will linger long over every part of each other.

'We shall enjoy making love and find even greater thrills with each other too. I love the way you dress for love – but if you had no perfume, no make-up, and were even in dull clothes, I would adore you just as much.

'I love *you*, Andrina. All you are and all you want to be. I want to be with you, in you, all around you, and somehow, when we talk I can feel almost in that state.

'Give me a sight of you soon.

I am,

Yours forever,

Bernard.'

Andrina wept after reading the letter, she thought it was so beautiful. She wept again that night in bed after Robert was asleep. The school holidays were over again and Robert was out during weekdays until after four o'clock. He was out a couple of evenings too at his karate club. But it still would be difficult to get a chance to be alone with Bernard. It always had been. She'd reminded him of this over the phone. Arranging to see him was like planning to walk through a minefield. Apart from the danger of people finding out, there was the problem of what to do with Jennifer. In a few months she would be three. Already she had met Bernard when he'd come home with Robert for a drink. She called him Uncle Benad, climbed up on his knee and showered him with kisses. Watching the scene, Andrina was consumed with jealousy. As quickly as she could she'd packed Jennifer off to bed. Then she'd felt ashamed and hurried back to the bedroom to kiss Jennifer goodnight again and tell her that she loved her.

But still she knew in her heart of hearts that it was a different kind of love from the obsessive, all-consuming passion she had for Bernard. Bernard possessed not only her body, not only her every emotion, but her mind. Hardly a moment passed without her thinking of him.

Over two agonising months passed before she and Bernard managed to get together. Her mother had been even more of a nuisance than usual. She had taken to coming to town more often and unexpectedly dropping in to see her.

'Mummy, you were on the phone this morning,' she would say. 'Why didn't you mention you were coming into town this afternoon? I might have been out.'

'You were going to do your shopping in the morning,' her mother would reply. 'Where could you have gone?' Or, 'You didn't mention to me that you were going out.' Once she'd nearly fainted when her mother had suddenly said, 'What about that big Pape?'

'Big Pape? Who do you mean?'

'You know who I mean. Bernard O'Maley.'

'What about him?'

'Have you heard anything about him? Or his brother?'

'His brother?'

'Don't keep repeating everything I say, Andrina.'

'But I don't know what else to say, Mummy. I don't know what you're talking about. Which brother? He's got three brothers. I've only met one of them – Frank.'

'I hope God strikes both of them down,' Sophie said. 'I hope both of them burn in hell.'

Bernard often called Sophie an old witch and she was certainly becoming more like one, at least in the way she talked and behaved. There had been such venom in Sophie's words, such an almost manic strength of feeling, Andrina was shocked and frightened. She desperately wanted to know why her mother suddenly brought up the subject of the O'Maleys but felt it was much too dangerous to ask.

Fortunately her mother was diverted by Jennifer who always demanded her 'nanna's' full attention and got it.

Later, after Sophie had gone, Andrina was left with fierce thoughts and longings for Bernard. It was as if the danger of her mother's curiosity about him had acted as a charge of electricity, of excitement.

That night in bed, while Robert was through at the kitchen table doing some school marking, she wrote to Bernard.

'My dearest one,

'I love you so very much – yearn to be engulfed in your strong hold, ready, willing – no, EAGER – to succumb to your manly charms and feel your love. No potion or elixir is necessary to arouse my deep feelings for you; the sight of you, to hear you speak my name, is aphrodisiac enough. Sensing your desire for

371

me releases my soul to cry out in glad response to you – to pursue your searching lips and find them on my face and neck and breasts and desperately await them travelling all over my body to arouse me to even greater heights. What creates that overwhelming desire? The essence of you – everything you are. My raison d'être. Is it such a crime to fall in love?

'I am alone, in bed, pouring out my love and desire to you in this letter. Having just showered and brushed my hair and teeth, I have slithered between the crisp, white sheets, naked and deliciously lotioned, experiencing the tortuous sensations of the cool bedlinen as I stretch out languorously and imagine you standing in the room.

'Silently, slowly, you approach the bed. Your eyes never leave me. You note the warm gloss of my hair brushed over the soft pillows, my arms outstretched awaiting you, the hint of pert nipples peeking from above the top sheet.

'Pulling back the covers you reveal my nakedness in its entirety and your arousal becomes apparent, inflaming my already surging desire. Body to body – skin on skin – my softness, your hardness. Your probing, my yielding, our own sexual rhythm, our own natural ebb and flow. Caressing, tingling, pulsating, stroking, sucking, nibbling, swallowing – a gourmet extravaganza.

'Gentle tender beginnings progress to a faster pace. A quickening of breathing, a desperation of purpose, bringing each other to the very brink of our climax. Now hot, now throbbing, plunging faster, deeper, stronger, pumping, thrusting.

'Simultaneous soft moans herald the ultimate moment. The juices flow – we are one.

'Oh, the deep, deep need to be yours again. I will arrange a time soon, my love.

'Yours forever,
Andrina.'

But it had been nearly Christmas before there was an opportunity. Robert's mother had become quite crippled with arthritis and her sister on the Isle of Skye said if Robert could manage to bring her in the car, she would look after Jean over the Christmas and New Year period. They seldom saw each other now and it was agreed it would be a great treat for them both. Robert wanted to take Andrina and Jennifer too.

'We would all stay with Aunt Betty over the festive season. Jennifer would love the beach.'

'The beach in the middle of December?' Andrina had laughed. 'No, I don't think so. Skye's a bleak place at the best of times. Anyway, my mother hasn't been at all well recently. My father doesn't seem so good either. I think I'd better spend Christmas and New Year with them. I'll go and stay in Bearsden for the few days that you're away.'

'I could take her up and come back here for Christmas, and go back up for her at New Year.'

'What? Make that dreadful journey four times in a week? It'll be difficult enough doing it twice.'

'I don't like leaving you and Jennifer,' Robert said unhappily. 'Christmas is a family time. And I was looking forward to seeing Jennifer's excitement when she wakes up and finds all her presents.'

'She'll have plenty of other Christmases with you, Robert. This time you can keep your presents until you get back. That way she'll have them to look forward to.'

Andrina could barely conceal her joy. At last she'd be with Bernard again. She'd make some excuse to get away from Bearsden on her own. She'd go to Bernard's flat – that enchanted place.

Everything there was magic to her – so much to her own taste and nature. And everything that she had chosen, Bernard found desirable. He had added touches of his own, of course: the erotic paintings, the jungle of lush plants, the black silk sheets and pillowcases, the tall scarlet candles burning at the altar of their love.

After Robert left, Andrina's father and mother collected her in their car and took her and Jennifer to Bearsden, but all the time Andrina's heart was singing through the flat in Sauchiehall Mansions. In her imagination she was swirling

373

around each room in sheer uninhibited joy. She was preparing herself for her lover. Bathing, perfuming, powdering her body. Inside, in secret, she was shivering with excited anticipation. She could not look at her mother, dared not meet her eyes. Passion and desire were burning from her with such intensity she was terrified her mother might see it.

'Bernard, Bernard,' every part of her moaned out to him. 'My love.'

Chapter Fifty-Five

Bridie wept when she read the poem. To her it confirmed and reflected what she had begun to fear. It was the first subtle hint of a separation to come. It was called 'Islands', and that was what she and Frank had become. They still loved each other but they were different, and the gulf of that difference would widen until they would not be able to reach each other across the divide. She had thought that only she had been aware of it, but the poem indicated that Frank had begun to feel the sadness too. She could hardly read the verses through her tears.

'There will always be you and I,
However we pretend that there's a 'we',
For when that word is used it must imply
That there's a single you and single me.

And though we try to bridge that gap each day,
In all the different ways that we can find –
In all the things we do, and all we say –
A trace of isolation haunts the mind.

We try each time we smile, each time we meet,
Stand together, play a game or walk
Hand-in-hand, or wave across the street;
And, most of all perhaps, when we just talk.

Or maybe most of all, when we two lie
With bodies intertwined in love's embrace,
And share each tender touch, each kiss and sigh,
We come the closest to excising space.

Yet even then a hint of self lies deep,
And final joy is felt to be one's own.
And when our minds are wrapped in separate sleep
They take their separate ways, and dream alone.'

She felt that Frank was taking his separate way. The Frank she had known in Garngad was no more. The serious, sensitive, devout youth taking Mass and attending the Boys' Guild. The pathetically optimistic young man who was always brimming over with impossible dreams and hopes. The scraggy man in his loose, ill-fitting suits over which his lank hair showered dandruff.

The make-up girl at the BBC had cured his dandruff. His hair was still straight. It still flopped forward over his face, but it was glossy and healthy looking. He now wore tight-fitting denims and blue open-necked shirts that brought out the blue of his eyes. He was no longer pathetic skin and bone. He was lean and fit. He had such confident vigour he seemed almost to swagger with energy. He had given up his job in the office. The insecurity of the future terrified her. She had an equally frightening feeling that he would succeed. In his continuing success, she believed, lay the seeds of their separation.

Parties they had now (and they had quite a few because Frank revelled in company) did not comprise of family. The family didn't feel any more comfortable or at home in the house in Botanic Crescent than she did. Occasionally Carragh and Scobie paid a visit. Sometimes Doris came on her own. But more often than not Bridie visited them.

At the parties Frank had – because they were all for Frank's friends – Bridie cowered in a corner of the noisy, smoke-filled room clutching at a glass of lemonade. (Her father had long since put her off any thought of alcohol.) She tried to keep smiling and looking intelligent, but it was always a relief to slip away to the kitchen to wash some glasses or make another pot of coffee. Or, if she could get away with it, to settle down at the kitchen table with a book. Frank's 'arty-farty friends', as her father called them, loved to talk. They talked very loudly and laughed even louder. They drank a great deal. Bridie worried at the amount of money Frank spent in the off-licence for these gatherings. They smoked continuously. They called each other darling and kissed when they met as if they'd not seen each other for years.

One man, a producer, kept calling her 'Dear heart'. She detested his hypocrisy. She felt hurt and insulted by it. She felt painfuly different, the proverbial square peg in a round hole.

Doris kept trying to help. Bridie was closer to her sister now than she'd ever been in her life. They would huddle together in the kitchen drinking tea and sympathising with one another while Frank was away in the other world of his imagination in his study. It was a four room and kitchen house, and Frank used one of the bedrooms as a study (as Steve Martin had done before him).

He quite often worked at night now – especially if he'd been at the BBC during the day. He'd shut himself in his study supposedly for half an hour. Invariably he would forget the time and never surface again until bedtime. Sometimes Bridie went to bed without him. Then he'd come hurrying through full of apologies, and he'd put her book aside and cuddle her and kiss her, as if she was a child and he was kissing the hurt better.

He was working hard at short stories and journalism now to try to keep a regular flow of money coming in. This was as well as the play writing. She had begun to hate his writing. Sometimes when, full of eagerness and enthusiasm, he gave her one of his stories to read in manuscript, her feelings showed and he'd cry out, 'You don't like it? What's wrong with it, Bridie? Be honest. Please tell me the truth. It's important to me to get it right.' In this respect – as far as his writing was concerned – he was as sensitive as he'd always been.

'No, no. It's fine. Honestly, Frank,' she'd manage. But even though she resisted the temptation to undermine him with critical words, he would still look worried, uncertain. His enthusiasm frittered away. He'd wander back to his study again, clutching the manuscript, wondering where he'd gone wrong.

His writing, like his friends, was something she couldn't cope with. His writing always won. It held him in an iron grip. She knew it would never let him go. No matter what she said or didn't say, he'd still beaver away alone in his sanctum, lost in a world of his own creation.

Doris said for the next party she should make a real effort. She still loved Frank, didn't she?

'Of course I love him,' Bridie muttered, lowering her gaze, afraid to meet Doris's eyes in case the agony of her love would be revealed. 'He's my husband.'

'OK,' Doris said. 'Why don't you borrow one of my outfits – we're both the same size – and let me make you up and do your hair.'

Bridie's eyes miserably twitched and flickered about. 'I don't know.'

'Oh, come on Bridie. You'll never get anywhere if you don't try. Give Frank a treat. Let him see how you can be. All his friends – women friends anyway – wear make-up, don't they? I wouldn't be surprised if some of those arty-farty men do as well.'

'Oh, all right then,' Bridie reluctantly agreed.

'Great.' Doris became quite excited and found she really enjoyed making Bridie's transformation. First she helped her into a short, tight fitting, low-necked dress. 'That shows a nice bit of cleavage,' she assured Bridie. 'Men like that.' Then she got to work on Bridie's colourless face. 'You know,' she chatted happily, 'I think I've got a talent for make-up. Maybe I should go in for the beauty business. Beauty salons are terribly popular these days. I think I'd quite enjoy it.'

She took great care, tongue absently peeking out, as she concentrated on applying rouge and lipstick and eye liner and eye colour and mascara to Bridie's anxious, upturned face. Then she energetically back-combed Bridie's hair and with many kirby grips and hairgrips and much hair lacquer, managed to keep it up in some sort of bouffant.

'Your hair's not really long enough to do it right,' Doris said, 'but at least I've managed to give it a bit of a lift.'

They both gazed in the mirror, Doris with pride at her handiwork, Bridie with shock and horror.

'Oh Doris, do you really think . . .'

'Great,' Doris enthused. 'Though I say it myself, I've done a terribly good job. Now I'd better go before Frank comes in. Time I went home anyway. Mammy'll be keeping my tea hot.'

'You could have had something here with me and Frank. You could stay for the party. Or come back for it if you'd rather. They usually start arriving between eight and nine.'

'No thanks, Bridie. Some of them are a bit weird for my taste. I don't know what they're talking about half the time. They make me feel uncomfortable.'

'I know what you mean,' Bridie said miserably.

'Never mind. You'll be a hit tonight. Frank'll be terribly proud of you.'

'Do you really think so?'

'He's got eyes in his head, hasn't he?'

After Doris left, Bridie put a pot of soup on to heat that she'd made earlier. She tried to remember what else she'd meant to have for the evening meal. After dinner Frank would help with the preparation of the party food. He enjoyed every aspect of entertaining. He'd happily fry cocktail sausages and spread sandwiches and sing to himself while arranging everything on the dining room table and admiring how the spread looked.

He used to help with the washing up, and Bridie had enjoyed sharing the task with him. She always washed and he dried and they'd chat together while they worked.

But he'd bought her a dishwasher. 'Every labour saving device,' he'd enthused. 'Every luxury, Bridie, just like I always said.'

She heard his key in the door and stood, with fast-beating, hopeful heart, waiting for his entry into the kitchen. She'd purposely not put on her apron so that he could see the full effect of the dress.

'Good God!' Frank gasped as soon as he saw her. 'For a minute I thought you were Doris.'

'She was here earlier and made me up for the party. Do I look all right?'

Frank closed his eyes for a minute. Then he opened them and said kindly, 'Bridie, please wash your face and brush your hair. And put on one of your own dresses,' he added.

'I look awful!' Tears gushed up and trickled down Bridie's cheeks. She had to grope off her spectacles to wipe at her eyes.

Frank came over and took her into his arms. 'I just want my beautiful Bridie, that's all, not a look-alike Doris or anybody else.'

'But I'm not beautiful, Frank.'

'You're beautiful to me.'

He cuddled her close and kissed away her tears. She tried to feel better. She assured him she was all right now and hastened to scrub every vestige of paint from her face and tug a brush through her hair. They had dinner and Frank told her all that had happened at the BBC and the latest fuss over the play about the bailie. He told her the plot of his next story.

Frank loved to talk, especially about his writing. He had always been the same. Eyes down, Bridie went on eating the food on her plate. For no apparent reason she felt resentment building up inside her.

'Damn him and his bloody writing!' she thought.

Chapter Fifty-Six

For the first time since he'd known Bernard, McPherson detected a sliver of vulnerability in the big man's eyes. It only lasted a second. McPherson took it for guilt.

'I want to talk to you. Can I come in?'

'You've picked a hell of an awkward time, McPherson.'

It was then it occurred to McPherson that Bernard probably had a woman in the house. 'It won't take long. I just have to get something straight.'

Bernard stood aside. 'Come through to the kitchen.'

'Funny time of day to be in your dressing-gown,' McPherson remarked.

'What I wear and when is my business.'

'Fair enough.' McPherson's anger began to show. 'But what about the play? Whose business is that?'

'Play? What the hell are you talking about?'

'You know what I'm talking about. The play your brother wrote.'

'My . . . oh, Frank? I thought he just wrote poetry.' He hesitated, remembering. 'You're right, he did go around trumpeting about a play he'd had accepted some time back. Must be over a year ago. Maybe two. What's it got to do with me?'

'That's what I'd like to know.'

'I'm still not with you.'

'You mean you haven't seen it?'

'I've been away on a job for months.'

McPherson was taken aback. 'I didn't think of that.'

'Are you going to tell me what all this is about?'

'I'll tell you what the play is about. It's about a Glasgow bailie who takes bribes, who gets involved, and gets other people involved, in graft and corruption.'

'Shit!'

'Exactly.'

'Listen. What do you think I am? Stupid? I hardly ever see Frank. Even if I saw him every day I wouldn't have said City Chambers to him, far less mention your name.'

McPherson calmed down. 'To be honest, Bernard, I didn't think it could be you. I just didn't know what to think. Who *could* it be?'

'How should I know? It's probably just Frank – his overworked imagination, or writer's intuition as he calls it. He used to always be rabbiting on about writer's instinct or intuition. He's my brother and I love the guy, but he's a nutcase. Always was. But I'll have a word with him if you like.'

'Thanks, Bernard. You never know, it might help. I've been hoping and praying it'll die down.'

Bernard grinned. 'Will I put a Catholic prayer up for you?'

McPherson took him seriously. 'It wouldn't go wrong. I've been on radio and television praising the way local government in Glasgow is run and making it plain how offended and insulted I and all my colleagues in the Chambers feel, and how I hope God will forgive these gutter-press journalists who care nothing for the truth or for the feelings of hard-working and honest representatives of the people.'

Bernard gave him a wink. 'That's the ticket, Bailie. You tell them.'

'Maybe it *will* all die down.' McPherson was beginning to feel much better and more confident. Cheerful even. Bernard had that effect on him. He liked the big man. Admired him too.

'Would you like a dram?' Bernard asked.

'No, I've interrupted you enough. I'll let you get on with enjoying yourself. You'll be good at that.'

'You're right there, Bailie.'

'A man of many talents.'

'Right again.'

McPherson laughed and made for the door. 'You must come to lunch soon. At the Chambers, I mean.'

'I didn't think you meant Bearsden.'

'I'll give you a ring.'

They had reached the front door.

'Take it easy,' Bernard said. 'Stay loose.'

McPherson laughed again and gave a wave before Bernard shut the door. He felt as if a ton weight had been lifted from his shoulders. Earlier, he'd slowly puffed up the stairs like a tired old walrus. Now, although he still kept a hand on the banister for support, he'd regained his proud and portly bearing. It had been foolish of him to get into such a state. It never did any good to panic. Bernard would never say a bad word about him. He should have known he could trust Bernard. He could trust all the contractors who employed him as a consultant too. Why should they bad-mouth him? He was too valuable to them and to many others. Why should he worry about an upstart scribbler like Frank O'Maley? Bernard would soon put him straight.

He wondered if he should tell Sophie that he'd been to see Bernard. He doubted, however, that his visit would be of comfort and reassurance to her as it had been to him. Sophie had a very twisted view of some things and people, and nothing could ever untwist her. Any time he'd tried it just made her worse.

No, better leave well alone. Let things take their course. God worked in mysterious ways, he'd tell her. Their faith would be rewarded. God would protect them. He would make everything all right. They went to church on Sunday morning and stood side by side and sang the hymns and listened earnestly to the sermon, and felt comforted. Andrina was staying over the weekend and sang a solo, standing like an angel in her white dress in front of the pulpit.

Both McPherson and Sophie felt proud, and pure, and uplifted. It was a special kind of happiness.

Afterwards he said to Sophie, 'We're very lucky, you know. We've a good daughter. Not only a good Christian but a really lovely girl. She suits white, don't you think?'

Sophie agreed. 'And a lovely grandchild.'

'Yes, dear wee Jennifer,' McPherson said. He was very fond

of the child. The church had started a crèche in the small hall and it was proving extremely popular. Sophie had helped collect funds to supply it with toys, and often took a turn of staffing it. Sophie was a wonderful worker for the church. Both the Reverend and Mrs Dinwoodie often said they didn't know how they'd ever managed without her. He too was a veritable pillar of the place and never spared himself to do whatever he could.

'You know,' Sophie said some days later, 'you were right, Andrew. We should always cling to the rock of our faith and trust the Lord to look after us. Things seem to have died down. There's been nothing more in the papers.'

He believed he had been right in saying this. God had looked after His own. No doubt, of course, this had meant allowing Bernard to oil a few palms and twist a few arms. This is what he meant when he told Sophie that God worked in mysterious ways.

He was also grateful to God that he was on good terms with the police. It helped being Chairman of the Police Committee.

Yes, God had been good to him. He in turn had been good to his family – to Andrina and little Jennifer. He had also tried to help Robert. More than once he'd told him, 'Look, Robert, I can easily use my influence to get you a better job. Or if you're still determined to remain in teaching, I could at least have you moved to a better school.'

Robert, however, was a very stubborn and foolish man. He not only wanted to remain in teaching, he insisted on remaining in Blackhill. Blackhill of all places!

'You'll never get promotion in a Catholic school, Robert,' he'd reminded him. 'Never as long as you're a Protestant.'

Apparently Robert didn't care. 'I believe in doing a worth-while job where I'm most needed,' he insisted. 'And I'm most needed in Blackhill.'

McPherson had remarked to Sophie, 'He's a bit of a masochist, if you ask me.'

Sophie agreed.

'And he doesn't look too happy with it,' he added. 'Have you noticed that look about him recently?'

Sophie nodded. 'He'll be worried about his mother. I don't think she's long for this world. That trip up north last Christmas was far too much for her. She's never been right since. The last time I saw her she told me she has angina now as well as her arthritis.'

McPherson looked suitably solemn. 'Robert's always been very fond of his mother.'

'I've never said he wasn't a good enough son. He's just not a good enough husband for our Andrina.'

McPherson agreed.

Sophie said, 'Even for his daughter's sake he should be looking more to his own future. Has Jennifer to grow up in that tenement in that rough part of town? I know it used to be a good enough area but there's so many awful types hang about the Green now, especially during the fair.'

'I've told him,' McPherson spread out his hands, 'I could lend him the deposit for a decent house out here. Something with a garden for Jennifer to play in. I'd give him a present of the money.'

'I know. It's very selfish of him to refuse. He can't even see that it would be far better for him as well as Andrina and Jennifer if he worked in a better school and lived in an area like this. He's always been gaunt-faced and lantern-jawed, but he's become quite grey-looking recently. It's all the tension of working in that awful place as well as the worry about his mother. But maybe once his mother goes, it'll be different.'

'I never thought of that.'

They both felt suddenly pleased with themselves. Everything would work out all right in the end. In time they would have Andrina and Jennifer living nearby. They would enjoy the pleasure of watching their granddaughter grow up among a good class of people, go to a good school, have the best chance in life.

McPherson experienced a pang of guilt when he found himself thinking in terms of class. He had nothing against ordinary working folk, most of whom were perfectly decent and good living. There were still people like his father, committed

Socialists, union leaders, still fighting their corner with all the old idealism and fervour. The world was changing, however. Power and profit were the things most sought after and admired.

Another new element had arisen, and with it a different outlook, a social transformation. Youth had taken over. A new generation was intent on defying and mocking the existing order of things and doing everything they could to shock and disgust. They dressed in a freakish, ridiculous manner. They stripped naked at festivals. They squatted in other people's property. If it wasn't hippies, it was so-called Mods and Rockers. Teenage vandalism was spreading like a rash. As were cases of arson and incendiarism. Telephones were being smashed by the thousand. Young boys were derailing trains and causing people to be killed. Addiction to heroin and cocaine had risen by a frightening amount. It was even worse with addiction to semi-addictive drugs. And of course the illegitimate birth rate had almost doubled.

What shocked McPherson more than anything was the different social attitudes, the different set of values nowadays: the Kray brothers had been included in David Bailey's 'Box of Pin-Ups' as the most glamorous figures of 'swinging' London; the 'Great' train robbery was being portrayed as some heroic wartime exploit; long-haired, arrogant youths like the Beatles were given MBEs by the Queen. Too many people in authority were paying too much attention to stars of pop and television and giving them a sort of status, even reverence. Society was in a very dangerous condition.

Yet there were still good living Christian folk around, and young people with a sense of decency and self-discipline. Once again he thanked God for his good wife, and his lovely daughter and grandchild.

He felt pleased with himself again.

And safe.

Chapter Fifty-Seven

The Orange Walk had a special trot, a jaunty swagger. It was held to commemorate the Battle of the Boyne in which King William of Orange – King Billy to Glaswegians – had defeated the Feenians.

It was a crush of orange sashes and rippling banners and flags and tootling flutes and banging drums. Fancy uniforms for men and women of blue and orange with big tammies, cocked to one side with long stiff feathers, rainbowed the streets. Hordes of men, women and children followed the bands. They wore their best clothes and proudly displayed their orange sashes. They came from all over the city and were aiming for Queens Park where they'd have a picnic, women would drink tea, children would play games and men would get steaming drunk. There had been a time, according to park officials, when everybody had cleared up afterwards. Paper cups and bags, lemonade and beer bottles, were gathered up and put in waste baskets or taken home. The Orange Walk left the park as they found it. But not now. The park attendants and the local residents dreaded their coming. The green and pleasant slopes of the park were awash with debris.

Ominous looking groups of people came to the doors of local residents wanting to troop in to use the toilet. Or they made what seemed equally suspicious and dangerous requests for drinks of water. The residents now locked their storm doors and hid silently inside, only allowing themselves the occasional peep from behind lace curtains as their normally peaceful area reverberated with reckless sound.

There was nothing silent about the residents of Garngad and Blackhill when the Orange Walk swaggered down Castle Street, past the town entrance leading to both these districts.

The Catholic residents turned out in force and shouted and

387

bawled at the Protestant marchers, 'Come on up here, you bastards! Come on, march down Garngad Road!'

Other abusive and provocative remarks were hurled at the 'Walk', but its marchers wisely never took up the challenge. Garngad was sometimes called 'little Ireland'. To trot through there carrying a King Billy banner was asking for it to be knotted round your neck. In Blackhill they'd be liable to shoot holes in it, and you as well. Jimmy and Martha Stoddart had been glad when they'd been rehoused in Castlemilk and were now well away from 'little Ireland'.

Jimmy Stoddart marched along, shoulders aggressively forward like a miniature John Wayne. Men like himself who belonged to Orange Lodges followed the bands proudly wearing black suits, black bowler hats and white gloves. An orange and blue velvet shoulder cape edged with gold fringes made a vivid contrast to some of the men's black suit jackets.

'Hey, Michael,' he heard Scobie Gallacher shout, 'there's your Proddie father-in-law.'

Keeping his eyes riveted on the man in front Jimmy Stoddart ignored Scobie, and Michael O'Maley, his big ugly-looking one-eyed son-in-law. He kept up the swaggering tempo of the trot.

'Ignorant rabble,' he told himself. Martha had been quite right. What had Caroline been thinking of, marrying a Green Grape? That one especially. He'd meant nothing but grief to her. She seemed, by all accounts, to be getting on better now that Michael had gone off the drink. But how long would that last?

The whole O'Maley family were no-users. To see Tony galloping and howling about the stage like a buck-toothed idiot was downright embarrassing. And that Bernard – some reputation he had, frightening the life out of folk.

As for Frank, he'd always acted like a right pouff – him and his stupid poetry. It was the luck of the Irish that had obviously protected Patrick O'Maley from serving half his life in prison. Everybody knew he made quite a business on the side selling things he'd nicked off trains. He was always boasting about his old army mate Bailie McPherson and how they both belonged to the Artillery Club. So he knew a bailie. So what?

It reminded him of the story of the carter who stopped at a pub and asked an amiable-looking man if he'd watch his load for a minute. The response to this request was, 'My man, do you realise I'm a bailie of the City of Glasgow?'

'Aye, OK,' the carter said, 'but surely to God I can trust you with my horse.'

It was a long walk to the Park and the temperature seemed to have crept up to boiling point. The air shimmered before Stoddart's eyes and his bowler was cutting into his head like a red-hot wire. Sweat oozed from every pore. It was purgatory wearing a suit, a stiff collar and a tie on a sweltering day like this. His new shoes hurt. His proud trot became a somewhat undignified hirple. In front, the bandsmen, equally sweating, abandoned their flutes for a time. The march depended on the monotonous, funereal beat of the drums.

Women began to straggle. Children whined. The bands, sensing the flagging enthusiasm, started up again and blasted out 'The Sash My Father Wore' with renewed vigour. Some folks were inspired to burst into song,

> 'Sure it's old but it's beautiful,
> And its colours they are fine.
> It was worn at Derry, Aughrim,
> Inneskillin and the Boyne,
> My father wore it as a youth,
> In the bygone days of yore,
> And it's on the twelfth I love to wear
> The Sash My Father Wore.'

Stoddart struggled valiantly to keep pace. Singing was beyond him now. Not only his feet hurt – a tight pain gripped his chest. He began to have difficulty in breathing. He tried to tell the man marching next to him.

'Aye,' the man said, 'I'm parched as well. To hell with the

389

picnic. I'm attacking the first beer crate I see as soon as we get to that fuckin' park.'

The pain in his chest grew worse. It took complete possession of him. The tramp of feet, the babble of voices, the cheeky tootle of flutes, the tum-tiddely-um-tum of drums, shrank to nothing. He hardly felt the crack on his head as he hit the ground.

'We'll have to go,' Caroline said. 'It's either that or Mammy coming to live here, and where would we put her?'

Michael groaned. The thought of living under the same roof as his mother-in-law, either in the Gorbals or out in Castlemilk, was enough to put him back on the drink.

His one eye squinted down at his wife. 'Just when we were getting on so well in our nice wee house.'

'I know,' Caroline sighed. 'But what can I do, Michael? She depended on Daddy and now that he's gone . . .'

'What worries me, Caroline, is she'll try and put you against me. She's always hated my guts. She could ruin our marriage.'

'No, never.' Caroline put a hand on his arm and squeezed it. 'I've stuck by you through thick and thin so far, haven't I?'

The anxious look still clung to his mis-shapen face. 'And that house'll be in her name now.'

'Maybe we could persuade her to let you go to the Corporation and ask them to transfer it into your name.'

'I can't see Big Martha doing me any favours, can you?'

'We could try. She's older now and practically helpless.'

'You're going to have a lot of extra work, and you've already got more than enough with three kids.'

'I'll manage. What else can I do?' she repeated helplessly. 'She's my mammy. I'm all she's got now.'

'OK, OK. We'll give up this place and go to Castlemilk.' His heart was heavy. He could hardly credit that such a nightmare could become a reality. Actually live in the same house as Big Martha Stoddart! As he told Scobie later, 'God knows how it'll all work out. That woman's enough to drive anybody to drink.'

Scobie laughed. 'You cannae drink in Castlemilk, son. There's no pubs.'

'A desert of a place. There's absolutely nothing for anybody.'

'Now, don't cross your bridges before you come to them, Michael. It might not be as bad as you think.'

'No pictures. No billiards.'

'Nice houses, I've heard though. Caroline'll be pleased you'll have a bathroom.'

'Oh aye, that's all we needed to make our life perfect. A bathroom in Castlemilk.'

'Well, you could look at it this way. You'll spend more time away from the place, what with travelling back and forth. You'll be longer with your mates on the building site in the Gorbals than with Big Martha in Castlemilk.'

'I hope to God the houses out there are made of better stuff than the new ones we're helping to put up in the Gorbals.'

'Aye, there's some cheap rubbish there and no mistake.'

'I've felt like telling my da to get his bailie pal to come and have a good look around, and speak to folk that are suffering dampness and God knows what else in the houses already put up. But I thought better of it. Nobody dare say a word to Da against Bailie McPherson.'

'I don't think it's so much the likes of him, son. It's the planners and architects – they've got it all wrong. They're not thinking of the Glasgow climate, for a start.'

Michael scratched his head. 'It makes you wonder, doesn't it? Guys like that with degrees and God knows what, and they design places with long corridors like prisons, and lifts that can't take folk's furniture, or stretchers or coffins.'

'Well, just be thankful for small mercies, son. Just imagine if Big Martha had one of the high flats. Think of trying to carry her coffin down from the fifteenth floor!'

Michael could have coped with carrying her coffin anywhere. The trouble was, Big Martha was alive. He hadn't seen her for ages. Even Caroline only visited her very occasionally because her mother criticised him so much.

'She's all right with Daddy,' Caroline always said. 'He does everything for her so I don't need to worry.'

391

Now they were both worried. But, as Caroline said, what could they do?

The night before they moved to Castlemilk, Michael lay in the kitchen bed watching Caroline sitting by the fire in her nightie, brushing her fair curly hair. When he'd first known her she'd had a sweet round face. Now it was plump with a hint of a double chin. Her body was soft and plump. She'd gained quite a lot of weight, but he still thought her a lovely woman.

She laughed, making her loose, unbrassiered and uncorseted flesh wobble. 'What do you think you're staring at?'

'My beautiful wife,' he said, but sadly. And after she put out the light and climbed into bed, he clutched her tightly against him. He felt ashamed of his fears but was suddenly at the mercy of them. 'I'm sorry, Caroline.'

'What for?' she sounded puzzled.

'All the awful things I did when I was on the booze. The way I treated you.' He couldn't understand what she saw in him, especially now when he was as ugly as sin.

'For goodness sake, that's all over and done with ages ago.' She cosied happily into his arms. 'You're my own good man. You always will be.'

'Blessed Mary, ever virgin,' he prayed, 'Saint Joseph and the infant child – let it be true.'

Chapter Fifty-Eight

'Oh, it's you, Doris! Come on in.' Andrina kissed her unexpected visitor. 'Nice to see you. Let me take your coat. It's an awful night, isn't it?'

'I know, I hate November. It's terribly depressing.'

'Hello Doris,' Robert greeted her when they arrived in the kitchen. 'How are you doing?'

'Fine, thanks.'

'Still working at Daly's?'

'Uh-huh. I'm in ladies underwear at the moment. We stock terribly good class garments.'

'Can I get you a drink? I was just going to pour one for myself and take it through to watch a programme on television. Unless you two want the use of the front room?'

'No,' Andrina said. 'We'll be cosier in the kitchen. You go ahead. I'll attend to our drinks.'

'OK. See you later, Doris.'

Doris smiled and coyly fluttered her Sandie Shaw eyelashes at him. She thought Robert was terribly sexy. There was something about his lean, hard body and the sensation of suppressed energy about him. A time-bomb ready to explode.

'Sherry or gin or vodka?' Andrina asked.

Doris settled herself in one of the chairs near the fire and giggled. 'You know me . . . Do you mind if I pull my boots off? They're absolutely killing me, so they are.'

'No wonder, with the size of those heels. I don't know how you manage to find boots and shoes with such high heels.'

'It's terribly difficult right enough. These white ones are really smart though, aren't they?'

'Is that enough gin?'

'Ta. I hope I'm not keeping you off your favourite programme.'

393

'No. I hardly ever watch TV. It's not often Robert watches it either, but there's this Japanese thing tonight and he's interested in anything Eastern. How's the family, Doris?'

Doris crossed her legs, revealing a large expanse of thigh beneath her black and white plastic skirt. 'Oh, Mammy's found the Bingo . . .'

'Bingo? What's that?'

'A numbers game. When Da goes out with his pals now, she goes out with hers. It's good to see her enjoying life for a change. I'm terribly worried about Bridie, though.'

'Your sister?'

'Uh-huh. I've been doing my best to help her, but nothing seems to work.'

'What's the problem? I thought you said her husband was doing great and they had a gorgeous flat in the West End.'

'So they have. That's the problem, I think. He's doing too well. He's got all these arty friends. Terribly glamorous, some of them. And poor wee Bridie so plain.' Doris lit a cigarette. 'Life's funny, isn't it?'

Andrina agreed.

After a couple of thoughtful puffs at her cigarette, Doris went on. 'There she is in that lovely flat with a successful husband who just showers her with everything. She's got a dishwasher, a washing machine and God knows what else. And she's as miserable as sin. She does nothing but moan and complain about Frank any time I go to see her. The last time, I told her – think yourself lucky you're not like me, I said, on my bloody tod – if you'll pardon the French. Bernard's not on his tod, of course!'

The last bitter remark was so unexpected, it nearly took Andrina off her guard. She nearly said, 'I know, he's off to Paris on a job with some of his men.' She jerked herself back just in time.

'I always said – he'll never be without a woman, him,' Doris continued. 'I didn't know at first if it was that Jane Ford or not. I just saw him come into the shop with this slimmer than slim creature looking as if she'd just stepped off the catwalk. I could have rushed at her and scratched her eyes out. Then I thought –what the hell? What good would it have done me? It wouldn't have got him back. I would only have lost my job and been worse off. So I just served her, sweet as pie, after he went off. He didn't see me there. There were quite a few girls and customers there at the time and of course he wouldn't even remember I worked there. He was never interested in anything I did. I heard him saying he'd meet her in the restaurant. One of the other girls went forward first of all but I elbowed in and took over.'

Andrina said nothing.

'I was curious, you see. I've always been dead nosy. She bought *terribly* expensive pure silk camiknickers and bra and suspender sets, and the most glamorous nightie we had in the department. I said to her, all innocent like – Is Madame purchasing for a special occasion? And she purred like a cat full of cream and said – I'm off to Paris tomorrow afternoon.'

'When was this?' Andrina asked quietly.

'Just today. And it *was* Jane Ford. She paid by cheque so I saw her name. You should have seen the clothes she was wearing. She's obviously loaded with money. Her father's one of Bernard's best customers, you know. Gives Bernard a lot of work. Are you feeling OK, Andrina?'

'What? Yes, I'm just upset for you. You must have felt dreadful.'

Doris sighed. 'I still do actually. That's why I came here straight from work. You're a terribly good friend, Andrina. My very best friend really. I know I can always talk to you and you'll understand. I always feel better after I've been to see you.'

'You must be starving.' Andrina got up and began fussing about in cupboards with her back to Doris. 'If I'd known you were coming I'd have had something really nice ready, but I'll soon rustle something up.'

'I should have phoned but my head was so full of what happened I couldn't think of anything else. I know me and Bernard's ancient news now. But it still hurts, Andrina . . . I still feel humiliated when I think of the way he treated me, the things he said.'

Andrina didn't turn round. 'What things?'

'About this other woman. And how he'd never loved me. Never for one second.' Doris began to weep and Andrina went over to nurse her head tightly against her shoulder.

'Don't worry, Doris,' she said. 'He'll get what's coming to him. Dry your eyes now and have another gin while I make a pot of tea and something to eat. You've made a right mess of your mascara now. You'd better go through to the bathroom and clean up your face before Robert sees you.'

'Aye OK.' Doris hiccoughed weakly.

By the time she came back, Andrina had made a mushroom omelette and plenty of chips. Doris was very fond of chips (liberally sprinkled with H.P. sauce and vinegar).

'The thing is,' Doris said in between mouthfuls, 'I haven't been able to have anybody since. I've lost my nerve, so I have. I just can't bring myself to trust a man any more.'

Andrina was sitting opposite her at the table nursing a cup of tea. 'I can understand it.'

'Between you and me, Andrina, my confidence in myself is just terrible. I mean, I try not to let it show. I can still be quite chirpy and cheeky at times, but underneath I could just die. I feel so terrible about myself.'

'It's not you,' Andrina said, 'you're all right.'

'But Holy Mother of God, Andrina. He had sex with me. He made me feel like a prostitute. He must have been just using me,' she chewed and blinked rapidly, 'if he never loved me.'

'Try to forget all about it. It's all in the past.'

Still blinking, Doris nodded. She even tried to smile. 'Sorry to go on about this.'

'It's all right.'

'But you're the only one I feel I can talk to.'

Robert appeared in the kitchen then. 'Any tea going?'

'Sorry,' Andrina said, 'we got talking and I forgot to take you a cup through.'

He winked at Doris. 'She neglects me dreadfully, you know.'

'I don't believe it,' Doris said. 'You've a woman in a million there, Robert Anderson.'

Robert dropped a kiss on top of Andrina's head. 'I know.'

'I wish I could make an omelette like this,' Doris said. 'It's as light as a feather. How does she do it?'

Robert spread out his hands. 'What more could any man want? A beautiful woman who can cook like an angel.'

Doris laughed. She felt more relaxed. Some of her self-confidence returned. The tea was putting some strength into her. She felt grateful to have such good friends.

'Give me a shout when you're ready to go home,' Robert said before disappearing away to the sitting room with his mug of tea. 'I'll give you a lift.'

'That's terribly kind of you, Robert,' Doris called after him. 'It's such an awful night. I'll really appreciate it.'

'See you later,' Robert said.

'More tea?' Andrina asked after he'd gone.

'Yes, please. What a nice man he is!'

'Yes.'

'And he obviously adores you.'

Andrina filled both of their cups then concentrated on sipping at hers.

Doris said, 'He's worth ten of that bastard. I'm sorry, Andrina, but I can't just put him out of my mind like that. When I think of what he's done to me – and as for that bitch – I should have bloody scratched her eyes out. Scarred her for life so that he would have got rid of her. He wouldn't have come back to me but he would have dumped her. Everything has to be just perfect for him. It would have been worth losing my job to spoil things between them. To get my own back on them both. Revenge is sweet, they say. I bet it is. Bastard, so he is. When I think of that big bastard . . . enjoying himself fucking that woman in Paris just now – excuse the language.'

'Drink up your tea, Doris.'

'Aye, OK hen.'

Will she never go? Andrina kept thinking. God have mercy on me. Make her stop talking. Make her go. But after she had gone it was shocking to be left on her own in the silence. It was terrifying to be alone with such rage, such anguish. She couldn't believe it of Bernard. She *wouldn't* believe it. He couldn't do this. Not to *her*. She couldn't bear it for him to be making love to another woman, to be taking her away to that beautiful love capital of the world.

She needed proof. She was going mad. She didn't dare let Robert see her. She crept through to bed and hid under the blankets and pretended to be asleep.

Tomorrow afternoon she'd go to the airport. She'd wait and watch. She tried not to shiver. She hugged herself, and dug her long nails into her arms until she drew blood.

Chapter Fifty-Nine

First thing next morning, after Robert had left for work, Andrina hastily dressed Jennifer and herself and dashed over to Bearsden. She didn't even take time to phone her mother.

'Andrina!' Sophie had an iron-grey dutch apron knotted round her lean waist. One hand clutched a washing up cloth. Behind steel-rimmed spectacles, her slate coloured eyes narrowed. 'What's wrong? You've never been this early before.'

'Aren't you going to let me in?'

The door was opened wider and as Andrina trundled Jennifer's push-chair into the hall, Sophie followed her.

'You never phoned.'

'I'm sorry, Mummy. I've had the most dreadful migraine. I've got an appointment with the doctor. I'll have to rush right back.'

'What's given you that? What have you been doing?'

For a moment Andrina lost control and snapped at her mother, 'This is bloody ridiculous! I've even to make excuses to you and give you reasons for feeling ill.'

Jennifer cried out 'Nanna' and held up her arms. Sophie lifted the child and carried her through to the kitchen. She gave her a biscuit and said, 'Who's Nanna's good girl?' Then she went on with wiping the table. She ignored Andrina.

The silence, the coldness, the shutting out nearly drove Andrina demented. She couldn't cope with it today. She wanted to weep. 'Mummy, I'm sorry,' she managed at last in a low tremble of a voice. 'I don't feel well, I didn't mean to snap at you. And I never usually swear. Honestly, I never swear, Mummy. Please forgive me.'

'If you're going, you'd better go,' her mother said coldly. Forgiveness was not so easily won.

Andrina left, weeping without tears. She had never felt so desolate, so distraught. She couldn't remember in all of her life her mother ever putting a comforting arm around her, or kissing her, or showing her the slightest demonstration of affection. Bernard made up for this lack of love. His love had encompassed everything she needed – including security and trust. She was in such a state she didn't know how she got to the airport and found the appropriate gate. In a daze she merged with the milling crowd.

Eventually she saw him. Tall, dark-eyed, always aware, always on the look-out. Not a hair out of place. Immaculate in his Armani suit and Gucci shoes. That slight swagger of his broad shoulders. And the woman. Blonde. Tanned. Expensively dressed in beige. They looked right together. A perfect pair. He put his arm around her as they passed through the ticket barrier. They were laughing.

Suddenly he was a stranger. Andrina didn't know him. She felt alone in the world. Terrified. She began running away through the crowd, away from the babble of people, the hollow echo of the tannoy, the deafening roar of the planes. Outside she took a taxi to Bernard's flat. She had a key and she opened the door and raced straight through to the kitchen. She grabbed the biggest, sharpest knife she could find. She began slashing at everything in sight: the kitchen curtains, the chairs, the dishes. She flew through to the hall wielding the knife crazily above her head. She ripped it through paintings in the hall, and in the sitting room. She tugged it through settee and chairs, all the time grunting and growling and snarling like a wild animal. With all her strength she scraped it down the wallpaper. She swiped at ornaments sending them crashing to pieces on the ground. She stumbled through to the bedroom and slashed and tore and ripped the black silk sheets and pillowslips to shreds.

Then she fumbled for her lipstick and wrote as large as she could on the wall, 'Welcome home, you bastard. I hope she was worth it.'

Rage protected her against hurt. Somehow she returned to Monteith Row and let herself into the silent flat. Already it was

400

getting dark. Rain was tapping at the kitchen window. The fire had gone out. The place had never looked so gloomy. She didn't want to be here. Nor did she want to go to Bearsden. She collapsed into a chair beside the table and sobbed brokenheartedly into the green and cream checked teacloth.

Soon Robert would be home and expecting his meal to be ready and she'd still got to go back to Bearsden and collect Jennifer. She dried her eyes and took deep breaths before starting to prepare her husband's meal. But still emotion was careering out of control. She felt resentment at the thought of Robert. She didn't love Robert. She'd never loved him. She realised that now. She'd married him to please her mother. Resentment immediately ballooned at the thought of her mother. She hated her. She wished her mother was dead. As long as her mother was alive, she'd never be free to live, to love, to be herself. If it hadn't been for her mother, everything would have been different. She would have been married to Bernard. He would have been all hers. They could have had a proper home together. Oh, how she hated her mother. As usual, however, guilt wormed its way in. Guilt frightened her. Fear diminished her. She locked doors inside herself for protection. But when Robert arrived she was able to greet him with a bright-eyed smile and a steak and kidney pie which he downed with relish and said it was the best thing he'd ever tasted.

He was sympathetic about the migraine she told him she'd suffered earlier, and offered to go and collect Jennifer while she relaxed and watched television. She agreed, and was soon left alone in the house again. It was then the memory sneaked back into her mind of how she had told Bernard to have a girlfriend, to lead a normal life. 'I've got a home and a husband and a child. You have nothing,' she'd said. 'I don't mind if you have somebody else too.'

But she *did* mind. That was the problem. She couldn't bear to share him. She loved him too much. She wanted him to be hers and hers alone. How could he love her and not want the same? But he did, of course. At least that's what he'd said. He'd wanted to marry her. Blind rage grew up inside her again. She

401

didn't care what she'd said, or what he'd said in the past. He was away in Paris right now making love to another woman. That was all that mattered. The thought caused her so much pain she nursed herself and rocked from side to side, witless with the agony of it.

'Bastard. Bastard,' she cried out loud. 'Don't you ever come near me again.'

By the time Robert returned she had washed the dishes and tidied up. She put Jennifer to bed and tucked her up with her dummy and teddy and left a nightlight burning. Jennifer was afraid of the dark. Unable to settle to watch television, Andrina busied herself baking some scones, a Victoria sponge cake, an apple pie and a batch of shortbread biscuits.

'Andrina,' Robert protested. 'Why on earth are you slaving away like this at this time of night? I thought you weren't feeling well.'

She gave him one of her perky smiles, eyes round and bright and sparkling. 'No, I'm fine. Absolutely fine.'

Robert stared at her. 'Sometimes I don't know what to make of you.'

'Don't make anything of me.' She fussed about with brittle cheerfulness. 'I enjoy baking and cooking. What's strange about that?'

'Come to bed. Leave all this and come to bed.'

Jesus Christ, she thought, don't let him touch me. 'You go,' she said. 'I can't leave the kitchen in a mess like this. My mother would have a fit.'

'Your mother's not here,' Robert said quietly. 'And what you do or do not do in your own kitchen is your own business. It has nothing to do with your mother.'

She almost laughed out loud. How little he knew about her, about anything. She could no more leave her kitchen in a mess than stop the world whirling round. It was an agony she couldn't possibly contemplate. Everything in her house, especially everything she had, everything she did, had to be perfect.

Like her mother she bathed every day, religiously manicured

her nails every evening, feet and hands, brushed her hair every evening until her scalp tingled, laid out clean underwear and clothes for the next morning. After every meal she meticulously brushed her teeth until they gleamed.

Everything in the house gleamed. Like her mother, she was always straightening things and plumping up cushions. She had to be the last to go to bed at night so that she could conscientiously check the perfection of everything before shutting each room door. If Robert was last, she had to creep up again after he was asleep and go around checking everything. It was impossible to rest, to sleep until she had done so.

'Your mother's not here,' Robert had said. But she *was* here. She was everywhere. Always. She was at her side, at her back, inside her head.

Then suddenly all the things she'd been doing over the years with Bernard hit her like a physical blow. It almost felled her. She felt sick with terror at the risks she'd taken. It was a miracle that her mother hadn't found out. How could she have taken such risks? A million times worse than leaving a kitchen in an untidy mess. Sweat poured from her and she paled at the thought. She must have been mad.

'Andrina, what the hell's wrong?' Robert strode across to her and gripped her arm. Shakily, she sat down. She was safe. She was safe. Her mother had *not* found out. She knew she would die if her mother found out.

'Oh, thank you God,' she kept thinking. 'Oh, thank you God.'

Robert shook her. 'Andrina what's wrong with you?'

Somehow she gathered her wits together. 'This headache,' she said. 'I told you. It just comes over me. For a minute or two I can't see . . .'

'I'll phone the doctor.'

'No, no. It's all right now. It was just a minute or two. It's just migraine. Rest and take a couple of painkillers until it passes, that's what the doctor said. I'll be all right. Don't worry.'

He helped her, half-supported her, through to the bedroom.

403

'You're trembling,' he said. He lowered her on to the bed. She sat like a child, allowed him to undress her and pull on her nightie. He tucked her in and undressed himself. He came into bed beside her and tried to gather her into his arms. She stiffened away.

'Please, Robert,' she said. 'Not tonight.'

'I only wanted to hold you.'

'I just want to be left alone to go to sleep.' But she didn't. She waited until his breathing became deep and even. Then, assured that he was sound asleep, she crept from the bed and the room.

Through in the kitchen she began to wash up the baking tins and stack them neatly away in their proper place.

Chapter Sixty

'Nobody would ever do this in the West End.' Bridie's mouth had taken an almost permanent droop and her eyes were dark with misery.

'Do what?' Carragh asked.

'Have a hing.'

Both women were at the open window of Patrick's house in Acrehill Street. Their folded arms were leaning on the sill. At the next window Doris had taken up the same position. They were watching Patrick and Tony and Michael and Frank and some other men of various ages, most of them unemployed, having a street race. This was one of the diversions the local corner boys had for passing the time and providing themselves some sort of challenge. It was obvious by the wild look in their eyes, the way their heads were thrown back, and their arms and legs going like pistons at full speed, they were giving the race their all.

'I thought you meant the race,' Carragh said.

'They wouldn't do that either.'

Carragh sighed. 'What's come over you, Bridie? You'd think Garngad and Blackhill were bits of paradise to hear you talk now. Look at your da.' Her attention was caught again by the race, which had been won by a shabby-looking man who was now trembling and choking and laughing in triumph. Scobie was staggering about as if he was going to have a heart attack. 'They're mad, the lot of them, but especially men of your da's and Patrick's age.' Carragh raised her voice to bawl, 'Scobie! Are you coming in for your tea?' In a quieter tone she added, 'Daft wee gowk!'

The three women withdrew into the room and shut the windows.

Doris said, 'I'm surprised at Frank.'

405

'Nothing surprises me about Frank any more.' The corners of Bridie's mouth drooped down.

'What about Frank?' Carragh asked.

Doris said, 'I thought with all his posh friends – you know – he'd be above carrying on with the likes of them out there.'

'Here you,' Carragh said. 'Watch your tongue, Miss High and Mighty. Your da's one of them out there, remember.'

'You have to laugh though, Ma.'

'Oh? What about?'

'Well, Da's wee legs whirring along and Tony galloping beside him with every buck tooth in his head showing, and Patrick taking the whole width of the road. What a pantomime!'

'Och well, they enjoy it.'

'I bet Michael let Francis Maloney win. I mean, Michael used to sprint up the Campsie Hills.'

'Maybe so, maybe so,' Carragh said. 'But don't let Francis hear you say that. Come on, you two, help me set this table.'

'Patrick should get married again. He's obviously hopeless without a woman. Look at this place. It's like a tip. Did I tell you I saw Bernard with that woman, Jane Ford? They came into the shop and . . .'

'Aye, aye, you told us, hen. At least half a dozen times. I don't think Patrick'll ever forget Maureen.' Carragh sighed. 'I miss her as well. She was a good pal. Many a good laugh we had – her reading my teacup. She asked me to keep an eye on Patrick. She knew he'd be a pour soul without her.'

'He's just too damned lazy to clean his house,' Doris said.

'Watch your tongue,' Carragh repeated. 'Honestly, you're a right miserable pair. I don't get many laughs with you, that's for sure.'

'At least I've a right to be miserable.'

'You should never have divorced your man.'

'He made me, Ma.'

'How could he make you?'

Doris shrugged and creaked lethargically over to the table in her PVC boots and skirt. 'He just did.'

'And as for you,' Carragh turned to Bridie, 'it's time you did something with your miserable face or you'll be losing your man as well. You were never a raving beauty, Bridie, and that dour huffy look does nothing to improve you.'

'It's just that Frank's changed, Ma.'

'Frank?' Carragh said. 'Him that was racing out there with the lads? Him that was kicking a football about the streets with them earlier? If you ask me, hen, it's you that's changed, not your man.' Of course, Carragh didn't realise what a traitor Frank was. To Carragh and Scobie, Frank could do no wrong. Bridie said as much to Frank later, after they'd returned to Botanic Crescent.

'I know what you were doing there today.'

'Visiting my father?' Frank suggested.

'More than that, and you know it. You were putting Blackhill under a microscope. You were just using everybody there. You're going to write about them, aren't you?'

'What's wrong with that? I'm a writer.'

'You'll betray them – your own kind. You'll make them out to be rotten.'

Frank's face turned grey with anger. 'Is that how little you know me or what I'm trying to do?'

'What are you trying to do, Frank? You tell me.'

'I'm trying to tell the truth. I'm trying to show what it's like to be brought up in an environment like Blackhill. What the place, what the system, can do to people. How it can affect their lives for good and for bad. I'm trying to show the whole picture so that people outside that environment can at least have some sort of understanding and compassion.'

'Oh yes? Is that what you were doing with your last play and the one before that?'

'I'm trying to tell the truth, as I see it. That applies to all of my work.'

'And of course it doesn't matter to you who gets hurt in the process.'

'What the hell's wrong with you, Bridie? You used to be all for my writing.'

407

'Was I?' she said sarcastically. 'Fancy that!'

He had reluctantly suspected for some time and now he was sure that Bridie was jealous of his work and the success it had brought. In his secret heart too, he knew that Bridie was floundering out of her depth. His anger melted away at the thought. Pity mixed with his love for her. He didn't know what to do. He couldn't stop writing any more than he could give up his new lifestyle and go back and live in Blackhill or Garngad or the Gorbals. He had experienced the hard life. He'd done his share of roughing it. Enough was enough.

He compromised by trying not to talk so much to Bridie about his writing, or to expect her to be the first to read his manuscripts. It was a terrible effort for him because he was always bubbling over with such enthusiasm and eagerness to share the joy of creation with her.

He forced himself not to invite people to so many parties in the flat. This went so much against his grain it was a real agony to him. People, all sorts of people, were eternally fascinating to him. But it was a special joy to be with creative people who had this God-given talent in common with him. One of his favourite quotations was by Robert Louis Stevenson, who said, 'If any man loves the labour of any trade, the Gods have called him'.

A sadness touched him. Because of the restraints and cautions he had to put on himself because of Bridie, or when he was with Bridie, the closeness they'd once had together was diminished. They had periods of silence that were awkward and strained, unlike the peaceful, loving, sharing quiet they'd once enjoyed together. When a silence stretched between them now, his mind frantically searched for something to say that had nothing to do with his work, or his colleagues in the Society of Authors, or the PEN Club, or the BBC.

He tried to build up her confidence by playing himself down. But when she took a lead from this, he felt resentment. She began reading his work again – the bread-and-butter short story manuscripts, a few poems he'd been commissioned to do for a literary magazine. Sometimes she'd do a serious criticism of which some points were valid and on which he acted. But there were a growing number of niggles and nit-picks. She began to sound as if she was only searching for faults. When she did manage to find any, she pounced on them and was maliciously pleased if she wounded him.

He locked his play in a drawer in his desk. It was the only locked drawer and he was thankful for it.

Yet they still had loving moments. They would still walk hand in hand through the park. They would still laugh together. They could still treasure moments of tenderness and physical closeness in bed.

It was the other closeness that was gradually disappearing, as if some terrible creeping paralysis had infected both Bridie and himself. He didn't know how to stop it. He didn't know what to say that wouldn't make her harder and more defensive and shrink further and further away from him. Words had become dangerous weapons between them. It occurred to him that this disintegration of a marriage would be a good theme for a play. He was shocked – not by thinking about using the theme – but that his marriage might, in fact, be disintegrating. His mind, his whole being, became torn between distress and the creative process. Gradually, the one form of suffering merged with the other until they became confused, and the dividing lines softened. It hardly mattered which was which.

He became withdrawn, absent-minded. Sometimes he didn't hear Bridie when she spoke to him. He shut himself away in his study for longer and longer periods. He was living partly in a dream world. He was gaining sustenance from it. Excitement was quivering in his loins, in his heart, in his head, in his very soul.

It didn't matter now about parties, or colleagues, or talking, or entertaining, or visiting, or thinking about or doing anything that would divert him or take him away from his desk. He had all the company he needed now. People were crowding together in his head. He could see them moving, hear them talking. He knew them better than anyone else on earth because he knew their innermost thoughts, their most intimate and truest feelings. They were creating a new world. He loved them like a father loves his children. A fearful urgency grew inside him. He mustn't die before they finished telling their story; or the house mustn't go up in flames. Burglars mustn't get their hands on the precious pages or destroy them. At the same time the excitement grew and grew. And the joy.

It was working. It was good. It was coming alive. *Really alive.* The characters were taking off on their own.

Hallelujah! Hallelujah!

He was a happy man.

Chapter Sixty-One

'Welcome home you bastard. I hope she was worth it.'

Bernard stared at the scarlet-smeared words, read them over and over again. He'd already wandered around the house. He felt not only devastated, he felt sad. The thought that he had caused Andrina to wreak such violence and destruction depressed him beyond words. His Velvet, soft and sweetly feminine, was not like this. He had driven her to behave completely out of character.

Her distress must have been unendurable. He was sorry. But what could he say that would change anything now? The truth would be no use. The truth was that he was so randy he had to have a woman much more often than every few weeks or few months. Yet at the same time, it made no difference to his loving Andrina. He had sex with other women, but he loved her and her alone. He had loved her from the first moment he saw her when she was only fifteen, and he would love her till the day he died.

He remembered her in all her stages, in all her moods, in all her styles. One day her dark auburn hair had been parted in the middle and plaited. It hung over each shoulder in long, thick pigtails. He remembered the time her full pouting mouth boasted its first bright coat of lipstick. He recalled the demure skirts and blouses that could not hide her provocative curves. When she had been pregnant he had watched her and followed her. She had worn a navy cord velvet coat with leg o' mutton sleeves, a swing back and edge-to-edge at the front. On a hot day she wore a navy and white striped dress with a white collar and navy and white shoes.

She'd long ago forgotten all about these outfits. She always marvelled at how he remembered every tiny detail about everything she'd ever worn.

The white tailored shorts she'd sported one hot summer's evening had been topped with a sleeveless white blouse. Her accessories were a broad gold belt, gold earrings and bangles. White and gold against the deep burnished gloss of her hair was striking.

The black satin basque, the lace-edged knickers, the black lace-topped stockings, the high-heeled black sandals.

The way she stretched and eased her arms high and piled her long hair on top of her head, her eyes innocent and inviting.

He loved the soft vulnerable curve at the nape of her neck.

How could he explain that he loved her now? She would never believe him. The strength and finality of her disbelief was all around him. Yet he had to try. He phoned her.

'Darling Andrina,' he began, but before he could say any more she hissed at him.

'Bastard! Don't you dare ever try to contact me again.'

He'd never heard any voice so charged with hate. He sat down on the wreck of the bed and supported his head in his hands. Depression weighed heavy on him, and for the first time in his life, he was attacked by a plague of indecision. He didn't know which way to turn, what to do, where to go. He couldn't stay here. Not tonight. Even the mattress on the bed had been slashed. He couldn't have a drink. He couldn't even make himself a cup of coffee. Every dish in the kitchen had been broken, his decanter of whisky had been smashed, every bottle of wine in the wine rack had been poured over every floor.

A sense of failure hit him with a wave of panic. He was a failure in personal relationships. He already had one failed marriage behind him, but the woman he wanted to marry wouldn't have him. He'd gone through a string of sexual partners. His latest one, Jane, was definitely angling for marriage and although he admired her in many ways, he didn't love her. Not as he loved Andrina.

A worry bell rang in his head. If he didn't get a grip on his personal life, the time might come when he'd fail in his business too. He couldn't afford to be indecisive in his business. He couldn't afford to panic. Indecision and panic could spell death, either for a client or himself. Or both.

He tried to banish Andrina from his mind but, surrounded by the wreck of the flat, the symbol of their wrecked relationship, he could not. The outer devastation was worming its way back inside him.

He suddenly strode out of the house and locked the door behind him. The click of the latch closed over with a sense of finality. It brought home the feeling of the end of an era. He leant forward, pressing his forehead against the hard wall of the landing. The deep coldness of the stone seemed to draw the heat and anguish from his soul like a leech. He straightened his neck and slowly closed his eyes. His jaw relaxed and he concentrated on his breathing. In through the nose for four slow seconds, the cool air trickled down to his throat, sucked down deep into his stomach. He held the air inside for another four seconds, before allowing it to dribble slowly, slowly out of slack lips. His chest empty, totally, he remained airless for the same time again. Then he repeated the cycle, kept repeating it.

Gradually his being cleared. His feelings marshalled themselves into a patina of normality. With a last deep sigh, he clattered down the darkened stairwell into his life once more.

He decided it was wiser to delay going to any of the pubs or clubs. Straight away he'd be on duty. He couldn't guarantee total alertness, not yet. Cobwebs of distraction still clung. He went to Pollokshields where Jane lived, cocooned in her big villa. Walking up the curving tree-lined drive, it occurred to him that he hadn't phoned. It would seem strange that, having put her in a taxi and said goodbye to her only a few hours ago, he should suddenly turn up on her doorstep. Again he struggled with indecision. What the hell was he doing? Just then he heard a rapping on glass and saw Jane waving to him in the lighted window of her sitting room. She hurried to open the door to him.

'Darling, I heard your step on the gravel.' She was flushed with pleasure. There was also what looked like a beacon of triumph in her eyes. His depression took another turn when he

413

remembered her earlier hints of marriage. She was a determined girl and, he later found, a recklessly impulsive one. She started saying things like, 'It seems a pity for me to be on my own in this big house and you on your own in that flat.' Soon she'd become more pointed. 'If we promised to endow each other with all our worldly goods, darling, you'd get a very good deal, don't you think?'

She was certainly loaded. Sometimes he asked himself, 'Why shouldn't I take this million-dollar chance of setting myself up?' The truth was he didn't care much one way or the other. If he couldn't have Andrina as his wife, no other woman mattered – except for regular sex. Entering the lofty hall with the chandelier sparkling down from the ceiling, he suddenly thought of his mother having to cope with a husband and four sons in a wee room and kitchen. It would have fitted twice into this hall and still have room to spare. He shook his head.

'What's wrong, darling?' Jane linked arms with him and walked with him into a room the size of a Hilton lounge.

'I felt bad,' he said truthfully.

'Oh darling, I felt the same. And it's so unnecessary separating like that when we'd been so happy together.' She wound herself around him. 'Move in with me.'

'Live together?' He knew perfectly well she meant marriage.

'Now, you mustn't tease.' She kissed the tip of his nose. 'You know I'm not that kind of a girl.'

He felt like saying, 'You could have fooled me!' They had been going at it hammer and tongs every night in Paris. And she'd enjoyed it. To the point of embarrassment, in fact. Every morning she'd rush out and buy him presents, gold cuff-links, gold wristwatch. She had been about to lash out on a gift of a Jaguar car. He'd just managed to stop her in time.

'Darling,' she enthused. 'You're worth it. You're a wonderful lover. I adore you. I'd do anything for you, give you anything.'

'Calm down,' he'd told her. 'What do you think I am? A gigolo?'

She'd thought that hilarious. 'You a gigolo? Darling, anything but. You're your own man. I know that. Anybody would know that just to look at you. I just admire you, that's all. I want to be with you all the time. For always.'

What the hell! he thought.

He took her quickly that night, almost brutally. Afterwards she lay in his arms and kept whispering over and over again, 'I love you, I love you, Bernard. We will get married, won't we? You want to marry me, don't you?'

Eventually he thought – why not? She was beautiful, she was wealthy, and most important, she was unattached.

'All right,' he told her, 'we'll get married.'

'Soon, darling?' she'd cried out in delight.

'As soon as you like,' he said.

Why not? After all, he too was unattached.

In the morning Jane wakened him with a kiss, then presented him with a tray the housekeeper had brought up. She was already showered and made-up and dressed for outdoors.

'Where are you going?' he asked.

She kissed him again. 'Take your time and enjoy your breakfast, darling. Then do your exercise routine. My trampet's under the bed. There's no need for you to worry. I want to do everything right and I'm so excited, I just can't wait. There's so much to see to: shopping for clothes, bookings to make. Absolutely everything to do with weddings has to be booked *ages* in advance these days. But don't worry. I'll organise the whole thing. See you later.'

He nearly said, 'Forget it!' But it was too late. The bird had flown, taking no chances, giving him no time to change his mind. Again he thought, What the hell! Life had to go on and, as far as he was concerned, it couldn't go on without a woman. It had crossed his mind more than once to ask himself why women found him so attractive. He'd stare at himself in the mirror and feel certain that innumerable men were far better looking than him. Yet he'd never once stood at the bar of a pub or club without a woman trying to get off with him. He had come to the conclusion that it was power, or the aura of power. Women seemed to find this irresistible.

It seldom worked the other way around. Jane's wealth had

given her a brick wall of self-confidence. She had always got her own way and was pushy with it. He would have to do something about that if they were going to have any sort of harmonious life together.

He struggled to concentrate on a future with Jane. What was the use of feeling suicidal about life without Andrina? He'd never actually had a life *with* Andrina. But those occasional snatched minutes, or hours, had been his lifeline. Those were the times when he had lived with every braincell in his head and every nerve in his body, every fibre of his being. They had kept his adrenalin pumping.

The twilight world of work was another world in which he walked a tightrope, existed on a dangerous knife-edge. He had always lived to the hilt, forcing himself to the utmost limits, no matter what he did.

After knocking back a glass of orange juice he pushed the tray aside, then padded through to the bathroom. Once shaved and showered, he returned to the bedroom. He pulled the trampet out and switched on the stereo. The throbbing beat of Deep Purple filled the room. He jumped on the trampet, bobbing up and down, side to side, shadow boxing, dancing, using imaginary skipping ropes, deliberately getting high on energy. After twenty minutes he was covered in a sheen of sweat as if oiled from head to toe. Drips coalesced on his eyebrows and pooled under his nose.

He lay on the floor and flung his legs over the bed. Hands on head, he began to crunch his stomach muscles into a tight hard wedge, lifting his upper body up to his knees. He managed four sets of sixty before collapsing back to the floor with a climactic grunt of release. Next he went over to two low stools and placed his hands on either stool. Then, breathing regularly, he began pumping out deep, stretched press-ups. He forced out the hundredth rep before slumping forward on to his towel. Slowly he stood up and shook his head, arms down, gently, before a final cool shower and rub down.

He thought, 'One of the first things I'll do in this house is get a top-class gym set up. He could see it now. Not just free weights and a lat pulley. No, he would indulge in high tech as well. Pec dec, definitely, and he'd investigate some nautilus equipment.

Positive action. Positive thinking. The absolute necessity. The survival kit. Downstairs he leafed through the phone book, found a firm of office cleaners and arranged for them to clean up the flat. He told them to call at his office for the key.

So far, so good. Back to work. Calling in at the pubs and clubs. Talking to his men. Scanning crowds with dark, sharp eyes. Supervising.

Pub owners, club owners anxiously waiting for him. 'Thank God you're here, Bernard. It was a bit dicey to tell you over the phone but . . .'

'Stay cool.' Dark eyes steady and piercing. 'What's your problem?'

Chapter Sixty-Two

They were married quietly at the Registry Office in town. Jane was Protestant, but didn't care one way or another. Nor did he. She hadn't been inside a church since her Sunday School days. He hadn't taken Mass since his divorce. Sometimes, thinking of his mother, he felt guilty. But guilt, like fear, was something he'd learned to cope with.

Jane wanted to go on a honeymoon abroad. It was their first test of wills. He couldn't take time off work after having been so recently on holiday in Paris. She had actually booked tickets for the Bahamas. She was in her element organising things and pushing ahead with her plans without any consultation. She was a regular and enthusiastic announcer of *faits accomplis*. He could imagine her in a few years time doing sterling work for charity on innumerable committees, bullying people to part with money.

'Cancel the tickets,' he said. 'Or cancel the wedding.'

She cancelled the tickets. There was no argument. He saw the fear in her eyes . Pushy or not, self-confident or not, she loved him too much to take any risks.

'Next year,' he said, 'we'll discuss a holiday together, and in plenty of time so that I can make the necessary work arrangements.'

He only mentioned the gym. Next day she had everything installed.

'Shit!' he said when he saw it.

'Darling, don't you like it? I thought you'd be so pleased.' Again the vulnerability filled her eyes. The bewilderment.

'Of course I like it. But when will you learn to discuss things with me first? We're supposed to be a pair – partners. Stop dashing off on your own bat.'

Nevertheless, they shared some satisfying times in the gym.

It was good that they had this interest in common. She was terrifically fit. And a real trier. Sometimes he had to laugh at her determined struggle with the weights. In some things she was as extreme and as determined as him. She was impulsive, however – he was not.

It was good to be seen with her too. Eyes turned to admire her glossy cap of blonde hair, her deep tan, her lean, long-legged figure. She was always immaculately dressed. It demoralised her when he refused to take her to nightclubs. 'Are you ashamed of me or something?' she'd ask, the defiance in her voice contradicted by the dark anxiety in her eyes.

He saw the desperation of her love for him. He realised how, without the slightest effort on his part (or even the slightest interest), he could shatter her confident façade. 'Don't be stupid,' he told her. 'I don't want to put you at risk, that's all.'

He had dozens of clubs on his books now, in Glasgow and in Edinburgh. He tried to explain the risks involved in accompanying him, but her hurt remained. She had no understanding of the dangerous waters, the treacherous under-currents, in these places. She had no idea of the kind of situation that could suddenly erupt that he would have to calm down. He had to be ready to deal with anything and everything in whatever way was appropriate.

He took her out for the occasional meal to a hotel or a restaurant instead, and each time she was as eager and excited as a child at Christmas. It was on one of these occasions, on a lovely spring day, that he and Jane bumped into Robert and Andrina. Andrina's hair was piled up on top of her head with wisps teasing down at each side of her face at the nape of her neck. She was wearing a white silk blouse with a high mandarin collar and high puffed chiffon sleeves with tiny buttons. Her shapely waist and curvaceous hips were flattered by a high-waisted, long and straight black skirt. On her feet were high-heeled black suede court shoes.

She looked stunning. It took every vestige of his control to calmly make the necessary introductions. Jane invited Andrina and Robert to join them. On the surface the evening went splendidly. Bernard was irritated by Jane's all-too-obvious pride in him. 'My husband did this; my husband did that.' It was embarrassing. He wished she'd shut up. It was as if he and Andrina had been together only yesterday. Nothing had changed. It seemed miraculous that their two partners never saw the electricity that fizzled across the table every time their eyes met. Everyone else in the world shrank into insignificance. There was only the anguish of love in his heart, the hot throb of passion in his loins.

His wonderful, sensual Velvet.

The next day he sent a bouquet of long-stemmed roses, one for each year he'd known her. The accompanying card said, 'To Velvet'.

Then he phoned her. And even the sound of her voice sent the adrenalin pumping. He said, 'Where can we meet?'

'Robert's on his spring break.'

'My house then?'

'What about your dear wife?'

The bitter twist in her voice made him shout down the receiver, 'The same as your dear husband. Jane or any other woman means nothing to me compared with you. Life goes on, Andrina, but so does our love for one another. I wanted *you* to marry me, remember?'

'Will she be out?'

'She goes to her Health and Beauty class tomorrow evening at seven-thirty. You know the house?'

She said, 'I know it.'

'Christ, Andrina, how I've missed you. I'm only half alive without you. I can't wait to hold you in my arms again.'

The phone clicked and went dead. Andrina had hung up. He knew however that she would come. He had felt the vibes of her passion winging over the telephone lines to him. He was excited. He was fully, vibrantly, electrifyingly alive once again.

For days and nights after she wrecked Bernard's flat, Andrina had wept and grieved, hated him and longed for him. When she'd read the notice of his marriage in the Glasgow Herald, she'd gone through the same gamut of emotion again. Gradually she'd settled down to a half-life – the kind of life, as far as she could see, that everyone else had. A normal, routine, ordinary, day-to-day kind of existence. Only, she was a better wife than normal. She was obsessively conscientious, a perfect housewife, a devoted mother, a cordon bleu cook. She went to church three times every Sunday and choir practice twice a week. Her mind bitterly discarded Bernard O'Maley. She was finished with him.

Yet, oh, in the stillness of the night, how she'd lain awake dreaming of her love. How she'd posed for him. How his eyes had devoured her. How his hands had caressed her. How his mouth had moved and licked and nibbled and sucked at every inch of her. How he'd entered her, and entered her, and entered her. And wetness had waited for him. And breasts had ached for him. Now the dream had become reality again.

She buried her face in the roses. She danced around the house. Only with feverish difficulty did she hide her rapture from Robert. He thought she was going to her usual choir practice and so no questions were asked. He only saw her leave with her coat on. He did not see how unsuitably dressed she was underneath for any kind of church attendance.

Next to her skin she wore a black satin basque above which the white of her soft breasts bulged. Black lace-topped stockings, a turquoise satin crossover dress that startlingly reflected the colour of her eyes, its tulip shaped skirt accentuating the sensuous bulge of her hips. In the secrecy of the hall she slipped on high-heeled shoes of the same vivid turquoise colour.

She travelled by taxi to the villa, got out at the gates, then walked up the drive with racing heart. What if Jane was still there?

He opened the door to her. The wicked thrill of being in another woman's home. What if Jane came back unexpectedly – suddenly appeared while she was parading and posing around the marital bedroom? While she was obeying Bernard's every carnal instruction?

They took their time. They pushed danger to its limits in the bed in which Bernard slept with his wife, and, as Andrina knew, in which they would lie together many times. As they would live and love in Robert's bed. As they would make love when Jane and Robert were in the house. As they had made love before, for snatched minutes, for dangerous indulgent hours.

She knew it was wicked. And it was the wickedness that drove her crazy with excitement.

Bernard confessed to her afterwards that since that night and their passionate reunion he hadn't been able to make love to Jane. 'I get so far,' he said, 'then I think of you and I can't go on.'

They made a foursome many times, met for meals in restaurants, entertained each other at home. Jane had become quieter, almost timid. She kept staring at Bernard with adoring yet apprehensive eyes. Often Jane and Andrina waited and talked while Robert and Bernard were at the karate club. Then they all had dinner when the men returned.

Jane and Andrina became friends.

Jane confided in Andrina. 'I don't know if it's my fault . . . if it's something I've done. Or something I've not done. It used to be so wonderful but . . . Bernard isn't the same any more. Half the time it's as if I didn't exist. Probably he doesn't mean it, Andrina, but . . . there's other times when he can be quite cruel. He makes it so obvious that he doesn't love me. He . . .' Miserably she hesitated. 'He's become impotent.'

So Bernard hadn't lied to her. Andrina felt grateful. At the same time, a knot of misery for the other woman twisted in her heart, making her shoulders hunch forward with the pain of it.

'It won't be you,' she tried to assure Jane. 'It'll have nothing to do with you. You're a beautiful, desirable woman.'

'Thanks, Andrina,' Jane said gratefully. 'The old self-confidence was beginning to sink. But I always feel better after I've been to see you. You're a good friend.' Suddenly tears filled her eyes. 'My best friend, really. I know I can always talk to you and you'll understand.'

God forgive me, Andrina thought, as she hushed her weeping

friend, and soothed her and patted her. But despite her misery, despite her sympathy, despite her guilt, despite everything, the strength of her feelings for Bernard remained. My wonderful, passionate lover, she prayed, hold me forever.

Then she hurried away to make Bernard's wife a comforting cup of tea.